# How To Start Living

# *(in the Zombie Apocalypse)*

# T.L. Walker

This is a work of fiction. All of the characters and events portrayed in this story are either fictitious or are used fictitiously.

**HOW TO START LIVING (IN THE ZOMBIE APOCALYPSE)**

Copyright © 2017 by T. L. Walker

Cover Art by Antonio Maldonado
of AZCS Technology/Dark Catt Studios
http://thecucoking.deviantart.com
http://AZCSTechnology.com
http://darkcatt.com

All rights reserved, including the right to reproduce this book, or portions thereof, in any form.

*This one is for
Jenna, for being one of the strongest
women and best friends
I've ever known.
(And for putting up with me for
nearly 16 years.)*

# Prologue

It's often said that it takes just the tiniest spark to light the largest fire of change - but to this day I can't say I believe that.

At least in my own life, it's taken nothing short of a disaster here and there to push me from complacency into action...and it's no different now that I've witnessed the end of the world as I knew it.

And no matter what I try to tell you, I'm *not* fine.

Oh, right, I guess I can't just jump into things quite that fast. For someone who used to agonize over every decision that she made, I certainly have come a long way. Shit, some of the people who knew me before would probably say that I'd lost my mind...but then, haven't we all?

Okay, okay, this time I really will take a step back and explain. Granted, I'm not a doctor or a scientist, so don't expect some detailed description of disease pathology. It also doesn't help that when the world started collapsing I was away at a week-long yoga retreat deep in the Blue Ridge Mountains. No television, no cell phone or internet service, just me and a few dozen other women eating bland all-natural vegan meals and forcing our bodies into *un*natural positions.

Actually, I'm being overly cynical about that. Had the world not gone to hell while I was busy perfecting my handstands, I would have returned to my daily life at least a little bit more relaxed than usual.

For a short while, anyway.

Unfortunately, no sooner had I eased my car down the retreat's several-mile-long winding drive and pulled out onto the equally winding state road, then I ran into someone. And then ran *over* them.

Talk about losing your Zen.

Now to be fair, the person had stumbled out into the road right in front of me, leaving me no time to stop. But all I could think was *Christ, can I live with the knowledge that I've killed another human being?*

(By the by, looking back at it now that seems like a pretty damn hilarious question. Ya know, considering how different things are these days. But I digress.)

I hadn't had a true panic attack in years, but you can bet your ass I had one then. Still, I somehow forced myself to stop my car, put it in park, get out and rush toward the body. "Are you all right?!" I cried – or at least, I *think* I said that...or something like it. In actuality, I didn't even feel like I was part of my own body just then, so I probably didn't say anything quite that coherent. More likely than not it was just a lot of screaming.

Of course, I'm not really sure what was worse – those few moments when I thought I'd killed someone, or the instant when I realized I hadn't.

Because you can't kill what's already dead...or in this case, *un*dead. I wasn't sure whether it was a man or a woman lying there in the road, but when it moaned I felt the strangest combination of relief and dysphoria. I'd like to believe that the latter was due to a concern that this person was suffering, but...well, I won't go there just now. It doesn't really matter. As I approached it (see, even now, I have a hard time thinking of it as a person!) the stench began to overwhelm me. *What the fuck?* Thanks to the bright afternoon sunlight, I suddenly realized that its clothes were ragged, its skin mottled, its shoulder-length hair tangled and filled with burrs, leaves, sticks.

And then it moaned again and rolled over to face me. I'll admit right now that I've not felt that afraid in my entire life. Sure, I've been scared shitless a few times since then, but come on. The first time you see a zombie, something that's not supposed to exist outside of fiction? There's really nothing like it.

The thing is, what followed was almost a sense of *excitement*. I don't know, maybe I'm more than a little bit crazy, but suddenly it was as if everything I'd ever read or seen or heard about the undead was running through my mind. As the zombie – which, in case it matters, was a woman - attempted to struggle to its feet, clearly intent on coming after me, I backed toward my car, threw myself inside, and locked the doors.

Yeah, I know, I know. What are the chances of zombies being able to figure out how to open a car door? But hey, one can never be too careful – and I'd realize later that there are several good reasons to always lock a door behind you. (As soon as you know that you're in a safe place, that is.)

I drove away before the zombie woman could even take a step toward me. In that moment, I had no way of knowing that this was anything more than some strange middle-of-nowhere occurrence...but I *did* know that I needed to get home and take stock of things.

And of course, check on my dog.

# PART ONE

## The Beginning Of The End

# Chapter 1
# The First Lessons

At twenty-nine years old, I'd made quite the comfortable life for myself. I lived in a beautiful little condo in the downtown area of a small southern city (I'm leaving out the city and state on purpose, here – can't have anyone knowing *too* much about me, even – or maybe especially – now).

I was in a stable yet boring relationship, and I had a job that paid the bills and allowed some fun on the side. Pre-zombie-apocalypse, this all seemed like more than I could have ever expected.

Who knew I'd turn into such an adrenaline junkie? (Yet again, that's something I'll get into later.)

I suppose it should have tipped me off, just how 'content' I was with my life, when the first and basically *only* thing that crossed my mind upon finding a member of the living dead on the road near my yoga retreat was *I have to make sure Holden is okay*. Holden being my dog, of course.

That's right, my live-in boyfriend of three years didn't cross my mind at all – I just wanted my dog.

Says something, doesn't it?

Now, because I don't want you to think I'm *too* cold, I will admit that after the initial panic and about an hour into my three-hour drive home, I did start thinking about my mother. She was alone, after all, still living on the farm she'd once shared with my father. She and I had our differences, but the longer I drove the more I knew that my condo would be just a short stop on the way to somewhere else.

I assumed that it wouldn't be too difficult to make it to the farm; even though I was on the road for several hours, I didn't see much of note. Once in a while I spotted a car speeding north as I drove south; a few times cars came up behind me and sped by, disappearing so fast that I knew there was no point trying to catch up. Yeah, here and there the sides of the highway were dotted with vehicles that had broken down or even clearly been in accidents before being pushed off the road, and while at first I slowed down to look, it turned out that the only bodies I saw had been half-dragged from wreckage and were pulled apart or chewed to pieces. In fact, even those entirely dead bodies were few and far between.

No one else seemed to care about getting a speeding ticket just now, but the car accident wreckage that I saw kept me from driving more than ten miles an hour over the speed limit. I mean, think about it – if most people are driving like maniacs and there are random zombies and who knows what else stumbling all over the place, isn't it best to keep your eyes on the road and pay attention to how fast you're going? Whether this was the end of the world or just some freak incident, I was too curious to find out what was going on to want to risk ending up dead – *or undead* – on the side of the road. Not to mention the fact that I couldn't stop picturing my sweet Holden; if anything I needed to make sure he'd been taken care of before giving in to the insane thoughts that kept popping into my head.

Granted those were three of the longest hours of my life, but when they were over I still *had* a life – at least for the moment.

*Drive carefully.*

*******

As I approached my little city, it became clear that eventually I'd have to get out of my car and walk. I was able to maneuver my little Volkswagen hatchback to within two miles of my condo, but soon enough the cars and loot blocked the way. I had no choice but to back up the street to a space where I would easily be able to turn my car around before finally parking and turning it off. At this point it still took several deep breaths to even calm myself down enough to think about what I should take with me. *As little as possible,* I somehow knew. Keys, of course, but a weapon was surely a must...

I got out of my car, shutting the door as quietly as possible, and made my way around to the back, where I quickly opened up the spare tire compartment and pulled out the wrench tucked inside. It was small, but what kind of girl carries heavy weapons in her yoga retreat luggage?

*Pepper spray!* Back to my purse, and armed with the spray and my wrench, I was as safe as can be. *Right?* "Right," I said out loud, then, "Talking to yourself already. Not a good sign, Charlie."

Yeah, that's my name, by the way. Well actually, it's Charlotte, but when I was a kid I was quite the tomboy, so 'Charlie' stuck.

Even after I became this yoga-pants-wearing woman who owns at least three dozen different shades of eye shadow.

Anyway, back to the story. So there I was, strolling up a creepily deserted street, the few high-rises that graced my home city looming not so far in the distance. I couldn't stop myself from eying my surroundings; of course, this was the best thing to do, though thankfully the only movement I saw was the random squirrel now and then, and once, the flutter of a curtain as someone peered out at me from inside their boarded-up home. The thought of stopping, knocking, and asking what the hell was going on was appealing for a moment – but just a moment, and then it was gone.

I'd never been one for talking to complete strangers, anyway.

It took me the better part of an hour to walk those two miles, but you know, slow and steady wins the race.

The city was as much of a ghost town as the country had been. "Where did everyone go?" I asked, well, no one in particular. The silence and emptiness were bothering me more than I would have admitted at the time, and as I saw my condo building just a few blocks ahead I broke into a jog.

The thing that came stumbling out of the narrow alleyway between two old buildings was clumsy and not particularly fast, but in my desire to be home I'd forgotten myself for a moment. Perhaps I have the yoga to thank, though, because even when the creature ran into me I was only caught off-balance for a split second.

Unfortunately, that was quite long enough for the zombie to realize that I was there, and alive, and that it wanted to eat me. I was able to dodge its mouth, but then – *oh my God, disgusting!* – one of its hands was tangled in my long hair. My pepper spray was more easily accessible then the wrench, but even though I aimed right for the thing's face, all I got in return was a hiss of annoyance as it continued to use its grip on my hair to pull me toward it.

Thankfully, it didn't seem to be very strong, and I suppose all of that running and rowing and yoga was good for something. "Fuck...off!" I shouted as I twisted away from its cold hands – leaving a lock of my hair behind – and finally slammed the wrench against its jaw. This earned me a brief moment of respite, just enough to break away completely, at which point I turned and bolted toward my condo building, ignoring the sound of the thing stumbling in my wake.

*Keys, keys, keys*! I yanked them out of my pocket, almost dropping them, but finally there I was in front of the doors. I was shocked to find that the power was still working and that my key ring card actually buzzed me inside; I can't even describe the relief I felt when the door swung shut behind me and locked automatically, though the ensuing echo didn't do much to still my pounding heart.

"Holden," I whispered to myself as I headed for the stairwell. We had an elevator, of course, but power or no power I knew that it wasn't a good idea to utilize that just now. Plus, it was only seven floors, right?

Well, it wouldn't have been so bad outside of the damn *smell*. The higher I climbed, the worse it got, until I was holding my shirt over my nose and *still* forcing myself to breathe through my mouth. *This is not good, this is not good...* For the first time, I wondered for a moment about my boyfriend Dave, but only because I questioned whether he'd thought to take care of Holden when things started going to hell.

But I knew the answer to that before I reached my floor. Dave had never been overly fond of my dog, and if I'd barely thought of Dave since I first realized something was wrong, the chances weren't good that he'd thought about me at all...let alone that he'd considered Holden.

My keys rattled against each other as I moved to unlock my door, and it was then that I heard it – a low whimpering, the patter of nails on my hardwood floors. My dog was in my condo, and he was still alive, but no sooner had I heaved a sigh of relief and shoved the key into the lock then I heard another sound: scratchings and moanings that grew louder and louder as I attempted to unlock my door. They were coming from the condo diagonally across from my own, and my hand wouldn't stop shaking; when the keys slipped out of it and fell to the floor my heart leapt into my throat at the noise they made. I bent down and scooped them up; this time, I was able to unlock the bolt, then the doorknob, and then I was inside my apartment and quickly pushing the door closed as Holden rushed toward me.

"Down boy, *down!*" I hissed, struggling to lock myself inside. When that was accomplished, I collapsed to the floor, Holden crawling into my lap as if he weighed far less than his full seventy pounds. I held on to him for several minutes, wondering how long he'd been alone. It smelled bad enough that I could tell he'd gone to the bathroom inside at least a few times, and when I finally pushed him away from me and stood up, moving through my condo, I wasn't surprised to find his food bowl empty and his water bowl bone dry. My stomach clenched – forget alone, how long had he been hungry and thirsty? I immediately filled both bowls and watched as he gulped down their contents before finally heading toward the bedroom to take stock of things.

There was my cell phone, right where I'd left it on the bedside table, but now there was a sticky note attached to it. Dave's bureau drawers and closet doors were open, the remnants of his clothes strewn everywhere. The message he'd scrawled on the small piece of paper simply said, "Going to my parents' house. Call if you can."

I thought about it. Really, I did. But in the end, when I decided to make a call, it was to my mother.

Not that it mattered anyway, because apparently even though the electricity was still working, cell phone towers were not, and I heard nothing but the bleep-bleep-bleep of dead communications when I tried to dial out.

As I lifted my hand and ran it through my hair, I remembered the zombie and how it had gotten hold of the length, and my stomach turned. I'd had a hundred different haircuts in my lifetime, but Dave had been adamant about me growing it out, so it had been long for years now.

Only suddenly long hair seemed more a dangerous fashion statement than anything else.

Scissors were in order. I was no hairdresser, but with a mirror and my sharpest kitchen scissors I made short work of my long brown locks. They fell to the floor in chunks, and while the result was a bit uneven and probably much shorter than it needed to be, it felt – in more ways than one – as if a weight had been lifted from me. I gathered up most of the hair on the counter and floor, tossed it in the trash, and put the scissors away, stopping to glance out my living room window. It was mid-autumn already, and the sun would be setting within the hour. I was stuck here for the night, but tomorrow...tomorrow I'd head on down to the family farm.

What about my friends, you ask? Oh, sure, I have friends here. (Or is it now more apt to say that I *had* friends?) But most of them were transplants like Dave, and if *he'd* left to go find his parents, I couldn't imagine that anyone else had stuck around. And even if one or two of them had, I doubted that they'd care to hear from me.

No, in times like these, I supposed that Dave was right: there's no place to go, really, other than home. In the meantime, I turned on the television...and got nothing but static. The radio had been the same in the car, so I didn't even bother with that. I drew my curtains, turned on the dimmest lights in my condo, cleaned up the messes my dog had made, and cooked myself a small meal. Then I packed up as many non-perishable items and comfortable clothes as I could. *So much for traveling light,* I realized – but at least now I would have Holden with me. He was some sort of retriever mix, and they were bred for hunting, right? Regardless, he'd already been full-grown when I'd adopted him several years prior. I'd always believed that he knew I'd saved him, and he was protective enough.

With that in mind, I snuggled down in a nest of sheets and comforter, Holden curled up beside me, and proceeded to lie awake listening for – "For what?" I finally asked myself. "Do you hear anything, boy?"

Holden merely let out a *huff* in response, so I wrapped my arms around him and finally drifted into a fitful sleep.

## LESSON LEARNED

*If you can avoid it, don't load yourself down – but always, always carry a weapon.*

*******

When I woke up, I was alone in the bed and I could hear Holden whimpering by the door. I forced myself to get up and move toward him, murmuring, "Shhh, Holdy, you've gotta be quiet." I knew that he had to go out, but I also knew that the less noise we made, the better. After peering out the window to the street below and determining that the city was still quiet and at least nearly empty, I allowed myself a quick shower and then gathered up my things, ignoring the fact that Holden had peed on the floor while he waited. "Come on," I said, putting on his harness and clipping his leash to it. "We're going to grandma's."

Loaded down with a duffel bag on my right hip, a messenger bag on my left, and Dave's little-used hiking pack strapped to my back, I quietly unlocked, unbolted, and opened my door. Holden crept out into the hallway first, immediately turning toward the condo across the way, his hackles raised. A low growl rose in his throat. "Shhh," I cautioned him, turning back to shut and lock my door behind me.

No, I'm not sure why I felt the need to lock it at this point in time, but bear with me here, okay?

Apparently we weren't quiet enough. Holden froze, watching my neighbor's door, growling louder and louder as the noises from within the condo rose as well. "Let's get out of here, boy," I insisted, and thankfully he obeyed.

I made sure to peer through the windows at the front of my building's lobby before moving out into the street, but again things seemed peaceful. *Is this some sort of dream? Shouldn't it be...crazier than this? More difficult?* I thought back to the handful of movies I'd seen about zombies and infected people and anything else that could even partially fit this scenario. It didn't take long for me to realize how sad it was that I'd never been a fan of horror movies and therefore didn't have much to go on.

The sun was bright but there was a chill in the air – an unseasonable one, even for this early in the morning. I led Holden out into the middle of the road; after the episode from yesterday I assumed it was better to stay away from open doors, alleyways, and cross streets – *and it's not as if you have to worry about getting run over*, I reminded myself.

Holden was clearly on edge, and as he kept an eye on our surroundings, I kept an eye on him. I knew that I could trust his senses far more than I could ever trust my own.

And at least now I had better weapons – Dave had left his giant Maglite under the bed, so between that and the knives I'd collected from my kitchen, I had a miniature arsenal at my disposal. A gun would have been preferable, but at least if I made it to the farm I would have several of my father's firearms to choose from.

I refused to think about the fact that those guns might not still be there, that my *mother* might not be there, that the farm itself could have been ransacked or worse, burned down.

We'd made it about halfway back to my car when Holden suddenly stopped in his tracks. He was alert, but his hair wasn't standing on end and he wasn't growling. (Or making any sound at all, for that matter.) I followed his line of sight and realized that there was someone peeking around the front bumper of a car not twenty feet away.

"Good boy, Holdy," I whispered, and then I called out, "I'm armed, but I just want to be left alone. And so does my dog – who, by the way, has been trained to protect me."

That last bit was a lie, but hey, no need to admit that I didn't have any idea how well Holden could, or would, defend me.

The person hadn't moved, and despite the fact that Holden didn't appear to be frightened or overly wary, I began to wonder if it was a *living* person at all. "I just want to be left alone!" I shouted again. "Do you hear me?" I raised my right hand, brandishing the butcher knife that was clutched in it.

Slowly the person stood, hands in the air. It was a dark-skinned teenage boy with rich black skin, his brown eyes wide with fear. "Please," he said, so softly I could barely hear him. "I don't have anywhere to go. You're the first real person I've seen in nearly two days. My family..." He paused and choked back a sob. "I don't have anyone. No car, not that I've ever driven a car..."

At this point Holden was straining at the end of the leash, his tail wagging furiously. He seemed almost distraught that the boy was upset, seemed as if he wanted nothing more than to run over and console the damn kid. I rolled my eyes. "Fine," I mumbled, bending down to unclip my dog's leash. "I'm going to let my dog come say hi to you. He'll be friendly if you are, so you'd best be nice to him. Hurt him and I swear I will chase you down and kill you."

I barely had the chance to stand up before Holden took off toward the boy, who stumbled backward for a moment as my sizeable dog wound himself around this stranger's legs. Tentatively the kid reached down and patted Holden's head; Holden responded by sitting obediently at the boy's feet. "What's your name?" I asked, taking a step closer.

"Mike."

"Well, Mike, there are plenty of cars just sitting empty, cars that are practically waiting to be...borrowed. And there don't seem to be any cops around to come chasing after you. Now tell me something – what the hell happened here?"

He looked startled. "What...what do you mean?"

I heaved a sigh. "I mean that I was out of town for a week, up in the mountains with no television or phone or Internet, and that I have no idea why I came back to a city that's deserted save for a few stray zombies wandering around."

Mike let out a low whistle. "Geez, lady, I don't know whether I'm jealous of you or feel bad for you. Thing is, no one really understands what happened – or if they do, they aren't telling. I know that most people left the city because there was news of an emergency camp being thrown together near one of the lakes up in the mountains...but some of us couldn't get out of here fast enough..." He trailed off, clenching and unclenching his hands. I could tell that he was trying to keep himself from crying.

"Your family...they're..." I didn't even know what to ask. Dead? Or *un*dead? All I knew was that if I left this kid here by himself, I'd feel like one hell of a horrible person. And Holden clearly liked him, which was usually a good sign.

On top of that, I'd always been one for taking in strays. It was another thing my mom had never understood about me, another thing that added to the rift that had started growing between us back when I was in high school.

Mike seemed unsure of how to answer me, and soon enough I gave in to that part of me that knew it would be shitty to leave him behind. "Come on, kid. I don't know if there's anything worth finding where I'm going, but if you want to come along for the ride, I'll allow it. For now. Don't think that I can't protect myself, though, and don't think that I won't ditch you first thing if you turn out to be too much of a burden." *Yeah right, Charlie, because you've been so good at that in the past.*

The look of relief that passed over Mike's face was gone almost as quickly as it had appeared. I grimaced. "Here, Holdy," I called out. My dog bounded toward me and allowed me to clip the leash back onto his halter. I gestured to the kid. "Let's go. You're going to walk ahead of me, because I don't know if you have weapons and, well, I'm not stupid. Keep an eye out for...things." I waited for Mike to move in front of me before I began following him. "We'll be staying right on this road," I explained. "I'll tell you when to stop."

I watched the back of his head as he nodded. "I can't thank you enough, ma'am."

"Don't call me ma'am. And don't thank me yet. I could stab you in the back right now and you'd never know what hit you."

He spun around, startled and frightened. "I'm kidding," I insisted, rolling my eyes and forcing a smile. "Now keep walking...or else." His back visibly stiffened at this addition, but he didn't turn around again and instead continued down the street, hands shoved deep into his pockets in something like defiance.

*Great, Charlie. Really great. You've picked up a petulant teenager.*

If my mom was actually home – and alive – she was going to just *love* this.

## LESSON LEARNED

*Never discount having a companion.*
*And by that, I mean [wo]man's*
*best friend.*
*(And by that, I mean a dog.)*

# Chapter 2
# Arrival

It wasn't quite noon when we reached my car. Part of me was surprised to find it right where I'd left it – and intact, at that – but you know what they say: Don't look a gift horse (or in this case, a gift *car*, maybe?) in the mouth.

I shoved Holden's leash into Mike's hand. "Stay right here," I ordered, then walked in a circle around my Volkswagen, peering inside to make sure it was as empty as I'd left it. Finally I opened the hatchback and divested myself of my bags, sighing in relief as I stretched out my arms and back. "Everything seems okay," I announced. "But before you get into my car, I'm going to pat you down." Mike's expression was mortified, but I merely shrugged. "Sorry kid, but I don't know you at all, and I'm not climbing into a confined space with you unless I'm certain you don't have any weapons hidden on your person. Now lift up your shirt."

His face scrunched in embarrassment, but Mike did as I asked. I waved at him to drop his shirt and then reached out with the back of my forearm, patting it against the outside of his pockets to make sure there was nothing in them. His wallet caught me off guard for a moment, but I asked him to show it to me and he quickly obeyed. Curious, I flipped it open, finding a student ID that named him a new sophomore. *Christ, he can't be but fifteen.* By the high school name, he was also clearly from the west side of the city, much of which was mired in poverty. Feeling suddenly guilty, I handed his wallet back to him. "Just one last thing. Lift up your pant legs." Again he did as told, and now that I at least knew he wasn't carrying any seriously dangerous weapons I jerked my head toward the car. "Put Holdy in the back seat, and make sure you buckle up."

"Can I ask where we're going?"

"Sure, you can *ask*. Doesn't mean I'll answer," I teased. I guess I shouldn't have been surprised when this didn't bring a smile to Mike's face. "All right, all right," I relented. "My mom has a farm about an hour from here. It'll probably take us quite a bit longer than that to get there today, of course."

"A farm?" Mike repeated softly.

"Yeah. Used to have a couple of horses, some goats, pigs, cattle, chickens. Pretty sure only the chickens are left now, though. It's not all that big, maybe sixty acres, but it's a veritable compound. Even has natural springs."

"So...there'll be food there?"

"Shit, kid, are you hungry?" I felt bad for not having thought of that before, but then who knew how long he'd been on his own, wandering around, hiding from other people – living or dead – and just hoping he wouldn't be seen.

"Little bit, yeah."

"Well...most of my food is in the back, but check that purse by your feet. I brought some granola bars back from my retreat...they're not all that good, but they'll do for now, I think."

It was silent for a while as Mike practically inhaled the two granola bars that he found in my purse. The drive took even longer than I'd expected – half of it was on the main roads that ran through my city toward the highway several miles away, and that meant a lot of slowly steering my way around wrecked or abandoned cars.

Driving a stick shift didn't make it much easier, and at first I was cursing myself for wanting what I'd thought of as a 'fun' car...until we reached the highway. I'd picked up my speed, knowing we were nearly halfway to the farm and feeling anxiety building in the pit of my stomach over what we would find – *or not find* – there, when suddenly an overturned tractor-trailer loomed in front of us.

"Shit!" I worked the clutch and brake at the same time, downshifting furiously, my heart in my throat as I wondered if, even driving manual, I would be able to stop in time. Somehow, though, I practically eased my car to a stop. Mike and I were left desperately sucking in air. My hands were trembling and my knuckles white where I was gripping the shifter and the steering wheel; in the backseat, Holden was whimpering softly.

"Can we get around it?" Mike finally asked.

"I think so." The median here was wide, flat, and grassy; on the other side, there was a large breakdown lane, but it was more than half blocked by the semi. There had to be room for me to maneuver around the truck...but if the median was our only choice, as seemed to be the case, there was a good chance that my sporty little Volkswagen would end up stuck.

"I didn't think you'd be able to stop for a moment there."

"I wondered that too. Wouldn't have been able to, if we'd been in an automatic. I would have hit that semi...or flipped the car. Maybe both." I was trying to sound nonchalant, but my heart was still pounding in my chest.

"What do you think happened here?"

"I think I'd rather not know."

"But how long do you think that truck's been like that?"

"Seriously, kid, *I'd rather not know.*" But he'd already forced me to think about it. Was there a body – or *bodies* – somewhere? What was on the other side of this semi? What could have caused it to crash like this? "I'm just going to try to drive around it. The median should be okay." Much as the idea of taking my fairly low-riding car off the paved road concerned me, I knew better than to think I could squeeze through on the other side.

"You think we can fit?"

"Oh, we can fit. There's no barrier blocking the northbound lanes of the highway, so we can cross over to there if need be...but you better be prepared to get out and push if we get stuck. And this time, I'm not kidding." As an afterthought, I added, "Do you know when it last rained?"

Mike shrugged. "Not since all of this started happening."

That was a relief. "All right, good. Hopefully this won't be too difficult, then." I backed my car up a bit and turned to the left, feeling the slight difference in traction as I maneuvered from pavement to grass. We rolled past the nose of the truck, and when I saw what was on the other side it was impossible to not gasp.

It had been an accident, and the stench of it filtered through the air vents of my car so quickly that within moments it had both Mike and I gagging. There must have been a dozen cars involved in the pile-up, and then of course the truck hadn't been able to avoid them. It couldn't have happened very long ago, or else it would have caused more wrecks – at least judging by how close of a call we'd had in avoiding running into the semi. But the *smell*... "I don't think this has been here long - "

"But it sure stinks like it has," Mike pointed out. I nodded in agreement.

"Maybe I'll just cross over to the other side of the highway for now..." I glanced to my left, where it seemed as if a good stretch of the road was clear.

*Slam!*

"Oh my God, oh my God, oh my God," Mike was suddenly shouting. A zombie had somehow made it into my blind spot and slumped right up to my car.

*Slam!*

Now a second zombie was assaulting the rear passenger door, and though they blocked much of my view as they clawed at the windows, I knew that there would probably be more coming. "Let's go, let's go, let's go!" Mike groaned.

"Slow and steady wins the race," I replied through gritted teeth. If I tried to speed up now, the chances of us getting stuck were much greater. As I'd moved closer to the dip in the center of the median, I'd felt my car straining. Not surprisingly, the ground was softer there, and now there was a third zombie and a fourth zombie clawing at my car, one of them even laying half across the hood and scratching at the windshield. Holden had backed up against the driver's side door in the back seat, pressing himself against it as he bared his teeth and growled at the undead just outside the opposite window.

And still we inched forward. Suddenly we stopped moving entirely and my back tires began to spit up dirt. At this point there must have been half a dozen zombies crowding around us, and perhaps it was the weight of the one who continually threw itself against the back window that kept us from getting completely stuck. All I know is that after a moment or two of sheer panic we were moving again, and by then I couldn't take it any more – I slammed my foot down on the gas pedal and my car fishtailed slightly, knocking a couple of the undead out of the way as the tires gained traction again and we barreled forward. I jerked the wheel to the right and swerved back onto the pavement, fishtailing yet again before my car found its purchase and we finally sped down the highway, the zombies growing ever smaller in my rearview mirror until we went over a small rise and lost sight of them entirely.

Only then did I slow down and pull off to the side of the road, sucking in air as if I'd been holding my breath for the past several minutes. *Hell, perhaps I was.* "You okay, kid?"

Mike nodded stiffly but said nothing in response – not that I could blame him. "Well. We're about halfway there, so let's just hope it's smooth sailing from here on in." I reached back and gave Holden a pat on the head before putting my car back in gear, glancing over my shoulder to make sure no other vehicles were coming (more out of habit than necessity, I suppose), and pulling back out onto the highway.

## LESSON LEARNED

## *Drive a stick shift. (Or at least know how to do so.)*

*******

I was once again driving carefully, still shaken by our experience with the wreckage. Mike tried to start up a conversation at one point, asking me about Holden's name. "Holden Caulfield. From *Catcher in the Rye*. You'd have read it in school at some point."

"Not me. They do that one...senior year, maybe? I didn't get that far before all of this."

"Shame. It's not the best book but it's a story I'd say everyone should read at least once in their lifetime." I paused, heaving a sigh. "Shit, sorry. Guess the word 'lifetime' is kind of a bad joke right now."

"Yeah," Mike mumbled, and we fell back into silence.

Once we left the highway we were relegated to winding country roads that forced even more caution, which meant that it was another hour before I finally pulled into the drive of my mother's farm. The gate was closed and padlocked, and I couldn't see any cars in front of the sprawling house... *But that doesn't mean anything,* I told myself. *If she was smart, she would have put her car in the garage, or hidden it in the back...*

"We'll have to climb over the fence. Can you take Holden's leash and harness off of him? He knows where to go. We'll leave the bags in the car for now...until we figure out if someone is home, I guess." *Please, please let someone be home.*

Once he was loose Holden squirmed under the fence, but instead of bounding up to the house as he usually did, he waited patiently as Mike and I climbed over the metal gate. "Good boy," I praised, patting him on the head. I continued up the drive, Mike and Holden on my heels, only to reach the house and see that all of the curtains – and even the shutters on the bottom floor – were drawn and shut. Still, I persisted. I gestured to Mike to follow me up onto the front porch, where I approached the door and knocked softly. We waited several long moments; nothing.

"This is your mom's house? Don't you have a key?" Mike finally asked.

I snorted. "No. I used to, years ago...but I never needed it. I so rarely came down here...let's just say that I've never really felt like I 'belonged' with my family."

(I'd almost said that I was the 'black sheep' – I just barely caught myself, in fact. As I'd aged I'd gotten better about not using certain non-PC terms, but until just then I hadn't really thought that someone might be offended by the idea of a white girl calling herself a 'black sheep'. Silly, right? I mean, who the hell has any right to care about something like this when the world's gone to such shit?

Or is it when the world's gone to such shit that things like that matter most? Damn, sorry, I'm probably getting too deep on you here. Moving on...)

I knocked again, a little louder this time. "Come on, mom," I called softly, stepping back from the door so that if she pushed the curtains aside on the windows she would be able to see who it was. "It's just me! Charlie! You know, your daughter?"

It felt as if at least another minute passed by before I saw a flicker of movement in one of the windows off to my right, but suddenly there was the sound of a bolt being turned, and finally someone cracked open the door.

"Charlie? Is that really you?"

*What the hell?* "*Joey*?! What are *you* doing here? Are you okay? Where's mom? Is she - "

"Calm down, Charlie. Mom's here, she's fine, she just...prefers for me to answer the door, these days." I saw the glint of a gun in his hand. "Who's that with you?"

"He's just a kid, Joey. His name is Mike, he's cool. I've got Holden too. Now will you please come unlock the gate so I can drive my car up and bring my stuff inside?"

"You're okay, right? You haven't run into any of...*them*?"

"Oh, you mean the fucking dead people walking around trying to eat me? Yeah, I've run into a few, but I'm fine."

"No bites?"

"Christ, no, no bites! Now come on, let's go get my car!"

"Just a second."

And my younger brother shut the door in my face. I pressed my ear against it and heard him talking to someone, then nearly fell over when he swung it open.

"Geez, Charlie, get out of the way. Come on, quick, let's go get the car. Put Holden in the house."

Holden didn't need to be told to go inside; he rushed by me and disappeared into the dim recesses of my childhood home. My brother and another guy stepped out in his wake, shutting the door behind them. I heard the bolt click back into place – my mom must have been right there the whole time – but I was too startled by the presence of a random stranger to say much about the fact that my mother had just locked all of us out of the house.

"Who are *you*?" I sounded more disgusted than anything else, though I wasn't quite sure why. The stranger was...well, shit, he was *cute*. Tall and muscular with sandy blonde hair that fell over his eyes in a way that could only be called endearing.

"I'm Luke," he said, holding out his hand. I looked at it warily, but before I could shake it Joey interrupted.

"We can finish the formal introductions later. Let's go get your car – and *fast*." He brushed by me and began jogging down the long drive, giving the rest of us no choice but to follow. When we arrived back at the gate, he said, "Climb over and start your car. Drive through, stop, and let me lock this...then we'll all get in and you can park around back."

It was the work of a couple minutes at most, but Joey's tone and demeanor made me more than a little bit nervous. He had me hide the car behind the house, and once we'd gathered the bags I'd brought from home along with the few things I had left in it from my yoga retreat, he insisted that I lock it. The house was clearly boasting nearly fortress-like security, and after he'd let us inside Joey bolted the door behind him again. Only then did he seem to relax at all.

"Joey, what the hell happened here?"

"Here? Not much. We ran into a bit of trouble with the neighbors a couple of days after we arrived...but other than that it's been quiet. Charleston, however..." At this, he glanced at Luke.

"You live in Charleston too, then?" I stuck my hand out to finish our exchange from earlier. "I'm Charlie, Joey's awesome older sister. How do you two know each other?"

Luke shook my hand. "Yeah, originally from Charleston. Just moved back there from Jacksonville a few months ago, after I got out of the Navy."

Joey interrupted me just as I opened my mouth to reply. "We're just friends, Charlie."

I raised my eyebrows. "And yet you ended up here, together? All the way from Charleston? During the...zombie apocalypse, or whatever this is?"

Joey rolled his eyes. "Charlie, Luke is straight."

"Ah. And you, dear brother, are decidedly not." I turned and wrapped my arms around him. "I'm glad you're here. And safe."

"It's good to see you, Charlie. I tried to call, before the phone lines went dead...mom told me to come here, but neither one of us could get a hold of you...where have you *been*?"

"I was at a yoga retreat in the mountains for a week." I blushed, because in that moment I realized how stupid that sounded. "No phone, no Internet...I didn't even know what was going on until I left there...and I still don't know, not really." I hoped he would take the hint, but instead Joey just glanced at Mike.

"And Dave?"

"He was gone when I got home yesterday. Left Holden there for God knows how long, no food or water. I gathered up my things and left this morning. Ran into Mike here on the way out of the city. He had nowhere to go."

"Same with me." My head snapped around; it was Luke who'd spoken, and he'd also taken a step toward Mike. "Though Joey did know me before...all of this."

My brother chuckled. "Yeah well, Charlie is known for taking in strays." I punched him in the shoulder. "Ouch! No offense, uh, Mike."

"It's all right. She saved my life. I'm just...glad to be safe."

"Shit!" I smacked my forehead with the palm of my hand. "I brought a few things, but *please* tell me you guys have some real food here."

"You may want to say hi to mom first, but yeah, we collected eggs this morning. Not sure how much longer the chicken coop will last, though. We're thinking about killing them and freezing the meat, just in case. Mom made bread yesterday, and you know her with the canning and jam making and all that. If it's just the five of us, we're good for a while."

"The five of us, and Holden!" I chimed in. "I brought some dog food with me, but it won't last very long. Maybe a week if I'm lucky."

Joey grimaced. "That dog better earn his keep."

I cocked my head. "I'm sure he eats a hell of a lot less than your friend. No offense, Luke, but I'm still at a loss as to who you are and why you're here."

"You're one to talk!" Joey jerked his chin in Mike's direction.

"Let's not have this conversation now, I guess," I relented, glancing at Mike. The poor kid had been through enough; the last thing he needed was for us to make him feel like he was a burden. "Anyway, safety in numbers and all that, right?"

"Right." It was Luke who spoke up, but I refused to look at him. If he thought that he could get in my good graces by agreeing with me, he had another thing coming. My brother wasn't known for choosing the best people as his friends, and I had a feeling that he barely knew Luke at all. Unlike Mike, Luke wasn't just a kid...*and he's certainly not as harmless, either*, I understood. Something about this guy seemed dangerous, to me; even though I couldn't quite place why, I knew that it would be best to keep him at arm's length.

"I think I'll go find mom. You ready to meet her, Mike?"

"I guess..."

"Don't worry." I gave him a small smile. "She's a bit old school, but she's not that bad." *Please be nice to this kid, mom.* An introvert to the core, my mother didn't seem very friendly when she first met people – and being a southern woman in her mid-fifties, she had some...interesting...ideas about race. We'd all been shocked that my father was more understanding of the fact that Joey was gay – my dad had been quite the hard ass – and as I led Mike up the dark stairway to the main floor of the farmhouse, I couldn't stop thinking about my mom's reaction to that situation. She hadn't talked to Joey for months...when he'd come home for Christmas last year he'd ended up turning around and leaving because of the way she was acting.

*Different times,* I told myself. *And Mike's just a kid who has nowhere else to go.*

*Shit, the world may be coming to an end and I'm worried about introducing a black kid to my mother. Priorities, Charlie...*

I eyed Joey and Luke before maneuvering past them, around the corner and through the living room and into the kitchen. "Mom? You gonna come say hi to me, or what?" I called out.

I heard the rustle of pages as she set down a book. "Coming, Charlie." She sounded so damn nonchalant that when she appeared in the doorway from the sun porch I wasn't surprised at how put together she appeared. "Oh, Charlotte. Your *hair*."

"Good to see you too, mom."

"When did you do that? Have your hair chopped off? And who did such a *horrible* job with it?" She approached me and touched my messy cut.

"I did it last night after some dead person got hold of it on the street near my condo. Figured it was better if they didn't have anything to grab onto."

She sighed. "Well, I suppose I can fix it up a bit. Let me get my scissors." She made to step around me, but I caught her wrist and stopped her.

"Good to see you too," I said. "I'm glad you and Joey are here, and safe."

"Well, why wouldn't we be?"

"Mom. You've *got* to be kidding me."

She withdrew herself from my grasp. "Whatever this is, I'm sure it won't last."

"Well I'm glad you're sure of that," I replied, my voice dripping with sarcasm.

"I see you've brought a...friend...with you."

I knew that she was just trying to change the subject, and this time I decided to give in and let her. Eventually she would have to face the fact that something very strange was happening, but if I let her have her way just now there was a chance she'd be a bit kinder to Mike.

"Yes, he's a friend...of a sort. Mike, this is my mom. You can call her Cheryl. Mom, I met Mike on the road today. Holden insisted that I bring him along." I was trying to make light of the situation, but my mother didn't find my explanation quite as amusing as I'd hoped.

"Just like you to credit your choices to your dog." She shook her head. "But you're here now, I suppose...and I expect you're hungry?"

"We are, yes."

"I'll cook something up. Power is out, but Joey and Luke can keep watch while we cook on the grill."

"You don't have power here? I still had it in the city..."

"I'm surprised at that." I hadn't heard Joey return from downstairs and almost jumped out of my own skin when I heard him speak up. "Most places lost it days ago. The cities..."

"Enough of that talk just now. We'll have some dinner, and then we'll need to make sure that we're closed up for the night." Our mother's tone brooked no argument, so we set about following her orders. *At least we'll get to eat.*

Joey gathered up one of our dad's rifles from the dining room table and handed Luke the sawed-off shotgun that my mother had inherited from her father. Mike was watching them with wide eyes.

"You sure you boys know how to handle those?" I grinned at Mike. "I don't think I've ever seen Joey here even *touch* one of our dad's guns."

"Come on now, I don't think you've used one of them since what, high school?" Joey pointed out.

"Fair enough. But what about Luke here?"

"Oh, you don't need to worry about me. Former military, remember?"

I opened my mouth, shut it, opened it again. *Way to go. What are you, a fish?* The problem was that all I could think of were sarcastic responses, and I knew that right then I should have been glad that my brother had made it home with some ex-military guy in tow. Who better to have around during the zombie apocalypse, right?

## LESSON LEARNED

### *[In most cases] There is strength in numbers.*

\* \* \* \* \* \* \*

"Listen, don't talk too much or...well, don't be too loud in general while we're outside. The grill and the cooking are bad enough. Yesterday we couldn't even finish heating things before..." Joey trailed off.

"Before...?" I prompted.

"Let's just say we had a lukewarm dinner."

"Why don't you use the generator and just cook inside?"

"We don't have much fuel. I convinced mom that we should conserve what we *do* have in case things don't get better before it starts getting really cold."

"Why don't you just drive up to the gas station? It's what, three miles away? Four?"

"I drove by it on my way in. There were cars everywhere...we'd need to pick our way through them to get to the pumps, and there are a lot of...those things...around. I thought it was probably too much for Luke and I to handle alone."

"I'm here now. Let's all three go. Not today, maybe, but tomorrow?"

Joey glanced at our mother, then at Luke. "I'm...not sure that's a good idea, Charlie."

"She may be right," Luke pointed out. "We could salvage more than just fuel, and with at least the three of us..." He shrugged. "I don't think it would be all that difficult."

"I'm glad you're so confident, but I don't think it's a good idea." Joey leveled his gaze at Luke. I watched the two of them for a moment, once again wondering how they'd met and how long they'd known each other.

"You boys can go back and forth about this for as long as you want, but the more time that passes the less likely it is that we'll find any gas or food or, well, anything at all, there."

I could see Luke watching me out of the corner of my eye. He grinned. "Once again, your sister has a point, man."

"If I'd known you would start taking her side on things as soon as she got here, I wouldn't have brought you along," Joey mumbled.

"I don't think he's so much 'taking my side' as he is listening to reason, but hey, you don't have to come along if you're that scared," I grinned.

"Charlotte, stop trying to press your brother's buttons. In fact, all of you be quiet while I cook this. Keep an eye on the fields – I would prefer to eat a proper meal this evening."

We were silent while my mom fried some eggs and grilled zucchini and squash from the garden. "We got lucky today," she said quietly, as Joey covered the grill and Mike and I helped her carry the food inside.

"I think we should eat this early every day," Luke suggested.

"Why?" I couldn't help but ask.

He glanced over his shoulder. The sun had just dipped below the tree line, but it was still very bright outside. "The darker it gets, the more active they are."

"I've seen plenty of them during the day."

"Have you been out at night yet?"

"No..."

"Trust me, you don't want to be."

I turned away from him and slammed the platter of food down on the kitchen table. "I'm really tired of no one being willing to tell me anything specific. What is this, 'protect the little woman'? I made it here on my own...I can certainly handle y'all telling me what you know. What you went through to get here. When all of this started, and how - "

"Damn, Charlie, calm down a bit. We'll have plenty of time to talk after we eat and make sure the house is locked up," Joey promised.

"If you say so." I refused to look at him and instead slid into a seat at the table, spearing a thick slice of zucchini with my fork and stuffing it into my mouth before I could say anything that I would regret.

The quiet that descended as the five of us ate our meal was awkward, yet in a way also welcome. As always I felt out of place here, to the point where I'd already begun to wonder how long I would be able to stay. And if *I* felt as if I didn't belong, I could hardly imagine what Mike was thinking. I knew that we were at least relatively safe here on the farm, but I also wondered if perhaps he and I would be better served finding our own way. Clearly my mother and brother and this random friend of his had their own situation figured out, and if they wouldn't even *talk* to me about it, how was I supposed to know where I factored in?

*Or if you factor in at all.*

I pushed the egg around on my plate. They'd only served me one – conserving food, I assumed – but it wasn't quite cooked all the way through, and I'd never really enjoyed runny egg yolks.

"Stop playing with your food, Charlie."

"Yes, mom." I rolled my eyes, but I did force myself to swallow the last couple of bites. As much as it pained me to actually obey her, I knew that I'd need my strength for our trip to the nearby gas station in the morning.

That, and I assumed it was best if I stopped acting like a petulant child, myself. Doing so probably would have been more amusing were we not in the midst of the zombie apocalypse, anyway.

While mom used a bucket of water to wash the dishes, Joey and Luke led Mike and I from window to window and door to door. Though the curtains were all drawn, there were stacks of plywood and boards set close to anything that could be a way into the house, all with crude latches or hooks attached that allowed them to essentially be locked into place.

"When did you guys do all of this?" I was shocked that mom had allowed it at all, but I kept that observation to myself for the moment.

"Few days ago. I think I said that it's been mostly quiet here, and it has...but only after we dealt with the neighbors." Joey grimaced. "That made for an interesting evening, and when it was all said and done we decided to keep the house boarded up as much as possible."

"So are you going to tell me what you mean by 'dealt with the neighbors'? Were they alive or...dead?"

"A little bit of both," was my brother's vague response. I was about to retort, to insist that he explain, when Luke spoke up.

"They were alive. At first. Your mother wanted to let them inside, and while Joe and I were trying to convince her otherwise...they turned violent. We ended up having to...well. Defend ourselves. We didn't have time to move the bodies before it was dark..."

"And they...came back, didn't they?"

Luke nodded.

"Does anyone have any idea why? Or at least know *how* all of this began? I missed the boat on any actual news, and it's kind of driving me crazy."

"I don't think anyone knows for sure. Before communications went dark, I heard that the origin was in Asia...some reports said India while others said China, and then the North Koreans put out that they'd done it on *purpose*, so who the hell really knows. Apparently wherever it started, they tried to keep it a big secret...and were able to do so for *weeks*."

"Until someone brought it here to the States," I stated.

Joey nodded. "It escalated so fast that most people didn't even know anything was happening until it was too late. Luke and I had to sneak out of Charleston in the middle of the night; they'd put the city on lockdown and were trying to keep people from coming *or* going. If I hadn't run into Luke on the street right after things started going to hell, I'd probably still be there...but he remembered me saying that my family had a farm upstate, and convinced me that it would be best to leave the city as soon as possible. We barely made it out alive, but don't repeat that around mom, okay? She thinks we had it easy, making our way up here."

"No wonder she's acting like this isn't a big deal, then! Joey, mom doesn't need to be sheltered from the world. She's probably stronger than both of us. I mean...even after what happened with the neighbors, you still think you can protect her? There is no 'keep it secret, keep it safe' with this, Joey. You're not Frodo."

"Who?"

*You've got to be kidding me.* "Tolkien? Lord of the Rings?" When he shook his head, I scoffed, "Never mind." Again I felt Luke's gaze on me, and this time I actually turned to face him – but the bemused look on his face only frustrated me more. "Come on, Mike. Let's go find a place for you to sleep."

Mike, who had been following us around in silence for quite some time now, glanced at the light filtering through the curtains of a second-floor window that Joey and Luke had yet to board up. "Isn't it a little early to go to bed?"

"Oh, you don't have to go to bed. I just think we ought to find you a room before it gets too dark. Of course...doesn't look like there will be much else to do around here, so sleep may be the best option you have."

"Mom's still got some of our old games and books, and we have some battery-powered lamps and candles...but again, we're trying to conserve," Joey explained.

"Well, after tomorrow, hopefully conserving won't be as much of a concern." Luke winked at me as he said this – actually *winked* at me. I rolled my eyes in disgust.

"Holden! Here, boy!" I called out. I heard his toenails clicking on the hardwood floors and finally he came trotting up the stairs into the loft area. "I'm going to get Mike settled and then go to bed," I announced, looking pointedly at Joey. Before he – or anyone else, for that matter – could respond, I turned and headed down the dark hallway that led away from the loft. "This is my room." I pointed to the first door on the left. "And assuming Joey is sleeping in his old room, and that his friend hasn't taken up residence upstairs, there's a pull-out couch in here." I strode to the door at the very end of the hall and swung it open. The windows in this room had been boarded up and left that way, but at least it was clear that no one else was utilizing it.

There was a jar candle sitting on the end table next to the couch, a lighter beside it. I lit the candle and helped Mike pull out the sofa bed, gathered sheets and blankets and pillows from the closet, and make it up for the night. "You'll be okay in here?" I asked.

"Yeah. Better than where I've been sleeping. Thanks again..." He paused, clearly unsure about what to call me.

"Charlie's okay." I smiled. I wanted to ask him what he meant, where he'd been sleeping. I wanted to ask him about his family. But as curious as I'd always been, it was hard for me to cross certain lines.

*Most lines, really.*

"All right. Thanks, Charlie."

"Let me know if you need anything. I'll be up early and I'll come get you. I'm not sure you should be wandering the house by yourself...my mom is acting more than a little bit strange, and Joey and his friend seem kind of jumpy."

"Can't really blame them."

"No. I suppose not. Goodnight, Mike."

"'Night."

I left him in the back room and let myself into my childhood bedroom, Holden close on my heels. My windows were boarded up as well, and another candle and lighter were on the corner of my dresser. It was almost as if my mother had known I would come home...or at least, she'd hoped that I would. I opened a drawer and dug out a ratty pair of sweatpants and a t-shirt, leftover from my college years when I would visit for a few days here and there, never arriving until I had to and often leaving before I was supposed to.

Once I'd changed, I carried the candle over to the window and pulled the plywood down. It was dark already, though it couldn't be much past seven in the evening, and I couldn't see anything except my reflection in the window, lit eerily by the flickering flame.

Suddenly Holden whimpered. When I turned to look at him, he was backing away from me and from the window, his hair standing on end. His whimper turned to a growl, and he gave me what could only be described as a pleading look. "What's wrong, boy?" I asked.

And then I heard it. The sound was so quiet that, had Holden not warned me, I probably would have missed it. I leaned forward and pressed my ear to the window. It had to be *them*...but the only way I could be hearing their sounds was if —

*They're close. Too close.* I stepped back from the window so quickly that I almost stumbled over Holden. He scurried out from under my feet as I set the candle down and put the plywood back up in the window, feeling my heart thudding in my chest. For a moment I thought about going to find my mother or Joey, about asking them if they could hear it too, but instead I moved toward the bed, crawled between the sheets, and invited Holden to lay down next to me. Once he was settled I blew out the candle and buried my head under the pillows. It was silly to think that I could still hear them; perhaps just knowing that they were out there made me feel like I could. Regardless, I lay there wide awake, feeling Holden trembling next to me, wondering if I would ever feel safe – *or sane* – again.

Obviously I should have known that safety – *true* safety – was impossible in this world. So how am I still alive? How am I still giving sound advice? Well, for now I'll just say that I got used to it. I've hinted before that I actually learned to *thrive* on the constant adrenaline caused by this crazy situation. I'm sure you don't quite understand how that happened – not yet. I know that I've been quite the whiny brat so far.

But the thing about the zombie apocalypse is that people change and evolve a hell of a lot faster than they would have otherwise.

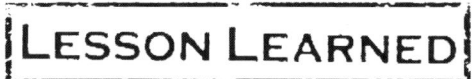

*Lay low at night. Like, really low.*

# Chapter 3
# Exploration

When I dragged myself out of bed early the next morning, I wanted nothing more than a giant cup of coffee. I knew better than to think I would get such a thing, so I scoured the kitchen and settled for an apple before making my way back upstairs to wake Mike up.

I opened the door to the back room to find him sitting on the edge of the bed, staring blankly at the wall. "You okay, kid?"

"Please don't call me that," he mumbled.

"Okay."

"Probably shouldn't use that word, either. 'Okay'. What a joke."

I wondered if he'd heard them too, last night, but I didn't have the heart to ask. "Hey, chin up," I said, forcing fake cheer into my voice. "You get to stay here with my mom while Joey and Luke and I run to the gas station. I'll even leave Holden with you guys. My mom's not such bad company...I mean, at least she's alive."

"You're funny." Mike's deadpan tone belied his words.

"I'm a regular stand-up comedian. Now come downstairs. I've got plans to discuss with the guys, and I'm sure my mom will find something for you to help her with, if you're so inclined."

He merely shrugged in response, but didn't hesitate in following me down to the kitchen. My mother was already there, and within a few minutes Joey and Luke joined us.

"Are you sure you want to do this?" Mom asked. She looked quite a bit more tired today than she had yesterday; I clenched my jaw shut to stop myself from pointing this out. I also glared at Joey, hoping he would take the hint and not speak the truth. It was clear that he didn't want to go to the gas station, but our mother didn't need to know that.

"We're going, mom. Do you want to keep cooking outside on that grill?" I leaned closer and whispered, "I heard them last night. I can tell you did too. If we're going to stay here, we need fuel, food, water. We're only going to the gas station today, but eventually we'll have to go farther. You might as well come to grips with that."

When I stepped away from her I realized that everyone was watching me. "What? Y'all know I'm right. We can't stay holed up here until we run out of the things that we need to *live*...and I don't see this getting better anytime soon."

"There's my glass-half-empty sister for ya," Joey mumbled to Luke.

I glared at my brother. "I heard that. So...what's the plan?"

"Handguns," Luke said. "But we won't use them unless we have to, so choose at least one other weapon as well. If you really want to kill these things, you need to get them - "

"In the brain, yeah, I got it."

"Right. Funny how fiction got that correct."

I shrugged. "Or maybe once upon a time it wasn't fiction."

"Touché. That said, we also figured out that if you get them in the spine – the neck is best, but a well-placed shot or hit or chop to the back can do it too – they lose mobility just like you or I would. The teeth still work, but if you're not stupid about it, well..."

"Understood. What do we have for weapons? I brought some kitchen knives, but please tell me you guys have something better lying around here."

"You know how Dad was. Here." Joey gestured for us to follow him into the dining room, where an array of tools and weapons was spread out across the long table. Hunting knives, hatchets, a baseball bat, some golf clubs, a crowbar, and even a sledgehammer.

"Do you guys have a preference?"

"Ladies first," Luke insisted.

After debating for a minute or two, I finally chose one of the larger hunting knives and the baseball bat. It had been a long time, but I'd played softball in my younger years and my father had always praised my strong swing. *Let's just hope he wasn't exaggerating.* Joey took the hatchet and a golf club, while Luke settled for another hatchet and the sledgehammer. He then gave each of us a handgun before tucking one into his own belt.

"We'll stay close together. This place could be overrun, but they seem to be slower, less active during the day. Maybe the sunlight annoys them, I don't know. We've got some duffel bags and backpacks waiting by the door with the gas cans, but we can't be stupid about this. Don't pick up any more than you can carry – we need to be in and out of there as quickly as possible."

Part of me wanted to disagree with or rebel against him; I barely knew this guy, after all. But everything that he said sounded logical, well thought out. "You've been planning this for a while, haven't you?"

Luke grinned. "Guess I just needed you here to convince your brother that it was necessary."

"Oh, I'm sure if you'd batted your pretty eyes at him enough, he would have capitulated eventually." As I was saying these words, I thought they sounded funny, but the hurt look that passed over Joey's face made me realize that perhaps they weren't. "Sorry," I mumbled to him.

He eyed me for a moment, then turned away. "Let's just get going. The sooner we put this little jaunt behind us, the better." The three of us loaded up the big farm truck with some gas cans and empty bags, then climbed in ourselves.

"Stay inside," Joey ordered Mom and Mike. "And don't worry about us being gone for a while. We have no idea how long this will take." I took note of the fact that our mother didn't acknowledge or agree to Joey's warnings, but before I could say anything he had backed out of the garage, turned the truck around, and sped up the driveway. He practically screeched to a halt at the gate; Luke got out to open it and Joey almost forgot to stop and let him back in once Luke closed the gate behind us. As we pulled out onto the road, I bit my lip and stared out the window to keep myself from complaining about Joey's driving. I figured that I'd already upset him enough for one morning. Instead I told them, "Put on some music." Luke looked at Joey, who shrugged.

"There are probably some old CD's in the glove box."

Luke opened it up and shuffled through the handful of discs before finally choosing one. It was a burned CD, no label on it at all, but everything else was clearly country or gospel, and I couldn't help but appreciate the fact that he grimaced at every single one of them. He slid the chosen CD into the player, and when the first song came on I almost laughed out loud. *If anything will cheer Joey up – at least a little bit – this will*, I told myself as I began to sing along.

"As I walk through the valley of the shadow of death, I take a look at my life and realize there's nothin' left...'cause I've been blastin' and laughin' so long that even my momma thinks that my mind is gone..."

Both guys turned to look at me, eyebrows raised, but when I continued to rap along with Coolio it took just a few moments for their stolid demeanors to crack. And then they were singing along as well, and we were all laughing, though far too soon the song and the drive were over and we were once again facing our ridiculous new reality.

We were forced to pull over a good quarter mile from the intersection where the gas station was located. We let a few minutes pass to make sure all was quiet before we gathered up our weapons, bags, and gas cans and climbed out of the truck. "I'd lock it if I were you," I reminded my brother as he started to walk away without doing so.

At least now when he rolled his eyes at me for ordering him around, it took just a few murmured lines of "Gangsta's Paradise" to put a smile back on his face. "Death ain't nothing but a heartbeat away...I'm living life, do or die, what can I say? I'm 23 now, but will I live to see 24? The way things are going I don't know..."

"All right, all right, shhh," Luke cautioned. I couldn't help but turn and stick my tongue out at him, which earned me yet another grin.

"I'd rather die smiling, thanks," I whispered, but after that I obeyed his warning to be quiet.

The closer we got to the gas station, the more difficult it became to pick our way between the haphazardly parked cars and the suitcases, boxes, and bags that littered the road. Most had been ripped open, their contents strewn far and wide, empty bottles and cans and every other type of trash one could think of littered across the ground.

"Maybe this won't be so bad," Joey murmured. "All this stuff everywhere...I think those...those *things*... are a bit too clumsy to figure out how to navigate through it. And there doesn't seem to be anything alive for them to eat, anyway."

"Don't be so sure that we're in the clear. Not yet. I heard them last night...a lot of them. And they couldn't have been all that far away." I shuddered when I remembered the sounds; it was almost as if I could still hear them...

"Oh. *Shit.*"

We were in the parking lot now and couldn't miss the cause for Luke's exclamation.

Someone had taken it upon themselves to lock what appeared to be dozens of people inside the station convenience store. Whether they'd been alive or dead at the time, I couldn't tell, but they were definitely *un*dead now – and despite how quiet we'd been in our approach, they had to have known we were coming. They were groaning, moaning, snapping their jaws, scratching at the windows and doors, piled up against the glass as they strained to escape and attack us. Not even the hum of the station's backup generators could cover the God-awful noises the damn things were making, and I felt my heart hammering in my chest as I stumbled back a step.

"So much for getting anything useful from the store." I didn't even bother to hide my disappointment.

"We'll damn well get at least one of the things that we came here for," Joey snapped, rushing over to the gas pumps. For a moment his initiative took my by surprise, considering how he'd been so against this trip in the first place – but only for a moment. Soon enough both Luke and I followed suit, taking up our places at the pumps on either side of him and hurrying to fill up our own cans. I couldn't help but glance up at the store every few seconds, but we were able to fill and recap the cans without any sort of incident.

"Maybe we should pick through some of this junk on our way back to the truck," Luke suggested. "If we can't get anything from inside, trying to salvage some stuff out here isn't a bad idea."

"Okay," Joey said warily. "But only *directly* on the way back. These things are already heavy enough." He hoisted his gas tank up a little, and headed toward the closest pile of belongings. I split off to his left and Luke to his right, and we slowly made our way back to the truck, stopping every few feet to poke through the piles of things left behind. Most of it was useless, though once in a while one of us would make a soft noise of excitement when we found a package of granola bars, a can of fruit or vegetables, a handful of MREs, even a few half-empty boxes of ammunition. I collected some clothing, too, because Mike didn't have anything other than what he was wearing, and I certainly hadn't packed much for myself, either.

Not surprisingly, Luke heard the noise first. He stopped, stood straight, held up a hand, and slowly turned his head to look over his shoulder. But by then, I'd heard it too – the sound of glass breaking.

What made me turn to look? Did I have some sort of death wish, that I didn't just grab what I could carry and run for the safety of the truck? Or was it just sheer curiosity?

Not that it really matters. I took that moment to glance over my shoulder, just in time to see the zombies spilling out of the station. If we wanted to get any of the things we had gathered – including the fuel – back to the truck, we had to move. *Fast.*

I grabbed hold of the gas can that I'd set on the ground, then hoisted the large bag I'd been filling with supplies onto my opposite shoulder. I didn't bother stopping to shove the clothes I'd chosen into the bag – I just ran, clutching t-shirts and pants in my free hand, feeling them flap against me as I went. Joey was already ahead of me, Luke close enough behind that I could hear his heavy breaths as he lugged a gas can in each hand, his back likely bent under the weight of the large hiking backpack he'd strapped on.

*Dammit, Charlie, if you're going to worry about someone other than yourself, worry about your brother!* It was my mother's voice in my head, and had I not been struggling to keep up the pace while somehow also keeping hold of the heavy gas can, I would have laughed. I could hear the undead coming up behind us, stumbling through the mess that was strewn across the road. *Their own things, perhaps.* They were snarling like a pack of wild dogs, so close behind us, *too* close...but there was the truck, not far ahead, just a few hundred yards away, and we were going to make it, we *had* to make it –

Just then, Joey tripped on something. I saw him go sprawling to the ground and let my momentum carry me forward, sliding to a stop next to him. I dropped to one knee and grabbed at his arm. "Let's go, Joey!"

"My...ankle..." he grunted. "And the gas can, I can't - "

"I've got it!" Luke swooped in, shoving the handle of his second into the same hand as the other one and then quickly scooping up Joey's. "Help him up, Charlie!" He moved on, not that I could blame him, and I had no choice but to struggle to my feet, pulling Joey along with me. *Don't look back, don't look back, don't look –*

I looked back.

They were there, practically on top of us, and I cursed Luke for not dropping the fuel and helping me carry my brother. Joey glanced over his shoulder and saw them too, and he let out a frightened whimper.

"*Fuck* that!" I screamed at him. "We're not dying like this, Joey! I don't care how much it hurts, *run*!"

Surprisingly, he obeyed. I was half dragging him, but at least now he was trying. And then Luke was there beside us, grabbing the last can from my hand and wrapping his arm around Joey's waist. A hundred yards and closing...fifty...twenty feet...ten...

"Get in, get in, get in!" Luke released Joey to drop the gas can into the bed of the truck. The door was already open and I shoved my brother toward it, swinging the duffel bag off my shoulder in the process as I prepared to climb in myself.

"Charlie!" Luke shouted. I turned, and there it was. What had once been a man was now gray-skinned and foul, half its cheek chewed off, its eyes glazed over with a gooey whitish film. My baseball bat was strapped to my back, and I immediately knew that there was no way for me to reach it in time. *The knife, you idiot!*

I yanked the hunting knife from my belt, but my slash was clumsy and the weapon merely got tangled in the zombie's disgusting flannel shirt. I yanked back, trying to work it loose, but at first this only succeeded in pulling the thing closer to me – until with a tear my knife came free, and I drove it upward, through what had once been an

Adam's apple, straight back through its upper neck and the base of its head. I leaned against the truck, bringing my leg up and kicking out, hard, to work the knife free. The thing crumpled to the ground – no death throes for the undead, I guess – and I could barely keep myself from gagging as Luke appeared by my side again, pulling me into the cab with him, depositing me in the passenger seat on his way to grab the wheel. He turned the truck around so fast that the door swung shut of its own accord and I was sent sprawling across his lap.

"It didn't get you, did it? No bites, no scratches, no blood in your orifices?"

"*Orifices?*" I couldn't help but repeat.

"Your eyes, your mouth - "

"I know what an orifice is." I shimmied off his lap and into the passenger seat. "I just can't remember the last time I heard someone actually use the word. But I'm *fine*." I turned to check on my brother. "You okay, Joe?"

He nodded, but his face was white and pinched with fear and pain. "We should have left when we had the gas," he whispered.

"And miss out on all the action? I think not. *Been spendin' most our lives, livin' in a gangsta's paradise...*" I sang softly. My brother merely scoffed and looked out the window, but when I cut my eyes at Luke I saw that he was smiling.

I guess that's the moment I became addicted. To something, anyway...

## LESSON LEARNED

*Knowing all of the lyrics to "Gangsta's Paradise" won't help you in the zombie apocalypse.*

* * * * * * *

Luke was speeding down the road at nearly eighty miles an hour, and though part of me wanted to remind him that we should be driving a bit more cautiously, I couldn't focus on anything except the fact that my hands and arms were coated in sticky blackish-red goo – what I supposed was the zombie version of blood – and that there was a rushing sound in my head. Looking back, I know now that it was an adrenaline high like nothing I'd ever experienced, a thousand times the strength of a runner's high.

It was, in a word, *amazing*.

My knife was still clutched in my hand. I wanted to put it away, but I knew that I should at least wipe it off. My shirt was already ruined, anyway, so I pulled it over my head and cleaned the blade.

"Christ, Charlie, some decency would be nice," Joey grumbled from the back seat. But when I looked at Luke, the corner of his mouth was quirked up.

"I guess 'decency' goes right out the window when one is covered in the blood of the undead," I shrugged.

"You should wash that off of you as soon as you can," Luke pointed out.

"Trust me, I'm counting the minutes. I'm not sure I could stand the smell much longer than that."

Everything still seemed to be in order at the farm – the gate had remained shut and locked, and when we pulled up to the house Mike opened the garage door so that we could park the truck inside. He was closing it again when my mom stepped into the garage and saw Luke and I helping Joey out of the truck. She blanched at the sight of us: her son, clearly injured, and her daughter shirtless and covered in blood.

"Charlie...Joey...are you..." Her voice trailed off as she reached out for us, her hands visibly shaking.

"We're fine, Mom. Joey fell and hurt his ankle, is all."

"But...you're covered in..."

"I had to, err...kill...a zombie. One good shower with a lot of soap and I'll be good as new."

"You had to...to *kill* one of them? What in the world happened out there?!"

"Mom, can we talk about this later?" Joey asked weakly. "I can't handle Charlie's stench anymore, and on top of that, I need to sit down."

"Oh, dear, of course, of course." Mom hurried back into the house while Mike helped Luke half-carry Joey inside. I followed in their wake, knowing that I would need someone to gas and fire up the generator so that I could take a proper shower. I watched our mother continue to fuss over Joey for a few minutes while Luke and Mike unloaded the truck, but finally I had to speak up.

"Um, not to say that Joey's ankle isn't very important, but we don't really know what is causing dead people to rise again, and, uh, I've got a lot of this stuff on my arms and hands and whatnot...Think someone could handle the generator so that I can wash it off?"

"I'll do it," Luke offered. "Mike, would you mind helping?" The two of them went back out to the garage, and several minutes later I heard a dull roar as the large generator kicked on.

"Thanks!" I practically shouted as they came back into the house, and I was on my feet and rushing up the stairs to the bathroom before they could respond. It had only been a little more than a day since my last shower, but it felt like an eternity, and though my adrenaline high was far from wearing off, my stomach was in knots and the smell and feel of the so-called 'blood' was starting to make me feel sick.

I knew that I couldn't waste too much time – time was fuel, fuel that we still didn't have enough of, at least not for luxuries like this – but once I was standing under that hot water and scrubbing myself down with my mother's homemade mint soap, it was hard to not forget myself. It wasn't until I heard a banging on the door that I realized how long I must have been in there, but that sound certainly broke me out of my reverie. I quickly rinsed off the rest of the soap as the banging continued, turning the water off and stepping out of the shower as soon as I could. I wrapped a towel around myself as I opened the door, and of all the people in the household (including my mother, the only other woman) it was Luke who they'd sent to fetch me out of the shower. As soon as he saw me standing there, dripping wet and clad in what now seemed to be a far too small piece of terrycloth, he spun away from me, mumbling, "Sorry, I didn't think – "

"That I'd actually open the door when someone knocked on it so urgently?" I joked.

"I...yeah, I guess. It's just...Cheryl is busy with Joe, and Mike's just a kid...someone needed to come up here and tell you..."

He couldn't seem to spit out the words, so I did it for him. "To stop wasting water and fuel?"

Luke glanced back over his shoulder at me, then quickly looked forward again. "Well, yeah."

To this day I'm still not really sure why I reached out and touched his elbow. "And that's the only reason you came up here?" I was teasing him, and lightly at that, so I was more than a little surprised when he turned around and looked directly into my eyes.

"I suppose I wanted to make sure that you were okay, after...what happened earlier."

"What happened? You mean...killing that thing?" He nodded, and I shrugged. "Of course I'm okay. More than okay, really. I feel..."

"Alive." It was a statement, not a question, and when I looked up at him I noticed a softness in his eyes that hadn't been there a moment before.

"Yeah," I agreed. "I guess that's it." My hand was still on his elbow, and almost without thinking I ran my fingers up his arm, taking hold of the edge of his sleeve and tugging it lightly, encouraging him to step toward me as I moved closer to him. My pulse was racing and my mind was clear of every thought except one – that I wanted to fuck somebody. Any half-attractive man who was both old enough and not related to me would have sufficed, I think, but in this case that left only Luke, who was here, *right* here, and of course other than my towel I was naked already, anyway.

So I let that fall to the floor.

"Charlie..." Luke's voice was strained. "I don't think – "

*Oh. Of course he doesn't want me like* that.

"I...okay, sure. Sorry," I mumbled, my face flushing in embarrassment. But as I bent to pick up the towel, he wrapped his hands around my upper arms and pulled me against him.

"It's not that I don't want to." His face was inches from mine, his eyes wide and sincere. "But if I'm not mistaken, what you did today...that's the first time you've done something like that. I don't want you to act on the way you feel now and end up regretting it later."

*You've got to be kidding me.* "I'm sure you think you're being very noble," I said, "but either one of us could die tomorrow, or the next day, or shit, even later this evening. So if I want this, and you want this, what's the point in holding back?"

He stared at me for what seemed like forever, and then, just as I was about to pull away in frustration, he finally covered my mouth with his. I let him kiss me for a minute, maybe two – I'm not quite sure how long it was. I lost track of time, because *damn* was he a good kisser...but I knew that we didn't have all day, so soon enough I began herding him toward my bed. He stopped kissing me long enough to breathe, "What about the others?"

"I can be quiet," I smiled. "Can *you*?" I pulled his shirt over his head and kissed him again, fumbling with the button of his jeans. He reached down and guided my hands, helping me undo them and then hurriedly kicking them off before dropping down onto my bed. I let Luke pull me onto his lap and I straddled him, thinking about how I'd never been with someone I'd known for so short a time, how I'd not been with anyone other than Dave in so many years...

But then I recalled that moment earlier in the day, that moment when I realized that I could actually *die*, and I suddenly understood that none of that ridiculous, self-conscious bullshit was worth considering at all right now. I leaned down, my nipples brushing against Luke's chest, and I felt more than heard it when he moaned softly into my mouth as I kissed him once again.

## LESSON LEARNED

*Get it while you can, where you can. (If you don't know what I mean by 'it', you're too young to be reading this.)*

\* \* \* \* \* \* \*

I sent Luke back to the kitchen well before I made my way downstairs. He couldn't have been with me for more than ten minutes, and I tried to tell myself that I didn't care if anyone suspected what we'd been up to...but better safe than sorry, right?

I ran a brush through my short but mussed-up hair and chose a worn pair of riding jeans and a soft, faded t-shirt from the few clothing items of mine that my mom hadn't given or thrown away. When I glanced at myself in the mirror, I had to stop myself from giggling. *Talk about a post-sex glow.* It had been good, too, *really* good, which had made it extremely difficult to be as quiet as I would have liked. *Enjoy it while you can, Charlie,* I told myself, *because it was a one-time thing.*

At least, that seemed to be the safest way to look at it just then.

Finally I forced myself to meet everyone in the kitchen. Joey was sitting with his foot propped up while Mom put dinner together. She was baking something in the oven; knowing her, she'd missed using that damn thing more than she missed anything else. Mike and Luke were picking through the stuff that we'd brought back from our run, and when he heard me enter the room Mike glanced up and gave me a grateful nod. "Thanks for the clothes," he mumbled. Then, "I'm glad you're okay."

I couldn't keep myself from smiling. "Thanks. I guess I'm glad I'm okay, too." I winked at him. I could see Luke watching me out of the corner of my eye, but in that moment I thought that it would be best to not meet his gaze. Instead I moved over next to Joey, and only then noticed that Holden was cowering under the table. "What's wrong with him?"

"I think he doesn't like the smell."

"The smell?"

"That awful stench those things give off. I mean it's okay now, at least to us...but he probably still notices it."

"Poor Holdy," I grimaced. I bent down to scratch his head; he sniffed my hand tentatively and let loose a small whine, but at least he let me pet him. "And you, Joey, how are you doing?"

"Freaked out. Ankle's sore. But I'll live."

"That's right you will, because you're not going out like that again. And to bring back what? Some gas for the generator and not much else." Mom wasn't looking at us, but I could hear her voice shaking and I almost felt bad for worrying her as much as we'd obviously done.

"We actually picked up some useful stuff, Cheryl." It was Luke who spoke up for us, and I wasn't sure whether I appreciated or resented him doing so. "Mike here needed some clothes, we must have a couple dozen MREs, and some of these bullets and shells are even going to fit in our guns. This, though...this is probably our best find." He waved his hand over the bottles of medication that were spread before him.

"Where did those come from?" I asked, bending down to pick up a bottle labeled 'Lortab'.

"You and Joey unknowingly grabbed a couple...I took some from the glove box of a car...found the rest here and there. Pretty much just picked up everything I saw without looking at the labels. Some of it is useless, but that right there is a decent pain med, and there are some antibiotics as well. What would be really nice is if we can wait a few days...hope that those things clear out of the immediate area...and then go back and pick that convenience store clean."

"Are you sure that's a good idea?" my mother grumbled.

"They were stuck in there for days – at the very least. They're going to be wandering around looking for their next meal, not hanging out in the parking lot drinking beer and waiting for us to come back." Luke was trying to make light of things, but he also had a point. Unfortunately, neither Joey nor Mom seemed to understand that.

"Are you *joking*?" my brother snapped. "Go *back*? We almost died!"

"There's nothing we need from there that we can't find a suitable replacement for here on the farm," Mom insisted.

"For now, maybe. But if we do end up needing anything, and if we can find it there, better to go back sooner, when there's less of a chance that the area will be crawling with those things." I knew that this wasn't what they wanted to hear, but I had to agree with Luke. "We'll give it a couple of days and talk about it again."

"You can try." Joey set his jaw and looked out the window, then suddenly sat bolt upright. "Uh...we have a problem."

The rest of us followed his gaze, and my first thought was, *what have we done?* I couldn't be certain that the dozen or more undead that were stumbling out of the woods were from the convenience store, but from what Joey and Luke had said, seeing this many of them all at once, during the day and this far out in the country, had to be rare. "The generator," I whispered.

"I'm on it." Luke was on his feet and out the door, and moments later the whirr of the generator was silenced and the oven clicked off.

"Sorry, Mom." Perhaps my apology was unnecessary, but at the moment I didn't know what else to say. "Joey, think you can at least get the kitchen window, if Mike and Luke and I take care of the rest?"

Before he could answer, though, our mother was already hoisting the plywood up. I shrugged and made my way to the living room, Mike and Holden following close behind. "You really think we have to do this?" Mike asked as we latched the first makeshift shutter into place.

"I'm not sure. I think we need to keep this house as quiet and unnoticeable as possible. For all we know, any flurry of movement could attract these things."

Mike was silent as we put up the rest of the plywood on the main floor of the house, working in tandem on the back windows while Luke and Mom fixed up the front ones. When we were finished, though, he stood staring at the last boarded-up window for a moment, and then asked, "Do you think we're really safe here?"

"For right now? Maybe. But forever, well...unless this turns out to be some fluke incident, not some country- or world-wide problem...I doubt it."

"You guys all set?" Apparently Luke had approached us from behind without my noticing; I nearly jumped out of my own skin at the sound of his voice.

"Yeah, we're done," Mike replied.

"Good. We should probably gather in one place and try to keep quiet. I'd say we could read or play a game, but...well, not much light left for that, I guess." Luke grimaced, and I found myself staring at him. There was something in his tone that worried me, something I couldn't quite place, but I knew better than to ask him about it just now. I had a feeling that anything he said would only upset the others, which was why he kept it to himself.

The problem was that I wanted to prove to him that I was strong enough to be his confidante. That I wasn't lying to myself about how bad things probably were, about how safe we would be if we stayed in one place for too long.

My chance came after we'd made sure the others were settled in the living room and Luke insisted on checking out the perimeter. "I'll help you with the window coverings," I offered. "Extra pair of hands, keep things steady, less movement and all of that..."

He hesitated for a moment, but then nodded. "Alright." I could tell that he was reluctant to allow me to tag along, but perhaps he felt it would look worse for him to refuse my assistance. Regardless, he turned his back on me and walked away, leaving me no choice but to simply follow in his wake. Even when we approached the kitchen window, he merely gestured for my help and avoided looking at me at all. "I'll hold it, you look."

I stepped up to the window and peered through the small crack. Without counting I could only guess that there were well over a dozen dead people wandering around the field behind the house. It appeared that they couldn't figure out the fence, as they just kept bumping into it, backing off, and then rushing forward only to run into it again.

"Well?" Luke pressed.

"They're at the fence. Can't seem to get past it. Unless these ones don't go away and their numbers really start racking up, we should be okay."

He let out his breath. "Good."

"Yeah. Good." I stepped back and waited for him to replace the boards, but when he turned around and made to walk away I stopped him. "Luke."

The look on his face was, more than anything else, resigned. "Charlie."

"You know this can't last forever. Us being here, I mean, and it being safe."

"I do, yeah, though I'm surprised you understand that as well."

I rolled my eyes. "I'll ignore that comment. Regardless, doesn't that mean that we should...I don't know...come up with a backup plan? And maybe a backup plan to our backup plan? I mean...what if these things never die...again? What if, no matter what, you become one of them? They'll just keep multiplying, and there will never be enough of the living to take all of them out, and we'll spend the rest of our lives fighting them..."

"Has it ever occurred to you that you may have an overactive imagination?"

"Trust me, I *hope* that's all this is. But if it's not..."

"Yeah. But if it's not." He sighed. "We need to get back to the others."

"But we'll continue this conversation later?" I pushed.

Luke furrowed his brow. "I suppose so. If you insist."

"Oh, I insist. You're not going to get rid of me that easily." I turned and started to walk away, then looked back to see him watching me thoughtfully. "Better come up with some ideas of where we could go, in case we need to leave at a moment's notice." *That's what I'll be doing.* Of course, maybe Luke would think about that...and then maybe he would think about what a burden Joey and Mom and Mike

– and yes, even I – could be. If I were him, I'd certainly consider a quiet disappearance.

*But you're not him,* I reminded myself, *and yet,* you've *already thought about that.*

## LESSON LEARNED

*Make your getaways quiet; make sure you're never followed.*

# Chapter 4
# Staying Alive

After eating a half-cooked meal that had also long gone cold, and then sitting around for several hours – sometimes in silence and sometimes talking quietly – we finally decided that it would be safest for us to all sleep in the same place. Luke and I had checked outside every half hour or so until the sun set and it was too dark to see. The number of zombies was growing, albeit very slowly...the problem was that none of them were wandering away, and several more appeared throughout the afternoon and evening.

When we finally decided to give up watch and try to get some sleep, the five of us gathered in Mom's bedroom on the main floor of the house, pulling out all of the old sleeping bags and blankets and pillows that we could find so that the guys would be comfortable. It had been a while since I'd been so happy to be a girl, because just now it meant that I got to sleep in the bed with my mother. Holden certainly didn't mind it either; he curled up between us, letting out a huff of breath, and soon he was snoring softly the way he always did after a long and tiring (or stressful) day.

I lay there in the bed that my parents had once shared, listening for the steady breathing that would tell me the others were asleep, but eventually it was obvious that none of us would be getting much of *that* tonight. "We should call them something. The zombies," I clarified.

Silence.

"Cannibals?" I suggested.

Joey snorted. "I think that implies that they're alive...that they *know* what they're doing."

"The military phonetic alphabet uses 'Zulu' for the letter 'z'." *Of course it's Luke who comes up with that.*

"Zulus? Ugh, no. Is that really the word they use now?"

"Well, yeah."

"It's a good idea, but I agree with Charlie, Zulu isn't a good name for them." I was surprised to hear Mom speak up. "Didn't they used to use 'zed'?"

"How very European," I joked.

"Zeds? I like it." It was Mike who agreed with her. I was surprised, but what did I know? Maybe he'd bonded with my mother while Joey and Luke and I were out playing "capture the supplies" against a team of undead.

"That's a much older call word, but hey, if this situation will do anything, it'll force society to take several steps back," Luke observed. *Is he just trying to make friends, all of a sudden?*

"Okay then, 'zeds' it is." Why not? I didn't much care; I was just hoping that if we talked long enough, some of us would fall asleep.

There was a long pause before Mike spoke up again. "You don't think...that they could be people again, do you?" It was a child's question, and there was a need in it that would have made my heart ache had I not been forced to kill one of the things mere hours before.

"No, Mike. I don't. And I don't think you'd want them to. Shit, if they knew what was going on, they probably wouldn't want to, either."

"Language, Charlie."

"Sorry, Mom." I was glad that she couldn't see me roll my eyes.

"It's okay, Cheryl." It was strange hearing a boy Mike's age calling my mother by her first name. "She's right. I just thought...my family..."

"What happened, son?" Mom asked, her voice soft.

It was several long moments before Mike replied. "I think it hit the bad areas of the city first. We didn't even know what was going on until it was practically at our doorstep. My mom wanted to get out, but my dad refused to leave. He thought we could hold out...and then my baby sister got attacked. It was just a couple bites and scratches...we thought if we cleaned her up, gave her medicine...but she died right there in her bed, and when she came back, she went after my mom. And when my dad and my little brother and me came home later that day, she came after us. Dad held her off and my little brother and I got away...we'd heard that there was a shelter set up at the YMCA, but by the time we got there it was..." He paused and took a shuddering breath. "I lost him there. I wandered around the outskirts of the city for two days before Charlie found me."

I hadn't asked Mike about his family because I'd assumed he hadn't *wanted* to be asked, hadn't wanted to talk about it, when maybe he *needed* to talk about it...only now that he had, I didn't know what to say. Joey had always been the more comforting of the two of us, and I was more than a little grateful when my brother spoke up. "Your family doesn't have to worry now. About surviving. About being cold, hungry, thirsty...when you think of them, try to remember that. *Only* that."

The problem was that Mike thought he was safe here, when that wasn't really the case. I could discuss the situation with Luke all I wanted, but what about the others? Would they leave when the time came, or would we be forced to wait until it was too late?

It was quiet again, and in the silence we heard them. "I wish they wouldn't - " I stopped myself. My voice sounded small and scared, and I hated the idea that I could be vulnerable like that.

"They're much louder tonight," Mom murmured.

"There are more of them nearby than usual," Luke explained. "A lot more."

"If they don't go away, we'll have to take care of them tomorrow." My stomach turned at the very idea, but was it in disgust or because I was – God forbid, *thrilled* – at the thought of doing so?

"You will do nothing of the sort. Look at what happened today!"

"That was different, Mom. We didn't know they would escape that store. We weren't expecting..." I paused and shook my head. "Anyway. If we go out and take care of some of them tomorrow, we'll have a plan before doing so. And if we can pare down their numbers, we'll be safe here for a little longer. If we can't, or don't, and they keep coming, they'll break through that fence any day. They may not be able to see us, or hear us, but we don't know what their sense of smell is like. We don't really know how much intelligence they have. We just can't *chance* it." I thought of the zed that had grabbed hold of my hair in the city. Had it gotten hold of me by chance, or had it known what it was doing? We simply didn't understand them well enough to be certain either way.

As I'd predicted, none of us got much sleep that night. The moans of the zeds rose and fell, and every rustle of movement put me on edge. But at least I used my time wisely, considering the types of places where we would be safest and trying to recall their proximity to the farm. And then there were the tasks I'd need to work on immediately – packing up some non-perishables, along with at least a couple sets of clothes for everyone. Maybe I was just being my usual glass-half-empty self, but *someone* had to make sure that we were ready to leave at a moment's notice. If the zeds didn't come calling, soon enough we had to expect that other people would show up – and if they did, and they happened to be more numerous and better armed than us, there was no way some simple wooden fences and plywood over the windows would hold them off.

When the gray light of dawn began filtering through the window coverings in my mother's bedroom, I finally allowed myself to get out of bed. She and Joey had fallen asleep at some point, but when I stood up and headed for the door I saw that Luke and Mike were also awake.

"Morning," I mouthed. Leaving off the 'good' seemed an obvious choice – what kind of 'good' was there in a morning that would begin with me doing what was essentially a perimeter check, followed by planning an attack on the undead that had wandered onto the farm throughout the night?

Mike nodded, rubbing his eyes, and Luke grimaced as he stood up. Our movements woke Holden up as well, and he jumped down off the bed, padding after me as I headed into the kitchen. I was starving, and thirsty, but I knew that getting a quick look outside and assessing our situation had to be first priority.

"You ready?" Luke had come up behind me without my noticing – *again*. I stood in front of the boarded-up kitchen window, refusing to turn and face him.

"As ready as I'll ever be." I reached up and undid the makeshift latches that held the plywood in place, and Luke took hold of the board, pulling it back just enough for me to get a glimpse of the outside world.

There were definitely far more zeds roaming around the field than there had been yesterday, but I knew that as long as we made our move soon, it was still a manageable number. I hadn't even realized that I was holding my breath until I let it all out in one long sigh, stepping back from the window so that Luke could replace the covering.

"How is it?"

"We need to take care of it soon, but I think we *can* take care of it, at least."

He nodded brusquely. "You sure you're okay with getting up close and personal with these things...again?"

"As I don't have a choice, I guess I'll just say, 'Sure!' and hope that you believe me." I forced a smile.

"There's always a choice, Charlie."

"Is there? Even now?"

Luke shrugged. "I can take care of things out there."

"And I can stay inside and...what? Cook? Clean? Do some other womanly thing?" I snorted in derision. "I don't think so."

"That's not what I meant. It's just...the best way to ensure survival is to not needlessly endanger yourself."

"Yeah, well, I don't want to just *survive*. I want to *live*." I spun on my heel and marched to the dining room table. "Now let's figure out a plan for getting rid of those zeds." Luke stepped up beside me to mull over the weapons that were spread out in front of us.

"One of us needs to create some sort of diversion, I think." He pinched his jaw between thumb and forefinger, his eyebrows drawn together as he mused over our best course of action.

It took everything in me to not reach up and brush his hair out of his eyes. "I run a lot. My guess is that I'm faster and you're stronger, so I'm probably the better...diversion." I had to turn away from him, unable to hide the smirk that came unbidden to my lips.

"Yes, I suppose you would be." Luke's tone was dry.

"Oh, lighten up." I gave him a light punch in the shoulder. "I'm about to become zed bait, and you the hunter! There's no *way* anything can go wrong."

The way he looked at me then...I swear, it literally made my heart flutter. I sure as hell don't think Dave had ever looked at me like that, with this crazy mixture of amusement and respect and concern...and something else that I couldn't quite place.

But then Luke looked back down at the table and frowned thoughtfully, and I told myself that it didn't much matter how he looked at me – not now when we had such a difficult morning ahead of us, at least. "Think we should do this now, before Cheryl or Joey has time to protest?" he finally asked.

"That's probably not a bad idea." I chewed on my lip for a moment. Part of me didn't want to essentially go behind Mom and Joey's backs, but I was also exhausted and in no mood to argue with them. Besides, Mike could always keep an eye on us from the house and raise them if things took a turn for the worse.

Speaking of Mike, he chose that moment to step forward. He was obviously nervous and uncomfortable. "Are you guys really going to do this?"

"We need to," I shrugged. "Or, well, *someone* needs to, and it just so happens that Luke and I are, at the moment, the most qualified. But you can help out, too. Is that okay?"

Suddenly Mike's nervous and uncomfortable attitude turned into one that was curious and excited. "Yeah, of course, anything!"

"We'll remove the coverings from those windows over there so that you can watch out for us. If it looks like we can't handle the situation, get Mom and Joey. They'll know what to do, and they'll need you to help them, too. Basically, you're a really, really important lookout."

I couldn't tell if Mike was disappointed or relieved when he asked, "You sure you don't need me outside?"

"I think two of us risking our lives like this is quite enough." I winked at him. "Besides, I'm used to incurring the wrath of my mother...it's not something you want to experience, trust me."

"I think it's about that time, Charlie. Choose your poison." Luke already had the hatchet and sledgehammer in hand, as well as a holster and gun strapped around his hips. I followed his lead with one of the smaller handguns, then grabbed the both my baseball bat and the same knife I'd used to kill the zed the day before.

"Trusty sidekick, here," I grinned, patting the knife. My heart was slamming in my chest, my hands trembling slightly, but I didn't feel fearful.

Okay, maybe I was a little bit scared, but mostly I was filled with something like anticipation.

"We should leave through the front. Mike, make sure you lock the door behind us. We'll go down the hill on this side of the house – we need to surprise them, only let them know we're there when *we* want them to know." Luke sounded self-assured, but when I looked at him I saw that his jaw was clenched, his lips thin, his eyes a bit wider than they usually were. He was tense and alert, but like me he didn't seem overly frightened. Something about that gave me strength.

"I'll follow your lead."

Luke nodded, but he still wouldn't look at me. I pursed my lips to keep myself from saying anything. We let ourselves out the front door and waited until we heard the locks click in place on the other side before creeping off the porch and around the corner of the house. Luke kept close to the wall, and when he reached the corner he stopped to peer around it. It was several hundred yards to the fence, and just beyond that I saw the zeds. There were at least a few dozen of them now, milling around much like the animals we'd once kept in the fields.

"Stay on this side of the fence. Run down the line to the right, away from the house." Luke squinted at the tree line in the distance. "How well can you climb?"

"Not very well," I admitted. "But if I remember correctly, there are some trees in there with low-hanging branches. I can probably get far enough up into one of them to at least be just out of reach."

"Good. We need to move." I followed Luke's gaze and saw that several of the zeds who were closer to us seemed to have noticed a change in the air. Maybe they smelled us, or perhaps they could hear us talking, even though our voices were barely above a whisper. "I'll be right behind you," he promised.

"I trust you." The words spilled from my mouth before I even thought about what I was saying, but the strange thing was how much I meant them. I hadn't truly trusted anyone in a long time, and I barely knew Luke – but here I was, trusting him with my life. *He proved himself yesterday morning. He got the fuel to the truck and came back for us.* But that wasn't entirely it, either. Somehow, he just *seemed* trustworthy.

I took a deep breath and started running. Once I was within a few feet of the fence, I stopped short and shouted, "Hey fuckers, come and get me!" And then I was off again, cutting to my right, moving along the fence line at a quick jog. It was hard to ignore the survival instinct in me that screamed *Run! Faster!* I glanced over my shoulder and saw Luke break away from the back of the house and sprint toward the pack of zeds, moving in on them from behind with his hatchet and sledgehammer at the ready. They were closing on me, though, and faster than I expected. I picked up my pace a bit, but found myself looking back once again when I heard a noise that could only be Luke picking one of them off.

He was swinging his sledgehammer as if it weighed nothing, and in the mere seconds that I watched him he took down three zeds. Unfortunately, the ones just in front of him had noticed the commotion and lost interest in me. I turned and began jogging backwards, even slower than before, cupping my hands around my mouth and calling out, "Over here! Weak female failing miserably at running for her life!" As I spun back around and ran a bit faster, I swear I heard Luke snort in amusement.

*You must be imagining things. Who has time to laugh when they're playing zed-killer?*

I was approaching the end of the line. The far end of the fence had fallen over long ago, and I wasn't quite sure what to do. Luke had wanted me to run for the trees, but was that really the safest route? If I did that, and the zeds didn't stay interested in me, we could end up in one hell of a situation. I looked over my shoulder and saw that he'd cut the size of the pack in half, at least – was it possible that was enough? *You know it's not.* We may not have to take out every single one of them, but the more of them we disposed of, the less chance there was that they would continue drawing this many of their friends here on a nightly basis.

I clenched my fists and did as Luke had suggested. If I remembered correctly, there was a large oak right at the tree line. My dad had once attempted to build a tree house for us in it; unfortunately, if it wasn't farm work he wasn't apt to finish things. But there was a chance there were still some boards nailed into the trunk, and that would make this particular tree easier for me to use to climb out of the reach of these things.

And hopefully take a few out myself, on the way...after all, I couldn't let Luke have all of the fun.

The ruins of our tree house were still there, all right – at least enough of them to give me a head start in climbing the tree. I pulled myself up and settled in on the third rung of the half-rotted makeshift ladder, keeping one hand pressed against the tree trunk, tightening my grip on the baseball bat and turning to face the zeds. A jolt of fear ran through me when I saw that even though some of them had followed me, most of them had turned their attention to Luke, and without even thinking about what I was doing I let out a bloodcurdling scream.

Well, it would have been bloodcurdling had any of the zeds actually been composed of blood that could curdle.

A few of the ones that had surrounded Luke turned their heads in my direction, giving him a moment of respite. I swung out with my bat and it connected with the head of the zed closest to me – but not hard enough. My grip on the tree kept me from using my full strength, and the thing merely staggered back a couple of steps before righting itself

– as best it could, shuffling corpse that it was – snarling, and coming at me again. I grabbed the bat with both hands, then braced myself against the solid trunk of the tree, and this time swung with all of my lefty might.

Yeah, I'm a lefty. And remember how I mentioned that my dad always praised my batting skills?

I heard the crack of the zed's skull. I hadn't connected well enough to collapse its head, but I'd definitely broken something, because this time it didn't just stagger backward – it collapsed like a puppet whose strings had been cut. *Success.* I half-turned and pulled myself up a bit higher on the tree, and when the next zed – a shorter one – got close enough, I was able to bring my bat down hard on top of its head. This time I was rewarded not only with a sickening crunch, but also with the sight of the top of the zed's skull sinking in a good inch. As it fell it even knocked one of its followers out of the way, and that one got so confused that it seemed to forget about both Luke and me entirely as it wandered off into the woods.

Another zed was approaching, but this time when I attempted to swing my bat my movement finally broke the rung that I was standing on. I slipped down the tree trunk, feeling it push my shirt up and scratch my back, and in my attempt to steady myself I dropped my trusty weapon. The zed was practically on top of me now, its arms stretched out and its hands grasping at my clothing. I knocked one of its arms out of the way as I reached for my knife, but with a lurch the thing was on me, knocking me off balance. I had no choice but to relinquish my grip on my knife or my position in the tree, and with a frustrated cry I fell to the ground. It wasn't far to fall, but it knocked the air out of me nonetheless, and the zed fell with me, pinning me beneath it. I struggled against its weight, stabbing blindly with my knife until I finally felt it connect with the side of the zed's neck.

But it wasn't any good – I hadn't hit the spine or the brain, and the thing's blackened teeth were inches from my skin. The stench was overwhelming, and though I hadn't eaten that morning I wasn't sure whether I was about to vomit or pass out. My vision was going black, and for a moment I thought, *Mom was right. We shouldn't have come out here.*

And then, suddenly, the weight was gone, the smell still there but nowhere near as strong. I took several deep breaths, and when my sight finally cleared I saw Luke standing over me, highlighted from behind by the sun so that I couldn't see the expression on his face, only that his shoulders were heaving as he tried to catch his breath. "You okay?"

"Yeah. Yeah, I think so. No bites."

"You're sure?"

I nodded.

"Good." He sounded more than a little bit relieved, and reached out his hand to help me up. I took hold of it, squeezing my eyes closed against the dizziness that threatened to overwhelm me as he yanked me to my feet. "We've done all we can here. We need to get back inside."

"What about the...bodies?" I grimaced, knowing that wasn't the proper word for these things, but still in too much shock to come up with something better.

Luke shook his head. "For now we're going to hope that their smell doesn't attract more zeds. Maybe later we can burn them, but we need to get inside and get washed up. I need to make sure..." He stopped, looking away from me.

"I wasn't bitten!" I insisted, and then I realized that he wasn't referring to me. "Oh. Oh, shit. Let's go." I took hold of his hand again and pulled him toward the house, trying to ignore the fact that out of everything I'd done this morning, this – the idea of him being hurt, or worse, infected – was the only thing that truly, deeply scared me.

## Lesson Learned

*Make plans. And then make backup plans. Several of them.*

*******

Mike opened the front door for us as soon as we stepped onto the porch. "Your mom's pretty pissed," he warned.

"She can deal with it. We have other problems." I ushered Luke to the closest bathroom and slammed the door behind us so that no one would know what was going on – at least not yet. "Take off your clothes," I whispered. He hesitated for a moment, but when I stepped forward to do it for him he shook his head and obeyed. "Where do you think they got you?" I asked as I began running my fingers down one of his arms, turning it over in my hands, eying it carefully for any bites or scratches.

Luke pulled away from me. "I don't know, it definitely wasn't a full-on bite…maybe a scratch, on the other arm."

Before he could protest I grabbed the offending appendage. Sprays of the red-black goo that served as zed 'blood' painted his skin – *why* hadn't we thought to wear long sleeves? I rubbed his arm with my fingers, smearing the gore as I looked for an actual injury. "I don't see anything," I finally told him. "Are you sure – "

"I felt something." Luke was adamant, peering stubbornly at his arm. Finally I reached for his chin and gently forced him to look at me.

"I'm sure you felt something, but whatever it was didn't break the skin. You're fine. You'll *be* fine. Think about something else – tell me how many of them we took out."

"All but a few, I think. There may be three left, four at most."

"We did good, then."

"Yeah…yeah, we did. But Charlie, you – "

"I'm fine, too. I am. More than fine, in fact." I stepped toward him and tilted my head up, searching for his lips. He kissed me softly before pulling back a bit.

"This is just the adrenaline talking," Luke murmured against my mouth.

"So what?"

"So, I don't want you to want me every time you're high from killing a zed or two."

"Or three or four," I reminded him. "And besides, I want someone, some*thing*, and my brother and Mike certainly aren't options."

I knew I'd said the wrong thing even before he snorted in disgust and jerked away from me. "You're a piece of work," he growled, pushing past me and letting himself out of the bathroom.

A moment later Mike stuck his head in. "Are you guys okay? What happened out there? I tried to keep watch, but at one point all I could see was the zeds milling around…and then you were kind of in the trees…"

"We took care of them. The majority of them, anyway."

"Is Luke okay? He seemed upset. "

"He thought he'd gotten scratched or something. By one of the zeds. But he didn't, and then he…didn't appreciate me teasing him about it," I lied.

"Oh. Well…he'll get over it." Mike smiled at me, and I felt I had no choice but to smile back.

"So. How angry is my mom? " I had to change the subject, and this seemed like the most appropriate question at the moment.

"About like you expected. "

*Of course.* "Guess I'll go face the music. " *Nothing like having all but one person in the house mad at you.* I had to assume that Joey would take Mom's side – he hadn't thought we needed to take care of the zeds near the house, either. And as I recalled the one who had lost interest in me so quickly, I wondered if perhaps they were right. I'd thought these things were mindless except for their desire for food – *living* food – but if it was *that* easy for them to essentially forget about meat that was just a few feet away…

"You sure everything went okay out there?" Though he was trying to hide it, I could tell that Mike was concerned. I suppose I wasn't surprised – I'd always been something of an open book. *That may need to change. And soon.*

"Wouldn't have said so if it hadn't." I gave Mike a quick smile and then turned away, heading toward the kitchen. I knew I would find Mom and Joey there, but Luke was notably absent. *He must have gone to wash off. You need to think about doing that soon, too.* Maybe I could make some quick excuses to my mother, go find Luke, apologize to him, *talk* to him, tell him what I was *really* thinking…

*No way in hell.* I would apologize for saying something crass, sure, but anything more than that would be too much. I wouldn't be throwing myself at Luke, not for any reason. If he couldn't deal with sex for the sake of sex, that simply wasn't my problem.

Or so I wanted to believe.

"*What* were you thinking? You could have been bitten – you could have *died!*" Mom snapped as soon as I walked into the room.

"With all due respect, if I'd been bitten, I would have died eventually."

"Do *not* play semantics with me, young lady. Those *things* were just wandering around out there. They would have gone away eventually – they wouldn't have had any food to keep them here."

"What do you think we are to them, if not food? We have fuel for the generator, but we wouldn't have been able to use it. Wouldn't have been able to go outside to use the grill, either. Sitting in this house with the windows boarded up, being as quiet as possible – what kind of a life is that?

Luke and I took our chances, and now we'll all have a bit of a reprieve."

"Just leave her be, Mom. You know you can't argue with Charlie. Besides, she smells freaking awful." Joey curled his lip at me. "I'm beginning to wonder if you're only doing this so that you can take a hot shower every day."

"Oh, absolutely," I sneered. "Risking my life for a hot shower really is the perfect plan, isn't it?"

"Just get upstairs. I'll show Mike how to turn on the generator. Keep it short this time, though."

I nodded. "What about Luke? He'll need to wash up too, why didn't you turn on the generator already? "

Joey shrugged. "He said he was going to use cold water. Don't know what his problem is, but he didn't seem half as pleased as you that you guys took care of those zeds."

"He thought one of them got him. Not sure how, or why, because I checked and he's fine. Guess he's still shook up about it, though. "

"Suppose so."

"Well, if you'll take care of that generator, I'll go wash this shit off me. I'll be done in a few minutes, promise."

"Yeah, sure." Joey clearly didn't believe me, but I could forgive him that considering he'd stopped Mom and I from fighting. Mike was helping my brother out of his chair, though, and I wanted to escape from the kitchen before she could start in on me again.

This time I made sure to shower as quickly as possible, not wanting them to send anyone knocking. After toweling off and pulling on some fresh clothes, I opened the door to find Holden waiting for me. He sniffed me tentatively and then wagged his tail. I bent down and scratched his head.

"I know you don't like the smell, boy, but you're probably just going to have to get used to this. The day may come when I don't have a proper shower to clean me up. Now let's go get some food…I'm starving."

Thankfully Mom had taken advantage of the generator being on again and was cooking something in the oven. "We've been out of meat since we had to eat the last of what was in the freezer, after the power went out and it thawed. But I'm baking some eggs in bell peppers, with rice and even a bit of cheese. It's the last of that, but...I thought you could use it after this morning."

I glanced at the kitchen table, where Joey, Luke, and Mike were all sitting. None of them would look at me, so I couldn't be sure if any of them had something to do with my mother's apologetic attitude – but at this point I was exhausted and just grateful to not be arguing, so I decided to take things at face value.

"Thanks, Mom, They'll be perfect."

"There are some pecans on the table as well, in case you need something to tide you over until I'm done cooking. Got them from the trees just before all of this started happening." She knew that I wasn't a big fan of pecans, but she must have realized that at this point just about any food would taste amazing. I slid into the chair next to Joey's and grabbed a handful of nuts from the bowl.

"Do I smell better?" I teased, leaning toward my brother and shaking my still-damp hair right near his face.

He grimaced and wiped some water droplets from his cheek. "Yeah. Thanks for the mini shower."

"Anytime, Joe, anytime." I looked over at Luke, who studiously avoided meeting my gaze. "You sure you don't want to grab a hot shower while you can?" I asked him, but he still didn't look at me; he merely shook his head 'no' in response. "Suit yourself." I turned back to Joey and Mike. "How's it look outside?" The coverings had been taken down from most of the windows, but I had no desire to peer out at the zed bodies littering the field.

"No new ones have showed up, and it looks like the few that were left have wandered off."

"Good." I couldn't hide my relief. "Good. Hopefully this will buy us a little bit of time. "

"A little bit of time? I'm certain we'll be safe, won't have to deal with something like that again, at least not for quite a while," Mom said cheerfully.

I glanced at Luke a second time, but he kept his eyes on the table. I couldn't help but roll my own eyes – I knew that he agreed with me, but it appeared that he was angry enough to refuse to back me up just now. And I was certainly too tired to deal with this on my own. "Sure thing, Mom," I hedged. I felt Joey and Mike level their gazes at me. They knew that I wasn't being honest, but it seemed that they weren't about to call me out or give their own opinions on the situation, regardless of whether or not they trusted that Mom was right.

"I think I'm going to go have a quick rinse. I haven't had a real shower in far too long. If the timer goes off, take those out of the oven and help yourselves." Mom smiled at us and left us alone. As soon as I heard her door close, I rounded on the guys.

"Luke said we should go back to that convenience store soon, and I agree. We need to stock up while we can. The farm appears to be pretty safe for the moment, and I doubt there are many zeds still hanging around that gas station…not when they were stuck in there for days. Joey, I know you won't be up for it, but Mike, if you're willing you can come along." At this Luke finally looked at me, surprised and maybe a bit concerned, so I quickly continued, "Of course, you'd stay in the truck as a lookout while Luke and I went through and gathered what we could. "

"I wouldn't need to stay in the truck." Mike looked hurt, clearly thinking he was still being left out.

"I'm sure you can take care of yourself, Mike, but trust me, after what happened last time we need to make sure one of us is keeping an eye on things from a safe place." It was a somewhat lame excuse, but after a moment he leaned back and crossed his arms over his chest.

"Okay. " He wasn't happy with the idea, I knew, but he'd get over it.

"Tomorrow, then? " I suggested.

"Can't sit still for a minute, can you? " Luke mumbled.

"Well, we can wait longer than that if need be, but I assumed we should go as soon as possible…just in case."

"If I know anything, it's that you don't argue with Charlie when she's made up her mind." Joey sounded less than pleased. "And if you think it will be safer to go tomorrow rather than wait…"

"Yeah, she's right about that, at least." Luke was obviously reluctant to agree with me, so when he did it anyway, I flashed an appreciative smile at him – a smile that he did his best to ignore.

"When are you going to tell Mom, then?" Joey asked.

"Not today. I think I've probably upset her enough for now."

"Yeah, well, don't go leaving before she gets out of bed tomorrow. I think she was angrier about that than anything else, this morning."

"We'll prep for the run and then tell her right before we leave. I just don't want to deal with her having hours – or longer – to try to talk us out of it."

"Fair enough."

The rest of the day passed by quietly. Our meal was finished without interruption, and though we did board up the windows again at dark, we also lit some candles and played – of all things – The Game of Life. "How ironic," Joey laughed when I set it out on the table.

"I don't know if it's exactly ironic, but it really called out to me just now," I grinned.

"You two," Mom sighed, rolling her eyes at us. Mike smiled uncertainly and even Luke's mouth twitched as he suppressed his own amusement.

The candles were burning low by the time we finished the game, but I made sure to mention that it had been worth it...if only because in the back of my mind I was able to hope that we would find replacements for them when we went on our run the next day. It was still fairly early – just before ten – when we all made our way to our respective beds. As I crawled into mine, Holden by my side, I tried not to think about Luke or about our argument. *If that's what you can even call it.* But no matter what I did, he was at the forefront of my mind – and for the first time in a long time, I found myself wishing that I wasn't sleeping alone.

And the more I thought about it, the more I wished that it was him by my side.

*Not that there's anything you can – or will – do about that. Especially tonight.* Instead I rolled over and wrapped my arms around Holden. He would just have to do for now.

## LESSON LEARNED

### *You can't be picky during the zombie apocalypse.*

\* \* \* \* \* \* \*

When I woke up the next morning, though, it appeared that Holden had gotten tired of my mildly suffocating embrace, having moved from his spot next to me and stretched out across the foot of the bed. I sat up and gave him a pat on the side. "Some comfort you are, Holdy."

My watch told me that it was just shy of seven, and I couldn't help but smile at the fact that in my old life, this would have been one hell of an early rise on a day when I didn't have to be anywhere at a specific time.

*But you* do *have things to do today,* I reminded myself.

I woke Mike up and we went downstairs. Luke was awake as well, and he informed us that he'd already put the two empty gas cans and some bags in the truck for our trip. "We can eat and then relax for a while, wait for Cheryl and Joey to get up. Once Cheryl knows what we're doing, we just have to hop in the truck and go."

"We should get going pretty soon. The earlier we leave, the earlier we get back, and I want plenty of time in case something goes wrong. Honestly, my mom *never* used to sleep this late."

"This is a pretty big change for her. She may try to act like nothing is wrong, but I'm sure she's stressed out, and possibly depressed."

I glared at Luke. "My mother is not *depressed*. She's stronger than anyone I've ever known."

"Did I say that your mother was weak? Being negatively effected by something of this magnitude doesn't make a person weak, Charlie. I'm sure your mother is quite strong – she raised you and Joey, after all."

Mike chuckled, but one quick look from me shut him right up. Wanting this particular conversation to be finished, I opened the pantry and grabbed a granola bar, tearing off the wrapper and practically stuffing it into my mouth to keep myself from saying anything else. Luke and Mike seemed to take the hint and found themselves some breakfast as well. We ate in silence, but when we were done Luke asked, "Is there another approach to that gas station? I'm thinking it may be a good idea to find one, see if we can get the truck right up to it."

"There are a couple of ways to get there…obviously they mean driving around a bit more, and it would take more gas if the first detour doesn't work and we have to backtrack and try another…but yeah, maybe we could find a way through." I was already mapping out the routes in my head and trying to recall how much gas was left in the truck.

Luke answered my unasked question. "We were at about half a tank when we got back the other day."

"We should be fine then, but if none of them end up working out we could be close to empty by the time we get back."

"Then we siphon fuel from another car, or stop using the truck," he shrugged. "It won't do us much good to have Mike on lookout in it if he can't see us or the gas station at all."

"In that case I can just come with you guys," Mike offered.

"I don't think so. You've been through enough – I don't want you risking your neck for some measly supplies." *Not yet, anyway.* The day would probably come when we had no choice, but for now…he was just a kid, and I felt some responsibility for keeping him safe.

"What's all this about supplies?"

Apparently none of us had noticed that Mom was awake. I couldn't be sure how much of our conversation she'd heard, but before I could even begin to explain anything Luke spoke up. "We talked about making another run to the gas station, and it's best to do it now. The farm is secure, and the area around the station probably isn't overrun with zeds anymore. But it's likely that neither of those things will last, so Charlie and I are going to go out again – and Mike is coming along as our lookout. He'll stay in the truck, of course; it's just that a third set of eyes is really necessary for something like this, and Joey's not in any condition to come along."

"I'm sure you're right about that, but is this really necessary?" my mother pressed. It was obvious that she didn't want us to go, but at least this time she was showing some restraint rather than simply insisting that we stay where we were.

"Yes, Mom, we're sure." I was firm in my response, but still surprised when she made no more protest outside of holding her hands up, palms out, and shaking her head in what appeared to be disappointment.

Luke gave her an apologetic smile. "And we really should get going. This run may take us a little longer than the last – we want to try to get the truck right up to the station, which means finding a different way around."

"We'll probably approach it from the south," I clarified.

"Well." Mom looked from me to Luke, then back again. "You know where you're going, at least. "

"Yes, Mom, I do."

"Off with you, then. After all, I don't want to be worrying about you for the entire day. I expect to see you back here in no more than a couple of hours."

Not wanting to look a gift horse in the mouth, as they say, I gestured to Mike and Luke and the three of us made our way out to the truck. Mom helped us with the garage door, and once we'd reached the road we made certain to stop and shut the main gate behind us again. "We'll try the longest way first; it's a lot of back roads, so it's more likely that they won't be as crowded even as we get closer to the store." I gave terse directions as we made our way across the main road that led to the station, driving several miles south before cutting back east and then finally north again. Though there were some cars parked along the road south of the gas station, we were able to maneuver around them. It helped that unlike the main road, the southern approach didn't have a deep ravine on the one side. That, and it appeared that the people who had gathered on this approach had been much more organized. *But they still disappeared.*

*Or died.*

"We really should have gone this way last time," I grimaced as we pulled right into the gas station parking lot.

Luke shrugged. "That experience made us think a lot more clearly. Now Mike...if you see anything, you give the horn one quick hit, okay? Just one. And...well, don't do anything rash. Charlie and I can take care of ourselves, you've seen that, so just lock these doors and stay low. You remember how to get back to the farm?" Eyes wide, Mike nodded as Luke handed him the keys. "If something happens to us, you get out of here as quickly as you can. Just go. Understand?"

"But - "

"No 'buts'," I interrupted. "If we can't make it back to the truck for some reason, for any reason at all, I *order* you to leave us here. Sometimes it's gotta be every person for themselves, Mike."

Before he could protest any more, I nodded to Luke and we gathered our empty bags and climbed out of the truck. I had my bat in hand and he had his hatchet at the ready; eying our surroundings carefully, we slowly approached the front of the store. There was glass everywhere from the other day, and as we picked our way inside we could see that it was a complete mess. Luke stopped, looked around, and sighed. "Look for bottled water, food, any sort of medicine – there's got to be things like cough drops, Ibuprofen, and the like somewhere in here. Shit, I guess at this point just pick up anything that seems even half-useful."

"Got it." I peered around, trying to note any movement in the darker corners of the store, but it seemed as if the place was in fact completely empty. I was relieved, but still not ready to let my guard down, so I barely paid attention to the types of food that I pulled off the racks. I tossed them haphazardly into my bags, then made my way toward the coolers, grabbing as many bottled waters as would fit in with the food. I nearly jumped out of my skin when I felt something take hold of my shoulder, but of course it was just Luke. "Jesus, announce your presence next time," I hissed.

He gave me an amused look. "Good to know you think so highly of me, but I'm not quite sure if I'm on the "Lord and Savior' level."

My mouth dropped open. "Was that a *joke*? You're suddenly *actually* talking to me again, and the first thing you do is crack a joke?!"

"Well, it put me in a bit of a good mood when I hit the jackpot over there." He made a vague gesture toward the back of the store. "Travel packets of almost every kind of over-the-counter medicine you could possibly think of. I grabbed everything they had, and some food as well. I see you've got the water." Luke nodded at my bulging bags.

"Yeah, and it's heavy, so if we could get out of here - "

I was interrupted by the short honk of a horn. Before I could do or say anything, Luke dropped his bags and dragged me down into a crouch, pressing his finger to my lips. "You stay right here – I'll go see what this is all about." I began to open my mouth, an argument already formed in my mind, but he just shook his head, stood up, and was gone.

Several long moments passed, and then I heard people talking – Luke was one of them, of that much I was certain. The other, I was sure, was a stranger. I couldn't make out what they were saying, but their voices rose and fell for what seemed a lifetime before Luke finally called, "Charlie, come out here."

I eased my bags off my shoulders and stood, slowly making my way outside. Mike had clearly obeyed my order to stay in the truck; he was nowhere to be seen. And off to the right stood Luke, facing three people – a couple who appeared to be in their early twenties, the young woman holding a little girl who was probably three or four years old. The man had a shotgun in his hand, but it was resting at his side, the barrel pointed at the ground. All three of the strangers looked frightened, their eyes darting from Luke to me and back again, almost as if they didn't quite believe that we were real.

Although they looked unassuming, I couldn't bring myself to be as trusting as Luke. I took my place at his side with my bat at the ready and my free hand cupped over the grip of my gun. I left it in its holster, but I wanted these people to see that even if Luke had let his guard down, I meant business. "What's going on?" I asked warily.

"Charlie, this is Daniel, his wife Lauren, and their daughter Mabel. They're from the town about five or six miles up the road, here." He pointed east. "They needed food, but when they tried to go to the supermarket and gas station closer to home, they were run off by zeds. Couldn't even get back to their car, so they just started walking." Luke looked pointedly at Daniel. "Did I get that right?"

The young man nodded. "Started walking yesterday. Had to stop for the night, though. Found an abandoned lot, fenced in. Broke into the shed and slept in there...or tried to. When we got up, those things were pressed against the fence at the back side of the lot. We let ourselves out the front and made a run for it. Still can't believe we got out of there alive."

"Mm-hmm." I crossed my arms over my chest and assessed the three of them. They were bedraggled and had some scrapes here and there, but otherwise they seemed okay. I didn't care for Daniel having a shotgun in his possession, but this was the South, after all. I nodded toward the weapon. "You hunt?"

"Deer. Turns out it was good practice."

"But we don't have many shells left," Lauren admitted.

Daniel glared at her. "Lauren! We can't go around telling people that. We don't know them from a hole in the wall!"

"And we don't know you," I pointed out. "But we won't bother you. We got what we came here for, and we can be on our way."

"Charlie." Luke was clearly exasperated. "Hold on a minute, folks," he said to the little family, then grabbed my upper arm and pulled me aside. "We can't leave them here," he growled into my ear.

"Why not? For all we know, he's an ex-con, and she's a...shoplifter. Or something," I finished lamely.

"Or he's just a young guy who worked a normal job not two weeks ago and is now left with nothing but the knowledge that he has to protect his wife and kid. That little girl is barely more than a toddler, Charlie. We can't just abandon them to fend for themselves, at least not without trying to help them. We should bring them back to the farm and give them some respite before we send them on their way."

I glanced over my shoulder at the family. Daniel and Lauren had their eyes fixed on the ground, obviously attempting to ignore us, but the little girl was staring straight at me. I didn't even like kids, but when I saw her wide, fearful eyes, I knew that I wouldn't be able to argue with Luke about this anymore. "Fine. But if my mom asks, this was your idea, and I do *not* agree with it."

"Your mother wouldn't want me to leave them out here either, not when they have a little girl in tow."

"We'll see about that." I turned on my heel and marched over to the family. "Daniel, I'll need to take your gun. You'll get it back eventually, though – we have plenty of our own." *There, make sure he knows that we're well armed.* "Luke, why don't you go get our bags. I'll take them over to the truck." I was a bit surprised when he listened to me without protesting at all – maybe he knew that he'd pushed my buttons quite enough. Daniel reluctantly handed his shotgun to me, and I gestured for them to follow. "It's going to be a bit of a tight fit on the way back. One of you will have to hold your daughter in your lap. I'm sure Luke will drive carefully, though."

Just then I saw movement over Lauren's shoulder. *Zeds.* No more than half a dozen, but that was quite enough to concern me. "Luke, we've got company!" I herded the family to the truck. Mike opened the door and the three of them clambered inside. I turned to see Luke striding toward us, loaded down with the bags of supplies from the store.

"We still need fuel, and I'd rather not come back here anytime soon," he said as he tossed his burden into the bed of the truck and grabbed the gas cans, setting them on the ground between us.

"Agreed. I'll pump, you hold them off?"

He nodded. Thankfully they were still quite a distance away – several hundred yards, at least. I filled the truck first, but by then the zeds were in the parking lot, picking up speed as they shuffled toward us, having noticed that there was, in fact, food close by.

"I don't want to let them get much closer," Luke said through gritted teeth.

"Use the gun, then," I told him.

"The noise – "

"Fuck the noise! We're going to be out of here in a minute or two anyway!"

Luke hesitated for another moment, then swore under his breath and pulled out his gun. He leveled it at the zeds, picking them off one by one. Each shot frayed my nerves just a bit more, but soon enough it was quiet again. I finished filling the gas cans while Luke scanned the perimeter. "Let's go," I finally said. He lifted the cans into the bed of the truck and moved around to the driver's side in silence. I looked around one last time, but didn't see anything out of the ordinary – and no zeds, either. I slid into the passenger seat and we were off, heading home with plenty of supplies – *and a few new burdens, as well*, I mused, watching Daniel, Lauren, and Mabel in the rearview mirror. I caught Mike looking at me, his expression a mixture of curiosity and concern; I met his eyes in the mirror and pulled a face. He grinned, shook his head, and then turned to look out the window.

The drive seemed to take no time at all, probably because I was more than a little bit nervous about bringing these strangers home with us. I cut my eyes at Luke several times, but he was focused on the road, his jaw set and his knuckles white on the steering wheel. *Good, he's worried too.* I didn't know why this pleased me so much; perhaps because he'd seemed so certain that bringing this family home with us was a good idea. When we pulled up to the farm, I got out of the truck and opened the gate, waving him through. "I'll walk," I mouthed, and he continued up the drive while I shut and locked the gate, taking a deep breath before following at a brisk jog, looking left and right to make sure that there weren't any unwanted visitors around.

By the time I made it up to the house, Luke had pulled the truck into the garage and Mike was ready to shut it behind me. Daniel, Lauren, and Mabel were huddled by the door that led into the house, and waited for us as we unloaded the bags of supplies that we'd collected from the convenience store.

"I'd better go in first." Luke adjusted the strap of one of his bags and knocked softly on the door, which my mother opened moments later. I saw her step aside to let him in, and I gestured for our new acquaintances to follow.

The next thing I heard was Mom's stern voice. "What's all this? Where are Mike and Charlie?"

"We're here, Mom." I squeezed into the foyer, Mike at my heels.

"Cheryl, this is Daniel and Lauren and their daughter Mabel. They showed up at the gas station while we were there. They had nowhere else to go, no car, and Daniel is almost out of ammo for his gun. I thought it would be best to bring them back with us, at least for now."

"It seems mighty convenient that they would appear out of thin air in the short time you were at the station." Mom looked at me out of the corner of her eye; I shrugged.

"I've got his gun, and they've got a child. Plus Luke insisted." I flashed him a sarcastic smile. He frowned at me and turned away.

Mom's expression – and voice – softened immediately. "Of course he did."

I rolled my eyes. *Is everyone but me under his spell?* Of course, as soon as I asked myself this I remembered the feel of his hands roaming my body, his solid arms supporting me, the way he looked at me when he was amused, or *didn't* look at me when he was frustrated with me... *Oh for fuck's sake, Charlie, pull yourself together.*

"We have plenty of room here," Mom continued. "If you want your privacy, you may want to sleep in the basement bedroom, but we can figure that out later. First let's get you some food."

By the end of the day we had inventoried our new supplies and Daniel, Lauren, and Mabel had made themselves at home. I suppose I'd known that the moment Mom laid eyes on that child, she'd never be able to insist that these people leave – not soon...and not later, either.

That evening we fired up the generator and allowed ourselves hot showers – all of us – while Mom cooked a big dinner. Vegetarian still, but at this point I wasn't sure I'd be able to eat meat again anytime soon.

And when dinner was over, Mom whispered something in Luke's ear. He nodded, smiling, and disappeared from the kitchen. I heard him rummaging around somewhere, and when he came back he had a bottle of wine in each hand. "There's plenty more where this came from," he announced. "Cheryl thought that we should celebrate our successful run today, and our new friends."

"The more the merrier, at times like these," Mom piped up. I raised my eyebrows – my mother had never been one to surround herself with people; in fact, she generally liked being alone. And the wine...well, that was an entirely different matter. Our father had been something of a teetotaler, and I was vastly curious as to whether Mom had started a wine collection before or after he'd passed away.

*Why do you even care? Just enjoy yourself for once!* Even as I told myself to do so, though, I wondered whether drinking this wine would really be celebratory, or merely a way to attempt to forget everything that had happened in the past few days.

Not that I let that stop me from accepting the large glass of the Veramonte Cabernet Sauvignon that my mother poured for me. We drank and talked, drank and boarded up the windows, drank and played cards. As the night wore on, one by one the others went to bed – Mabel fell asleep in her father's arms, and soon after that Daniel and Lauren said their goodnights. Mom was next, clearly tipsy from the two glasses of wine she'd enjoyed. Mike stayed up until I called him out for nodding off, at which point he grumbled at me and went upstairs.

I had lost count of how many glasses of wine I'd drank when Luke suddenly excused himself to help Joey to the room they were sharing. I leaned back on the couch and closed my eyes, losing myself for a moment as I scratched Holden's head and breathed deeply, wishing that I could calm myself down enough to meditate. But the sound of footsteps startled me out of my reverie, and both Holden and I sat up straight, peering into the darkness. The candles had long since been put out, and my eyes weren't adjusting fast enough. The thought that it could be Daniel crossed my mind, and I called out softly, "Who's there?"

"It's just me, Charlie."

*Luke.* Basically the last person I expected it to be...but if I was honest with myself, the only person I *wanted* it to be. "I thought you'd gone to bed."

"No. Just helping Joey. His ankle - "

"Is probably fine. He's milking this for all it's worth."

"I'm actually worried it's broken. He doesn't want to worry your mom, but he's in more pain than he's letting on. I'm thinking about fixing up a splint for him. If it doesn't heal properly..." I felt the couch cushions shift as Luke sat down just a couple of feet away.

"Too bad none of us is a doctor...unless Daniel or Lauren is holding something back."

"I had some medical training when I was in the service. It'll suffice so long as nothing really over the top happens."

"Well aren't you just Mr. Perfect." The words were out of my mouth before I realized that yet again, I was saying something I shouldn't.

Maybe the alcohol had loosened Luke up a bit, though, because he just snorted and said, "I've got my good qualities, even if some people don't want to see them."

"And you understand the art of sarcasm. How endearing."

"Shut up, Charlie." I felt him move toward me, and suddenly his hand was on my shoulder, turning me to face him. "What you said yesterday – about me being the only available guy – did you mean that?"

"Well I'm sure as hell not about to put the moves on my brother or a fifteen-year-old boy," I replied weakly. I knew that this wasn't the answer he was looking for, but then he hadn't really asked the right question, either.

"You know what I meant. But if that's the way you want to be, then just forget it." Exasperated, Luke released me and leaned back into the couch. I could see his outline as he balanced his elbows on his knees and leaned forward, pressing his fingertips to either side of his head and massaging his temples.

I bit down on my lip. I knew what the truth was, but I just wasn't sure if I should – or even *could* – say it. It had been a long time since I'd dated, if that's even what you could call this…but Dave and I had played coy games with each other for nearly a year before we finally buckled down and had the "we like each other and should be in a relationship" discussion. And how in hell did a discussion like that even factor into this world, anyway?

"What do you want me to say?" I finally asked.

"Huh?"

"I need to know what you want me to say."

"Jesus, Charlie, you're ridiculous. I want you to say what *you* want to say." He paused and drew a deep breath. "I just want you to be honest with me, is that really so much to ask? Especially now that we've risked our lives together not once, not twice, but *three* times?"

*He has you there.* I squeezed my eyes shut for a moment. "No, I suppose it's not too much to ask. The thing is, though, I'm really not sure what to say. I mean…we barely know each other." Silence. Apparently he really was going to refuse to give me any guidance. "Fine. You're attractive, I'll give you that. I don't really know much about your friendship with my brother, but he seems to trust you, which is a pretty big deal – Joey…has a hard time trusting people. And whatever you did for my mom, she's smitten with you as well."

"I'm not asking about how Joey or your mom feels about me, Charlie. I'm asking why you…wanted me. Or rather, asking you to clarify what you said about wanting me."

"Yeah…I know," I admitted. I grimaced, glad that the darkness hid my expression from him. "The problem is, things aren't the way they used to be, and they'll very likely never be that way again. If I saw you pass by on the street in my old life, sure, I would have given you a second look. If I'd gone down to visit Joey – which in and of itself probably wouldn't have happened – and he introduced you to me, and we talked, I'm sure I would have known that you were the type of guy I'd like to get to know better. If my brother had brought home someone else, someone who wasn't you, who I maybe wasn't as attracted to, or who was kind of an ass, then…well, I guess I probably wouldn't have thrown myself at that person. But he brought *you*, and…well, here we are."

"Yeah. Here we are."

The silence between us stretched for several long moments, until finally I couldn't take it anymore. "Was that a good enough answer for you?" My voice was so low that when Luke didn't reply for quite some time, I wondered if he'd even heard me. I had just about resolved to go to bed when he finally spoke.

"For now, yeah, I suppose it was. "

"For now? Luke, I'm sorry, I just – "

He kissed me then. He was so quick about it that I hardly even noticed that he'd moved toward me, but then his mouth was hot on mine and our embrace lasted so long that when he finally pulled away – just a bit – I was practically gasping for air. I reached for him again, and he laughed softly, holding me back just enough so that my lips couldn't find his. "Does your offer from yesterday still stand?" he whispered.

"Yes. If you'd like to come upstairs – "

"I would."

I groped for his hand, found it, and we stood. Holden followed us up the stairs, but when I shut my door behind the three of us I said, "It's the floor for you, boy. At least for a little while." I fumbled to light the candle on my nightstand, and when its flame was casting flickering shadows on the walls Luke sat down on the edge of my bed and pulled me into his lap. "Will you stay with me tonight?" I murmured into his ear. I felt him nod, and then I searched for his mouth again.

This time, he let me kiss him.

## LESSON LEARNED

*Never pass up the chance to collect supplies.*

# PART TWO

## Three Months In

# Chapter 5
# Farm Life

"We have to leave." My chest was heaving, my arms shaking with exhaustion. "We can barely go outside anymore, and there are no stores left to raid around here, anyway. If we don't go soon, we'll be overrun."

"Mom's not going to like it."

"She's right, Joe. Every day we stay here is one day closer to us not being able to leave at all." Luke sounded as tired as I felt. I wanted to lose myself in his embrace, I wanted to sleep for a day or a week or a month, I wanted to never have to leave my bed again. Of course we didn't have that luxury...not that I believed that either one of us would put up with just hiding away and waiting for death – *or was it un*death*?* – to come find us.

"If you hadn't always agreed with her before you started sleeping with her, I'd wonder about you, Luke," Joey sighed.

"Not in the mood, Joey," I warned.

"When are you ever?"

I knew that he was teasing and I forced myself to smile at him. Before I could reply, though, Lauren rushed into the room with a bucket of water and some cloths. "Better wash up. You know how Cheryl feels about the smell of those things."

"It's pretty much permeated the entire house by now," I pointed out. "Not that I won't try to get rid of it, anyway." *But what's the point?* The question went unasked, but it was there nonetheless, poisoning the air between us as much as the stench of the zeds did.

So much had changed in the past few months that I barely remembered the person I'd been or the life I'd lived before this. I mean, I'm no idiot – of course I'd known that when the dead began to rise and shuffle around looking for people to eat, things would never be the same again – but as time had passed, we realized more and more how little we knew about what was going on. We were sheltered here on the farm, so when the first of what we now called 'super zeds' showed up, we didn't know what to do, or how to handle it.

I guess I need to backtrack a bit. After all, a lot can happen in three months, and in this world it seems like any and everything can happen, period. So let's see…where did I leave off…

Oh, that's right. The farm was safe, we had plenty of food and water and fuel, and our original group of five had grown to eight. And there were still eight of us now, but with every day that passed I wondered more and more how much longer that was going to last. You see, we were out of fuel except for what was in the vehicles, and we knew better than to siphon from that. We'd had to start rationing food, though thankfully we were still getting just enough to eat. We were okay with water, thanks to the natural springs on the property, but collecting it had become a pretty big hassle. In fact, that was what we were just doing outside – filling up on water – and let's just say that it didn't go so well.

*But didn't you have the zed problem under control, at least on the farm?* you ask. Well, sure we did – until they started learning.

Sounds crazy, doesn't it? I mean, I'm still not sure that 'learning' is even the proper word for what they were doing. They hadn't started talking yet, anyway. But in the beginning they were slow, stupid, quick to lose their focus – if you could even call it that. What they had now, three months later, may still have only been motor function, but it was certainly far more of it than they had right away. It appeared that when they first rose from the dead, they were almost like infants – it took them hours, at the very least, to even pick themselves up, to move from whatever position they'd been in when they died.

And after that they stumbled and shuffled like – well, like toddlers, I suppose. This phase seemed to last days, possibly even a couple of weeks. As we didn't know where they'd all come from in the first place, or how long ago any of them had died, it was hard to tell when they stopped being toddlers and became, in a sense, 'adolescents'. We figured that was the best way to refer to this particular stage, if only because it was when they were most easily distracted. Faster, steadier on their feet then they'd been at first, but still generally, well, stupid.

The problem was, about a month and a half into things, it was like a switch went off. Suddenly we started encountering zeds that moved nearly as fast as we could. Not only that, but they could figure out stairs, and then fences. Eventually it was ladders, simple doors, how to use their feet and fists to break through glass...

So yeah, there's really no other way to describe it other than to say that somehow, some way, they were *learning*.

We started calling them super zeds right after the day we made a run to the closest supermarket and saw one of them look at its hand, make a fist, and punch the glass window separating it from us. Especially when the zed right next to our ingenious buddy followed suit and took its fist to the glass as well.

We barely made it out of there alive that morning, and what we were able to gather in terms of supplies was meager at best. Still, we assumed it must have been some sort of fluke. We allowed ourselves a day off to recoup, and then we – quite stupidly, mind you – returned to the same supermarket.

Did they know that this was the type of place that would attract the living? I don't think it had gone quite that far, but we couldn't deny that the parking lot and the store itself were both crawling with zeds, far too many for us to handle. "We're okay on food. We should go," Luke said, obviously regretting our decision to attempt another run, period.

I nodded my agreement, and in the backseat Joey and Mike remained silent...but we all knew, in that moment, that things had changed. That the balance was no longer in our favor. The scales were tipped the other way.

Not two days later, the farm saw its first zed in weeks. Luke and I took care of it, but by the end of that week there were more, and more, and no matter how often we killed them, there were always new ones to take the place of the ones that we got rid of. We killed off the chickens, then, wasting more meat than I'm willing to admit...but it was our only choice, what with the noise they tended to make.

And now here we were – tired, above all, and more often than not hungry, thirsty, dirty, smelly. "It's not worth it anymore," I grumbled as I wiped the zed goo off my skin. "There's got to be some kind of shelter or home that wasn't overrun. I mean...what about the military bases, or the National Guard? What about FEMA? The Red Cross? Something, *anything*..."

"I'd like to think that the military was able to get things under control somewhere, but I just don't know if we can trust that to be the case," Luke admitted. "And FEMA is worthless." His lip curled in disgust.

"Fine, whatever. I still think we should pack up and try going back to the city. We're just too exposed here, and at least up there if we want to go on a run there are plenty of stores within walking distance."

Luke took hold of my arm and gently pulled me out of the room and down the hall a bit, so that we were away from the others. He bent his head so that his mouth was right next to my ear. "You know I agree with you, Charlie, but this is something we need to discuss as a group. You and I promised that we would stop making decisions without consulting the others, and we need to stick by that. If we don't, things will fall apart."

I tucked my chin into my chest and mumbled, "You mean faster than they're falling apart now?"

"I heard that, and yes. Now come on, let's get upstairs and enjoy what little daylight we have left. " Today's water run had taken longer than we'd expected. It seemed like every ten feet there was another zed stumbling toward us, and now that they were quite a bit faster than they'd been at first, dispatching them took more time and effort. On the rare occasion that we met with a newly-turned zed, it was practically worth a celebration over how easy they were to take out. Not that any of them had been that easy today.

"We can't go another day without talking to them about this. And by 'them', I mean my mother. She seems to be the only one who is oblivious about the fact that we need to leave the farm."

Luke ran his hand through my hair, which I still insisted on keeping cropped close to my head, and pulled my face close to his. "She's stubborn. Just like someone else I know," he murmured, and then he kissed me.

Despite the fact that we were both absolutely disgusting – I couldn't remember the last time we'd had proper showers, or been able to really brush our teeth – he somehow still made me melt inside. What had begun as a mere physical attraction had progressed more than I wanted to admit, though I continued to insist that this was merely due to the fact that we were constantly in danger, constantly living on the edge – which, as I was so fond of reminding him, made me constantly horny.

"Break it up, you two!" Joey called from the other room.

"How does he *always* know?" Luke pulled away from me. I chuckled, allowing myself a moment of amusement despite how shitty things were for us just then.

"Seriously, it's like he's got some sort of radar. I'm telling you, if we *do* ever leave here, we need to find somewhere that affords us a bit more privacy."

Even as I said this, though, I knew that if we wanted to stay safe, we'd have to stay close...and staying close would never afford Luke and I the space we desired. In fact, if we somehow found our way to the city, to a shelter or to some other sort of group home, it was likely that we would lose what little privacy we had here at the farm.

"Come on, guys. The longer you take, the less time we have to enjoy ourselves before we have to prepare for tonight!"

Joey was right, of course. All new concerns had cropped up with these stronger, faster, and in a way *smarter* zeds. Because the farm was never truly clear of them, we kept the windows boarded nearly all the time – there were just a couple of hours in the afternoon, when the sun was brightest, when we could take the coverings down and enjoy some proper light. And on days when it was cloudy? Well, forget it.

We'd then learned that once it was dark outside, even the tiniest flicker of light through a crack could pull the zeds toward the house like a damned beacon. Strange, how they could detest the light during the day, but be drawn to it at night. On the other end of the spectrum, they seemed to be more sensitive to sound during the daytime – though Joey's theory was that they were all being so loud at night, moaning and groaning and making God knows what other noises, that they simply didn't have the capacity to hear much else.

The truth was, I personally didn't much care about the 'why' of it all. All I knew was that our world became smaller and smaller as time passed. We slept, we woke, we tried to live...and more often than not failed miserably at it. We talked, we ate a bit here and there, and then we talked some more. Talked in circles, really. And then it was always time to sleep again, because there was really nothing else to do once the sun had set.

I'll tell you this much – I was tired of living like a rat in a cage.

And yes, every time I had that thought I couldn't help but recall the song.

The thing was, I had long since realized that there was no coming back from this life. Shit, sometimes I wondered whether, if I woke up and realized that it was all a dream, I'd be able to go back to jogging and yoga and puppy play dates and watching Dave occupy himself with his phone nearly every moment of every day. I was *useful* now. I was strong. I was even independent – as much as I cared about Luke, as much as I enjoyed him, every day I reminded myself that at any moment he could be gone, and so I knew better than to rely on him or his presence.

Mom was on us like a hound after a fox the moment we stepped into the kitchen from the basement stairs. "Were you able to get the water?"

"Wow, no 'glad to see you're okay', no 'how was it out there', nothing like that?" I asked, knowing that my sarcasm would frustrate her – and that this was not the best time for me to act like an idiot. We were all constantly on edge these days, and of course the discussion about leaving the farm was once again looming over our heads...whether Mom liked it or not.

"I don't have time for your attitude, Charlie. Michael's fever is worse; he needs a cold compress."

My stomach turned. "Worse?" Mike had come down with what should have been a mere cold, but without proper heat in the house it had progressed to what Luke thought was at the very least bronchitis. We had plenty of over-the-counter medications, but nothing to treat a real infection – and I was fairly certain that if he was still getting worse, he was likely now dealing with one hell of a case of walking pneumonia. "I want to see him."

"You know that I can't allow that. Just wet a washcloth for me, please." Mom had taken it upon herself to care for Mike alone. The rest of us weren't allowed to see him at all, and she herself even kept us at arm's length. I knew that she was right, that this was the only way to possibly keep anyone else from getting sick, but I felt bad for both her and Mike. Still, I did as she asked and let her go about her business, following her into the living room after handing her the wet cloth, only stopping at the bottom of the stairs when she turned and glared at me. Hands on my hips, tapping my foot in a combination of annoyance and concern, I watched her disappear up the stairs, heard the door to Mike's room open and close.

"So much for having that talk, huh?" Luke whispered in my ear.

"I'm hoping that Mike's being sick will help convince her to leave, but now wasn't the time."

He shrugged. "If you say so."

"You disagree?"

"I suppose I don't disagree, per se…or maybe it's that I understand where you're coming from, but knowing that Mike is still suffering has made me impatient."

"When were you ever *not* impatient?" I reached for his hand and gave it a quick squeeze, remembering all too well how he had needed me to tell him how I felt and what I wanted from him so soon after I'd first invited him to my bed.

Luke snorted. "Trust me, once upon a time I was. Truthfully, I was far too patient about everyone and everything. But Cheryl needs to understand that Mike needs treatment, care that we can't offer him here…and there's not even anywhere nearby for us to go in search of antibiotics or anything else that would really help him. She cares about him…she'll see the light."

"I'm not sure if I find it heartening or *dis*heartening, the fact that you're suddenly on my side about this."

"Come on, Charlie, don't play that game. I told you that I agreed that we needed to find somewhere to go, but I honestly didn't think we would be able to convince the others – especially your mother – that this was the case. Mike's situation changes things. Now can we stop talking in circles and have something to eat?"

Joey, Daniel, Lauren, and Mabel were already sitting around the kitchen table, spooning cold canned vegetables into their mouths with a resigned sort of disgust.

"What do we have today?" I sighed, sliding into the seat next to my brother, doing my best to avoid looking at Mabel. The more time that passed, the more she seemed drawn to me like a damn magnet, and between my mother, Joey, Luke, and Holden, I had quite enough on my plate without having to babysit a child, thank you very much.

"Your all-time favorite…green beans!" Joey said with forced enthusiasm.

"I swear, you were put on this Earth to try me," I groaned, picking up a fork and pulling an open can toward me. I detested green beans – to me they'd always tasted like dirt – but food was food and these were better than some of the junk we'd picked up at the convenience store.

"Likewise," Joey quipped.

I ignored him and reminded myself that I wasn't in any position to be picky, as I held my breath and forced down a couple mouthfuls.

"Guess I'm glad we've got just the one to raise," Lauren said, kissing the top of Mabel's head. "You two seem a bit old to be going at each other like cats and dogs, yet you do it just about every day." I knew that she was teasing us – it had taken weeks, but once Lauren and Daniel had come out of her their shells, they'd become just as much members of the family as Luke and Mike.

Holden ambled into the kitchen just then. I called him over and held my fork out. He slurped the green beans off the end of it, wagging his tail and giving me such a hopeful look that I stood, picked up the can, and dumped the meager remains of it into his bowl.

"Charlie..." Joey shook his head.

"What? He has to eat too, and I can't stand the things anyway." I ran my fingers lightly across the top of Luke's back. "I need to get into some different clothes. If Mom comes around, keep her down here and come get me. It's time we had a...group discussion."

Luke nodded solemnly, but Joey rolled his eyes. "Great." I chose to ignore him – this time, at least – and left them to stew over the impending debate.

## LESSON LEARNED

*Know your zeds.*

\* \* \* \* \* \* \*

I smoothed out the road atlas that I'd found in a bin of junk at the back of the garage. "God, I miss the internet."

Luke smirked. "That makes one of us."

"Yes, thank you, I don't need to listen to your social media diatribe again." I almost laughed, remembering the time Joey had made a joke about Luke not having Facebook – it had turned into quite the rant. "I don't think I've ever seen you so passionate. Well, outside of the bedroom, anyway." I elbowed him gently, and when he wrapped an arm around my waist and pulled me close, nuzzling the back of my neck, I allowed myself that brief moment of enjoyment.

But brief it was, because somehow I had to convince everyone in this house that returning to the city – or at least the outskirts of it – was our best course of action. I ran my finger along the highway that skirted downtown, leaning forward and peering at the roads, trying to place important landmarks – the hospital, the schools, anywhere we might find other people, or at the very least, more food, safer shelter, and above all, medicine for Mike.

"What's this?" Luke pointed to an area just southeast of where I'd marked the hospital.

"Oh. There's a park there…it was used for most of the city's rec events. The zoo is next to it. " I rested my pointer finger beside his, suddenly wondering what in the world would have happened at – or to – the zoo, when everything went to hell.

"Interesting." Luke pulled his hand away; I glanced at him, noting the thoughtful look on his face.

"You think so?"

"I do. I mean…fences. Cages. An area for them to care for sick animals…"

"Exactly, Luke. *Animals.* Some of them dangerous. No way will we be able to make the others believe there's a good reason to drop in and visit the *zoo*. This is going to be hard enough as it is."

"Hey, I'm just saying that we should keep it in the back of our minds, in case we don't get anywhere with the hospital or any of the schools. I'm still concerned that those places will be overrun, and if Cheryl isn't exaggerating Mike's condition, any medicine will be better than no medicine."

"Let's just make sure we can convince them to leave at all, first."

"So that's why you wanted all of us to get together? Another 'discussion' about leaving the farm?" Mom had snuck up behind us. She'd been doing a lot of that lately. I'd gotten to the point where her doing so at least didn't make me practically jump out of my own skin, but this time it sure as hell gave me a bit of a jolt.

I took a deep breath. "Deal with it, Mom."

Joey sauntered into the room. "Uh-oh, at each others' throats again, are you? Let me tell you, Charlie, you're a lot less frustrating when it's not me you're picking fights with."

"Who's picking fights?" I asked. "I'm simply trying to do what's best for the group as a whole. And the group includes Mike, who is sick and needs some sort of care, or at least proper medication, neither of which we can find here."

"Maybe we should wait for Daniel and Lauren," Luke reminded me carefully. "They put Mabel down for a short nap, so just give them a few more minutes."

*A nap*. Sometimes I wished that I could lie down for a nap – not because I was tired, but because every once in a while, I truly didn't want to get out of bed. Mostly on the days when we weren't planning on leaving the house, which was why I generally kept my feelings about wanting to stay in bed to myself, not even mentioning them to Luke. But sometimes I would catch him looking at me with a strange expression, and in those moments I was fairly certain that, no matter what I didn't tell him, he knew it all anyway.

Knew that he was dating a zed-killing maniac, I mean. Seriously, talk about enjoying the small things – every time I took one of them out, a thrill went through me like nothing I'd ever felt before. Most days, it was better than sex.

But I digress. This certainly wasn't the time for me to be losing myself in memories of the many life-or-death moments I'd experienced throughout the past few months. Instead I asked Luke to check on Daniel and Lauren. "We need to get this over with." He shrugged, as if he didn't understand why I was in such a rush – despite his claims of being impatient, he was certainly more patient than me – but he did as I'd asked, anyway.

Finally we were all gathered around the kitchen table. I chanced lighting some candles, hoping that the sun, which hadn't quite yet dipped below the horizon, would hide any flickers of light from inside the house. I pressed the tip of my pointer finger to the small area that represented my city. "We're exposed out here on the farm. In the city there are more options to find supplies, buildings where we could live several stories above ground and have more than one escape route, and maybe even other people to trade with."

Joey exchanged glances with Daniel and Lauren. "We've been safe here so far, Charlie. And you've got to remember, we have a child with us now. This isn't just you and Mike fleeing to the countryside – if we leave, it's a huge undertaking. Packing, deciding how many cars to bring and which ones, planning for everything from breakdowns to accidents to...well, who knows what else."

"She's right, though." I was surprised to hear Mom speak up, and downright shocked at what she said. "Mike needs better medical care than we can offer him here, and at least a couple of us would need to be with him. Of course, I won't *make* anyone leave this place if they don't want to." She turned and gave me a hard look. "And neither will you. Even if that means that some of us go our separate ways."

Luke's eyes met mine; he clearly hadn't been expecting this, either. "I don't know, Cheryl. That may be jumping the gun just a bit. Charlie and I will have to go - "

Mom raised her hands, palms out. "Of course you will. And you've both done a very good job of protecting and taking care of us. But I'm not leaving this place. It's my home. I'd prefer to remain by myself, of course, as doing so would mean that I wasn't putting anyone else in danger...but unless you're running some sort of dictatorship here, you need to give everyone the choice to go, or to stay."

I rolled my eyes. "How lovely that in your old age you've become such a revolutionary. Christ, Mom, you know that Luke and I would never feel right about taking Mike and leaving the rest of you here to fend for yourselves. I'm not saying you couldn't, because sure, for a while you probably could. But if these zeds continue to become more dangerous...no one is going to last much longer. Might as well make the most of the days or weeks or whatever we have left, and not spend them hiding away in this house and waiting for the food to run out, or waiting for the day when we have no way to get water from the spring, or for the house to get overrun."

"Cheryl is allowed to have her opinion, Charlie," Luke said carefully. "Just like no one can force you and I to stay here." He turned toward my mom. "I'm guessing you've talked to Mike about this."

She nodded. "He's miserable, and in pain, and he wants to go."

"We'll go as well," Lauren piped up. She reached for my mother's hand, clearly wanting to apologize for deciding to leave. "We don't want to, not really, but we just...we have to think about Mabel. If she got sick, or injured, and everyone else was already gone..."

Mom waved her off. "Of course, dear. I know you've said you wanted to stay, but I always knew you'd leave. And Joey, I don't even want to hear your protests or arguments. You know you want to go, and I'll not have you staying here just for my sake."

"We can't leave you completely alone, Mom," I sighed.

"I've been on my own for quite some time, Charlie. I can do it again."

"We'll leave first thing in the morning," Luke interrupted. "Anyone who is coming with us needs to pack up while there's still some light in the house. Cheryl, I really do hope you change your mind about this, but none of us will argue with you." His tone was firm, and this time it was Joey and I who exchanged a look. I wondered if my brother really meant to leave with us, especially after all of his protesting about the very idea of leaving at all – and I also wondered if he and I would actually be able to leave Mom behind.

Nonetheless, I nodded my reluctant agreement to Luke's suggestion, then called for Holden and made my way up to my room. I'd been sharing it with Luke for months now, of course, but something deep inside of me persisted in calling it 'mine'.

And now I had to decide what I would be bringing with me. So much would have to be left behind – traveling light is the way to go during the zombie apocalypse, remember? – but the weather being what it was, clothing that could be layered and blankets were a must. Then there was food, and water – we'd have to make a trip out to the spring in the morning before we could leave, that was for sure. I dug out my bags and began poking through drawers, carefully choosing the best clothing items I could find and packing everything in the expert manner I'd learned from years of regular travel. I'd learned a tough lesson when I left my condo in the city, throwing things into bags like it didn't matter what I brought with me.

*My condo...* I couldn't *not* wonder whether I'd be able to get back there at some point. And why not? If it wasn't any more dangerous in the city than in the country, tacking on a trip to my condo as part of a supply run – once we were up there and settled, anyway – wouldn't be too much of a hassle, right?

*Don't think about that right now. You've got other things to worry about.* My mother, for one. I wanted to believe that she would change her mind, though of course I knew that wouldn't happen. I recalled Luke's comment about how she and I were the same kind of stubborn – he'd said something along those lines, anyway – and realized that there was no point in hoping something would change. We would go, she would stay, and I would very likely never see her again. These past few months had been trying, but I supposed that they'd also been good for us, for our relationship. I hadn't spent this much time with my family in over a decade, after all, and what had once been grudging affection and respect had grown into a cooperative living situation that had allowed us – and our new-found family members – to survive.

I sat down on the edge of my bed and heaved a sigh, looking around my dimly lit room and for some reason recalling that cliché about not being able to go home again. The crazy thing was, I'd done so, and the only reason I was leaving was because I had no other choice

"How's the packing going?" I looked up to see Luke standing in the doorway.

"Very funny. I've done some. I was just...thinking."

"About your mom?"

"Sort of, yeah. And about the farm."

"Not changing your mind, are you?"

"You know I'm not. I guess...well, strangely enough, when I was growing up I always wanted to leave this place. And I did, as soon as I could, and only came back to it when I had to. But now...well, as much as I know that we *need* to leave, that doesn't make me *want* to do so."

"Understandable. We had a good thing going here, for a while." He stepped into the room and sat down beside me. I could tell that he wanted to wrap his arm around me, but he didn't – he'd learned my moods, and knew that I wouldn't care to be cuddled right now. Instead we just sat there in silence for several minutes, his arm pressed gently against mine.

Finally I heaved a sigh and stood up. "Guess we better finish packing up while we still have some light."

It was a restless evening to say the least, and when we did finally go to bed Luke and I both tossed and turned for most of the night. As the first gray light of dawn began to seep through the cracks of the window coverings, we dragged ourselves out of bed, exhausted, and began loading our things into the two cars we'd chosen – mine, of course, and the truck as well. The water run was the last thing we needed to do before getting on the road, because of course we wanted to make sure that we had enough water to take with us, as well as leaving some for Mom. *Don't think about what she'll do when it's gone. She's in good health. She knows how to use a gun.*

The sun had broken the horizon by the time Luke, Daniel, and I snuck out the back door and made our way down to the spring. We stumbled across a couple zeds along the way, but nothing that the three of us couldn't handle together. I ran offense and Luke brought up the rear, with Daniel between us carrying the majority of the water jugs. It wouldn't be quite so easy on the way back, when any noise we'd made had time to attract more zeds and when we were all loaded down with our water burdens – we'd learned that the hard way these past weeks, as more than one of us had experienced a close call. Or, as in my case, upwards of a dozen close calls.

"Nine," I heard Luke hiss from behind. I passed my bat from my right hand to my left and then spun to that side, giving myself a moment of windup before swinging as hard as I could, the satisfying *crack* echoing through the woods as I connected with the zed that was rushing toward me.

"They'll have heard that," Daniel mused. I nodded and picked up the pace to a jog. How quiet we'd been up until then was our only real cover; that near-silence was broken now, and the faster we did this, the better.

Not that we could really tell the natural springs to hurry up. I watched one direction, Luke the other, while Daniel filled each jug to the brim. A couple zeds came stumbling up the path we'd used, and each time Luke or I ran up to meet them, hoping to keep them at bay. In the past this had worked much better, of course – nowadays it was as if they remembered having heard us, and they just kept coming. *Fuckers.*

"One last stressful trip to the old watering hole before we go," I grunted as I picked up one of the jugs. The guys gathered up the rest, and after I took a moment to switch my baseball bat for my hunting knife, we slowly made our way back to the house.

We'd made it less than a few hundred yards before the first attack came. They approached from behind this time, and with the noise that we ourselves were making none of us heard them until they were practically on top of us. You see, it's a funny thing, the way zeds run – now that they *do* run, that is. They still shuffle, sort of. And you know, they're still essentially brain-dead, so they don't care how they look or how clumsy they actually are. (Which, while not as clumsy as they used to be, is still way more than us.) It makes for a pretty funny picture, when I think about it...but at that moment, however amusing the zeds looked as I turned and saw them launch themselves at Luke, I sure as hell wasn't laughing.

## LESSON LEARNED

*Take joy in the little things while you still can.*

# Chapter 6
# Runaways

Luke shouted, dropping the jug that he was carrying. I cringed as it burst open, but that was all of the attention I could afford for some water when one of the few people in the world who I'd ever truly cared about was obviously in danger. I bent low to set my own jug on the ground as I rushed toward Luke. Out of the corner of my eye I saw the jug topple over, cap still on – a brief moment of respite as I brandished my knife, yelling as loud as I could, wanting to distract the zeds even though all the while I knew that it wasn't three months ago and that none of this would work.

Luke was struggling with one of them now, having not been able to get his hatchet in hand fast enough. I was at his side then, the blade of my knife flashing in the tree-filtered sunlight as I stabbed at each of the attackers in turn, picking them off one by one. And then Luke was in control of his own weapon, and the head of his hatchet was buried in the zed's skull.

Gasping for breath, my heart pounding, I clutched at Luke's shoulders and made him look at me. "Are you okay? Did it – "

Wordlessly, he held up his right hand.

His pointer and ring fingers ended at the knuckles, blood gushing from where the zed had bitten them off.

"No," I whispered. Then, louder, "No. What the *fuck*, no, no, no – "

"Shut up, Charlie. Get me my hatchet."

I could hardly bear to let go of Luke, and I was shaking so much that when I *did* obey him, it took several attempts for me to pull the hatchet from the zed's head. When I was finally able to retrieve it, he calmly told me to wash it with the rest of his water and then bring it to him. I made sure that it was as clean as possible, wiping it off on my shirt and then rinsing it again before holding it out to him. But he shook his head, reached up and tore off one sleeve of his shirt, and then spread his hand on the half-rotted log next to him.

"Take them off."

"I – *what*? No, Luke, I can't – "

He gritted his teeth. "Take them *off*, Charlie. *Now*. The longer we wait..." His voice trailed off, and I knew what he was thinking. That this was a shot in the dark anyway, and if we didn't do it soon there was probably no way at all that it would work.

I raised the hatchet, took aim, and brought it down as hard as I could. Luke screamed in pain, maybe louder than I'd ever heard anyone scream in person, and yeah, I'm ashamed to admit that my first thought was about how many zeds all of this noise would attract.

"Wrap it up. Tight," he said weakly. I turned and saw Daniel staring at us, his face white with fear.

"Keep watch," I hissed before turning back to Luke and tying the piece of his shirt around the stumps where his fingers had been. He clenched his jaw, breathing hard through his nose, but when I was done he sucked in one more breath and blinked slowly.

"Help me up."

Again I obeyed, though immediately this time, and when he was on his feet and leaning against me Luke said, "Let's go. Quickly as possible."

Somehow we made it back to the house without another incident, despite – or perhaps because of? – me alternately cursing at and praying to God the entire way. Once there, our immediate departure for the city was forgotten as Mom rushed to find the few medical supplies we had left. Once the hydrogen peroxide and gauze were located, though, I had to turn away. I'd done my duty – *more* than my duty –

and I'd never been one for vast amounts of blood and gore anyway. The zeds were different. There was no lifeblood that flowed from them when they were shot or hacked or stabbed. Killing them was like running over someone in Grand Theft Auto; it was a game to me, and they didn't matter.

Luke was resting comfortably by noon, but only after insisting that we leave at first light the next day. Mom even agreed with him, noting that now we had two people in the house who were in dire need of proper medical care. The rest of the day was spent in awkward silence, and when I tried to crawl into bed with Luke that night he pushed me away.

"Get out of here, and barricade me in. I don't know what will happen, if what we did will work, how fast I'll...change...if it doesn't." His eyes were clouded with pain, but otherwise he seemed lucid. As much as I didn't want to leave him, I couldn't stand how worried he sounded. In that moment I would have done just about anything to give him peace of mind.

There was no water run the next morning, that's for damn sure. Our goodbyes were faster than I'd thought they'd be, and somehow more somber as well. Luke had survived the night, but he was already running a low fever, and so it fell to me to drive him and Mike in my car while Joey took Daniel, Lauren, and Mabel in the truck. I held back tears when I asked my mom one more time if she would come with us, but she just shook her head and gave me a sad smile.

"You come back and check on me sometime, if you can. But for now, get those boys of ours some help."

And then we were gone, up the driveway and down the road, speeding toward the city with all thought of driving safely forgotten. When we passed by the wreck that I'd almost crashed into on mine and Mike's journey to the farm, I noted that some of the cars were gone, and wondered what had been in the eighteen wheeler and whether anyone had broken into it to see. I hadn't thought about it when we'd passed by that first time, and now we clearly didn't have a moment to lose, not for a truck that had probably long since been emptied of anything valuable. Besides, while Mike had tied an old scarf around his face, he was coughing incessantly; when I glanced at Luke in the passenger seat, his face was pale, his eyes closed. The hospital was only another half hour drive, maybe a little longer if we ran into any snags...I reached over and rested my hand against Luke's cheek – he was burning up, now, but was that just because he was weak, or because his injury was infected, or because he was on his way to –

*No. Don't think about that. We caught it, he just needs proper treatment and he'll be fine.*

I took the long way around the city and approached the hospital from the southwest. It was strange to drive down what had been a major road and see that the traffic lights were dead, most of the parking lots empty, and not a single car was driving by. I glanced in my rear view mirror and saw Joey hunched over the steering wheel of the truck, following me far too closely for comfort.

"Are you sure this is a good idea?" Mike mumbled. I met his eyes in the mirror, noted that Holden was stretched out across the backseat with his head in Mike's lap, then refocused on the road in front of me.

"I don't know," I admitted, "but we really don't have much of a choice. Not now, with..." I stopped myself from saying his name, but Luke knew I was talking about him. He opened his eyes and turned toward me, giving me a small smile.

"You don't have to talk about me like I'm not here. My hand hurts like hell, but I'm not dead."

I tried to ignore the fact that he didn't say he wasn't dying, just that he wasn't *dead*. "I just thought you were sleeping."

"Nah...too much pain."

"I've got some of those Lortabs..."

"Thanks, but no thanks. I want to be lucid in case..."

*In case we get to the hospital and find help. In case we get there and don't find help. In case it's a wash and we have to figure out another option.* There were too many different scenarios to count running through my head, so I merely nodded in response.

Soon enough the hospital was looming just in front of us and to the left, and I could tell as we approached that this hadn't been one of our better ideas. Cars were parked haphazardly on the sides of the road now, in the lawn at the front of the building, all over the parking lot...many of them were blocking each other in, and some of them had clearly tried to ram their way out of the lot. The hospital itself was dark, most of its lower windows smashed in, the doors open wide to the elements – and to the zeds. Surprisingly, I didn't see any of those wandering around – perhaps they knew that this place was dead, useless – but I was fairly certain there were still some stuck inside. Even super zeds couldn't figure out how to get out of the maze that was a large hospital, right? And in that case, could we – or maybe, rather, *would* we – chance going in to look for medication?

"Doesn't look good," I sighed.

Luke chuckled weakly. "I'm not sure I'm surprised."

"Joey and Daniel and I can go in and poke around…"

"I don't think that's safe." Mike pointed to one of the windows on a higher floor. It was intact, but as the sunlight glinted off it I saw movement – something throwing itself against the window. It had to be a zed that had heard our cars. "Those things have probably been trapped in there the entire time. They'll be – " He stopped, breaking into a fit of coughing.

"Yeah." I knew what they would be – hungry, maybe weaker for that, but possibly more dangerous for it, as well. "But we need to try…"

"No, we don't." Luke was firm. "Rather, *you* don't. You've done enough for all of us, Charlie, as have Joey and Daniel. We should find another place. The closest school, maybe…"

"That'll be the high school," Mike said. I nodded, rolled down my window and gestured for Joey to pull up next to us. He did, and Daniel rolled down the passenger side window of the truck.

"We're going to try the high school." I jerked my chin at the hospital. "There are zeds in there, probably a lot of them, and all it would take is one of us opening the wrong door…"

"Don't have to tell me twice," Joey grimaced. "Lead the way."

The high school was even closer to the city center than the hospital had been, and it wasn't long before the roads became impossible to navigate. We were able to get within a mile or so of the school, but I knew that it would be up to me and either Joey or Daniel to walk the rest of the way and check things out. As much as I didn't care for the idea of doing a run with just one other person as backup, we certainly couldn't leave Lauren and Mabel alone with Mike and Luke in their current states. Lauren could fend for herself, of course, but asking her to protect them as well as her own child was a request I simply couldn't make.

I pulled my car over and Joey followed suit. By the time he and Daniel had climbed down out of the truck, I had my knife and gun tucked into my belt and my baseball bat in hand.

"No offense, Joey, but I'm taking Daniel on this one. Someone needs to stay with Lauren and Mabel and the guys, and Daniel is a better shot than you. I'll leave Holden here as well, though."

Joey shrugged. "You're not hurting my feelings. I know I'm better with this than with a gun." He patted the hatchet that was strapped around his waist.

"Yeah, your aim is shit, but you've got more upper body strength than anyone but Luke." With this, I glanced into my car. "I won't ask you guys to sit in such a confined space with them, but you may want to stay outside and really keep an eye on things. Hopefully…" I stopped myself and shook my head.

"We'll be fine." Joey reached out and squeezed my shoulder. "If it comes down to it, Lauren – and Mike and Luke – will fight if they truly need to. You just figure out if we can get what we need from the school and then get your ass back here."

For a moment I actually thought about giving my brother a hug. I'd never been one for displays of affection, though, and in the end my ingrained nature won out. "Will do," I nodded, turning away from Joey's touch. "Come on, Daniel." The young man's face was set in grim determination – he opened the truck door and said a quick goodbye to his family, then came back to my side.

"Lead the way."

We moved quickly, half-running up the road, darting around the cars that had been abandoned in front yards, on sidewalks, and helter-skelter all over the street.

"Damn," Daniel muttered. "What happened here? Why didn't these people just keep going?"

"Who knows. It's like this on the other side of the city too, closer to where I lived – ah, shit." A small group of zeds – no more than half a dozen, but enough to concern me – had appeared just in front of us and to the right. "Don't use your gun unless you have to," I reminded Daniel as he moved to my left side. He knew better than to get between me and the zeds – the only person who still tried to do that nowadays was Luke, and he…

*Don't fucking think about* that *right now.* The zeds were already picking up speed. They'd clearly heard us talking, and I cursed our stupidity. We'd been so careful, so quiet, until just a few moments ago…though I supposed that it was better to have them in front of us and realizing we were there than hearing us pass by and approaching from behind, where we likely wouldn't have noticed them quite so soon.

We stepped behind one of the cars, putting it between us and the zeds. We could see over it and therefore keep an eye on their approach, but it at least acted as a sort of shield, something to slow them down a bit.

Or so we thought.

No sooner had the first of the group reached our little roadblock then it grabbed hold of the car and scrambled over it. The others followed suit, like so many ants boiling out of their hill. I stepped back as quickly as I could, barely missing their grasping hands – but I hadn't looked behind me, and my foot caught on something. Next thing I knew, I was flat on my back with the wind knocked out of my lungs and a zed throwing itself off the roof of the car, aiming to land right on top of me.

I rolled to my right and heard the thud as it landed where I'd lain just a moment before. I scrambled for my knife, lashing out with it as I felt a hand grab hold of my arm and haul me toward what, I didn't know.

"Stop!" Daniel shouted, and I realized that it was him, not some zed, whose hand was wrapped around my bicep. I struggled to my feet, and we continued to stumble backwards until we ran into another car. Once again the zeds were far too close for comfort, but then I had an idea. I stepped to the left, then spun to the right, cracking one of the zeds across the back. It was driven into the side of the car, its head slamming against the window. As it fell to the ground I knew that it wasn't completely taken care of, but for now it was down for the count, and that had to be what mattered. Thankfully Daniel followed my lead, leaping out of the way just in time so that we were behind the zeds. As much as they'd evolved in however long they'd been reanimated, they were still essentially brain dead – and for the moment, we had the upper hand. I rushed forward, swinging madly, slamming two more of the zeds back into the car and knocking them off their feet, while Daniel stabbed out with his knife, catching a third in the cheek and driving forward until his blade was buried so deep in the zed's head that I knew it was finished. Daniel pulled back, but not quickly enough.

"Duck!" I ordered, but he hesitated, and for a moment I thought I would hit him – but then he dove to the ground and my bat connected with the temple of the zed that had almost gotten close enough to bite Daniel.

We made short work of the ones that were still moving, but I knew that we had to keep going. We'd made quite a bit of noise, and if there was even a single zed around I was certain we'd see it soon if we didn't make our way directly – and quickly – to the school.

## Lesson Learned

*Act fast.*

\* \* \* \* \* \* \*

It wasn't much farther, perhaps a half mile at most, but I set a grueling pace. By the time we stopped short of the chain link fences surrounding our destination, Daniel was panting and even I had to take a moment to catch my breath. We both stepped up to the fence and looked around the schoolyard, then at each other.

"Looks abandoned," Daniel shrugged.

"Which seems too good to be true. Should we find the entrance?"

He nodded his agreement, but just as we turned to do just that, someone called out, "Don't move!"

Without even thinking about what I was doing, my hand went to the butt of my gun – but Daniel reached out and stayed me. He jerked his head to the left, then to the right – *No* – and I followed his gaze.

There were people standing on the roof of the school – at least three that we could see, the closest being the one who'd spoken to us, while the others were on either corner. *Lookouts.* And that meant that there was something here to protect...

"You can leave those guns of yours right there and be on your way. Do that, and we'll leave you alone. Try anything else, and...well, I wouldn't try anything else."

"It's a *kid*," Daniel mumbled.

"That's rich, coming from you," I whispered.

"Go on, then. Don't forget to leave your guns."

"Just our guns, hmm?" I replied. "What's so important about them, then?"

"Oh, we've got plenty of other weapons. And a few guns, too." The kid – I could tell, now, that it was a teenage boy – raised his rifle. "Don't make me use this one."

"We don't want any trouble," Daniel informed them. "There's a group of us, though, and the others will come looking if we don't return. So I don't think we'll leave our guns."

The boy aimed his rifle at us. "My aim isn't that great, but I'll hit you. And then you'll be injured, and you'll bleed, and one of *them* will get you. If you have friends, and they come looking, note that we have a fence, and brick walls, and – "

"Oh, *please*," I interrupted. "You won't use that thing on us. If you do, you'll attract every zed for miles. May take some of them a while to get here, but do you really want to give up your spot that completely? I'm guessing you haven't done so yet, or you wouldn't feel so cozy and safe behind such weak protections as these." I grabbed hold of the old chain link and shook it a bit. I was taking a chance even doing this, knowing that any zeds nearby would hear the rattling – but I had to hope that the kid was bluffing. We had more guns back at the cars, of course, but to give up even two of our supply…well, it would be more of a loss than I cared to think about.

Daniel was staring at me, wide-eyed. Much as he must agree, I suppose he hadn't expected me to be so forward, so sure of myself…whereas I just figured that I didn't have a choice. "What are you *doing*?" he hissed. I shrugged, but obviously my response had confused – possibly even *concerned* – the kid with the rifle. I saw him look to his left, at the guard on that corner of the school roof, and then lower his weapon.

"Just get out of here!" he finally yelled.

I gave Daniel a lopsided grin. *See?*

"How about this – one of our people needs some medicine. If you have what we need, perhaps we can do a trade?" We'd packed every bit of extra ammunition that we'd found throughout the past few months, and I couldn't help but think that if some of it was unusable for us, it may fit one of the weapons these people had. If that was the case – and if this school had at least some of the meds we needed – then each of us had possession of something that was almost priceless to the other.

"If you think we're letting you in here, you're fuckin' crazy, lady."

"Did I say that? No. We need – well, antibiotics would be best, and a lot of them. I see you've got a rifle there, and we have some ammo that we can't use. Something tells me that would be more than a fair trade…*if* you can help us out."

The kid gestured for one of his friends. The other person – it appeared to be a girl – approached him, and they conversed for a few moments, both of them gesturing wildly. Finally the girl shook her head and marched back to her spot on the corner, and the kid yelled, "We aren't so sure about this, but I'll check with the others. You'll wait right there if you want any chance at all of getting those meds. Leave, and you damn well better not come back."

"Understood," I agreed. I turned to Daniel. "I'll keep an eye on these guys – you put your back to the fence and watch for zeds. We've caused quite a ruckus and I'll be shocked if none of them show up…especially if this takes a while. But we *need* those antibiotics. And if they didn't have any at all, they would have told us to go away. Again."

"I don't know. I don't like it. What if there isn't a single adult in this place?"

"He went to talk to someone, Daniel. I've got to assume – at least for now – that whoever is 'in charge' isn't just another teenager. Anyway, this kid clearly understands that we're offering them a good deal…and shit, I don't know, look at Mike. He survived where his family didn't, and he's still alive now. Maybe him being with us is a big part of that, but he can certainly take care of himself to some extent. So what's to say that other kids his age couldn't do the same?"

"I'm not saying they couldn't, but I *am* saying that I don't trust them. Teenagers can be pretty damn stupid, in case you don't remember, and they're worse when they're grouped together like this."

"Bad high school experience, huh?" I felt a swell of empathy for him – while my years in high school hadn't been horrible from beginning to end, they hadn't been all that great, either. Certainly not something I'd want to relive. And he was right, when teenagers were grouped together there was bound to be trouble. The question was whether or not the ones holed up in this school had succumbed to that – and I wasn't sure if I wanted to know the answer.

We took care of a couple zeds while we waited, but finally, about fifteen minutes after the kid had disappeared from the roof, I saw him and another person approaching from the far side of the school. It was an older woman who looked to be in her fifties, and something about her screamed school nurse, probably because of the stern look on her face as she said, "Offering bullets for medicine, are you? To a *child*?"

I glanced at the boy, who was maybe a couple of inches taller than me with messy dark hair and the patchy shadow of a beard just barely growing around his jawline. I couldn't help but chuckle. "A child? This kid? He tried to force us to throw down our guns, threatened to shoot us…if that still constitutes a child, well…" I shrugged.

"He's just following orders. Be glad he came to get me, and not someone else. Thankfully he was either smart enough – or stupid enough – to figure out that I'm the only person who knows exactly what's in my office." She and the boy looked at each other; he swallowed hard and turned away all too quickly for my liking. *What the hell is going on in this place?*

Yet even as I thought that, I understood that I wanted to know even less now than I had before. *Just get the meds and get outta here, Charlie. Get Daniel and yourself back to the others and drive away. Find somewhere else to go. Preferably somewhere far from here.*

"All right, let's pretend I believe that you're not in charge here. You may know what you have in terms of medicine – we need antibiotics at the very least, by the way – but then how do I know that you have the authority to give me what I need?"

The woman strode up to the fence, practically pressing herself against it, her nose just inches from mine. "Right now, I have the authority. The one who usually does is out scavenging, or so she calls it, and if we do this quickly we maybe won't get caught. I can get you some antibiotics, but my stores are limited and you certainly can't have it all. I'll throw in a few other things that I think will help, based on the fact that you need antibiotics at all. You give us every bit of ammo you can't use. If I think it's enough, we're done."

"I don't know how quickly you expect this to happen. It's getting late in the day and we have to go back to our…camp…and then come all the way back here." I could only hope that she hadn't noticed my hesitation as I changed the word 'cars' to 'camp' at the last moment.

"'We'? Oh, I don't think so. One of you stays right here. We'll help keep watch over that one. The other goes back for the ammunition. I told you, we don't have very much time."

"And then what? We travel back to our place in the dark? Lady, do you even know what you're suggesting? "

"You listen to me, child. You go now, without your medicine, or we do the trade and you go as soon as it's over, no matter that it's light or dark. In my experience, they're equally dangerous."

Her eyes were glittering as she stared me down. For a moment I had considered consulting Daniel, but now I was worried that he wouldn't understand that taking the time to do the trade would be better. *And not just because it's not his loved ones who are sick.* The thought popped into my head and was gone just as quickly – or so I wanted to believe. I couldn't even look at him as I spoke my verdict.

"Fine. Daniel, you stay. I'm faster." *And I have less to lose.* I was gone before he could protest, gone as soon as the woman nodded her head in agreement. I heard him shouting my name as I ran, but I forced myself to ignore it. I was the one taking most of the risk, going all the way back to the cars by myself, then having to return to the school alone as well. But if I did it fast enough, if this all went smoothly, maybe we could make it back with the medication before it was completely dark.

So I ran for Luke, and I ran for Mike, but really – more than anything – I ran for myself. Because I'd left my mother behind, and I didn't want to lose my friends. Because I sure as hell didn't want to die, either.

Because I was selfish.

And I made it. Passed a few zeds along the way, and forced myself to take several detours in hopes of throwing them off my trail, though of course this added several minutes to my trip back. When I arrived, slightly winded, empty-handed, and alone to boot, the looks on the others' faces and the questions on their lips were almost more than I could bear.

"Daniel's fine. I just need the extra ammo – the stuff we can't use," was all I said in explanation.

"Charlie, what – "

I cut Joey off with a wave of my hand. "There's no *time*, Joey. Just help me dig out the shells and bullets we have that won't fit our guns, as many of them as we can find." I headed around to the back of the truck, Joey on my heels and sputtering protests the whole time. I yanked bag after bag out of the way and finally my fingertips brushed the side of the box that I knew held our found ammo. "Empty one of the backpacks. I need something that's easy to carry." My brother hesitated for a moment. "Joey!" I snapped, glaring at him. "Do it!"

It was the work of a few minutes at most, finding what I needed, transferring it to the pack, and strapping that to my back as tightly as possible. I dropped my bat off in my car, noting that both Luke and Mike were passed out, neither of them looking well at all. I'd wanted to say goodbye again, maybe tell them both that I loved them, but I realized that it was probably best that they didn't know I'd come back only to turn around and leave again. Not now, anyway.

"Daniel and I will both be back soon." It was the last thing I said before running off again, and deep down I knew that it might be a promise I couldn't keep. But the words were out of my mouth before I really thought about that, I suppose – and then I was gone, racing back up the road toward the school, my right hand wrapped around one of the backpack straps and my hunting knife clutched in my left hand. I jogged, then I ran, and then I sprinted, hoping that I would be outrunning any zeds that came after me. I simply didn't have time to stop and fight – and besides, if I dragged a few zeds back to the school with me, so be it. *Let them use their damn guns on the real threat.*

The sun was setting already; I swear that I could see it disappearing bit by bit as I ran. By the time I reached the school fence, having to cut several hundred yards to my right to reach Daniel's side, the sky was more purple than blue.

It was twilight, and we were running out of time.

The nurse now had a large paper bag in her hand, the top rolled down to keep its contents intact – *and hidden*, I noted with chagrin. The kid was still with her, and Daniel looked none the worse for the wear, so I set my pack on the ground and bent to open it. I held up one of the half-empty boxes of ammunition, label out so they could see it.

"I'll give you what you can use, nothing more. You know what kind of guns you have, I take it?"

The woman and boy exchanged a glance. "Well enough," the kid finally said.

I rolled my eyes. "You're agreeing to make this exchange when you clearly don't have the authority to do so, and on top of that you're not even certain what kinds of firearms you have?"

"You are trying my patience, young lady," the nurse snapped. "We are doing you a favor. My guess is that you need this medicine more than we need that ammunition. So show us what you've got and we'll go from there."

"My name is Charlie, by the way," I heard myself saying. "And this is Daniel." I suppose that part of me hoped that telling these people our names would help our case – and admittedly, I was curious about who *they* were, as well.

"Dominic." The kid poked his chest with his thumb, then gestured toward the woman. "And that's Mrs. Downing."

"*Dominic,*" the woman snapped, shaking her head at him.

"Hey, he's just being polite. I told you our names, after all." I flashed my teeth at Mrs. Downing – baring them more than smiling with them – and she pursed her lips, glowering at me until I sighed and looked away.

"Go on," she insisted. "Show us what else you have."

"You too. " I gestured to the paper bag. "Guess I'll need you to tell me what's what in terms of the meds you're giving us."

"How about one for one? You show her some ammo, she shows you some medicine. We don't have time for all of this arguing," Daniel pointed out.

Mrs. Downing's eyes met mine; we both nodded slowly. "I showed you mine, you show me yours," I said.

I couldn't help but glance nervously at the sky every few minutes after that. It seemed that the trade took forever when in all actuality it couldn't have lasted more than ten minutes – and only that long because Dominic was hemming and hawing over some of the ammunition, while I was asking Mrs. Downing twenty questions about every medication she showed me. When we were finally done, the bullets and medicine squeezed through the holes in the fence, Mrs. Downing nodded brusquely and backed away. "Watch them go, then come inside. Immediately," she ordered Dominic.

## LESSON LEARNED

*Be prepared to trade.*

\* \* \* \* \* \* \*

Once she'd turned her back on us, I leaned in close. "Bit skittish, isn't she?"

Dominic's eyes were wide. "We all are."

"Clearly. So…who really *is* in charge, here?"

He shook his head. "You don't want to know. And Mrs. Downing is right, you really should go. If they come back, or if they run into you along the way…"

"Who's 'they'?"

This time it was Dominic who leaned in close. "The leader's name is Jia. She was a junior here, before all of this went down. There were a lot of us here after hours the day things went to hell, and most of us just…stayed. We thought it would be safe to go home, eventually, but it never was. And then she took over things, and now…we can't leave. She hunts people down when they try. Makes…examples…of them." He looked downright nauseated, and something about his expression made my stomach turn as well. I took a step back from the fence.

"Come on, Daniel. We need to go. "

He leaned in, his mouth right up against my ear. "I don't know, Charlie. Do we want to leave them here after hearing that?"

I turned my back on Dominic and started walking away, my steps brisk and determined. Daniel followed after a moment, and when he touched my arm I jerked it away from him, shaking my head. "We're going," I hissed, breaking into a jog. Thankfully he didn't continue to protest; I heard him pick up his own pace, and soon we'd left the school behind us.

There were no streetlights, not anymore, and even if I'd had a flashlight I knew that it would have been stupid to use it. Twilight was fading all too quickly – it seemed as if the whole world was in shadow, with pockets of black where the buildings and cars were located. I couldn't run as fast as I had earlier – I could only turn my head from side to side, constantly peering into the darkness, watching and listening for zeds and still uncertain as to whether I'd notice them approaching, anyway.

We heard them first, of course – the strange noises that were somehow neither moans nor cries – but they seemed distant enough, and we were at least halfway back to the others. "Charlie..." Daniel panted, and I could hear the fear in his voice.

"Shut up and keep going." I lengthened my strides, heard him grunt behind me as he did the same. *We just need to get back to the cars, then we can drive a bit farther out, away from these zeds and from that damn school.*

But they seemed to be gaining on us. We would have no choice but to dive into the cars and go, and I knew that even then it would still be a close call...although at this point we had no choice. If I was judging correctly, the number of zeds after us just now was more than even Daniel, Joey, Lauren, and I could handle together. *Maybe if Luke and Mike were well...*

But that didn't – *couldn't* – matter just now. They weren't, and the best thing for us to do was to get the hell out of here as soon as possible.

Thankfully, Joey had been smart enough to hole up in the truck. I heard Daniel break away as I dove for my own car. The door was unlocked, and as I shut it behind me I heard the truck engine roar to life. I followed Joey's lead, not taking even a moment to check on Luke or Mike before glancing over my shoulder and revving my car up the road in reverse. I spun it around, waited a moment to make sure that Joey was following me, and took off.

"Where're we going?" Luke mumbled. I reached over and patted the back of his bandaged hand – it was far too hot and dry for my liking, though, and I snatched my own away, fear rising in the back of my throat like bile.

"I don't know. Away from here, that's for damn sure. Daniel and I had some zeds after us just now…we barely outran them."

"The…oo…"

"Hush, Luke, you don't need to talk. I'll figure something out; I always do."

"Nnn…no. Go…go to…*zoo*."

He'd put too much emphasis on the last word for me to mistake it for anything else. At first I'd thought he'd been exclaiming in pain, that trying to talk was too much for him, but no, he was telling me to go to the damn zoo. Again. I bit down hard on my lip. He was fevered, he didn't know what he was saying – or so I tried to tell myself, though deep down I knew that wasn't the case.

He'd talked about the damn zoo before he'd been bitten, after all.

I chewed on the inside of my cheek. If I wanted to take the most direct route to the zoo, I had about a minute to make this decision. I glanced at Luke – he seemed to have lost consciousness. *Get away from the zeds, find a place to park, get some medicine into him and Mike.*

I knew what I had to do. I turned down the road that skirted the south side of downtown and ended near the highway that ran into the city. There was a park situated off this road, just before it ended – and the zoo was part of that park. At the very least it was a wide-open space, a space that was hopefully empty. It was far too late to try breaching the fences at the zoo, but if we set up in the middle of the park we'd see anything that came our way.

*You'll also be exposed*. I understood that much, but I suppose I'd become so used to not being completely safe that I could accept the negatives of any situation…as long as there was at least one positive.

Mercifully, we arrived at the park some time later and found that it was – for the most part, at least – empty. There were cars here and there, but so far as I could see, no people or zeds wandering about. The area where the zoo was located looked like nothing more than a black void, so I turned my car away from it and eased out onto one of the sports fields. It was overgrown, now, but my guess was that it had been used for soccer before this whole apocalypse thing happened.

Joey parked the truck next to my car, close enough so that when we opened the front doors they nearly touched – it wasn't the best barricade, but it was something to cover at least one angle of attack. "We'll need one person on top of each vehicle. You take the truck – Lauren's a good shot, and small enough to sit on top of my car. Daniel can keep an eye on Mabel and Holden. I'm the one who got the lowdown on these meds from the school nurse, so I guess I get to play caretaker."

My brother snorted. "Such a fitting job for you."

"Yeah, tell me about it. " I didn't even have the energy to argue with him, especially not when I knew that he was right. Sick people had always made me uncomfortable, and the idea of dispensing medication that I had so little information about was scary in its own right.

I waited until Joey and Lauren were situated before reaching for my backpack and digging through it for the proper boxes. I had to turn the interior lights on in my car to see the labels, but finally I found the two that Mrs. Downing had pinpointed when I'd told her about Mike's pneumonia and Luke's 'injury'. I tried to forget the way she'd looked at me – out of the corner of her eye, clearly not believing my story of a minor cut that had gotten infected. I had to believe that I could save Luke, though of course at this point my mother would have pointed out that I always had to believe that I could save everyone. "That's my Charlie...always taking care of everyone and every *thing* except for herself," she used to say.

But Luke was a part of me now. There was no denying that.

Water bottles in hand, I shook Mike and Luke awake and pressed their respective meds on them. "You both need to drink a lot of water with these." I held out the water; Mike reached for his, but Luke pulled back.

"Can't drink more than we need to. Not until we find a place to replenish our supply," he croaked.

"Oh no, don't you dare. What you *need* to drink happens to be a lot more than usual, and that's what you're going to do. What was the point of us coming up here, of trying to find a way to help you, if you aren't going to actually *try* to get better?"

The only answer I got was Mike's hacking cough, but then I heard him twist the cap off his water bottle and gulp it down. "Mike's obeying me, at least," I pointed out.

Luke sighed – or at least I hoped it was a sigh, and told myself that's what it must have been. Because if it wasn't, it was a long and ragged breath that didn't sound human, causing my heart to thump hard in my chest until, after several moments, he finally took the other bottle from me. He fumbled with it, his bandaged hand stiff and clumsy, and though I itched to help him I also knew better than to try. We'd saved each other's lives countless times, Luke and I – but we didn't *help* each other. Not like that.

We didn't need to.

The night felt long, but maybe that was because it was strangely uneventful. We could hear zeds nearby – at times their usual night sounds, and once the noise of a few of them stumbling around in the woods at the edge of the park – but they never appeared. Not that we could see.

Somehow, that put me on edge more than if we'd spent those hours fighting the damn things.

At the first hint of dawn – which was, thankfully, the glow of an actual sunrise forming on the horizon – we piled back into the truck and my car and left the field behind, turning back into the large parking lot and then following the winding road that led through the park to the zoo, which had been carved out of the hillside that separated the park from one of the city's historical residential areas.

I couldn't help but cast anxious glances at both Luke and Mike. I thought that Mike looked and sounded a bit better, though I hoped that I wasn't just being optimistic. Luke, however...he had a bit more color, perhaps, but his sleep had been restless and now that he was awake his eyes looked almost panicked.

"We're going to the zoo, just like you wanted. I've got a good feeling about this." I tried to smile but was certain it looked as forced as it was. Luke, for his part, merely grunted and leaned his head back. His breaths were deep and measured, but I could tell that this was because he was trying – hard – to control them.

Eventually the truck and my car could go no farther driving side by side as we were. I threw on my parking brake and got out, nodding to Joey to follow me. It wasn't light enough to see much here, where the trees leaned over the path to the zoo's gates – but as we approached them, it was clear that someone had really battened down the hatches when everything went to hell.

Joey and I exchanged a glance. "You think there's still anyone here?" he whispered.

I brushed my fingertips across the front of the giant padlock that held together the two ends of the long, heavy chain that was wrapped around the gate. After a moment of thought, I nodded.

"What makes you so sure?"

"At least some of the people who worked here would have truly cared about the animals." I paused, smiling wanly. I knew that Joey wouldn't understand that like I did; he'd never been much of an animal person and obviously thought I was nuts for still having Holden with me now. "Combine that with the fact that this entire place is surrounded by walls and fences – most of which probably have razor or barbed wire worked in — and I'm telling you, someone would have stayed."

"Smart girl. Now turn around and be on your way."

It was a woman's voice, low and gravelly and distinctly southern, and despite what I'd said to Joey about knowing that people must have stayed behind, it scared the shit out of me — figuratively, I mean — to actually hear someone speak up. Ever the peacemaker, my brother immediately raised his hands, palms out, while I — the warrior sibling — couldn't help but drop my own hand to the butt of my gun.

"I wouldn't do that if I were you. I've got my own weapon and I *will* use it. So scram."

*Scram?* I choked back a laugh. Who in the world *was* this person? "Listen — we don't mean any harm. We're a small group, we have a child with us, and two of our friends are sick. We tried the hospital and the school…we didn't know where else to go." I knew there was a chance that I was giving this woman too much information, but I couldn't even *see* her — she clearly had the upper hand, and maybe if I played to that…

There was a long pause. I turned my head and listened, wondering if I was hearing things, or if there were indeed two voices now, both speaking far too quietly for me to understand what they were saying. This time, when someone finally responded to me, it was a man. "You won't find any help here, either. This certainly isn't a place for children and sick people."

"Come *on*, Charlie — let's just go." Joey was already backing away.

"No," I hissed, but I did take a single step back from the gate and reluctantly raise my hands in supplication. "I guarantee there is something we can do for you. Several of us are better shots than you've probably ever met. One of our men is a hell of a tactician — "

The woman interrupted me. "Shots. How many guns do you have?"

*Do they not have guns?* That was it, then – the thing that we could offer them – but I also found myself wondering how they thought they could keep us at bay if they only had…what?

"If you think we don't have guns of our own, you're mistaken." It was the man again, and although I was fairly certain that he was lying, I decided to humor him.

"But you could always use more. The zeds – zombies, I mean – must give you trouble? Or…" I remembered the school, the fact that Dominic and Mrs. Downing had been so frightened of whoever was in control there, the fact that their leader had been conspicuously absent… "If you haven't had problems with other people yet, I can almost guarantee you will, eventually – but not with us. Believe it or not, we're the good guys."

Silence. I let the seconds tick by; it must have been half a minute or more before I decided to once again mention where we'd been. "I'm not sure what's going on at the school, but I got the feeling the people there are trouble. I'm telling you, if you haven't had issues with them yet, you will."

I could hear them arguing again and decided to let them finish. Joey was watching me intently, but I merely shook my head, slowly, and waited for a response.

"Okay. We're going to open the gate and bring you in for a chat – but you'll leave your weapons with one of our men. We won't suffer armed strangers in our presence," the man finally announced, sounding more than a little exasperated.

Joey made a choking noise. "Go in there unarmed? Screw that."

I shrugged. "Can't be much worse than staying out here."

"This is a one time offer – take it or leave it!"

## LESSON LEARNED

*Sometimes, you just have to walk away. (Literally...or figuratively.)*

# Chapter 7
# Taking Chances

"We'll take it," I agreed quickly, before Joey could interrupt me. "But you'll need to let all of us in, and one of our men will stay with yours to keep an eye on our things."

"You're not really in a place to be setting terms. "

"We're not stupid enough to leave our weapons with one of your people and not watch them at all – so you'll have to trust us at least that much. "

"Fine. Get ready to pull your vehicles through the gates as soon as we open them. And know that if you step out with any weapons in hand, we will shoot you on sight."

"Understood." I spun on my heel and jogged back to my car, Joey shuffling along behind me. I could tell that he was angry, but I didn't have time to worry about that; Mike and Luke needed help, and at the moment it seemed to me like this was our last chance to find it for them.

"What's going on?" Mike mumbled as I climbed back into the driver's seat and put my car in gear.

I pasted a smile on my face. "We're going in." I eased my Volkswagen toward the gate as a tall, slim, dark-haired man pulled it open. Joey had the truck so close to my bumper that I almost felt like tapping my brakes in warning – but then what would I do if he hit me? *Something tells me there aren't very many car repair shops open these days.* I couldn't help but chuckle to myself.

The man was shutting the gate before Joey even had the truck in park. "Stay in the car for now," I told the guys as I slowly pushed open my door and stepped out, hands in clear sight. I glanced to my left and saw Joey doing the same, and followed his gaze to the woman who had a gun trained on us. She was older than our mother by a good ten years or more – her hair was white, but she was standing straight and tall. Despite the weapon in her hands, she was smiling pleasantly.

"Good morning, folks. I'm Virginia; he prefers to be called Richard." She jerked her head toward the dark-haired man. "The rest of your people going to get out and meet us, as well?" This was more an order than a question.

"The two friends in there are sick." I jerked my head back toward my car.

"I'll get the others." Joey leaned back into his own vehicle. I couldn't hear what he said, but Daniel's expression was grim as he nodded. A moment later, he and Lauren and Mabel were climbing out of the truck.

"Daniel here will be staying with our things," I announced. "I can get Mike and Luke out too, but they're going to be a bit slow."

"I'm not sure we want them in our facility if they're…sick." Virginia grimaced. "They can stay in the car. Best warn them that if they make any move to get out, I'll do what I have to do."

I rolled my eyes. "We wouldn't have come through your gates if I thought any of us would cause you trouble."

"We'll see about that. " The man who 'preferred to be called Richard' was standing in front of my car now. "Come with me."

As we made our way down the wide but winding path, following it deeper into the zoo, I noted that most of the enclosures were overgrown, their residents – *former residents?* – nowhere to be seen. I remembered this zoo from before, though I'd only been once. I'd dragged Dave here for an after-hours craft beer festival, an event that had turned into another failed attempt at reviving our 'dating life'.

"Miss? *Miss*."

I started, my eyes refocusing on Richard, and realized that I'd stopped walking. "Sorry," I mumbled. The man pursed his lips, but then turned and strode away again.

Joey appeared by my side. "What the hell was that? Are you okay?"

"Geez, I'm fine. Spaced out a bit for a moment thinking about the last time I was here."

"You've been here before?"

"Just once, a couple of years ago. And it was…different."

"Of course it was. There were other people here, maybe a lot of them. Families. Children." Joey's tone was bitter.

"Not just that. Take a look around. Shouldn't a zoo have animals?" I kept my voice low, not wanting Richard – or Lauren and Mabel, who were following close behind – to hear me. Joey glanced around and nodded his head, once.

"And…this is a small zoo, isn't it?"

"Oh yeah. He's taking us on a pretty circuitous route."

"What have we gotten into, Charlie?"

I pressed my index finger to my lips and glared at my brother before whispering, "Maybe he doesn't want us to see a certain area of the zoo, but that could mean any number of things."

"Sure, and none of them good."

Before I could respond, Richard beckoned to us and veered off to the right. By the time Lauren and Mabel caught up with Joey and I and we turned the corner together, Richard was holding open the door to a building that was almost entirely hidden by vines. I could hear the hum of a generator, but I still wasn't ready for the harsh fluorescent lighting of what was clearly the zoo veterinarian's office.

"This was just my workplace, at one time. Now it's the only home I have."

It was the first thing this stranger had said that made him actually seem human. "You were the vet, then? " I couldn't hide the relief that I felt, knowing that this man had actually been employed here. I knew that Joey was watching me, but I kept my eyes on Richard.

"I was. Which means that I'll be the one to take care of your friends…if we can come to an agreement."

"Should we get down to business, then?"

"In a few more minutes. I think you should have a better understanding of our situation before you make any promises to us. Let's go have a seat; the third member of my team should be back soon."

"There's just three of you, then?" Joey asked in disbelief. "If that's the case, why not tell us before? Or…why suddenly tell us *now*?"

Richard stepped into a room on the right side of the hallway; we followed him and waited for a response. He perched on the corner of his desk and gestured to the chairs in front of it. I took one, Lauren and Mabel the other, while Joey leaned against the wall behind us.

"Yes, there are only three of us. Surely you understand why I didn't care to admit that right away; as for telling you now, well…it would be a very short matter of time before you found out. I assumed that you would appreciate my honesty."

I made sure to speak up before Joey could do so. "It certainly helps that we didn't have to…find that out on our own, I suppose."

Just then a young man burst into the room. "Everything is good for now, Doctor Rich – " He caught sight of us then, and his mouth dropped open.

"Ethan, these people are guests of ours." Richard stood and laid his hand on the young man's shoulder. "Say hello."

"He – hello." Ethan spoke slowly, haltingly, but I could tell that it wasn't just from shock.

Richard must have seen the look on my face. "Ethan here is Virginia's son. They were two of the zoo's best volunteers. They spent a lot of time here…and happened to be here when…"

"Everything went to hell," I finished. Richard nodded; forcing a smile, I stood and held my hand out to Ethan. "I'm Charlie."

He gave it a wary glance, then looked away without offering his own, merely mumbling, "Nice to meet you."

I shoved my hands in my pockets and faced Richard. He had a look on his face that said he would explain later; I decided to bring the conversation back around. "Here's me being honest, then – the two guys in my car need immediate assistance. I got them some medicine but...they're in bad shape. Especially the blonde one. Luke." I hated the way my voice cracked when I said his name.

"And in return, we get…?" Richard was stern, insistent even.

"Our protection," Joey snapped.

"And equal access to our weapons," I promised, hoping that my brother's attitude would go unnoticed.

Richard stared at Joey for a few moments. "Equal access?"

"Equal access," I repeated.

"What kind of weapons, Doc – "

"Guns, Ethan. So I help with your friends, and no matter what happens…"

"We assist you in return, for as long as we're welcome here."

"I suppose that's a deal we can agree to." Richard held out his hand, glancing at Ethan as I withdrew my own hand from my pocket and shook Richard's. The young man looked away from us and scuffed his feet against the ground; Richard sighed and released his grip. "Let's see to your people."

He led us back outside and down the same path we'd walked earlier, though this time Ethan trailed behind us. He seemed oddly wary of Mabel in particular, and though I couldn't know for sure, I thought perhaps he was autistic.

Sara, a friend of mine from college, had worked with autistic children; she and I had talked about our jobs on a regular basis, and I'd learned quite a bit from her...

*Don't think about that. Don't think about her, or any other friend.* Chances were I'd never know what had become of my friends or extended family, so there was no use dwelling on such things.

It was the sound of a dog barking – Holden, I knew immediately – that pulled me back to reality. Richard turned to me and started to speak, but I held up a hand to stop him. "Holden doesn't usually bark, not unless something is seriously wrong. You better hope that he and the rest of our people are okay." I broke into a run, calling over my shoulder, "Joey, stay with Lauren and Mabel." I heard Richard pick up his pace as well, but I doubted he could catch or keep up with me – months of dodging zeds had made me a solid mass of muscle built for running, while the good doctor had been holed up behind his fences, safe and sound.

But nothing could have prepared me for what I saw when I rounded the last corner of the winding path and burst into the open space by the front gate. I practically skidded to a halt, my first reaction being to take a step backward, though I nearly stumbled and fell as I did so. My jaw dropped open of its own accord and for the first time in a long time I was frozen in place, completely unsure of what to do.

My dog was barking at a fucking *elephant.*

## LESSON LEARNED

*Always assume that things aren't quite what they seem.*

\*\*\*\*\*\*\*

"Not *again*." Richard had stopped beside me. "Ethan! Take care of this!"

"What do you mean, 'not again'?"

"Get your dog to stop making a racket and we'll talk."

I crouched down and whistled softly. "Holden!" I hissed. "*Holden!*" He stopped barking, but hunkered down and growled as he backed away from the elephant. Ethan was approaching it from the side; I could tell that he was talking to it, but the words were murmured, indistinct. The rest of us were frozen where we'd stopped as the young man finally reached out and touched the animal's shoulder. Moments later they were walking away, heading the opposite direction into the zoo, and then suddenly Holden was bounding into me, nearly knocking me to the ground. I sat down and tucked my arm over him, holding him tight until he calmed down, at which point I finally fixed my attention on Richard. "What was *that* all about?"

"This is a zoo," he shrugged.

"Ohhhh no. No way. You were too pissed off just then to act like it was actually no big deal. Do your animals escape often?" I didn't even bother to hide the sarcasm in my tone.

"Hush, girl." I turned and saw Virginia standing over me, hand held out to help me up. I eyed it warily, but took it nonetheless. Once I was back on my feet she glanced in the direction Ethan had gone. "I'm sorry that happened today of all days. It's not a regular occurrence. El – that's her name – is an escape artist, and from time to time Ethan doesn't chain her gate properly."

"Wonderful." I grimaced. "Any lions or tigers or bears wandering around?"

"Don't worry about all that. There really aren't many animals left." Virginia was so matter-of-fact that it made my stomach turn.

"You didn't…" I couldn't even bring myself to say it.

"We did not *eat* them," Richard snapped. "We're not…barbarians."

"It would have been like eating a pet." Virginia shuddered. "No, we just…knew that we couldn't feed them. And we didn't have enough bullets to put them out of their misery. So we let them go."

"You…let them go? As in, opened the gates and let them out into the city? What the hell made you think they would survive that?"

"Probably most of them didn't. But perhaps some of them did. It's more of a chance than we could have given them if we'd kept them locked up here in the zoo."

"Fine, whatever, let's say that the ones that are gone don't matter. Which ones did you keep, and do I have to worry about something worse than an elephant being around every bend?"

Richard's shoulders sagged. "Just the elephant. Some monkeys hang around from time to time, but they never come down to the ground. They assume we would try to cage them again, I think."

"How astute," I said drily.

Virginia eyed me the way only a mother could. "There's goats and chickens as well. We had an interactive petting zoo, taught city kids how to collect chicken eggs, showed them how to milk the goats. Sold some goat milk products, soap and the like, in the gift shop."

*That* was interesting. "Well. I can't argue with that. We came from a farm, but it hadn't really been a working one, and…" I stopped and swallowed the lump that was building in my throat. I couldn't think about the farm right now, let alone *talk* about it. "Anyway. Let's just get Mike and Luke inside, please. We can finish this discussion later."

"Are they contagious?" Richard asked.

"To be honest, I don't know. We tried to keep the kid, Mike, away from most of us when he started feeling sick...but we're all fine, and I think we still should have caught it, if it was contagious."

"And the other?" *Damn, he won't let up, will he?*

"Contagious..." I thought for a moment, then shook my head. "No, I really don't think so. Look, can we talk about this in private?" My people knew about Luke's hand, of course, but I wasn't sure that Richard would want Virginia or Ethan to know.

The vet leveled his gaze at me for a moment, then sighed and nodded. "Alright then. You can park the car over there." He gestured to a large alcove-type area in front of what had once been a Siamang enclosure, according to the almost silly ornate sign hanging above the empty cage. "It's small enough to be hidden from sight if you pull right up to the edge; we can move it later. Virginia will show the others where to keep the truck while we get these boys to my office."

I didn't think Luke *or* Mike would care to be called a boy, but I merely set my jaw and nodded. "They'll need help walking all the way back there."

"I've dealt with sick lions, pregnant orangutans, and a hundred other things. I think I can handle a couple of sick men."

*I really fucking hope so.* If he couldn't help Luke, I doubted that I would find someone else who could. Not in time to save him.

Holden paced nervously as I moved my car; in the passenger seat, Luke was barely conscious. Mike still seemed to be faring better, and I knew that I couldn't let Richard see what was wrong with either of them – but especially Luke – until we were well away from the others. "Mike, when I get out of this car, you need to ask for that man's help. I need to stay with Luke. Do you understand?" Mike nodded once, slowly, in response. "Okay. Here we go." I slid out of the car, dragging my backpack over my shoulder as I did, and immediately moved around to the front passenger side to deal with Luke. Mike opened his door and set his feet on the ground. He was obviously still weak, and with me preoccupied, Richard stepped forward voluntarily.

We moved a lot slower on this second trip back to the offices. Luke was practically dead weight and dragged me down with every step; eventually I waved Richard on, insisting that I could find my way, promising that I wouldn't leave the beaten path.

For once, I actually meant it when I made that promise. I had no desire to get lost in this zoo with Luke leaning on me like he was. And he needed medical care. Fast.

But I also needed to talk to him. I wasn't sure how much we should tell this stranger, and as soon as I saw Richard and Mike disappear around a bend in the path, I staggered to a halt.

"Luke." I waited. "*Luke!*"

"Huh?" He was groggy, but at least he was hearing me.

"In case you haven't noticed, we're at the zoo. I'm bringing you to see the vet. But Luke, listen to me. *Don't tell him you were bitten.* Not right away. I'm hoping he just...doesn't ask the right questions. Maybe it's not the bite at all, you know? Maybe it's just infected from – "

"I...I don't...don't think we should lie. "

"Are you sure? He may hear you've been bitten and simply write you off. "

Luke seemed to take hold of himself then; suddenly he was standing on his own; I lost my grip on him, and then he took one slow step, and then another, and another, up the path.

"Fine!" I called out, exasperated. "Fine! But at least let me help you."

We moved faster now, though it was still several minutes before I had Luke settled in a chair in Richard's office while the vet examined Mike. I was impatient, but I also didn't want to alarm this man. *He may be our only chance.*

Finally Richard stepped back. "He said he's had medicine. You remember what you were giving him?"

"Yeah, sure..." I set my bag down and rummaged through it. "This."

Richard peered at it for a moment and then finally nodded. "Good." He turned back to Mike. "I think you just need some food and water and a good long rest, maybe for a day, two at most. Keep taking those while you're at it." He gestured at the box in my hand, and then finally approached Luke. "Now, what's wrong with you?"

We exchanged a look, and in that moment Luke knew that I still had it in me to lie. "I was bitten," he admitted, then quickly rushed on to say, "We took off the fingers well below where the zed got hold of me, but I've been..."

"He's just been out of it," I interrupted. "Weak. A bit feverish, yeah, but truth be told I'm more worried about the method we used to remove the fingers than the bites that started this whole mess."

The veterinarian was trembling, and I instinctively knew that it wasn't in fear – he was angry. Really, really angry.

"You brought an *infected man* into this zoo? You saw our few strengths, our many weaknesses, and you decided that it was *okay* to put us in this much danger?!"

"Please, please, we'll leave as soon as you've looked after him, if we have to," I pleaded, wondering just how royally we'd fucked things up. "He's fine right now, he's still alive, he's still *lucid*. I wouldn't have brought him in here otherwise – "

"Tie me down," Luke said suddenly.

Both Richard and I turned to face him, asking, "What?" at the same time. It was almost comical.

But Luke wasn't laughing. "You must have ropes here, or at least more chains than the one that's on your gate. If you're so worried about me dying and then rising up to attack you, just *tie me down*."

I looked at the vet; he was still watching Luke, his gaze wary. "All of you, stay here. I'll go get some rope...or something. But not before you answer this – has anyone else in your group been bitten?"

"No," I replied quickly. "Just Luke. I swear it."

Richard hesitated for a moment. "You haven't been bitten?" he asked Mike.

"No, sir."

"Right. Okay. Like I said, *stay here.*" He left us then, and was gone for several minutes. He'd shut us in the office, but we still heard a door open, some rummaging – he wasn't far down the hall – and when he came back, he had a large tube of zip ties and a thick coil of soft rope. I tried to help Richard as he led Luke to his desk chair and began securing his legs and arms, but he wouldn't have it. "I'll make sure he's secure myself."

Luke's eyes met mine, and without him saying anything I knew that he was thinking, "I told you so." At that point I didn't even want to consider what Richard would have done had we waited any longer to tell him about Luke's bites; I merely nodded my head in agreement. *Yes, you were right.*

Finally the vet seemed confident that Luke wasn't going anywhere. Richard had zip-tied Luke's hands together behind the back of the chair, then used more zip ties to bind his feet as well. The rope was wound around his chest, his upper legs, and the chair so many times that I almost wanted to laugh at the absurdity of it all.

"Help me wheel him into the light," Richard ordered. I immediately obeyed, then knelt to watch him unwrap Luke's hand and tell him about the bites.

"It was a clean chop," the vet murmured, "but a dirty blade, I'm guessing?"

"I definitely wouldn't have called it clean."

Richard stood and walked away, pacing in front of his desk for a minute before finally saying, "I think – I *think* –

we just need to cut away some flesh, clean the wound, and re-bandage it. He'll have to stay locked up, at the very least – and alone – but I believe that if we do that, I can reassess the situation tomorrow. That may be all he needs. Or..." Here he paused, looked down at the floor, and cleared his throat.

"Or?" I prompted.

"Or we may need to take off the hand. At least. Maybe even the whole arm. Regardless, what we do...it will need to be a quick decision. But after that, I think he'd have a perfectly good chance of survival."

*Survival.* There was that damn word again. *But this isn't your decision.* "What do you say, Luke?"

"Do it. We'll...we'll figure everything else out tomorrow." There was no heart behind Luke's words, but he said them nonetheless, and so the veterinarian went to work. He wheeled the desk chair into a clean room, Luke still tied down despite the fact that he seemed more with it than he had in days. Richard insisted that Mike stay in his office; I had the feeling he would have tried the same with me, but I shoved my way in behind them.

Luke eyed me, his gaze still a bit unfocused. "You sure you want to be in here? I have a feeling this won't be pleasant."

"Nothing about anything is really pleasant anymore. And yeah, I want to be here for you. Hold your hand." *Your other hand, anyway.*

"Yeah, thankfully I still have the one good hand." Luke's smile was pained, but at least he was making some attempt at humor again.

I favored him with a coy smile. "For both our sakes, hmm?"

Luke rolled his eyes, but Richard was too busy prepping to take note of my lewd comments. By the time he turned back to us I'd put on my most innocent expression and stepped forward to entwine my fingers with Luke's. It was awkward, doing so around the rope that bound them to the chair; I could even feel the edge of the zip ties that held them together cutting into my wrist, but then the vet reached around and cut through the plastic, pulling the injured appendage out of the ropes and setting it on the portable table that he'd placed next to the chair. He immediately grabbed a roll of duct tape and wound several strips of it around Luke's arm, binding him to the small work surface.

I eyed Richard with trepidation. "Is that really necessary?"

"Maybe not, but I don't trust you, I don't trust him, and I don't know what will happen here. I've never seen anyone who's been bitten...not anyone still alive, I mean."

"Right." I knew that he was trying to tell me that this was probably a waste of time, a worthless attempt to save a life already doomed, but I didn't want to believe it – *couldn't* believe it. Not really.

The next hour was a blur of pain for me as Luke clung to my hand, breath hissing through his teeth as he clenched his jaw against the torture of Richard poking and prodding at his severed fingers. On a good day Luke knew his own strength...but I had to face the fact that the good days were probably long gone. So I bit my lip and let him squeeze, reminding myself that whatever I was feeling, he had it much, much worse.

Finally the vet was binding the hand up again. Luke's eyes were glazed over and I was surprised that he hadn't passed out. "Where will he be staying tonight? He needs to lie down, not be tied upright in this chair."

"We have a holding cell for sick animals. He'll be safe in there, though the best I can do is some blankets on the floor. We don't exactly have a plethora of beds around here."

"Fine. Whatever. I'll need some blankets as well. I'll be staying with him."

Richard glanced at Luke. "That's probably not a good idea."

"Do I look like I give a shit? I'm not leaving him." I refused to complete the thought – that I couldn't leave him to die alone. Not Luke. He deserved better than that.

Especially from me.

The vet shrugged. "I'm well aware that I can't stop you."

"But I can."

We both turned to Luke; I rushed to his side, ready to protest, but he gave me a weak smile and shook his head. "Charlie, you can't be left alone with me, and no one else should be put in that kind of danger. We don't know what will happen."

"I'm staying," I insisted. "You couldn't stop me if you tried."

"Maybe not *now* – "

"Good, so we can discuss this again when you're better and decide to punish me for not listening to you."

Luke chuckled, but it was half-hearted at best. "When have I ever punished you?"

"Every damn day," I murmured, thinking of how on edge I was regarding him...because in the end, the realization that the thought of losing Luke was more worrisome than anything else about this world in which we'd found ourselves was almost frightening.

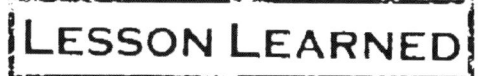

## LESSON LEARNED

*Tell the truth...*
*whenever you can justify it.*

# Chapter 8
# Zoo Life

In the end Luke didn't have enough energy to stop me from bedding down on the floor outside the holding cell. It was a barred-in alcove nestled into the back wall of the room next to the one where Richard had treated him. Though it must not have been scrubbed down in months, it still boasted the faint smell of strong cleaning products, and under that, the unmistakable odor of animals.

"Are you sure you want to stay in here?" Mike asked, wrinkling his nose in disgust.

"Could be worse."

"What about your brother, and Daniel, Lauren, Mabel? What about Holden?"

I closed my eyes and took a deep breath. "Mike...I'm exhausted. And the truth is, I don't want to leave Luke. Plain and simple. If you could make my excuses to the others and look after Holden for the night, I'd really appreciate it. I know you're still not feeling one hundred percent, but...I need tonight. Just in case. Hopefully tomorrow will be easier."

After a long pause, Mike finally nodded. "Okay." He looked over my shoulder at Luke, who was sitting against the far wall of the cage, trying to rest. *Or just pretending.* "See you in the morning, man," Mike said.

Luke opened his eyes and grimaced. "Yeah, Mike. Of course." But there was no conviction in his words, and with one last worried glance at me, Mike finally turned and left us.

I'm not sure how much time passed; it could have been an hour, or several of them. All I know is that I'd drifted into a restless sleep, but was woken by the sound of slamming doors, followed by Lauren stumbling into the room with Mabel on her hip, practically dragging Holden behind her with the help of a makeshift leash that had been tied to his collar. I hadn't seen the little girl cry in months, but somehow her wide, frightened gaze was even more disturbing than her tears. Thankfully my dog distracted me by rushing to my side to lick my face like he hadn't seen me in days.

"What's wrong?" I pushed Holden away and tried to rub the sleep from my eyes, but I was too groggy and couldn't focus. It took me a moment to realize that Lauren wasn't looking at me, but at Luke.

"They sent us to keep an eye on Luke. You're needed outside. The zeds, Charlie…they're at the gate, a whole lot of them, and a couple even got into one of the empty cages at the back, too. Virginia said we must have made too much noise today…probably drew them from miles away…"

I was already on my feet. "Don't worry about Luke. He'll be fine. If he wakes up, tell him I'll be back soon." I had to hope that would be the case, anyway.

"And if he's not fine?"

"He *is*," I snapped, then paused when I saw the hurt in Lauren's eyes. "But if something happens to him while I'm gone, he's locked up tight. He can't hurt you or Mabel, okay? And I'll leave Holden here with you as well."

She nodded warily, and I took that as my cue to leave. *Weapons, weapons, where would they have put our weapons?* I had to assume they'd let me use one of theirs if they expected me to help out, but something felt wrong about not having *my* knife, *my* gun…even my bat.

I didn't know the layout of the back half of the zoo, but I knew how to find the front gate. I went there first, sprinting down the path, hoping that I wouldn't trip over anything considering how dark it was and that I could barely see a foot in front of me.

Virginia was there, ordering Ethan and Mike around in a low hiss. I couldn't hear what she was saying, but as they all seemed to be armed with some sort of prods that had been tipped with knives, it was the work of a moment to figure out that they were jabbing at the zeds through the gate. Thankfully it had been built to keep people out as much as to keep animals in, and even some of the more emaciated zeds were only able to press themselves against the bars in fruitless attempts to get at the fresh meat they sensed just beyond.

"Hey!" I called out, as quietly as I could. Both Mike and Virginia spun around.

"No! Keep at them!" the older woman told him.

I rushed forward. "Lauren sent me to help."

"No, no, not here, we can handle this." Virginia turned to stab at another zed.

"I didn't know where else to go – I don't know my way around this place!"

"Right." *Jab.* "Right." *Stab.* "Ethan, show her to the old giraffe pen."

"*Enclosure*, mom," Ethan replied, exasperated.

"*Go*, son," Virginia insisted. "Take your spear."

*Spear?* "I need something too. You guys took our weapons, remember?"

"Richard and the others have plenty of things for you to use. Now follow him!" Virginia jerked her chin in the direction Ethan was moving. He was walking fast, but unevenly, and I quickly caught up with him.

"How could the zeds have gotten into an enclosure?" I asked as I reached Ethan's side.

His eyes flicked toward me momentarily, but then he looked straight ahead again, and remained silent.

*Shit. Of course he doesn't know what a zed is.* "Sorry, the zombies. Undead. Whatever you guys call them. I mean, if they can't get through the front gate..."

I trailed off. As far as I could see, he wasn't even really listening. Hearing my words, maybe, but focusing on them? Probably not.

I'd just have to see it for myself.

It was several minutes before we finally caught sight of Daniel. He appeared to be holding a gate shut, and there were several zeds scattered on the ground around him, though thankfully none of them were moving.

"What the hell? Daniel, where's Joey? And Richard?"

He turned to me, his face pinched and white. "In there."

And he gestured at the pen.

"But *why*?"

"This door's broken. They needed someone to keep an eye on it, stop more zeds from getting into the zoo this way."

"Wait. Wait. *More* zeds? How many got through?" I'd already broken into a cold sweat, and I could feel the adrenaline pumping even harder than just a few moments before.

"Don't worry, we got the ones who came through already." Daniel nodded at the bodies on the ground. "But they're going to need help. The zeds just keep falling in."

"*How?*" God, it was like pulling teeth, getting answers from him. And all the while, Ethan was standing off to the side, staring at his 'spear' and chewing his lip.

"Jesus, Charlie, I don't know how this zoo was built. Just get in there and help them!"

"It's the hillside. The fence up there was just chain link. It probably fell down. They never paid enough attention to it...there were only a couple giraffes in this enclosure."

I turned toward Ethan, but bit my tongue and collected myself before simply saying, "I see. Thank you. And this door?"

Ethan peered at it. "Broken after," he stated, his voice flat and emotionless.

I knew better than to ask any more questions just now. "I need a weapon."

"There." Daniel pointed at what appeared to be a pile of junk just off to the side of the gate. I strode over to it and bent down, my lip curling in distaste.

"You've *got* to be kidding. Where are *our* things?"

"I don't know, they put them away somewhere, didn't have time to get them. Shit, Charlie, just pick something and *get in there!*"

I groaned and snatched up a pair of gardening shears and some sort of post-apocalyptic mace – an aged strip of wood with some nails jutting from one end. Daniel cracked the door open and I slipped through. It clanged shut behind me and when I turned to glare at him I suddenly realized how dark it was.

I froze.

*There was a moon tonight, I know there was.* It may have only been a half-moon, but it hadn't been this dark a moment ago.

I could hear the zeds in the pen, their moans punctuated by Joey and Richard's grunts as they fought. I chanced a look at the sky, which had clouded over in that sudden way of early spring nights in the south. *Fuck.*

I stepped forward, willing my eyes to adjust. They did, and none too soon – a zed that had gotten past the guys was just a few feet away and coming right at me, its mouth a bloody maw as its grasping hands reached out.

I brought the gardening shears up and drove their tip into the underside of the zed's chin. Suddenly I stumbled, slamming into the zed and driving it to the ground beneath me. I dropped the strip of wood as I fell, and when I landed on top of the zombie, gardening shears sandwiched between us, I could think only of getting away from its bite. I released my weapon and rolled to the side, but whatever those shears had done was good enough. The zombie lay twitching on the ground, somehow incapacitated but definitely not completely dead. I decided to abandon the shears, scooping up the wannabe mace as I rushed farther into the enclosure, following what I hoped were the sounds of both Joey and Richard still fighting off zeds.

Joey caught sight of me first. He had his back to the hillside, which loomed like a black wall not fifty yards away. "Charlie! Finally!" he called out as he slammed what appeared to be a brush axe into a zed's temple. The weapon lodged there for a moment; Joey leaned back, lifted his right foot, and gave the zed a good hard kick. It fell to the ground, but he almost did, too – I had to jump forward and catch his arm. When he was steady again I let go.

"Dammit, Joey, be *careful*."

"Are you shitting me?"

I spun him around to face the hillside. "That's where they're coming from?"

He nodded.

"Then don't turn your back on it. Otherwise, nice work right there." He hadn't actually been very smart in his handling of that zed, but at the moment I figured it was better to praise him rather than nitpick.

Joey pointed off to the left with his weird little axe. "Come on. They're getting in over here. Thank God Ethan reminded Richard that this area wasn't well contained. We got the few that had stumbled through the broken gate, but they've been pouring in pretty regularly thanks to all the noise. It only just started slowing down a bit. That's why I was over there, chasing a few of the wanderers."

By now we were moving slowly; the closer we got to the breach in the hilltop fence, there were more zeds littering the ground – and I could see movement here and there that proved they weren't all rendered harmless.

As the first drops of rain pattered down on my head, Richard staggered into my path, lurching away from one zed as he bludgeoned a second one on the head with a hammer. *Wonder if it's the same hammer they used to make* this *piece of shit*, I thought to myself as my half-assed mace connected with the first zombie's neck. I'd been startled, though, and my swing wasn't hard enough – this zed was moving slower than the others, and its neck was still meaty. *A new one.* I almost lost myself for a moment there, wondering who it had been not so long ago...but my blow had only knocked it from its path, and I quickly collected myself, stepping forward to drive the nail-tipped end of my weapon into its face.

Richard was bent over double, clutching his chest. "Someone needs to get up there," he wheezed, pointing at the hillside, "and fix that fence."

"Not gonna happen until the morning, Doc," I replied as the rain began to fall in earnest. "Take a break. Joey and I've got this for now. He said it's slowing down?"

The veterinarian nodded. I could see in his eyes that he didn't want to give up, but at the very least he was having some sort of asthma or panic attack. At the worst...

*He's fine. Anyway, you've got bigger problems right now.* And I did – I could see the glints of metal a few dozen feet above where the fence was mangled and collapsed. Just now, though, it was quiet. "I'll watch the fence," I told Joey. "Take care of the ones that are still...moving. But do it fast."

I was surprised when my brother obeyed without question. Richard had backed even further away, but I could still hear him gasping for air. "Try to make less noise," I hissed. If the zeds heard the sounds that they associated with food, they would come. If they heard other zeds moaning, they would come. *Thank God no one's been stupid enough to use a gun.*

"Richard," I murmured. Then again, when he didn't respond: "*Richard!*"

"Yes, yes, what?" he finally grunted between breaths.

"I know we need to fix the fence, but first can we find a way to bar that gate? At least then we can keep them contained and not need so many of us dealing with this. You'll have to do it; none of us will know where to find anything. Joey and I can handle this ourselves for a bit, but you need to figure that out *quickly*. Please," I added as an afterthought.

"I – right, yes, of course. There's a storage building..."

"That's all well and good, but we don't need to know the details. Just take care of it, okay?" I was almost surprised at how nice I was being when every part of my body was tensed for attack. I heard Richard murmur his assent and move off.

Suddenly I realized how *weary* I was. The adrenaline that had been pumping through me just moments before must have run its course, and I found myself reaching up to rub the back of my hand across my eyes, cringing at the stench of the zombie goo that had caked my sleeve and splattered all over my skin.

*When was the last time I slept through an entire night?* I couldn't remember, and tonight was proving to be as bad as – or worse than – those in recent memory.

Joey stepped up beside me, wiping the flat of his blade on his pants. "I think they're all *dead* dead now," he informed me. But I didn't respond, which prompted him to ask, "You okay?"

"Yeah. Just tired."

"Well it's about time. I've been exhausted for *months*."

I snorted. I knew he was just trying to lighten the mood, but at the moment I couldn't handle it. "I'm only human, Joey."

"Could have fooled me. Especially these last few months. I really didn't want to have to call you out here to help us, but when it got to the point where I didn't think Richard and I could handle it on our own, I had to send Lauren for you. Plus it was the only way to get her to take Mabel away from this. She didn't want to leave Daniel."

"You guys seemed to be doing okay." It was only half a lie; they'd certainly taken care of the majority of the zeds without my help.

"Only because they finally stopped pouring through that hole like an undead waterfall."

"*Undead waterfall?*" I repeated, choking back a laugh. "That's horrible. Though it would maybe make a great parody song...you know, don't go chasin' undead waterfalls...stick to the – "

"Aren't you just hilarious," Joey interrupted, shaking his head, but I could see that he was having trouble holding back a chuckle. "That's what it looked like, and that's all I'm gonna say about it. Honestly, Ethan remembered not a moment too soon that the gate to this pen was broken. We barely made it back here in time to contain them at all. I don't know, Charlie. Maybe coming here wasn't such a good idea. Clearly the noise from earlier today is what drew the zeds to the zoo in the first place, and who knows when that damn elephant will get loose again. And it's not as if we can even count on their fences." He jerked his head toward the hillside.

"I never said we needed to stay here forever," I assured him. "But Richard may be able to help Luke. I can't discount that and just run away again at the first sign of danger."

Joey's eyes sought mine; they were shining in the dark, his eyelashes clumped together from the rain. "Charlie...that's the problem. You don't run away from danger anymore. *You seek it out.*" I stared at him for a long moment, my jaw clenched as I tried to think of a response, *any* response – but suddenly he whipped his head around to look at the hillside. "Did you hear that?"

I followed his gaze and concentrated on listening; for a moment all I heard was the sound of raindrops hitting leaves and ground and the bodies around us. But then there it was – the low, keening moans of a group of zeds. *But how* many? *A few? A dozen? More?* "Maybe the rain will confuse them now that it's quiet down here," I whispered. My brother nodded, but I could tell his hopes weren't high.

A minute passed, then two, and I was about to breathe a bit more easily when I heard the cracks and snaps of brush and branches. And then there they were – one, two, three, four, five zeds, stumbling through the break in the fence, tumbling and sliding down the hillside. The fall held them up, and I began to step forward in hopes of taking them out while they were partially incapacitated, but Joey stuck out an arm to stop me.

"There could be more."

As much as I hated the idea of waiting, of allowing the zeds to haul themselves to their feet and move toward us, I knew that he was right. I nodded and tightened my grip on the end of my makeshift mace.

"Don't swing until you see the whites of their eyes," Joey mumbled.

That time, I couldn't help but laugh.

## LESSON LEARNED

*Complacency is no longer possible.*

\* \* \* \* \* \* \*

The zeds were moving toward us now, and these ones were *fast*. "*Joey*," I snarled. "There's no more coming."

"Just *wait*," he replied. "Wait..."

"No!" I argued. "*Now!*" They were practically on top of us when I stepped forward and swung my weapon at the closest one. There was a sickening thud as the nails bit into the zed's cheek, and it took all of my strength to rip them free. The zombie reeled, slamming into one of the others and taking it to the ground. Before they could get up I moved in and smashed my mace down on their heads, again and again and again, until I was certain they wouldn't be getting back up. I spun around to look for my brother, but the rain blinded me for a moment...and then suddenly another zed was there, too close for me to swing at. I braced the length of wood in both hands and drove it at the zed's chest, but it had already started reaching for me, the ground was a mess of slick mud, and I lost my footing.

We went down in a tangle of limbs.

Looking back, I've wondered if I really did press the attack too soon, or if everything that happened next was simply inevitable. I heard Joey call out and felt his hand close around my forearm. He pulled me off the zed, yanking so hard that even as he let go to raise his axe the force he'd used propelled me across the muddy ground.

From that moment on, my memories of that night are nothing more than flashes of horror. A lightning bolt splitting the sky, highlighting the edge of Joey's blade as he drove it down to take out the fallen zed once and for all. The return to black and the rumble of thunder that didn't quite cover his cry of surprise. Me, screaming his name, feeling like I wasn't even in my own body as I struggled to regain my footing.

A thud as Joey fell to the ground not a foot away, another flash of lightning showing him reaching out to me, his mouth open as he tried to call out to me, the gaping hole in his neck rendering him incapable of speech.

The moan of the zed that fell on my brother as I reached for the axe that had slipped from his grasp.

The feel of that axe as I took hold of it, the handle still warm.

The madness that came over me as I tackled the zed, forgetting my own safety in my need to kill it, kill it, *kill it*...

I woke with a start, the sunlight from a nearby window warm on my skin, and my first thought was, *Just a nightmare. Thank God.*

Until I realized that I was lying on Richard's desk. The vet himself was standing over me, eyes wide, face white. I sat up so fast that we nearly knocked heads; he took a step back and raised his hands as if to ward me off. "Careful now," he said, but the way he was looking at me belied the calm tone of his voice.

"What happened? Why am I here?" I suddenly realized how much pain I was in; my arms ached in ways they hadn't for months now. I looked down at them, covered in caked blood and gore, and felt my stomach lurch. "No, no, no, no..."

Another flash of memory. A pulverized zed at my feet. Turning and falling to my knees at Joey's side. Clutching at him, refusing to let go even as someone tried to pull me away...

"Charlie. Charlotte. Right? Charlotte? You're safe, okay? We're all safe. The pen – "

"Where's my brother?"

"I don't think – "

"You said *we're all safe*. Where's my brother, Richard? Where's Joey?"

He took another step away from me. "I'm sorry, Charlie."

"You're sorry? *Sorry?* Where is my brother? Don't make me ask again!"

The vet closed his eyes and drew a deep breath. "He was already gone when we got there. We...we made certain he wouldn't...come back. And Mike and Daniel carried his body back here. We've got it locked away until we can give him a proper burial."

"Show me."

"Charlie, that's probably not a good idea."

"Don't say my name anymore." I turned, braced myself on the edge of the desk, and set my feet on the floor. "Take me to my brother."

"Okay," he relented. "Okay. Come on."

I followed him out into the hall. He turned left and stopped at the very next door. "We had to put him in here. It was either that or lock him up with your other friend."

"I thought you said he was..." I stopped, shook my head. I couldn't bring myself to repeat it.

"Well, yes, but...better safe than sorry."

"How cliché." The words were out of my mouth before I even realized what I was saying. *Are you seriously being flippant about this, right now?*

What the fuck was wrong with me?

Richard gave me one last concerned look before unlocking the door and pulling it open. I pushed by him as he fumbled for the light switch, falling to my knees in front of Joey's body, which had been propped up against some shelves. His clothes were still wet and muddy, but I could tell that someone had washed his face and neck. They'd also covered his bite with some gauze, and I couldn't help but feel grateful that someone had taken care of him. *You sure as hell didn't.*

"Sorry, Joe," I whispered. I wanted to turn my head away, but I made myself keep looking at him as I stood and backed out of the closet. "We need to bury him. I don't want him locked up in a closet like this."

"It may need to wait until tomorrow, and I'll need your assistance. The boy, Mike, too. But the front gate is secure – the storm probably helped. All of the noise..."

"Yeah, great." I stopped myself; I was snapping at him for the wrong reasons. When I spoke again, it was to ask the next dreaded question. "How's Luke?"

"I've only had a moment with him, but he appears to be improving. And if that continues at its current rate, it will likely be safe to release him from confinement as early as tomorrow morning. He's alone right now…well, except for your dog."

I wish I could say that such good news lifted some of the weight from my shoulders. But no, I wasn't ready to allow that.

Not yet, anyway.

Instead I braced myself and headed back down the hall to check on Luke. And Richard was right – he looked half himself again. I, on the other hand, was such a mess that the moment Holden caught wind of my stench he skittered away to cower in a far corner. I decided to brush off his rejection for now, and instead crouched down in front of Luke's cage, wrapping my hands around the bars in a vise-like grip. I wanted to touch him, but not with zed guts – *and Joey's blood* – all over me.

"Hey," I greeted him. "How are you feeling?"

"Physically? Better. But..." Luke trailed off, shaking his head and looking away.

It was almost a relief, the fact that he clearly already knew about Joey. The fact that I didn't have to speak the words myself.

"Yeah." There were a dozen things racing through my mind, things that I wanted to say, but somehow I couldn't bring myself to spit them out. "Yeah."

We sat there, so close and yet so far away, and neither of us spoke a word. People came and went, but none of them said anything to us until well after midday. It was Mike dropping in for the second time, and he finally spoke up. "Charlie, we need help out here. If you're able."

He sounded so downtrodden that I had to turn and face him. "Help?" I repeated.

"Yeah. Virginia and Ethan are keeping an eye on the front gate, but Mabel hardly slept last night and she's keeping Lauren busy. The rest of us didn't get any sleep at all. We need to get that enclosure secured and post a guard to keep an eye on it until someone can fix the fence."

I gave him a sad smile. I could tell that he was practically dead on his feet, and I didn't have the heart to tell him no. "Sure, Mike. Just...give me a few minutes, okay? And please take Holden with you, I'm sure he needs to go out."

"No problem. I'll wait outside. Come on, Holden." My dog didn't even give me a second look; he trotted over to Mike and followed him through the door.

When they were gone I looked back at Luke. "I don't know if I can do it."

"You should, though."

"I know. I'll come back as soon as I can."

"Don't worry about me, Charlie. I'm too busy worrying about you."

"Hey, then maybe that means we'll both be fine," I said with false brightness.

As I stood to leave, I thought about telling Luke that I loved him – but something stopped me. It was almost as if saying it so soon after Joey's death would cheapen it. "I'll see you in a little while," I told him instead. And then I went to find Mike.

He was waiting just outside the long, low building. I turned and stared at it for a moment, truly seeing it for the first time. *It's practically a bunker*, I mused as the heavy main door slowly clicked shut behind me.

"You ready?" Mike asked. I nodded, and he led me down the path, Holden snuffling along behind us as we made our way back to the pen where Joey had made his final stand against the zeds. "Lauren has Mabel in the truck back near the front. We haven't moved it yet because of the noise," he explained.

After that we walked in silence until we reached the broken gate. It appeared that Richard and Daniel had been passing the time piling up the zed bodies that littered the enclosure, though what they meant to do with them, I wasn't sure. Burning would be best, but we couldn't risk that now – even once the fence was fixed, lighting a fire that big would be dangerous.

*But it won't be long until we can't handle the smell of them.* "Have there been any more?"

Mike glanced at me out of the corner of his eye. "No."

"Good. Let's get this door fixed, and I'll take first watch."

"You sure?"

I shrugged. "I feel better when I'm being useful."

That wasn't the whole truth – mostly I just didn't think I could stand being in that building with Luke locked up in a cage and my brother's dead body just down the hall. But Mike didn't need to know that. *If he's not already thinking it, best not put it in his head.*

"As long as Richard thinks it's okay, we'll all sure welcome the break," he smiled.

*As long as Richard thinks it's okay?* "Oh, I have to run all of my decisions by Richard, now?"

"Come on, Charlie, you know I'm not saying that. You...well, you were in pretty bad shape last night. We'd all understand if you needed some more rest."

"I'm fine, Mike. And keeping busy will help."

Once we got Richard and Daniel to give up zed-moving duty, it didn't take long to fashion a proper bar for the gate – and then, at my insistence, set a couple of extra boards across it just in case. I was finally able to shoo them away soon after we were finished, and once they were gone – even Holden wandered off after Mike – I lowered myself to the ground. I crossed my legs, staying several feet from the bars but keeping my back to the pen. Regardless of whether or not I'd be able to pick out the spot where my brother had fallen the night before, I couldn't stand the thought that I might.

But I knew that I'd hear the zeds coming. *Or at least falling down that hill.*

The early spring morning was cooler than usual thanks to the rain, but soon the sun was beating down on me. I needed a shower more than ever before, yet somehow the idea of washing off the proof of what had transpired seemed as bad as baking in it the way I was just then.

It was Mike who brought me food later that afternoon, Holden still meandering along after him, and Mike who sat with me in silence as the sun disappeared behind the hillside that I refused to turn and face. Finally, after not saying anything for several hours, he finally asked, "Aren't you tired?"

"From what? Sitting here?"

"No. Leaving the farm, and your mom. Me being sick. Luke being hurt. The trip up here." He paused. "Last night."

"So are they just making you into their scapegoat? You get to be the one who has to follow me around and make sure I'm okay? Come on, kid, you're worth more than that."

"Actually, Richard wanted to come out here, but I told him I'd do it. I thought you'd rather talk to someone you know."

"I don't *need* to talk to anyone," I insisted – and then I immediately realized my mistake. "But yeah, I'm glad it was you." Wondering if my earlier silence had unnerved him, I reached my arm out and draped it over his shoulders. "Holding up okay?"

"Yeah. But...how long are we going to stay here?"

I knew he wouldn't like my answer. "Until Luke gets better. Then we'll all sit down and figure out what happens next." I chewed on my lip, wondering how to say the rest of what was on my mind. "Hopefully we won't have to stay too long." I pulled away from Mike and stood, finally turning to face the enclosure behind me. "Or much longer at all."

## LESSON LEARNED

*There's a time and place for some things, but grief isn't one of them.*

∗ ∗ ∗ ∗ ∗ ∗ ∗

I slept like the dead that night. Yes, I know, very funny – but I did. Even though my bed was just a pile of rough wool blankets next to Luke in his cage, being near him calmed me.

And I'm sure the shower helped, too. Richard was hesitant to use the generator, but Virginia guilted him into it. "Look at the poor girl, Richard! She's been wallowing in gore the entire day!"

I'm not sure what was more ridiculous – her calling me a 'poor girl', or the bit about me 'wallowing in gore'. But the idea of a shower (especially a hot one) was too tempting to pass up. "I really should scrub down. Make sure none of this shit got where it shouldn't have." I forced a laugh, but Richard suddenly looked half panicked.

"Good thinking," he said brusquely, and the next thing I knew the generator was grumbling and I was led to a bathroom at the far end of the building. It was only equipped with a small stand-up shower, but I wasn't in a position to complain – or even to care.

I'm not sure I'd ever been so grateful for hot water in all my life. Holden was still a bit wary of me afterward, but eventually I was able to coax him into sleeping on the floor next to me.

The next morning I woke early and sat up to find Luke standing over me, smiling. Though the past several days had clearly taken a toll on him, I was relieved to see that he was up and ready to go. I stood and we hugged each other through the bars.

"I'll go find Richard," I mumbled into Luke's neck.

He moved his head until his chin bumped mine, and we shared a brief kiss. "Yeah, I could use one of those showers you told me about last night," he said as he finally pulled away.

"Oh, very funny," I automatically replied, then bit down on my bottom lip, my jaw tightening as Joey pushed his way to the forefront of my thoughts.

Luke, having realized his blunder a moment too late, closed his eyes and took a deep breath. "Let's just get me out of this cage."

I nodded and left the room, thankful that Richard hadn't bothered to lock us in for the night. Holden followed me out, but ducked through the very next doorway. I peered in after him and saw Mike sit up in his own makeshift bed and scratch Holden behind the ears. "Morning," I said softly. "Can you take Holden outside for a few minutes? I have to talk to Richard."

"Yeah, no problem. Good luck."

When I knocked on the veterinarian's office door, a hoarse voice called out, "Come in." I opened it to find several candles blazing and the early morning sunshine pouring through the windows.

I shielded my eyes and caught a glimpse of Richard's drawn, pale face. "How long have you been awake?"

He shrugged. "I couldn't sleep. I needed to find these." He waved his hand over the messy pile of maps and blueprints that were strewn across his desk. "I knew they would help us get that fence fixed...you see, I don't know where they stored everything..."

"We're not going to get anything fixed if you don't get some rest. You're probably the only one who knows this place well enough to figure it out."

"I'll sleep later. I need to utilize the sunlight...I'd like to get that fence repaired first thing tomorrow." He then blew out the candles one by one.

"I came to talk about Luke."

"I figured. Much better, is he?"

"Yes. And we need his help, especially if you want to get started on the fence so soon."

"Of course. Give me a minute to straighten up, and I'll come check on him."

When I returned to the room I shut the door behind me, glancing over my shoulder as I approached Luke. "He'll be here in a minute. He looks terrible, he hasn't slept at all. Just thought I'd warn you." The last thing we needed was for Luke to say the wrong thing and irritate Richard into insisting that he stay locked up.

But when the vet arrived, he barely gave Luke a second glance before pronouncing him well enough to join the rest of us. My eyes met Luke's; he gave me a crooked smile as Richard finally unlocked the cage.

"So where do we start?" I asked as Luke moved to my side and entwined his fingers with mine.

"I've got to work on figuring out the best way to get up there to repair that hole, but first I need to show you where you can..." He stopped and glanced out into the hall.

*Joey.* "Right. Of course. Let's go."

There was no sign of Mike and Holden, but I had to believe that they would keep each other safe. Luke and I followed Richard back around to the front of the park, where we cut off to the left, moving along the southeastern edge of the zoo. In the far corner, behind where, if I remembered correctly, they'd once kept some turtles and flamingos, there was an area of softer ground.

And beside it, two shovels.

"I'll need your help later today, but for now...I thought it would be best..." Richard gestured helplessly.

"Yeah. It probably is. Thanks."

Once the vet was gone, I turned to Luke. "You sure you can do this?"

"You'll have to handle the heavy lifting, but I can certainly help."

"But...your hand..."

He glanced down at it; Richard had re-wrapped it the night before, so it was protected – but also ungainly. "I'll do what I can."

Luke was right – I did end up having to do most of the heavy lifting. But even as my skin was coated in dust, even when I broke into a sweat and lost that just-showered smell, I kept digging. The hole still wasn't deep enough for my liking when Mike came to find us, but it was carved out and almost halfway there. "El was freaking out again. Ethan calmed her down, and they fed her what they could, but you need to come back to the office."

"I'd rather not stop now," I told Mike.

"Richard wants to talk about the fence. He thinks he's got it figured out."

"Where's everyone else? Where's Holden?"

"Waiting for me to bring you guys back to the office."

"*Everyone?* There's no one watching that pen, or the front gate? And he sent you back here *alone*?"

"Daniel's at the pen. We took Virginia away from the front gate, but that thing's not going anywhere. Or letting anything in. And *you'll* be with me on the way back."

Mike had a point, but that didn't mean I liked it – or that I liked how sure he was that we would go back with him. Unfortunately, I knew that the longer I stayed here, the longer the front gate would remain unguarded. "Fine. Let's get this over with." I pretended that I didn't notice the look of relief on Luke's face as he handed his shovel to Mike; the two of us made much faster work of he grave than Luke and I had been doing, and soon – *too soon, or not soon enough?* – we had gently rolled Joey into the hole and seen his body disappear under the dirt.

I was afraid to wallow, and instead made myself a silent promise to come back on my own as soon as I could. "Let's go," I announced, my tone brooking no argument. I almost set my shovel down, but then I realized that without it, I was empty-handed. Weaponless. I clutched it tighter.

It was almost eerily quiet as we walked back toward the front of the zoo. *Too quiet*, I thought, craning my neck to look past the gates as we approached them.

Suddenly Luke stopped walking. "Charlie," he murmured. I began to turn toward him, but from the corner of my eye, saw him shake his head. "Grab Mike and get behind something."

"What about you?"

"You need to go forward. I'll go back. Confuse them." There was a short pause. "*Now!*"

Somehow I didn't hesitate. I dove toward Mike, who was still strolling along, ignorant of any danger. I grabbed hold of his hand, shouting, "With me!" as I pulled him toward my car, which was still parked just off the opposite side of the gate.

For a moment, nothing happened.

And then a shot rang out. I shoved Mike hard; he slid to the ground behind my car, crying out as his arm scraped against the pavement. The bullet hit the ground not far behind me as I propelled myself forward, the shovel flying from my hand as I landed beside Mike with a *thud* that knocked the air out of me.

"Dammit!" someone cursed. "I said *no shooting!*"

I gathered myself and peered across the open space, looking back and forth until I spotted a flash of white that could only be Luke's t-shirt. He was crouched down in a cluster of trees next to one of the enclosures. Satisfied that he was safe, I pressed myself against my car and crept to the back bumper, sucking in a deep breath before looking around it.

I still couldn't see anyone. I jerked back behind my car again to find Mike staring at me with wide eyes. I pressed my finger to my lips; he nodded.

It was Luke who spoke first. "I know where you are, so you might as well step on out and tell us what you want!"

"I don't think so. Something tells me you're not in charge. Find me someone who is."

It was a young woman speaking, that much I could tell. I saw Luke looking toward me, and in that moment I knew what I had to do.

Willing myself to believe that the girl had meant it when she'd said 'no shooting', I stood up and strode out toward the gate.

Before the world went to shit, I wasn't one to take charge – not in any situation. But now it was almost second nature, and somehow I knew that we didn't have time to fetch Richard. "I suppose you're looking for me, then. Now how about you return the courtesy and come on out." I did my best to keep my tone flat and my eyes from wandering. Luke may have known where these people were, but I sure as hell didn't.

Nothing happened for several moments, then finally the girl said, "Sure, why not," and stood up from behind one of the boulders that lined the path up to the gate.

I'm not sure what I'd been expecting, but it certainly wasn't anything like this girl. She was slight, her movements fluid, and I knew from a glance that she was *tough*. It wasn't just her shaved head or the handgun she kept pointed at me at all times – it was her aura of control, the cold look in her dark eyes.

"Where did you come from, and what are you doing here?" I asked. I knew she was likely from the school, but playing stupid seemed like the best bet right now.

The girl smirked at me. "What, no polite introductions?"

I had to stop myself from rolling my eyes, and instead forced a smile. I almost introduced myself as Charlie, but at the last second I said, "I'm Charlotte. And you?"

"Jia."

"Great. *So* nice to meet you, Jia. Now tell me what you're doing here."

"Some of my people were out on patrol and saw a lot of zombies heading this way. When they reported it, I sent out scouts to check on things. Imagine my surprise when they reported back to me that there was a group of people living at the *zoo*. The zoo! I mean, once I got over how ridiculous it was, I realized that it's actually kind of brilliant. So I decided to come see it for myself."

"You mean you decided to arm yourselves and then sneak up on us. Not quite as innocent as you're trying to make it sound."

"Hey, I get it. You don't know us. But we don't know you, either. We're just trying to watch our own backs." Jia glanced behind her. "Come on out, guys." At her behest, five more teenagers stepped out of their hiding places on either side of the path.

She was right about one thing – I didn't know her, or any of the others. But I *did* know that there were those back at the school who took issue with her leadership. *I just need to figure out how to use that. If necessary.*

I had a bad feeling that it *would* be necessary. "Now yours," Jia said, cocking her head.

"I don't think so. You had plenty of time to watch us already." For a moment I was torn between scolding and praising her; thankfully she interrupted my thoughts before I could say anything stupid.

"True," was her flippant reply.

"Where do you call home these days?" I asked, glancing at several members of Jia's group.

But none of them would meet my eyes, and then Jia waved me off. "Oh, we're from here and there. It doesn't really matter now. I've seen what I came to see, so we'll be on our way." She began to turn, her companions immediately mimicking her in an off-putting manner...and then, when she stopped and turned back to face me, again they followed suit.

It was more than a little bit creepy, but it was swept from my thoughts with Jia's next words. "We'll be back tomorrow. Be prepared to receive us, or this time I'll allow them to shoot."

I lost my composure, then. "Receive you? What the hell is that supposed to mean?"

Jia was no longer smiling, and though her words sounded logical, there was nothing friendly or agreeable in her tone. "You may have things we need. We probably have things you need. We'll trade."

I couldn't help myself. "And if we don't want to trade?"

The girl spun away from me again, took a few steps, and then called over her shoulder, "You'll trade. That's how things work now."

*Be careful what you wish for.*

# PART THREE

## Lord of the Zeds

# Chapter 9
# The Real Enemy

Before I could speak again, I felt a hand on my shoulder. I knew it was Luke; I shrugged him off and took a step forward.

"Charlie, *no*." He was quiet, but firm. I glanced at him, then looked back at the group of teenagers. Each one paused to check back on us in turn – an oddly planned exit that sure as hell didn't do anything to ease my mind – and then they rounded a bend and I lost sight of them.

"This is bullshit, Luke. They're a bunch of kids – "

"Kids with *guns*," he pointed out. "We need to find the others. There needs to be two guards on this gate at all times, and they need to remain hidden as much as possible. And we need our firearms back. First things first, okay?"

The idea of once again having a gun strapped to my leg calmed me a bit, and I nodded.

Leave it to Mike to bring up the one thing I sure as hell *didn't* want to think about. "And the broken fence?"

Luke reached up to wipe his forehead with the back of his hand; at the last moment, he realized he'd raised the injured one, and he let it fall back to his side. "First things first," he repeated.

We fell in behind him as he broke into a jog. "They probably don't even know about the fence," I tried to reassure Mike.

"They were following the zeds, Charlie. They know about it."

"Fine. We can't worry about that now, then." *Should, but can't.* The enclosure was built in such a way that anyone entering through the broken fence could be kept at bay for quite some time...but a dozen people? Or more? People who may have weapons far superior to ours?

Forget it.

Richard was pacing outside of 'headquarters'. "Where have you been?" he called out when he saw us.

"Get inside!" Luke ordered. For a moment the veterinarian looked stunned, but then he braced himself and stood his ground.

"I *was* inside – we all were – waiting for *you*!"

"Richard, please, something's happened. Let's just go inside." I marveled at how quickly Luke was able to calm down; my heart was thudding in my chest, there was a roaring sound in my ears, and I itched to *do* something, *anything*.

I decided on pushing by the vet and letting myself into the building. "Come on, Mike," I beckoned. He followed without hesitation, and the door hadn't even clicked shut behind us when Luke pushed through it with Richard on his heels.

"The office. Now," Richard ordered. We moved down the hall, which was only dimly lit by the sun filtering through the small, barred window in the main door. There was more light pouring from the open door of his office, though, and we entered to find Virginia, Ethan, Lauren, and Mabel seated around the room. Holden leapt up from Lauren's side and bounded toward me, but stopped short when I didn't bend to greet him. He whined at me, and I shushed him.

Richard stormed in and rounded on us. "What the hell is going on?"

I looked at Luke, who glanced pointedly at the others – but I shook my head. "They need to know, and we don't have time to play telephone with this information." I stepped closer to Richard, directing my words at him; I could feel everyone's eyes on me, and as I spoke I eventually forced myself to meet each of their gazes in turn.

"Before we came here, we stopped at the hospital, and then the high school, trying to find medicine for Mike and Luke. It was just Daniel and I at the school; we traded them some ammo for the meds we had when we got here.

"The people we gave the ammo to made it sound like they were being lorded over by some kid. They didn't even want her to know that we *existed*, so they sure as hell weren't planning on telling her about our little deal."

"What the hell does this have to do with my zoo?" Richard snapped.

I almost threw my hands up in frustration. "Because this girl, they were *afraid* of her, and just now she showed up at your front gate with five other kids, all armed to the teeth. She demanded that we let her into the zoo, demanded that we trade with her. *Tomorrow*."

Richard looked confused. "Trade? Trade what?"

I closed my eyes and took a deep breath. "I don't know. Whatever she wants us to trade. Or maybe she doesn't want to trade at all, and it's just a ploy to get inside the zoo. Either way, it's not good. Trust me."

"How do you know this girl is the problem?"

Mike stepped forward. "I went to school with those kids. I didn't get a good look at all of them, and I probably wouldn't know all of them by name, but a couple of them...well, a couple of them were pretty big assholes *then*. Jia, though..."

I eyed him. "What about Jia?"

"I...I don't know. She's...different, now. I mean, I didn't know her well. She was a senior this year, and I was just a sophomore. Seeing her around, though...I guess I always thought she was a little bit keyed up, but she was like...a model student. Second in her class, on the debate team, in band, and I think she was some sort of state gymnastics champion too."

*That explains the way she moved.* "But did she really look or seem different to you?"

Mike reached up and touched his hair. "She shaved her head. I think her hair was pretty short before, but – "

I tapped my foot impatiently. "I chopped my hair off too, Mike. It's the smart thing to do. " *Though shaving it is a bit extreme.*

"Yeah, but Charlie, I don't remember her being so...well, so scary. She used to do morning announcements, and I mean, she always sounded pleasant. That girl you talked to today was..." He gestured helplessly, unable to find the words.

"Emotionless?" I prompted.

"Yeah. Yeah, something like that."

"It doesn't matter," Richard interrupted. "They can't get in here."

Virginia shocked me by speaking up next. "Don't be stupid, doc. This place isn't some kind of impregnable fortress. Who knows how many of them there are, or how many guns they have. It would only be a matter of time before they *found* a way in."

I wish I felt relieved that she was on my side, but hearing how little she trusted the zoo's defenses was pretty damn disheartening. "So what do we do? Somehow I don't think letting them in and then simply hoping for the best is really an option."

"We could try gathering what we can to...trade...and bringing it to the front gate. Then they wouldn't need to come in at all," Richard said. He folded his arms across his chest, as if daring someone to disagree with him.

Luke shook his head. "I don't think she'll agree to that."

"I dunno," Mike mumbled. "We could at least *try*..."

"Mike. Not a minute ago you were talking about how much this girl has changed. Do you really think the person you saw today will suddenly give up her very specific request to come into the zoo?"

He shoved his hands into his pockets and kept his eyes on the floor, but he finally mumbled, "Probably not. But like I said, we could still try. What about El?"

"She's an *elephant*. She likes Ethan, but she's not going to do our bidding, " Richard snapped.

"Forget the elephant, " I agreed. "I'm not even sure we want Jia and her people to know about it, to be honest. And anyway, even if we can 'try' to stop Jia from coming into the zoo, it will probably need to be a last-ditch effort. We have to come up with something else. Scare them away, somehow...or...maybe..." I stopped, almost hating myself for what I was thinking. It was the old me, the pre-zombie-apocalypse me, rearing her overly-cautious head and saying, *Just make them think you've left*.

"What? Maybe *what*?" Richard pressed.

"Give me a minute!" I snapped. I knew I shouldn't lose my temper, but I couldn't concentrate with everyone staring at me expectantly – especially when I couldn't differentiate between the ones who were hoping that I'd come up with a solution...and the ones who were hoping I would fail.

What I really needed, more than anything, was to talk to Luke, *alone* – but something told me we wouldn't be allowed out of this room until we'd all come to some sort of agreement.

Or if I had it my way, some sort of *decision*.

"Okay. One way or another, they're going to get into this zoo. I hate to admit it, but we need to face that fact. So we're going to bring them in here, which means someone needs to clear out the entrance to this building." I saw both Richard and Virginia open their mouths to protest, but I shook my head, and before they could say anything, continued, "If they can't see what they're walking into, it's going to go a lot harder on us. Now Richard...please tell me that there are places in this zoo where we could tuck things away and these kids would be none the wiser?"

"Yes..."

"Okay. Let's assume that we're still being watched. We need to gather up what we can, and Richard, you can put it away. The fewer people who know where it's hidden, the better." I paused, and couldn't help but grimace. "I hope you're a good liar."

"He can put on a poker face when he needs to, " Virginia assured me. "But no one knows this zoo like Ethan. He really should help. And we'll need him to check on El, especially if things get...hectic."

I couldn't help but hesitate, much as I hated myself for doing so. "He won't tell them anything...by mistake?"

Virginia glared at me. "Ethan is very protective of this zoo, and proud of how much he knows."

"They won't know my secrets," Ethan said. I was surprised – he spoke so little – but I took a deep breath and smiled.

"Thanks, Ethan. You'll be a big help." I stepped into the center of the room. "We have to assume that they've seen all of us, so there's no point in hiding. I don't care for it, but they'll be less likely to question whatever supplies we choose to show off if we're up front about other things." *I hope.*

"And if things go bad?"

The fact that it was Mike who asked that question – Mike, who *knew* this girl Jia – didn't sit well with me. I glared at him for a moment, then reassured the others, "It won't. Not this time. But we'll have to be prepared for the worst. They may only start with depleting our stores, but if any of you have read a dystopian novel or seen a movie set post-apocalypse, you know that it won't end there. "

Luke cleared his throat. "That's a bit doom and gloom, Charlie."

"Perfect for the times, then," I snapped. "Now we better get to it. Gather what we can salvage – what we can *hide* – here in Richard's office. And then Richard and Ethan can work on moving those things to...well, wherever they can hide them."

For a moment everyone hesitated, but when I opened my mouth to order them out of the office, they moved before I could speak. I shut my mouth again and let them go – even Holden skulked out on Mike's heels, barely giving me a backwards glance as he did so.

But Luke didn't follow. He watched the rest of them leave and then rounded on me, taking me by the shoulders. His grip was gentle, non-threatening, but I shrugged him off nonetheless. "I know you're going to chastise me. Don't bother. If now's not the time for harsh realities..."

"They're already scared, Charlie. You don't need to make it worse."

I turned away from him. "They're not scared enough. I'm going to go back to my car, see if there's anything in there we can give them. If they're watching us, they'll see me."

Luke nodded. "And they'll think they have proof of our honesty." He wasn't happy, but he was playing along – and I supposed that was all I could ask of him. "You want me to go with you?"

"No...someone needs to keep an eye on things here, and you're the only one I trust to pay enough attention to what they're doing."

"I'm not going to spy on them," he warned.

"I didn't say that! Jesus, I'm not an idiot. I meant it when I said most of us shouldn't know their little hiding places. Just keep them from doing anything stupid, please?"

"I'll do my best."

"Your 'best' should work just fine. You damn well know how to lecture."

"Yeah yeah, love you too."

I smiled automatically, and then stepped forward to kiss him on the cheek. "You're hilarious."

The corner of Luke's mouth quirked up, but he stepped back and waved me away. "Get back here soon, okay?"

"Of course." I reached out and squeezed his hand before stepping out of the room. Halfway down the hall, I realized that I probably should have told him that I loved him, too. I turned back, prepared to sneak up on him, but when I peeked into Richard's office Luke was far too engrossed in his hand to notice me. He was rubbing the bandage, his jaw clenched.

I spun away, pressing up against the wall outside the room. *You're overreacting. He's fine. It's just tender from the treatment.*

After several deep breaths, I'd half convinced myself that was actually the case...and besides, I needed to check out my car sooner rather than later.

But I would also make it a priority to ask Richard to tend to Luke's hand. *We need him right now*, I told myself, but what I really meant was, *I* needed him right now.

And I knew that the *needing* had to end.

I took another deep breath, set my shoulders, and forced myself to leave Luke – and my concerns about him – behind.

## LESSON LEARNED

*Sometimes you have to pick the lesser of two evils.*

\* \* \* \* \* \* \*

Despite my original promise to Luke, I took my time rifling through my Volkswagen, opening every obvious compartment, poking through what was left in the car slowly and methodically, all the while hoping that Jia or her people were watching.

In the end it was still mostly for show, as the coins, cell phone charger, and paperwork that I turned up were all useless. I did find a half-empty bag of old Easter candy, a pack of Camel Crushes with two cigarettes remaining, several lighters (though only one of them worked), a roll of paper towels, a used but intact gift bag, and a horrible seminar-on-CD – "Self Discipline and Emotional Control" – that my boss had loaned me God knows how long ago. I remembered trying to listen to the CDs, remembered how terrible they were, and my first thought was to break the damn things...but then I realized that they were the only ones I had other than the old mix in the truck.

I left them in the car. *Just in case*. But as I turned to head back to the offices, I made it a point to start eating the candy. I knew that if anyone was watching they would probably take note of this, and if I admitted to doing it there was always the chance that they would be more likely to believe me about other things.

*They're teenagers. How much damage can they really do?*

Besides, even though the candy had melted and re-formed and was clearly stale, I loved every bite. I saved some for the others, too – one last thing to enjoy before tomorrow's shit show.

How did I know it would be a shit show? I just did. It was the way Mike talked about Jia. The fact that we were relying on Richard, who was fairly passive, and Ethan, whose only thought was protecting the zoo as a whole. There was Virginia, of course, but I couldn't get a good read on her. And Lauren and Daniel needed to protect their daughter.

*And Luke*...We didn't always see eye to eye, but I knew that I could rely on him.

The problem was that there was still a large part of me that simply didn't *want* to rely on him. *But you don't* have *to*.

Perhaps knowing that should have made a difference. It didn't.

The rest of the day passed in some sort of haze. We collected what we could, hid a good portion of it, left a selection for Jia and her people to pick through. The whole thing left a bad taste in my mouth, and it didn't help that I couldn't even look Luke in the eye.

When the sun was so low in the sky that we could no longer see it from inside the zoo, we gathered in Richard's office again. "That's enough for today," Luke insisted. "If there's anything left laying around...I guess we'll just have to assume it's a loss."

"Or hope that these kids aren't smart enough to see the use in some of it," I said, knowing that I sounded a lot more hopeful than I felt.

"Positive thinking," Richard replied dryly.

"It's my forte." The words were out of my mouth almost before I realized what I was saying; certainly before I remembered that Joey wasn't there to call out my obvious sarcasm.

No one spoke for a long moment. "What about guards for tonight?" Daniel finally asked.

"I think it's best if we just keep someone at the door to this building for now, and then send a couple people to the front gate at first light," Luke suggested. "We...we should stay together as much as possible." I could feel him watching me, but I forced myself to focus on poking through the supplies we'd stacked around the office.

"Are we sure we want to allow them in here? " was my only response.

"Yes. I think that will lend even more weight to the idea that we aren't hiding anything."

"I was just thinking...it's so...*enclosed*."

"And they're just kids, remember?"

Despite my own use of forced sarcasm, I couldn't stand it coming from Luke. "You know what I meant when I said that."

Luke shrugged. "Just trying to lighten the mood." I wanted to believe him, but then he winced and rubbed at his bandaged hand.

"Are you okay?" I asked, realizing too late that my tone was harsh, almost argumentative.

"Yeah. Hurts a bit, but we need to save what little medication we have."

I nodded. It was all I could bring myself to do; I knew that he wasn't telling the truth – or at least not the *entire* truth.

*Or maybe you're just being paranoid.*

That voice inside my head was getting to be a bit much; this time I brushed the thought aside like it was nothing more than a fly buzzing by my ear. "Get some rest tonight. I'll keep watch with Holden."

"Sleep isn't going to help, and it's your plan, so it's you we all need tomorrow. I'll guard the door."

Looking at Luke just then, I knew that this was an argument I wasn't going to win. "Okay. But at least keep Holden with you. I know he's a bit of a baby at times, but he'll hear things well before you do."

Luke shrugged. "Can't say I'd mind the company."

"I mean, we can always keep watch together. Or someone else can sit out there with you."

"Charlie, I'll be fine. I just meant, you're right. Holden would notice something's up well before I could. And if I need to I can send him back inside, give you guys a warning without abandoning my post."

I almost cringed. I hadn't thought about it that way; leave it to Luke to one-up me, whether he meant to or not. "Let's see how everyone else is doing."

Within an hour we'd done all we could. The pile of goods left in Richard's office – the things we'd be trading, as it were – was pathetic, but something told me we still hadn't held enough back. Not if we wanted to survive.

"Let's hope they actually mean to do an exchange of goods," I said. I meant to sound encouraging; the others' faces told me I didn't.

"I'm sure they do," Luke insisted.

"Right. I'm sure they do," I repeated.

We all went our separate ways, then – Richard, Virginia, and Ethan settled down in the office, while I joined Mike, Daniel, Lauren, and Mabel in the room where Luke had been kept. There were plenty of blankets, it was dark, it was quiet...but it was clear none of us was going to sleep that night. I tossed and turned, maybe dozed here and there, but finally I gave up, wrapped myself up in one of my blankets, and ducked out of the room.

The hall was so dark that I couldn't do anything but shuffle along. When I got to the door I peered out through the reinforced glass, but the night was inky black, the moon completely obscured by clouds.

*Who knows what this darkness is hiding?*

I figured that thought made it official – I was beyond paranoid.

I pushed the door open.

The sky was still black, but I could feel in my bones that before long the horizon would be gray. I looked to the right and saw that Holden was sitting up and staring at me almost expectantly, but Luke had fallen asleep. This was so unlike him – to slack off on his watch – that I could only stare at him for a moment. Finally I opened the door wider and beckoned to my dog. "Inside, Holdy," I whispered; he immediately obeyed. I pushed the door shut behind him, and when I heard it click into place I turned to face Luke again.

Somehow that small noise was what caused him to sit up and rub his eyes. "Charlie?" he mumbled, squinting at me. "Is everything okay?"

"Yeah. I...couldn't sleep. Are you okay out here?"

"Of course. I guess I just...drifted off..." Luke sat up suddenly, half panicked as he peered around. "Where's Holden?"

I moved toward him and brushed my fingertips along the length of his arm. "I let him inside. I think that's what woke you up."

He looked up at me, blinking. "Right. Sorry."

"Don't be." I smiled, letting the blanket fall to the ground as I deftly slid my yoga pants and underwear off with a quick pull-and-kick. I straddled Luke's lap, bracing my legs around either side of his waist and reaching up to massage his temples. He closed his eyes again, but only for a second. "You should be resting," he insisted.

"I'd rather be here with you," I said, running my hands through his hair and down the back of his neck, pulling us closer together until our lips met. I'd worried that he would be hesitant, but in fact it was the exact opposite. He wrapped his arms around me, hitching me forward until our bodies were pressed against each other, and I rocked in his lap to the rhythm of our kiss.

Eventually Luke pulled back. "Aren't you cold?"

My only response was to wiggle my arms loose and pull my shirt off. "I think I'll be okay."

He bent his head and brushed his lips across the tops of my breasts as his hands deftly unclipped my bra clasp and slipped the straps down my arms. My nipples went hard in the chilly night air, but then Luke cupped one breast in his hand and his mouth covered the other and I found myself arching my back and squeezing my legs tighter around him.

"It's been too long," Luke murmured against my chest. I reached around and grabbed hold of his hair, pulling it just enough to make him look up at me.

"Let's remedy that," I breathed before once again covering his mouth with mine. The sex was brief but amazing; I had to bite down on Luke's shoulder to keep from crying out, and I could hear him mumbling beneath me, though I couldn't make out what he said. We came together, shuddering and grasping at each other and doing our best to not make too much noise. It had been years since I'd done it like this, so out in the open, having to silence...well, everything.

I'd forgotten how amazing it was, the thrill of the possibility of getting caught, the need to keep quiet.

I clutched at Luke, knowing that I needed to move but not willing to let go just yet. The zeds, those damn kids from the high school...*Luke's hand*. So many threats right in front of me, but for once I was going to allow myself a peaceful moment in which I wasn't thinking about how it may be the last one of its kind.

Finally I stood, gathering up my clothes and shivering as I put them back on, relishing the wetness between my legs. For someone who had never wanted children, it somehow still felt sexy knowing that the remnants of our coupling dampened my thighs.

"Shouldn't you go...change?" Luke murmured, as if reading my thoughts.

I waved him off. "I'll be okay. I think I'll just stay out here with you for the rest of the night."

He moved as if to relinquish his seat, but I shook my head. "Oh no, your watch, your chair." I gathered up my blanket and settled down on the ground beside him, resting my head against his leg. "I didn't say I was going to stay awake."

"Didn't say it, but I know you will."

He was right, of course, but I just laughed and wrapped the blanket tighter around myself. It wasn't long before Luke was snoring softly, and soon I was having trouble staying awake as well – until I heard a hitch in his breath. I slowly lifted my head, listening carefully. It seemed like I waited forever, but no – there it was again.

Moving as quietly as I could, I stood up and shifted my position to one that allowed a better look at his bandaged hand, and at first glance it seemed just fine.

But then he wheezed a bit, and his hand fell to the side, wrist up. Just then the cloud cover dissipated just enough for the moon to shine through, its light making his skin appear milky white...and highlighting the dark veins that were lacing up the inside of his arm. *Too dark.*

Black. Black veins fading to gray and then finally the blue-ish color that mine were. *The color his were when his arms were propped on either side of me that time at the farm...*

I balled my hand into a fist and bit down hard, willing myself to not cry. I backed away, half-tripping over the blanket as I did so, catching myself in time to watch Luke take a long, shallow breath and cross his arms around his midsection.

When he didn't wake up, I moved toward the door, but paused for a moment before opening it.

If I ran and fetched Richard, what would happen? The only thing I could imagine was amputation; definitely at the elbow, *but to be safe...* Except then Luke would be out of commission for whatever took place when Jia returned – and there were only a few hours left until that happened. Would that amount of time mean life or death for Luke?

*What would he want?*

But in that moment, I convinced myself that it didn't matter. I knew what Luke would say – that we needed to take care of this outside threat, and then deal with his arm.

Which meant that I had to get Richard involved, because every part of me was screaming that this couldn't wait. I let myself back into the building, my heart leaping into my throat when I heard a scrambling noise coming from just inside the door. I only released the breath I was holding when I felt Holden winding himself around my legs. I bent to scratch his ears. "Hey, boy. Go sit with Luke, okay?"

Holden hesitated for a moment, but when I straightened he finally slid out the door. I pushed it shut, settling it into position so that the only sound was that of the latch bolt clicking into place, and made my way up the hall to Richard's office.

The lights were still off, but I was surprised to find that the door was ajar. Just barely, but the thought that he hadn't even shut it, let alone locked it, made me wonder how much I had been underestimating his trust in us. Either that, or he was stupid – though it was clear that wasn't quite the case when the creak of the door opening caused an immediate stir in the back of the room.

"Richard, it's Charlie," I whispered. He gave a grunt of acknowledgement, and after a bit more shuffling and scraping his battery-powered LED desk lamp clicked on. I blinked in the sudden light, so much more centered and filtered than outside.

"What's wrong?"

I knew that the panic in his voice was probably because he thought that something was happening with the Jia situation. "We're still on track for tomorrow," I heard myself reassuring him, an automatic reply, me putting off the situation at hand.

I choked back a laugh. *The situation at hand.*

Was I finally losing it? *Wait. How many times have I asked myself that, recently?*

Richard stepped around his desk, walking toward me with one arm outstretched. "Charlie?" he said, his tone half concerned, half frustrated.

"Sorry, yeah, I wouldn't have woken you up, but..." I stopped, drew in a breath, but when I opened my mouth to speak, nothing came out. I cleared my throat and steeled myself. "It's Luke. His hand."

The vet's arm fell to his side and he closed his eyes for a long moment. "He didn't seem right. The more time that passed, he didn't seem right."

"He's not. His breathing is...well, it's wrong." *It isn't the same.* "And his veins...it's like the infection is just moving up his arm. Fast." *Too fast.*

"Where is he now?" Richard was already rolling up his sleeves and heading for the door. I hung back, and he turned to me. "Charlie, we may have to act immediately. *Where is he?*"

"Outside. Sleeping. Holden's with him, I – "

But before I could finish explaining myself, before I could tell Richard that I knew Luke wouldn't agree to let us help him right now, the vet made a disgusted noise in the back of his throat and spun away from me, through the door, racing down the hall toward the tiny patch of light at the entrance.

For someone who reveled in the rush of adrenaline that I got when killing zeds, I couldn't bring myself to follow. Instead I made my way to the clean room where Richard had first treated Luke, turning on more of the battery-powered lights and washing my hands in the bucket of cool water we kept there for that very purpose. These were tiny acts of hope, ones that I was fairly certain wouldn't make a difference. If I knew anything about Luke, it was that he was stubborn. At least as much as I was, and if I'd been in his shoes, I wouldn't let anyone take off my arm. *Or even half of it.*

Holden entered the room first, skittering to a stop behind me and taking a stance that was fearful yet protective. Luke stormed in a moment later, Richard hot on his heels, shutting the door behind them just as Luke came to a halt, bending his face toward mine as he poked me emphatically in the shoulder, hissing, "What the *hell*, Charlie?"

I jerked back, out of his reach. "You need *help*, Luke. You've been getting worse all day, and your arm, look at it!"

"Help? Who are you to say when I need *help*?" he growled, turning away from me to face Richard. "You think you can fix this?" He stuck out his arm, and in the glaring light I saw how much worse it truly was. The infection hadn't progressed in the minutes since I'd last seen it, at least not that I could tell, but the concentrated LED lighting showed what natural moonlight couldn't – the faint mottling of his skin, the little branches of bigger veins, how black they were where they first appeared, creeping out from under the bandage that ended just past his wrist.

Before Luke could move, Richard stepped towards him and grabbed hold of his arm. The vet peered down at it, and though Luke's muscles were tense and he was clearly resisting, it was obvious that Richard was stronger than he looked.

I guessed you'd have to be, to work with certain zoo animals.

It was only a matter of seconds before Richard let go of Luke's arm. "The only thing we can do now is take it off here – " he jabbed at a spot just above the elbow – "and hope that's good enough."

"Or take off the whole damn thing, knowing it's likely neither option will actually work? No thanks."

*My sentiments exactly*, I thought, but this wasn't me, this was *Luke*. He'd let us chop off fingers in hopes of preserving his life; that was more than I think I would have ever allowed. "We need to do *something*," I said, more than a little bit aware of how desperate I sounded.

Luke looked over his shoulder and shook his head in disbelief. "What about tomorrow? You'll need me. You know you will." He faced Richard again, and I saw the vet's face fall, as if he knew what Luke was about to say. "They already know I'm here. How will you explain it if I'm locked away with a stump for an arm just hours after they saw me moving around the zoo? Best-case scenario, we look weak. Worst-case scenario, we look weak and *stupid*. You can't do this."

I couldn't help but shudder. He hadn't said "You can't do this *right now*" – and I could tell by the way he was standing, facing off with Richard, every part of his body ready to spring into action – that he would never agree to us removing his arm. *Or even part of it.*

Richard finally spoke up. "If you won't sign off on an amputation like that, I can't do it anyway." He kept his eyes on Luke, and I knew that it was because he couldn't look at me. If Luke had been unconscious, Richard would have taken his arm off at my order...but Luke had said exactly what he needed to say. Richard's main priority would always be protecting his people and probably even his animals, and right now, to do that properly, he needed Luke in one piece.

"What are you going to do about the fact that you are getting worse by the hour?" I snapped, forcing the two men to recognize my existence. "We'll be lucky if they don't take one look at you and see that you're...that you're..."

But I couldn't finish. The truth was, I didn't know what to say. Luke's eyes met mine, but I found that I couldn't hold his gaze. I jerked my head down and growled, "I hope you can figure out a way to make him presentable, Richard."

And with that, I stalked out of the room, Holden on my heels.

We'd already left the door unguarded for far too long.

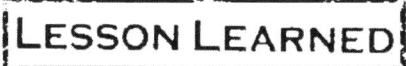

*Sometimes the worst enemy comes from within.*

# Chapter 10
# Off Script

The tops of the trees across the way were brightening with the rising sun when I heard the door open and then close off to my left. I kept staring straight ahead, though I could see Richard in my peripheral vision.

"I've been keeping an eye on him. I gave him some more medicine and he fell asleep almost right away. I woke him not that long ago and re-bandaged his arm. Tried to...clean things up a bit."

"And cover the evidence?"

Richard shifted his weight from one leg to another. "Yes. Right up to the elbow, just...just in case."

I couldn't help it; I turned around slowly and peered up at him, smirking with the knowledge at how stupid all of this was. "I guess we have to hope that Jia and her people aren't observant enough to see that half his arm is wrapped up, now. You know, when it wasn't earlier."

"Stop it, Charlie." Richard's tone chilled me. He spoke the words quietly but firmly, an order I would not be allowed to refuse. Still I felt myself opening my mouth to speak, but before I could formulate a proper retort – something damned unusual for me, especially these days – he continued, "Luke is alive, and he'll remain so for...well, it will be long enough. I could have taken his arm against his will, and there's a very good chance he would have died on that operating table. I'm a vet at a zoo, not a surgeon. I've performed duties beyond the norm from time to time, but I've never amputated a limb. Not even on an animal."

"There's a chance we could have convinced him. *Together*," I hissed. I felt Holden bump my leg with his head and wished that something so simple would make me feel better. It used to, but not anymore. Not now that everything had changed, anyway.

"No, there's not." Richard's words had a finality to them that I hadn't been expecting, and suddenly I understood that Luke had told Richard things. That at this moment in time, Richard knew more than I did about the man I loved.

I covered my face with my hands. I couldn't bring myself to continue arguing with him – in that moment, I felt more defeated than anything else. "Then we just go on with the plan? Can he even handle that?"

"As long as they don't stay here past the end of the day – or longer – he'll be fine. I can give him a bit of a boost right before they arrive...whenever that is."

"She didn't give a specific time." I cursed myself for not insisting on that, for not even thinking to ask, if I was honest with myself. "I'd guess soon – full dawn, I mean – or if she's dramatic, high noon."

"Do you know if they went back to the school yesterday?"

I shrugged. "No clue. We were all a bit too busy to attempt some sort of reconnaissance mission, weren't we?"

"Think about what I'm saying, Charlie. If they went back to the school – which I presume they must have, not knowing what they'd find here or what to bring with them yesterday – they wouldn't turn around and march right back. Noon, I think."

"Dramatic," I spat.

"What did Mike say?"

I realized just then that I hadn't even thought to ask Mike what time he thought she would arrive. *He's the one person who knew Jia before.* I looked up; this time, it was Richard who was smirking.

"Fine. Your turn to keep watch while I go talk to Mike."

As I headed back inside, clenching my fists in frustration and anger, I kept telling myself that Richard could have asked Mike himself. I almost convinced myself that he'd already done so, until I realized that Mike wouldn't have confided something like that to anyone other than myself or Luke. Possibly Daniel or Lauren, but even that was unlikely. Holden gave a soft whine and I bent to run my hand down his back, trying to reassure both of us.

Mike was right where I'd left him, though he was no longer asleep. "What happened?"

Apparently we hadn't been as quiet as I thought. Part of me wanted to hold back, to not reveal how bad things really were, but one look at his face told me that would never suffice. I jerked my head toward the door – somehow, the others were still sleeping – and he followed me out into the hall.

"It's Luke," I admitted. "The infection is spreading. He won't let us take care of it because of...because of this thing with Jia."

Mike turned his head away. "I'm sorry," he mumbled.

"No, I'm sorry. For what I'm about to ask, even though I have to ask it. It's dawn. When will Jia show up? Now? Or..." I trailed off, somehow knowing that it would be best to let him answer without being led into doing so.

"After what I saw yesterday...I'm sure she left people nearby, but I think she must have gone back to the school. And if not now – if not dawn – I think maybe she'd try for as close to noon as she can make it." He paused, biting his lip for a moment before concluding, "If she's not the person she used to be...and I don't think she is...then yeah, it will be noon."

I nodded. "Dramatic." I don't know why I couldn't let go of that word, why I so badly needed someone to agree with me.

"A bit, yeah. And she'll probably think we expect her now, that after waiting a few hours we'll let our guard down."

"I don't know how long Luke can make it, how long he can fake being okay." *Why am I telling him this? Him of all people...*

"He can. He will. He's Luke."

My first thought was, *But for how much longer?* Except this time I stopped myself from voicing that particular concern.

"Charlie?"

I re-focused on Mike, only then realizing that I'd completely zoned out. "Yeah, Mike, sorry. Just...worried."

The one thing I couldn't do was lie and tell him that I was only worried about today.

"You should rest. Or try to," Mike corrected himself. "Richard or I can take the watch. I'll go talk to him."

"I think I need to talk to Luke. Take Holden with you, at least. And if you need me..."

Mike stared at me for a long moment, then finally nodded. "Okay. C'mon, Holden." I waited until I saw him and my dog slip outside, then steeled myself and headed for the clean room. *See, dumbass? You've never even thought of it as an operating room.*

I could hear Luke snoring as I let myself in. This now-familiar noise was softer than it had been earlier, and I was relieved when, even after listening for nearly a minute, his breath didn't hitch the way it had when we were outside.

*Maybe something Richard did actually bought us more time.* I allowed myself that moment of hope, knowing that it had to be a brief one. I doubted there was any such thing as giving Luke enough time to rest – I knew how things were going to turn out, with him.

I think I'd always known I'd lose him. *One way or another.*

I didn't bother turning on any lights as I approached Luke's side. I doubted that the strangely bright glow of the emergency lamps would do either of us any good, so instead I settled myself on the bed next to him and reached through the darkness, placing my hand on his shoulder and squeezing lightly. "Luke. It's Charlie. Can we..." I stopped myself. "No. We *should* talk."

Luke had stopped snoring almost the second I'd touched him. I pulled my hand back and waited until he cleared his throat and replied, "Yeah. We should."

"About what's going to happen today. About what to do if you can't handle the meeting with Jia. She won't be here for hours."

"It's not morning yet?" Luke sounded confused. *Too confused.*

"Well, yeah, it's dawn. But she's not here. I talked to Richard and Mike...we all agree she won't be back until noon. We should send a couple people out to the front gate soon...me, and at least one other person who's already been seen. But not Mike. I'd rather she not have any more chance to recognize him than she already has."

"Or will," Luke reminded me.

"Right. And you're not going either, so I guess it should be Virginia. She was the last person at the gate before those kids revealed themselves...they must have seen her, must have been watching us long enough for that."

"They've probably seen Richard, too, you know."

"Probably."

I may have agreed with him, but Luke knew what I was really saying. That between Virginia and Richard, the latter was far less expendable.

These were the decisions we had to make, now.

"It should be me, Charlie."

"Not anymore, Luke." Those words were weighted ones, too. "Go back to sleep, if you can. Save your strength, and all that," I said, knowing that unless he got up and moved around it would only be a matter of minutes before he was basically unconscious. "Richard will know when to wake you." I felt for his head and kissed the top of it – willing myself to not think too much about the heat emanating from him – then stood and shuffled back in the general direction of the door.

"Charlie?"

I paused my search for the exit, but didn't respond.

"Charlie, you know that I'm not just giving up. I don't want to die...or worse, be one of those things. But if I was missing an entire arm, I'd be nothing more than a burden to everyone. Especially you. I can't let that happen. I know you wouldn't, either, if you were in my shoes."

"You don't know that." I began moving my hand along the wall again; mercifully, I found the seam of the door almost immediately, fast enough so that I was opening it before Luke could reply, trying to tell myself that I didn't care whether he even would have said anything at all.

Richard was outside where I'd left him. "I'm headed to the front soon. I need Virginia to come with me. She was the last person guarding the gate before we met our new little friends, and I don't want them to know about all of us if we can help it."

"You think you're going to be able to hide *people*, too?" he asked, incredulous.

"Just Lauren and Mabel. I don't think there's any way Jia or her people could have caught sight of them. If they did, and call us out on it...well, I'll think of something."

"*You'll think of something*?" Richard spat. "Are you – "

I held up my hand and shook my head. "Having a child in our group is a weakness, and it's one I don't doubt they'll exploit if they find out. So I'm going to do my best to keep that from happening. Oh, and tell Mike to shut Holden up, too. Not with Lauren and Mabel, though."

"Where do you propose they go?"

"I'll leave that to you and Ethan. Listen, I trust you guys, okay? Please trust *me* on this."

Richard glared at me. "You may be crazy, but you're no idiot. You know this is a bad idea."

I shrugged. "It's all I've got. Can I at least trust you guys to find them a safe place to stay? And I hope I don't have to clarify that it can't be anywhere near the supplies."

The vet's face turned bright red, and I could tell that not one part of him wanted to follow my order – but I wasn't going to back down. "I can't promise anything. You better hope Ethan knows of somewhere safe. Those places are few and far between..."

For a moment I thought that perhaps he was going to finish his thought, but instead Richard gave me a curt nod and stalked away. *These days. Few and far between these days,* I thought.

Virginia appeared less than ten minutes later. "You okay with this?" I asked before she could get a word in edgewise.

She gave me a look that was something close to sly. "I was just getting myself ready, darlin'," she said, speaking quietly enough that no one hiding even just outside the fences could have heard her. Her face remained completely stoic, but there was steel in her tone.

I was surprised to find my mouth quirking into a smile as I gave a simple nod in response, then turned and gestured for her to follow me down the path. Virginia showed me her watch; it was still early, just past seven.

We had a long wait stretching ahead of us.

Once we reached the front gate, we made ourselves comfortable on the rock fence that bordered the tree line directly across from it. I'd been worried that Virginia would have trouble sitting in silence when that was all I could stand at the moment, but she sat and stared straight ahead with me and never uttered a word.

I was surprised to find that it was Joey, not Luke, who came to mind that morning. I suppose that part of me was still in denial about how dire Luke's situation was, but I couldn't stop thinking about what Joey would be doing if he were still here. *If he were still here.* I felt a tightening in the back of my throat but refused to let the thought – the *feeling* – take hold.

The sun crept slowly upward, the air growing hot and heavy, which is what finally prompted Virginia to speak. "It's going to rain later," she murmured.

I nodded. I knew this weather. It was only a question of whether it would happen this afternoon or sometime this evening...and whether or not Jia and her people would still be here when it did.

"Is that good or bad, you think?"

I shrugged. There was no way of knowing.

Virginia didn't speak again, though eventually she held out her wrist and pointed to her watch, which read ten minutes to noon. The thing probably hadn't been exact in ages, but the sun was high in the sky and I wanted to greet Jia on my feet. I searched for some part of me that was scared, but found nothing. I was entirely aware that this wasn't a good thing, not really, but at the very least it might make this child despot uncomfortable.

Shit, it made *me* uncomfortable. But I shook that feeling off, too. I stood up and approached the gate, already understanding that Virginia would follow my lead. Somehow I had requested the perfect partner for this particular situation – almost against all odds, if I was honest with myself.

We continued our vigil just feet from the gate, but we didn't have to wait long. As soon as I heard them – which, thanks to the midday silence, was before I saw them – I glanced down at Virginia's watch. With a small margin of error, Jia was right on time...and as she approached, I silently reminded myself to thank Mike for his input, while at the same time wondering what the hell these kids planned to trade with us when they didn't seem to be carrying anything other than some basic necessities.

I made certain that it was me who spoke first. "You'll need to leave your weapons here. One of your people can stay to watch over them – Virginia will stay, too." I nodded toward the older woman, and she mustered a kindly smile, something she certainly hadn't done when she'd met me at the gate not that long ago. But I knew what that smile meant – she was giving them the good ol' Southern 'fuck you'…just without saying the words, "Bless your heart."

Jia cocked her head. "And what about *your* weapons?"

Deep down, I'd known she wouldn't give in immediately. I tried to hide my reluctance. "I'll leave mine here as well. We've gathered the rest up with everything else. I made sure that the only arms my people kept on their persons are short-range ones. You never know when a zed might turn up."

*Fuck.* It was silly, maybe, to be angry with myself for letting that term – *our* term – slip out, but I couldn't ignore the bemused look on Jia's face. "Zeds? Interesting."

I shrugged, trying to appear more nonchalant than I felt. "Have to call them something."

"I suppose one does." Jia continued to smirk, but I refused to ask what *she* called them.

"Do you agree to leave your weapons here or not? It's the same deal I was given when I first came through those gates. Trust me, you want to take it."

The girl stared at me for several long moments, and I knew that she was trying to figure me out, trying to decide if I posed any threat. Maybe she wondered whether I had some master plan to shoot them all down the moment they started surrendering their guns.

I wasn't sure if it was a good thing or a bad thing when she nodded. "We will. And someone will stay here to watch them. And she'll stay too." Jia jerked her head toward Virginia.

"That was the offer," I reminded her coolly. I could have sworn I saw a flicker of anger in her eyes, but when she spoke again she was calm and collected.

"Good." She looked at one of her people – a mousy girl who had the same hard look about her that Jia did – and then turned back to me. "Allie will stay. I suggest you open that gate before I change my mind."

I turned away to hide my grimace. "Virginia?"

"Of course, dear." She pulled out her key ring, and the first thing I noticed was that it was a lot less full than usual. I glanced at the group of teenagers on the other side of the fence; Jia was watching Virginia almost greedily, while the rest of them were alert, scanning their surroundings, keeping an eye on their leader, or studying me.

I couldn't help but worry about the others, about their ability to keep a straight face. *Please keep your shit together, guys.*

One by one the padlocks clicked open, and Virginia slowly unwound the chains. I didn't believe that she was being so methodical on purpose, but Jia was clearly in a hurry. "Any day now," she said, finally looking up at me, obviously expecting me to hasten the process.

"I'm sure you know what happens if we make too much noise, and I don't think any of us want to attract the zeds." *Now that they know the word, might as well use it.*

Jia glared at me but didn't say another word as Virginia slowly pulled the last bit of chain through the bars and set it carefully on the ground. As she opened the gate, she turned her back on the kids for a brief moment, just long enough for her to glance at me, her expression the only proof I needed that she would be completely in control over this Allie girl while I led Jia and the rest of her people through this farce of a trade.

In fact, Virginia almost seemed more prepared than I was to fight these children...should the need arise. I inclined my head in thanks, just barely, but in the end Jia was too busy shuffling her followers through the crack in the gate to notice our exchange. I still didn't feel great about leaving Virginia alone with this girl Allie, but I told myself that Virginia could handle her.

When they'd all filed through the gate – eleven of them, by my count – Virginia looped one chain around it and secured it with a padlock as they divested themselves of their guns.

"We'll be keeping our knives," Jia said. "In case of...zeds...of course."

"Of course," I agreed.

"Lead the way, then."

I crossed my arms over my chest. "Here's the thing. You're here to trade, right?" I had to swallow the 'supposedly' that was on the tip of my tongue. "But it doesn't look like you brought much with you."

Jia nodded. She'd obviously been expecting this. "Don't worry – our offerings are forthcoming. Remember, I'm the one running this trade – you don't get to see our goods before we see yours."

"Well, you suggested this trade in such a way that we simply couldn't say no," I reminded her, not bothering to keep the mocking tone out of my voice.

"So very true." Jia smirked at me. "We are locked in here, and are leaving our guns at the gate. We could be walking into an ambush, but I'm choosing to believe you aren't that stupid. Either way, by my last count we outnumber you almost two to one...and that's just based on the people I brought with me. So again, I'm the one running this trade. We look first, we take first, and then we give...in our own time. Now, I highly suggest you bring us to those offices. Immediately."

There was nothing I could do, and I wanted to kick myself for losing my temper. *So much for not showing her your weaknesses.* "Actually, no. I'm going to tell you which way you are going. Six of your people will walk ahead; the other three can follow you and I. That is, unless you want to leave your knives behind, too."

Jia snorted. "No matter what, it's ten to one."

"Which is exactly why I assume you don't have any problem with that arrangement. Especially as I have no reason to believe this trade will benefit us in any way."

She shrugged. "It's a new world, *Charlie*, and we have the upper hand here. To the point where I feel completely comfortable acquiescing to this nonsense."

I almost opened my mouth to respond, then decided that I would let her have that one. I pointed to the right. "The offices are that way. It's a bit of a walk, but just keep on the path until I tell you to turn right."

"Is it the only right turn?" Jia asked, her eyes glittering.

"Yes," I sighed. "But I'm not sure of the exact distance, and it's hard to see the entrance if you don't know where it is. Guess you'll just have to trust me."

"Trust has no place in this world," was Jia's cold response. "But I think you know what will happen if you try anything, and you care too much about your friends here to let that happen. Or maybe..." She gave me a sly look. "Maybe you simply value your own skin enough to not take any risks here today. That's something I can respect, at least."

I stared back at her, hoping that all she saw was my blank expression. Finally she chuckled and waved me off. "Well, whatever it is, I'm fine with your little rule." She pointed to six of her people – three boys, three girls – and they started down the path. I followed, Jia immediately falling in step beside me. I could hear the footsteps of the others close behind us – two girls and a boy. Strangely, I found myself wondering whether I would ever know their names. *Maybe it's better that you don't.*

We walked for several minutes, and though I refused to look back at the people behind me, the ones in front kept glancing over their shoulders at Jia. Not that she ever acknowledged this – I could see her eyes darting from one side to the other, and I had an uncomfortable feeling that she was taking mental pictures of her surroundings.

That she was *memorizing* everything she was seeing.

I was unnerved, but thankfully we were almost at the office building. "There's a small turnoff just up here on the right," I pointed out. "I know it doesn't look like much, but you'll be able to see a chair and a door."

By the time Jia and I reached the entrance, the rest of her group were gathered close to the door, peering at their surroundings, their hands on the hilts of their knives. "Calm down, guys," Jia ordered. She turned to me. "This was much more well-hidden before, wasn't it?"

This time it was my turn to smirk. "I was fairly certain you wouldn't follow my directions if I told you to walk straight into a dim alcove that looked like it was formed from vines."

"You think that would have scared me?" Jia laughed.

"Who said anything about scaring you?" I shot back. The silence stretched between us, but Jia never broke eye contact.

When she finally spoke, her voice was cold and hard. "Open the door."

*She thinks she can't be frightened.* This was probably the most important thing that I knew about this girl just now, but I didn't have time to think about that at the moment. I turned and backed toward the door, trying to keep my eyes on as many of them as I could.

I rapped my knuckles against the hard steel three times; it swung open almost before I withdrew my hand. Richard was there, looking as stern as he ever had, though I doubted his expression would have any effect on Jia.

"There are six more of us inside," I announced, speaking louder than I would have liked, wanting to make sure that everyone heard me. "I'll let five of your people go in with Richard here, and then I'll lead the rest of you in myself."

"You're very concerned about how many of us there are. How many people do you *actually* have here, *Charlie*?"

She said my name like it was some sort of a curse; the first thought that crossed my mind was *maybe she's right*.

"Like I just said, there are seven of us here...and Virginia back at the gate, of course," I replied without hesitation. We stared at each other for a long moment, and then Jia actually *chuckled*. I smirked at her. "Seven against eleven isn't bad considering you're on our territory."

"Very true. But if you think there are only eleven of us, you're woefully mistaken."

"I don't doubt you have more people outside these walls," I admitted. "The thing is, I'm more concerned about what's inside of them."

This time it was one of Jia's followers, a tall and slim yet scrappy-looking kid, who laughed. "You have no idea, lady." My eyes met his, and I didn't move until he looked away. Satisfied that at least one of them knew that I was tougher than they thought, I beckoned him and four others to follow Richard. Jia and the rest – two boys and two other girls – crowded around me, pulling Jia back behind them, but I shoved out my elbows and slowed them down.

I rounded on them. "Enough. You may do things differently, but we aren't going to separate you just to take you down. After all, you don't even have any long-range weapons just now, remember?"

Jia stepped through her companions' barrier; they parted like the Red Sea at Moses' command. She looked calm and collected. *Assured.* "You're right. We don't have any weapons, and you are...well, I don't know what you are. I only know that I'm shocked you've survived this long." She paused, peered around me into the dim hallway that split the concrete block of the building we called home, and shrugged. "Then again, you have a nice setup here."

All the things she wasn't saying were practically written on her face. She thought we would be eaten alive if we had to survive outside, and I knew that was probably true about a few of us, even if I didn't count Mabel in that equation.

Still, something like hope welled up inside of me just then. *She's underestimating us. Severely.*

I headed inside, straight to Richard's office. He and the five who'd gone with him were still standing in the hall, and his face was red, his posture tense. "...think I'll let one of you stay out here? With only your word that you won't – "

"That's enough, Richard." He clenched his jaw, but didn't say anything else. "Go on in. They can leave someone out here; tell Luke to come out in the hallway and keep watch." I turned to Jia. "One person. Your choice."

She looked over her shoulder and jerked her head; one of the girls, tall and lanky with rich sepia-toned skin, a head of gorgeous black curls, and the face of a movie star, stepped into the light. I immediately noticed the scar that ran across the bridge of her nose and down one cheek, a slash that hadn't cut deep but had still left its mark. Somehow it made the girl even more beautiful, despite the size of it and the fact that it was still raised and red. "Monika," she said, sticking out her hand.

But before I could grasp it, Jia coughed, and Monika immediately withdrew her gesture.

"She's a bit too friendly sometimes, but trust me, she can take care of herself." Jia shouldered past me then, but not before I realized that she'd spoken with something like *affection*.

I had to pull myself back to reality, finally gesturing to the others that they should follow their leader. "Take them in with you, Richard. Get Luke. I'll wait out here while you do. Just keep an eye on them."

Richard obviously wasn't happy with the situation, but he only hesitated for a moment before disappearing through the door behind Jia and several of her companions.

"Hey, Monika. I'm Charlie," I said, keeping my eyes on the door even as I tried to figure out the best ways to ingratiate myself with Jia's people.

"We know your name."

"We? The collective 'we'? Or..."

There was no answer, so I chanced a glance in Monika's direction. She was staring at the door, too, and there was color in her cheeks that hadn't even been there when she'd attempted to introduce herself to me.

*But is it because of my question, or because she can't see Jia?* At the moment, I had a feeling either reason was equally probable.

I half expected Jia to return with Luke, but it was one of the boys who stood in the doorway after Luke stepped out into the hall. "Luke, this is Monika," I told him. His eyes met mine and I took a deep breath, hoping that it disguised me dipping my head at him. Of course he wouldn't know *exactly* what I was trying to say, but he would understand that there was something important going on.

"Come on," doorway kid ordered.

"As if I would miss this," I muttered, squeezing by him, my elbow knocking his just hard enough so that he would know that he was in my way and I wasn't having it.

I ignored the fact that he scoffed at my little display; once I was in the room, my attention was on Jia again.

She'd waited for me.

"Gang's all here!" she said. She was smiling, her tone cheerful, and that almost scared me – because neither her expression nor her words were fake. "And apparently so are all of your supplies." She continued staring at me, narrowing her eyes.

I rolled my own. "Yeah. This is what we're left with. Seven people living inside these walls for so long...what else did you expect?"

Jia sighed and shook her head. "There's not much here worth trading for."

"Well, what are you giving us in return?"

"I think I've already made it clear that it doesn't work like that. Not quite yet. We take what we want, and I'll send a group back with some things for you. Our choice."

"That doesn't seem like much of a fair trade," Richard hissed, causing Jia to finally turn her gaze on him.

"There's no such thing as a fair trade. You're lucky we still have a nurse, or you would be coming back to the school with us."

I couldn't help it – I finally snapped. "Fuck that! You wanted to see what we have, there it is. No one said anything about taking people – or even *threatening* to take them."

Jia cocked her head at me. "Damn. You really *are* sheltered here, aren't you?"

"What the fuck are you talking about?" I could feel everyone staring at me, could feel the extra tension my loss of temper caused, but right then I didn't care.

"We always take someone with us. Insurance, you know? Don't worry, whoever we take will be treated just fine." She paused, pointed to her people, then to the supplies we'd thrown together. "You know what to look for." They moved forward and began picking through our things, taking the best of what we had, stuffing items into their bags and their pockets.

"You'll have a hard time getting out of here with all of that and one of our people," I pointed out.

"I think not. One of your people will go with us. Willingly. They always do, once they know what will happen to their friends if anyone tries to stop us."

"You might outnumber us, but right now, *here*, we have the upper hand. And you're not taking any of my people."

Jia's eyes glittered with malice. "We can leave the supplies, and take more people. We can take the supplies, and take no one, and then swarm your pitiful little compound from the breach in the back fence and any other undefended spot we find, and kill every last one of you. Take your pick."

"I refuse to force anyone here to be your captive."

"Force? Who said anything about *force*? I choose the captive, and that person agrees to return to our base. Very simple."

"*You* choose?" Somehow I knew that she wouldn't take me, the one she perceived as the leader of our little group. I waved my hand in Ethan and Daniel's direction. "You already said you didn't need Richard, and I know you aren't thinking about me, though I'd go if you were. So it's Ethan, Daniel, Virginia – "

"Oh no. No, no, no. None of them. The one in the hall. What was his name?"

My stomach turned, but I did my best to ignore the sickening feeling in my gut and instead forced a laugh. "Luke? What the hell is he going to do for you?" I hated saying it, but in a way, I spoke the truth. Luke was sick, possibly even dying, and although there was a good chance Jia hadn't noticed as much, it wasn't as if she would be able to get him to fight for her. *Not in his current state.*

"He's going to keep *you* at bay," she replied, grinning at me like the Cheshire Cat.

## LESSON LEARNED

*Never forget that there's no such thing as a fair trade.*

\* \* \* \* \* \* \*

Somehow I knew there was no getting out of this, but I was shocked that Jia hadn't picked up on the fact that Luke was injured. I wasn't sure if that was something I could even use to my advantage, so rather than mention it, I forced a laugh and said, "My word is what will 'keep me at bay'. Taking one of us won't change that. But if you're so worried about me, wouldn't I be your first choice?"

Jia waved me off. "Please. You're more trouble than you're worth – I've known that since we started watching you people. Besides, they need you to keep shit together more than they need military man out there."

*How did she know?* I shook my head to clear it. "I won't make him go."

This time it was Jia who laughed. "But you know he will. And even if he didn't, my next choice would be him." She nodded in Mike's direction, though thankfully he was watching the others too closely to notice. "He looks like he belongs in a school." She smiled at me, some twisted version of a "mother knows best" look. "Maybe I should make you choose, after all – between your big handsome boyfriend out there...or the kid."

I didn't want to think about what she may have seen that led her to assume that she knew me – *and Luke* – so well. I didn't want to think about how long they'd been watching us. "You're right. Luke will do it. But if one of us goes, one of you stays."

"Of course, of course. It's actually Bobby's turn this time."

The tall, slim boy from earlier stepped forward, smirking. "You don't seem to mind drawing the short straw," I noted.

He shook his head, his smirk turning into a shit-eating grin. He looked like he was about to say something, but then Jia caught his eye and he merely crossed his arms over his chest and looked up at the ceiling, back to smirking now and still obviously amused.

"I completely expect you to keep him under lock and key," Jia admitted. "We'll be doing the same with your...Luke. And if we return with our goods and Bobby has a single mark on him, you *will* pay."

"How do I know he won't rough himself up and blame it on us?" *He sure as hell looks like he would do just that.*

"He knows better. They all know better. You see, unlike you, I run a tight ship."

It dawned on me then – that's how she knew that Luke had military experience. That's why she was so – *her*. "Tight ship? Either you're a lot older than you look or you're a military brat."

I don't know what made me say it, and I wasn't sure if I was finally one step ahead of Jia or if I'd simply made things worse – because when she spoke, her voice was level. "My mother was an Army Ranger, actually."

"Is that supposed to scare me?"

"If you let it," was all she said.

"I think I'll be okay."

"Good. So, Bobby will stay here, we'll take Luke, and you'll see us again in three days."

I had to bite down on the inside of my cheek to keep from snapping at her again. "I've lived in this city for the better part of a decade. I know where the school is. You don't need three days to get there and back."

"Who said anything about *needing*? That's the way we work, and you have to accept it."

*Why three days?* I was burning to know what nonsense Jia cooked up in this waiting period of hers, but of course I knew better than to ask.

That question would be for later. *For Bobby.*

Finally Jia's people finished picking through our supplies, and I knew the only reason any of them were left was because they couldn't carry anything else. "That's good enough for now," Jia said. "But before we go, just one more question."

My heart leapt into my throat. *Please not Lauren and Mabel...* I raised my eyebrows in pretend surprise. "What, not ready to leave our little safe haven quite yet?"

"More than ready, actually, but I find myself wondering...where's your dog?"

I wanted to be relieved that she didn't seem to know about Lauren and Mabel, but when I opened my mouth to respond I realized that *I* didn't even know where Holden was. Thankfully I caught myself, though not as quickly as I would have liked. "Richard put him up. He can be...protective."

Jia cocked her head again, a habit of hers that was already beginning to annoy me. "From what I saw, he seemed friendly enough. But I suppose he would sense when you're...upset."

"He senses a lot of things. That's one of them, but not the one you'd need to worry about. Still, I'll introduce you to him, if that's what you're getting at. Who knows, maybe he would like you just fine." I was being nonchalant despite not really knowing how Holden would react if she insisted on seeing him; I couldn't help but hope that she would hear the not-so-veiled threat in my words, no matter how inaccurate it may be.

But Jia only shrugged. "Maybe next time."

I gave her the coldest smile I could muster. "If you insist." *How long would it take to teach Holden to respond to some sort of 'attack' command?* A stupid question, of course; I knew there was no chance in hell of that happening in just three days.

*Just three days*...but shit, if they took Luke, what would three days do to *him*? I'd been so worried about the idea of Jia taking someone at all that until now I hadn't thought about his arm, about the infection that seemed to be spreading faster all the time.

"Richard, take Bobby somewhere...safe," I ordered. "Daniel, take the rest of these people outside." I simply mouthed *Stay here* to Mike before facing Jia again. "I'll have a minute with Luke before we leave this building." It wasn't a request, wasn't a suggestion, and I willed her to see as much and not push me any further.

"Of course you will," she replied, every word weighted with judgment.

"Whaddaya say, boss?" Bobby interrupted. I looked over to see Richard standing by his side, tense as always.

Jia looked irritated. "Go on, then." We watched as Daniel herded the rest of her people out of the office. Richard and Bobby followed, and although I worried that he wouldn't have an easy time of it, locking the kid up, I knew that I had to focus on what I would say to Luke. I gestured for Jia to go ahead of me, frustrated with this time-consuming parade.

We met Monika and Luke just outside the door; I was more than a little shocked when Jia actually motioned to the other girl and they walked down the hall. Jia didn't even look back, though Monika did – but not at me. At Luke.

"She told me. I could only hear bits and pieces of your conversation, but she told me."

"Luke, you don't have to – "

"Yes I do. You know I do."

"But your arm..."

"That's exactly why I have to go. I'm done for, Charlie. I know it, Richard knows it, and goddammit, *you* know it."

"But *they* don't."

Luke actually laughed, then. "You going soft on me? No, they don't. And that's going to be their undoing. *I'm* going to be their undoing."

"Some of them are probably innocent," I reminded him, thinking of the school nurse, and of Dominic.

"Probably, but Charlie...we're way past that, now."

"This is biological warfare," I said carefully. Carefully because he was right, because I knew it was our best option, maybe even our only option. Carefully because while I wasn't quite sure that I cared, I knew that deep down, *he* did.

"I have to improvise here. This is the only solution, and it is what it is."

"You hate that phrase." How many times had I said it to him these past several months? *How many times did he tell me it was nonsensical?*

"I need to do what I can to protect our people." He didn't say "to protect you", but the insinuation was there.

"They're going to lock you up, anyway. You don't even know – "

Luke smiled sadly. "I'll get myself out as soon as I can – you said it yourself, there are people in that school who are innocent. Who knows what they wouldn't do for a chance to change up Jia's little regime. I'll hide it for as long as I can, of course – Monika told me I'll be there for three days. At this point I'm pretty sure that's plenty of time. You're the one who will be in the most difficult position. Someone will need to sneak out of here early, probably by the forty-eight-hour mark, and come keep an eye on the school...then make it back here to fetch more of you when everything comes crashing down around that girl."

"Luke, this is crazy. You can't – "

"I can. I will. Just do me one favor, Charlie."

I clenched my eyes shut, took a shaky breath, and nodded.

"I'll do what I can on my end, but if you can help it, don't let me get out of the school. And make sure I'm not a zed for too long." His tone was devoid of all feeling, and I knew then that there was no way to change his mind.

"I'll make sure," I promised. "I'll take care of everything."

Luke drew me in close and hugged me tight, practically squeezing the air right out of me. "I know you will," he murmured into my hair, before loosening his embrace and leaning back, tipping my chin up with one hand to kiss me softly on the mouth.

There was no passion in his kiss; it was simply gentle and warm and lovely.

*Just the way a goodbye kiss should be.*

I heard Jia push the door open, and her voice rang down the hall. "That's enough. It's raining, and we have our own *safe haven* to get back to."

Fast as I could, I leaned in and whispered, "Keep an eye out for the school nurse, Mrs. Downing. She's in her fifties maybe, her hair's mostly gray. And Dominic. Young kid, short, mop of black hair."

Luke nodded, his hair brushing my lips, and I finally stepped away from him. We didn't even bother to look at or touch each other as we made our way out into the rain; it was hardly more than a sprinkle, but I could see darker skies moving in over the trees and knew that soon enough we'd be caught in a downpour.

"I'll take care of things from here," I told Daniel. I could tell that he was grateful, but thankfully he didn't say anything in response, and Jia didn't protest as he turned and let himself back into the building.

The twelve of us walked back to the front gate, keeping a brisk pace. We arrived back to see Allie pacing miserably in the rain while Virginia sat off to the side under a tree. Both of them had their guns in hand and spun to face us when they finally heard our footsteps.

"We're all set," Jia said. Virginia looked to me as she trained her gun on Allie, but when I shook my head she lowered her pistol.

We took turns gathering up our weapons, but when I moved to hand Luke a knife, Jia stepped forward and grasped my wrist, clenching her hand around it so tight that I knew she was trying to cause pain – but my adrenaline had taken over and I didn't feel much of anything.

"Absolutely not. We're not stupid – he'll travel with his hands and arms free. But no weapons."

"Fuck you. God knows what could happen on your way there!"

"He's been injured and he's still alive. I have a feeling that between that and the training I'm sure he's had, Luke here can take care of himself. If we get attacked, he can run. But I'm sure as hell not letting him have a weapon."

I opened my mouth to protest, but Luke spoke first. "As long as my hands are free and I can run if I need to, I'll be fine."

"Yes, you will. Just don't try to use this as a way to escape. It won't go well for you – or for your friends back here," Jia warned.

"I figured as much." Luke sounded so nonchalant that I almost wanted to believe he actually wasn't worried.

Jia smiled again. "See? We're all in agreement. You can see us out, and we'll be back at the same time three days from now."

I nodded to Virginia, who opened the gate for them as quickly as she could. There was thunder rumbling in the distance; I guessed we had maybe ten minutes at most before the storm arrived in full force.

As I moved forward to help Virginia chain the gate behind Luke, Jia, and her people, Jia once again turned toward me. "Of course you know we'll be keeping an eye on you. Several pairs of them, in fact. See you soon!"

My hands clenched around the chains that I was holding in place, and I only allowed myself to let go when I heard the second giant padlock click shut. "Let's get back to the office," Virginia said. I was glad that she wasn't trying to reassure me.

"Yeah. They'll be watching our gate for us, I suppose."

"Someone will come back here when it stops raining. Maybe two people."

I turned and stalked away. Virginia was right; two of us needed to be guarding that gate until Jia returned. But who? We had to keep hiding Lauren and Mabel, and after what had transpired earlier, I sure as hell didn't want Jia – or any of her people – watching Mike for any extended period of time. *And we have to sneak two more out the back as soon as we can...*

There was safety in numbers, but ours were dwindling.

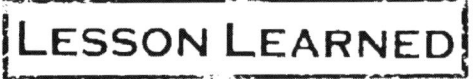

*Know how to improvise.*

# Chapter 11
# Strength

By the time we let ourselves back into the office building, Virginia and I were drenched. It was my fault – the rain grew heavier with each passing minute, but still I walked as slowly and steadily as I could.

I hated the fact that someone had been able to watch us so closely; hated that someone might still be watching us now. With the zeds, you knew what you were going to get – the freshly killed, slow and clumsy, or the ones who smelled of rot and gore and moved so fast you could almost believe they were alive – the ones who could get close enough to catch you if you weren't quick enough. *Or strong enough.*

Somehow, I must have allowed myself to hope that there would be a chink in Jia's armor. Even if the people we'd met at the school weren't happy with their situation, I knew they wouldn't outright help us. Even if the girl from the roof hadn't been part of Jia's crew today – even if Dominic, the nurse, and the nine kids tagging along with Jia and Luke were all the people she commanded – well, she still had a healthy soldier inside our walls and nearly twice our own number outside of them.

*Probably more.*

We were inside and almost to Richard's office when Virginia stopped and faced me. "We need to ask Mike how many people might be at that school."

"Why? That's just putting pressure on him when there's no way he could give even a rough estimate."

"I think you underestimate him," Virginia stated. "Go on into the office. I'll find some of the others and we'll sit down and talk about what we will do."

*What we* will *do. Not what we* can *do. What we* will *do.*

Something about Virginia's demeanor just then made me yearn for my mother. "Just make sure to leave, you know, some 'things' where they are. And Richard or Daniel will have to stay with this Bobby kid. Maybe try to talk to him."

"Richard, I think." Her eyes met mine and I understood that, as long as Lauren and Mabel were locked away in secret, Daniel had the potential to be a very weak link in our already-eroding chain.

Mike was the only one left in the office. "Ethan went to grab a few of the items we were hiding. Daniel came back for a minute, but then he said he wanted to get a better look at Bobby."

"Do you know him? Bobby?"

"No. I mean, I could have seen him before, but there were like...over two thousand kids who went to my school. I don't think he was in my grade..."

I waved him off. "It's fine, Mike. I was just curious. Richard is going to guard the kid, but once Ethan, Virginia, and Daniel are back, we need to know everything you do about that school and how many people might be there. Even if it's just guesswork, okay? No one expects you to be one hundred percent right...about anything. We just..." I paused, closed my eyes, and took a deep breath. "Anything you think of could help. Even the smallest detail..."

"You have a plan," Mike said, and when I saw how relieved he was, my stomach flipped.

"Not exactly," I finally replied. "But we will."

I just couldn't imagine that it would be a very *good* plan.

Virginia and Daniel arrived first, and we all sat on the floor, forming a circle that Ethan joined a few minutes later. He didn't say a single word as he handed out snack-sized bags of peanuts and set a bottled water in the center of our circle.

"Okay," I finally began. "Obviously Mike knows the most about the school, but does anyone else have a clue about what's going on there?" I fixed my gaze on Virginia. "Is there anything you haven't told us?"

She shook her head. "I'd almost like to admit that we betrayed your trust and kept something like that from you. But no...we've been so sheltered here, we had no idea. And before you came, there were so few of us – even if those kids had come poking around the park, even if they'd walked our perimeter, the chances of us seeing each other..."

"You saw *us*," I snapped.

"You had *cars*," Ethan interjected. When I looked at him, he was staring at his unopened bag of peanuts, and he didn't look happy.

I relented. "Okay. Okay, fine. You don't know anything, and we as a whole don't know much more than that. Daniel and I saw the school, but it looked mostly deserted. The people we talked to seemed like they would be interested in the idea of removing Jia from her throne, as it were, but we can't count on that. And numbers-wise...she could have a dozen people, or hundreds." I turned to Mike. "This is where you come in. How many of those two thousand or so kids could be there?"

He chewed on his lip for a bit. "We had a full day of school, and that evening things really started going to hell. Before I went to bed that night they'd already canceled classes and started telling everyone to remain in their homes."

Daniel spoke up. "It wasn't so bad down where we were, not that fast, but all of our radio stations were city ones, of course...and I was hearing some pretty crazy things when I was driving home from work that day. Must have been about four in the afternoon."

I was thankful for this information; I didn't want to have to have to admit to anyone else that I'd been safely tucked away at a yoga retreat while the world collapsed around me. "This...this could be good. I'm sure some people went to the school when things got bad – we certainly can't be the only people who would have tried – but how soon did Jia take charge..." I rubbed my hand across my forehead as if to wipe away any hopeful thoughts that could be cropping up.

Mike stood up and began pacing. "I can't tell you when Jia took over, but she would have been at the school after hours. Her and maybe a couple hundred more kids, plus a few teachers. Football practice, clubs...it was close enough to the beginning of the school year, there was a lot of that stuff going on."

*A couple hundred. She could have hundreds of people.* "Okay, maybe not so good after all."

Virginia glanced at Ethan. "If parents getting out of work were hearing about things on the radio, many of them would have called their kids to come home. Maybe some of them didn't listen, maybe some of them didn't check their phones in time, but I doubt more than a few dozen kids ended up in that school for good."

"There's still the problem of how many people went there afterward, thinking it might be a safe place," I pointed out.

"And who would have let them in? Maybe some slipped through, if they were other students, other teachers, family members...so a few dozen more? And how many would have actually survived?" Virginia paused and looked at each of us in turn. "Something happened there, I'm sure of it. No matter who Jia and her people were before all of this...they're still kids. Kids who act like they're part of some militia. That doesn't happen overnight."

"But other things do..." I heard myself say. We'd experienced it once, back on the farm. Saw a woman attacked by a small pack of zeds, heard her screaming, and couldn't get to her in time. Something in me had clicked the moment I heard her screams subside, and I'd gone after the zeds, anger and adrenaline fueling my slaughter. It was

Joey and Daniel with me that day, and I remembered being thankful that Luke hadn't seen me lose my mind.

It wasn't something I liked to think about, but now it was also the only reason I knew that three days was more than enough time for Luke to turn. Because I'd insisted on bringing the woman's body back to the farm, and I dug her grave myself, with Luke keeping watch, obviously not understanding my need to do this one kindness.

But I forgot to bash this stranger's head in. All of us had. I was lost in my fit of madness, while Joey and Daniel were clearly having trouble digesting the situation as a whole – what I'd done, what I was insisting on doing.

She turned before I could even finish digging the damn grave. Both Luke and I were so shocked at first that she was already writhing around, a brand-new zed trying to find its feet, before I threw him the shovel and he drove it down into her face as hard as he could.

He'd had to do it two more times before she finally stopped moving.

It was Daniel who finally ripped me away from dwelling on the sickening sound the shovel had made. "Charlie?" His voice was soft, hesitant – *scared*.

I turned to look at him. "If Virginia's right, we could have a chance. With Luke there, we could maybe take care of this whole mess."

Virginia looked at me, her eyes bright with concern. "What do you mean, with Luke there? He's their *prisoner*." The way she said it, I wondered if she thought I'd lost my mind.

*And she doesn't even know how much you've questioning your own sanity lately.* I shook my head to clear it, but Virginia took this as me disagreeing about Luke's status. "Charlie, you know they'll lock him up – maybe even tie him up – the moment they get back to the school." She spoke slowly, making her calm tone only seem *more* forced.

"Yes, Virginia, I know," I said, hating how tired – how *defeated* – I sounded just then. I looked around the room, making sure to acknowledge each of them in turn before continuing, "Luke's infection started spreading again. And the more it spreads, the faster it spreads. He doesn't have three days."

My admission was met with silence, so I finally explained, "This was his plan. He'll get loose before he – "

"Jia and most of her people might be kids, but they're not idiots," Mike snapped. "He'll die there. Alone. And then they'll take him down, maybe before he even does any damage. Why didn't you let them take *me*? Luke would have had a chance here. Richard could have saved him!"

"Some people don't want to be saved," I said, knowing that I wasn't only referring to Luke. "Besides, what's done is done. Now we have to figure out how to carry out the rest of Luke's plan. Ethan, is there paper in here somewhere? And pens?"

The only acknowledgement I received was Ethan standing up and moving around behind the desk. He opened one drawer, took something out, and then bent to open another. I heard that one close, and when he returned to our little circle he had a fistful of writing implements in one hand and several sheets of computer paper in the other. "Thank you," I said as he handed everything to me.

I laid out a few pieces of paper and handed everyone a pen before bending to draw a large box on the corner of the paper closest to me. I wrote "ZOO" inside of it, but suddenly Ethan knocked my hand aside. "The zoo isn't *square*," he said, clearly exasperated.

Out of the corner of my eye, I saw Virginia lean forward. "Of course it's not, Ethan. Charlie knows that. But we have to draw a map, and quickly. Things can be different shapes."

My hand hovered over the paper as Ethan stared down at what I'd done. "Will everything be a different shape?" he finally asked.

"Yes, of course," his mother replied brightly. "All straight lines." She looked at me, and I gave a quick nod.

Ethan sat back and took a deep breath. "What else will be on the map?"

"The school, for one. I think it would be somewhere over there." I gestured across the circle to my left, at the paper in front of Daniel, but Mike shook his head. "It's farther west than that." He turned the paper horizontally and drew the hospital and school. It was all too close, but I understood what he was trying to do.

The map took us another twenty minutes or so, and in the end it was a messy patchwork that barely even approximated the city. But we knew how to get from point A to point B, and I'd told them that two of us needed to go keep watch on the school. In the end, it all came down to choosing who would go and who would stay.

"You're stuck here," Virginia told me. I knew that she was right, but hated it all the same. "And to be honest, so are Ethan and I. Whoever goes needs to be fast."

"Lauren," Daniel said. "She runs. Did that half-marathon in Charleston once. She's not the fastest person out there, but she can do the distance. Probably better than any of the rest of us."

"She's safe right now," I reminded him. "They don't even know she's here."

"So they won't miss her when she's gone. Trust me, Charlie, if we tell her what we need, she'll want to go. If we don't tell her...well, that'll have to be on you."

Before I could respond, Mike spoke. "I'll go with her. I'll stay behind, and she can come back."

I rounded on him. "No. Jia is already too interested in you. If you get caught – "

"Then I get caught. You and Virginia and Ethan need to stay here. And I won't stop Daniel from telling Lauren that we need her, which means he needs to be here for Mabel. Richard is out because he's our damn *doctor*. And anyway, I'll find the school – and a spot we can use to keep an eye on it – faster than anyone else here." Before Mike even finished his tirade, I knew that he was right, and it took everything in me to not remind him that we were all I had left. My mother must be gone by now, Joey was dead and buried, and I would never see Luke alive again. Yes, Daniel and Lauren and Mabel had joined us early on, but only Holden and Mike had been with me since what I considered the very beginning. *Of the end, anyway.*

"First thing tomorrow, then," I relented. "Ethan, can you find a way to get Mike and Lauren out of here without being seen?"

He sat up very straight and nodded. "Yeah, I know just where to take them."

I let myself relax a bit. I knew that I could trust Ethan; he hadn't failed us so far. "Show Lauren where you've stored things. Only Lauren, okay? She can take what she needs, and they don't know she's with us." I didn't bother saying anything more – the implications were obvious. If she was caught, they might not think to ask her about the zoo.

Or at least I hoped that was the case.

"Some of us should get some sleep," Virginia suggested, "and Charlie, you need it most." I opened my mouth to protest, but she held up a hand and shook her head. "Mike can sit outside the door first. He'll need more rest later. Trust me, there's no way anyone outside this zoo could see him. Mike, once the rain stops – my guess it that won't happen for a couple of hours yet – come get me and Daniel and one of us will take your spot while the other goes to the gate. Charlie, we'll wake you up when it's your turn."

"You must be crazy if you think I'm actually going to be able to sleep right now."

Virginia ignored me and turned to her son. "Ethan, can you go get some of the medicine Richard gave you to hide? Look for the bottles with my name on them."

Ethan nodded and disappeared through the door. Mike gave me an almost apologetic smile as he picked up one of the chairs and lugged it out into the hall.

"What about Bobby?" I asked. "I *need* to talk to him."

"You will. Before you take your shift, if you want. But not right now. Richard can handle that kid for a while...we need your mind clear for what's to come."

"And you think knocking me out with a bunch of meds for some indeterminate amount of time is going to make my mind *clear*?" I scoffed.

"It's better than no sleep at all," Virginia shrugged. I glared at her, my jaw clenched tight to keep me from saying things I knew I shouldn't. The worst part was that she was right – as busy as my mind was, I could feel my body falling apart. I was weak, barely able to keep myself from shaking – although my whole being was still tense from the encounter with Jia, I hadn't gotten proper sleep in days and eventually I would collapse. *Probably sooner rather than later.*

Eventually Ethan returned and Virginia rifled through the little orange containers he'd brought back with him, finally popping one open and handing me two elongated white pills. "Ambien," she informed me, closing my hand around it. "Let's go find you some water and a place to lay down."

"I brought water," Ethan said, holding out a dusty bottle of Dasani.

"Thanks," I replied, hoping I sounded more grateful than I felt. *You need to sleep, stop being such an asshole.*

I could tell that Virginia was trying to figure out where she could put me, so I took it upon myself to head for the door. "I'll take the bed Luke was using."

Virginia coughed. "Are...are you sure?"

"So what if it's morbid? It's a bed," I grunted, making my way to the clean room as fast as I could, hoping that Virginia wouldn't follow me.

She didn't, and once I'd closed the door behind me and settled myself on the bed I gave in and swallowed the pills, washing them down with half the bottle of water before setting it on the medical stand that was still positioned close by. I lay back and stared into the darkness, my eyes slowly growing accustomed to the dark room. At some point, I seemed to drift into a strange immobilized state – not quite awake, not quite asleep – and I was frozen in place as I hallucinated people climbing through the single high window on the wall to my left. The worst part was that they weren't even zeds – they were nameless, faceless people, but the Ambien and my own personal terror kept me prone, my brain trying to make my arms or legs move and my body refusing to respond.

The next thing I knew, there was a hand on my arm. The dim but warm purple of twilight was filtering in from the window, and when I opened my eyes my first instinct was to look up at it. The bars were still in place, and when I turned back to the person trying to wake me, it was Mike's face that I saw.

"We're not safe," I mumbled. "Nothing is safe. I can't promise to keep you or anyone else alive."

Mike sighed and pulled away. "You don't have to, Charlie. We need you, but not for that. It's on us to stay alive. You can't be everyone's hero."

I squeezed my eyes shut again, trying to work the sleepiness out of them. "That implies I'm someone's," I joked as I stretched my arms and legs out and sat up, swinging my legs over the side and waiting for a wave of dizziness to subside. I knew it had to be the meds wearing off, but I needed a jolt of caffeine – or something similar – if I was going to be watching the front gate soon.

"Yeah, I guess I forgot, you're trying to be our anti-hero," Mike replied, shaking his head at me.

"You read a lot of comic books before, didn't you?"

"Whenever I could get my hands on them. Found some of yours back at the farm but didn't really think I should bring them along when we left. Let me tell you, veterinary texts are nowhere near as fun."

I realized yet again that I had next to no idea what everyone else had been doing since we reached the zoo. Even when we were on watch, we'd had more down time than not. "I imagine they aren't," I snorted. "But hey, maybe we'll get into that school and snag some books from the library. I'm guessing you never had time to read *The Scarlet Letter*? Or *Heart of Darkness*? Damn, those are the only books I remember from my junior and senior years."

"Yeah, you're showing your age, alright. But nope, didn't get to those. We were supposed to be starting...*Old Man and the Sea*, I think. We'd just finished *I Know Why the Caged Bird Sings*."

"Maya Angelou." I nodded approvingly. "I loved her. Didn't really appreciate Hemingway in high school, but you should read that one. And some of his other books. I had a bit of an obsession with him a few years back, visited all these places where he lived, read a bunch of books about him. I could tell you some stuff that would make you really appreciate his writing in a way I never could when I was your age."

"We'll see," Mike grinned, and I knew that he was mostly humoring me. "But for now, you get to keep an eye on the gate."

That was our life at the moment – no time for reading lists or book discussions or bonding over anything positive like that. *But maybe, if we can end this thing with Jia once and for all...*

"Yeah. Back to the old grind." I finally stood up, stretching again before making my way to the open door.

"'The old grind'? Now you're *really* showing your age," Mike called as I left him behind. I lifted my right hand and gave him the finger.

"Holden's coming with me this time. Can't believe I let someone who's probably never even read *Catcher* keep an eye on him so much lately."

"I told you I hadn't read it right after I met you!" Mike reminded me. I stopped, the sudden memory of our drive to the farm overwhelming me. I turned and gave him a sad smile, tapping the side of my head.

"Yup, my memory's already going. See you later, kid." I waved and stepped backward through the door, turning on my heel and striding toward the front of the building as quickly as I could. I didn't know what would happen next, but if I could leave Mike with some positive memories...well, that was something.

I hoped.

## LESSON LEARNED

*You can't save everyone.*

\* \* \* \* \* \* \*

Virginia was at the door, Holden stretched out on the ground by her side. "I thought he could use some fresh air," she said as he stood, stretched, and ambled over to greet me. I bent down and scratched his head, burying my face in his fur for a moment. He smelled awful, but I didn't care. Being close to him calmed me.

"Thanks," I told Virginia. "I'm going to take him up front with me. I'm guessing Daniel is there?"

"Yes, and I imagine he's ready to come back and spend some time with his wife."

"What about Richard?"

"Mike is coming out here and I'll be giving Richard a break and watching that boy for a bit."

I stood back up and gave her a shrewd look. "You guys really don't want me anywhere near Bobby, do you?"

"Correct," Virginia replied matter-of-factly. "Jia and her people know enough about you. If he ends up back at that school, we don't want them knowing any more."

"I'll have my time with him."

"If there *is* time, maybe Richard will take you to see him. But Charlie, think about the group as a whole here, not just about what you want. I'll see you when your shift is over."

Virginia was dismissing me, and my head was still too fuzzy to think of a way to continue the conversation. "Come on, Holden." I walked away, my dog trotting along beside me. I tried to push the whole Bobby situation out of my head, but I knew that I would end up dwelling on it throughout my watch. *Screw Virginia. Screw Richard,* I thought to myself...but even as I did, I realized that they were making the right choice.

Not that I would allow myself to admit that any time soon.

When I reached the gate, I saw Daniel standing in front of it, staring straight ahead. I couldn't even tell if he was looking *at* the gate or *through* it, but I had a feeling it didn't matter. He was in another world. Thankfully he started as soon as he heard me approach; some part of him was still on guard. "Go on back to headquarters," I told him. "Your turn to rest."

Daniel scratched his head and sighed. "As if I could."

"I think you will," I insisted. He gave me a confused look, but I just waved him off. "Go on. Enjoy it while you can."

He held my eyes for a long moment. Finally he nodded, though I wasn't sure if it was in understanding or simply because he wanted the conversation to be over. "See you later," he said, then leaned in to whisper, "There's some water and snacks stashed behind the rock wall. We had to bring something out here with all of us stuck watching this damn gate for hours. If you go into the little nook and sit under the trees, there's almost no way someone could see you, anyway."

I squeezed his shoulder before he walked away. I hadn't thought about food since I'd woken up, but now that I knew it was there I realized I was starving – and that I had no idea when Holden had last eaten. If Daniel had seen anything out of place, he would have hinted at it. I hoped that things would remain calm for the next half hour or so; only then could I justify tucking myself away to get some food in my stomach.

Once Daniel had disappeared down the path I approached the gate. I stood there for several minutes, Holden close by my side, but I didn't see or hear anything out of the ordinary. *It's almost too quiet.* I wandered down the fence line, first to my left and then back to the right, stopping to listen several times. I was almost relieved when Holden eventually stopped following me and headed back to stretch out against the stone wall. I knew that if he didn't sense anything, we were safe – *for now*. I waited as long as I could, waited until it was truly night, though with a bright moon that bathed everything in a white light that seemed far too pure for this world.

Finally my grumbling stomach got the better of me and I made a beeline for the nook across from the gate, unbuttoning my jeans along the way, hoping that if anyone was watching me they would assume I was just going to the bathroom. The small cache that I found after fumbling around a bit – it was much darker back under the trees – included a warm soda, which I gulped down so fast that I could barely quiet myself when I needed to burp. I almost laughed at the ridiculousness of it all, but I was too busy trying to dig some beef jerky out of its bag and hoping that

I hadn't already been gone too long. I passed a piece of the dried meat to Holden and then gestured toward the little pond on the other side of the wall. "Go on, boy." He gave me a cautious look before clambering over the stones and lying down by the water. I couldn't imagine that the jerky or the water in the pond were healthy for him, but I tossed him another piece before forcing a couple down my throat, guzzling as much water as I could, redoing my pants and then heading back to the gate, straightening my shirt as I walked across the open area. Once again I stood and listened, and once again I was greeted with an eerie silence.

The night stretched on in just that way. Richard arrived not long after the sky began to lighten, the first hints of dawn, but even then it was hard to leave the front gate. *If things don't go badly, this is where Jia will return.* I knew that I was being ridiculous, so I relented when Richard insisted on taking my place – but I wasn't ready to go back to headquarters, especially not if I wasn't going to be allowed to pay Bobby a visit.

"I'm going to scout the perimeter. Who's at the door?"

"Mike, though we should probably give him a break soon. Daniel is in the office."

I assumed that meant that Daniel had had his time with his wife and daughter. "I'll get Daniel to take over for Mike when I get back there, but someone needs to make sure that back pen is still secure."

Richard looked uncertain, but after a long pause he assented. With no time to repair the back fence, we couldn't go any longer without checking things out, making sure that no zeds – or people – could get in through our makeshift fix. I didn't bother saying anything about Bobby; I simply whistled quietly for Holden and made my way up the opposite path.

After all, this may be the last chance I had to visit Joey's grave.

The hard rains had nearly flattened the mound of earth that covered my brother's body, but the sun had baked everything dry while I slept. I dug into my back pocket and pulled out the little drawstring bag that I'd found in my car. It had probably once held something that wasn't useful in this new world – a USB drive, I thought. Who knows where that had gone, or even what had been on it. *It doesn't matter.* The little padded black bag was the only thing I had that would allow me to carry a piece of my brother anywhere I went, so I plunged my fingers into the hard-packed earth, palming just enough of it to fill the bag halfway. I knotted it shut and tied it to one of the front belt loops on my jeans before taking a moment to brush as much of the loose dirt as I could back into place. "I don't know what's gonna happen, Joe," I whispered, pressing my hand into the ground. "But if I leave the zoo, I hope you know that I'm not really leaving you here alone." I reached up and squeezed the pouch before standing and moving back to the path. I took a right, bracing myself for the worst as I made my way toward the breached pen.

As I got closer, I used the tree line for an extra bit of protection, practically tiptoeing, tensing every time Holden's nails clicked against the pavement. Was it odd that I found myself wondering if I should trim them? I wasn't sure. All I knew was that the broken fence was our biggest weak spot, and I hated myself for not insisting that someone check on it sooner.

And yet, when I finally approached the fence, I realized that everything was silent. Even in the zombie apocalypse, there was wildlife – especially birds. They'd long ago stopped singing the way they had before, but that had only made the other sounds more prevalent. The branches rustling when they landed, the beat of wings as they fled from approaching threats. The fact that I'd heard nothing of the sort all night was more than a little disquieting.

See? Even when wallowing in my own anxiety, I can still make puns.

The enclosure was just the way we'd left it, the gate sealed shut and not a single zed wandering around inside.

I knew better than to assume that this was pure luck. I gazed up at the top of the hill, where I could see the ragged edges of the fence still gaping open.

Despite the sun beating down on me and the thick mugginess of the post-storm air, the hair on my arms stood up. *They're watching you.*

Holden whined. "I know, boy," I murmured, standing as still as I possibly could, my eyes darting left and right, hoping to see something, *anything*. I waited several minutes before finally giving in and moving on, continuing to my right, forcing myself to not look over my shoulder as I made my way back to the office building. When I reached it, I saw Mike sitting in the chair by the door, and I stood back for a bit, watching him fidget. He was obviously exhausted. I sighed and moved toward him, Holden bounding in front of me, stopping only to nose Mike's hand, begging to be petted.

"Your turn to sleep," I told him, forcing a smile. "Go grab Daniel; he can keep watch here for a while."

"What about you?" Mike asked.

I shrugged. "I've got things to do."

"You know you're not supposed to talk to Bobby."

"Yes, thank you, that's been made very clear." I hated how exasperated I sounded, but Mike's eyes met mine and I saw his own frustration. "Sorry. I'll stay here until Daniel comes out. Then I have some things to go over. Make sure the others stay where they are."

After all, someone had to make sure that Lauren understood what she was getting herself into – and something told me that Daniel wasn't that person.

Mike bit his lip but nodded his ascension. He left Holden and I outside the door and within minutes Daniel came out. My first thought was that he looked like a dead man walking, and I tried to push that observation out of my head as Daniel dropped into the chair without saying a word to me. Before I went inside I reached down and squeezed his shoulder. "It's just reconnaissance. You said it yourself – she's fast. And she's smart." I pulled away, but paused in the doorway. "None of you have ever been a burden, Daniel. And now it's Lauren's time to shine."

He didn't say anything. He was upset, maybe with me, but there wasn't anything more I could do, and certainly nothing I could *undo*.

By the time I reached the office, Mike had already disappeared. Lauren and Mabel were sitting on the floor, well away from the windows' line of sight. If Virginia was right, this was unnecessary, but I appreciated it nonetheless. Our half-assed map was still spread out on the floor; obviously anyone who'd been in the room had gone out of their way to leave it undisturbed.

I sat down next to Lauren. "Where's Ethan?"

"With Virginia." *Great, everyone but me gets to hang out with that Bobby asshole.*

Mabel started squirming in Lauren's arms. She whispered, "Don't touch the papers," before releasing her daughter to play with Holden.

"Over there," I said firmly, and Holden gave Mabel a quick lick on the cheek before retreating off to the side.

"He's a good dog," Lauren observed.

"The best," I agreed, smiling as I watched Holden stretch out on the floor and allow Mabel to clamber up on his side.

"You know I need to go."

"Yeah. I do."

"Daniel..."

"He suggested it. He doesn't want it, but he knows it's what's best. I don't want anyone to go, least of all you or Mike." I paused. "You're my people."

Lauren looked at me. "We know, Charlie. But we're our own people, too...and it's past time for me to carry my own weight."

"Just...promise me you'll remember how to get back. If not, Mike – "

"I'll remember. I've practically memorized this – " she gestured at the papers – "and I'm good with directions. As long as it's light when I return, I'll be fine."

"And if it's dark when you're on your way back?" I asked, knowing it was a possibility.

"Then it will be harder. But that doesn't change anything. And it might even help that it will be dark when we head out."

"You'll leave tonight, then?"

"Yes."

I didn't know what else to say. I assumed Mike was in Luke's old bed now, so I gathered a few of the ratty blankets Jia's people had left behind and made myself a nest in the far corner of the room. We sat in silence for some time, and I was left wondering who would come to tell us what was next. The light coming in through the single high window became steadily brighter and warmer, and in the end, it was Virginia who came for us. I felt my stomach twist at the sight of her.

"Who's with Bobby?"

"He's sleeping."

"You really believe that?"

She shrugged. "It doesn't matter. I'm the messenger now, and we need to do a bit of shuffling. Can you go grab Daniel from the door and send him to me?"

I knew that they were still doing everything in their power to keep me away from Bobby, and a childish anger reared its ugly head. "You look like shit," I told her.

"I'm sure. I'll be waking up Mike. He'll get you at the door and you can relieve Richard at the gate."

*This is it, then.* I'd apparently wasted a lot of time not sleeping; I knew I wouldn't be relieved before dawn the next day, which meant that Ethan would help Mike and Lauren sneak out while I was on watch...and who knew if I would ever see them again.

The only thing I could think of to say was a quote from a TV show I'd watched once upon a time. I held my hand out to Lauren. "May we meet again."

She cocked her head. "I know where that comes from."

I smiled indulgently. "It wasn't always a bad thing. And Lauren – you know that we'll take care of Mabel. And Daniel, if he needs it. No matter what."

Lauren glanced at Mabel, who was napping with her head on Holden's chest. "I know. But here's hoping it doesn't come to that."

"Time for you to get going, Charlie. And you should keep Holden with you," Virginia insisted, and as much as I hated taking my dog away from Mabel just then, I knew that she was right.

"Holden, come," I ordered. His head jerked up and he blinked at me for a moment before easing his way out from under Mabel's head. Lauren rushed over to replace him, and somehow the little girl continued sleeping. As I left the room, I decided to make one final request. "Virginia, can you please go stay with Bobby until Richard gets back? I doubt he's sleeping, and until he leaves here, he's a threat." She sighed at first, but then nodded her agreement. Knowing that was all the agreement I was going to get, I made my way out the door.

By the time I reached the gate, the sun had set and the sky was once again the pale purple of twilight. "You're going to have a long shift," Richard warned me.

"So are you. No rest for the wicked." It took everything in me to not smirk at him, knowing that he would be relieving Virginia, continuing their attempt to keep me from Bobby. "Anything I need to know about?"

"No. Quiet as the grave," Richard replied.

It was a sad attempt at a joke. "That's what worries me," I sighed. "I'll take it from here."

Richard bobbed his head in a brief acknowledgement; I turned away and didn't bother watching him leave. This time Holden refused to leave my side as I paced behind the gate, but as the sky became darker and I was once again left with nothing but moon- and starlight to see by, I finally sat down facing the entrance, folded my legs into the butterfly pose and tried to tell myself that I was comfortable sitting like that on the unforgiving pavement.

Hours passed; I couldn't count them, and they probably felt longer than they were, but eventually I knew that Mike and Lauren must have left, and here I was guarding the zoo when only Daniel and Mabel remained from my original group. For the first time since before everything had started, I couldn't tamp down my anxiety, and I found myself wondering whether maybe Richard and Virginia and Ethan were actually in league with Jia and her people already. *If so, they're damned good actors.* Deep down I knew that it wasn't very likely that they'd dealt with Jia before – at least not directly – but I couldn't stop thinking about how badly they could betray us now, if they really wanted to.

I don't know what time it was when Holden first heard the noise. He was stretched out next to me, his chin on his paws, watching the gate just as I was, when suddenly his ears perked up and he lifted his head. By this time the moon had dropped in the sky and everything seemed just a bit lighter, though the birds were still quiet. I laid a hand on Holden's shoulder.

"What's up, boy?"

He let out a low growl, something he'd rarely done before or since the world had gone to shit, and I immediately jumped to my feet. I moved toward the fence, narrowing my eyes, craning my head, and breathing through my nose, wondering for far too long how soon it would be before I finally sensed what Holden had.

In the end, it was the crackle of a radio that caught my attention. Whoever possessed it was hiding just up the hill to my left, likely either prone in the underbrush or perched on a tree branch. The second time I heard something, it wasn't just a crackle – it was a broken message that included the words "all...return.......attack".

Holden was beside me, his hackles raised, and then I heard someone whisper far too loudly and harshly for someone who was supposed to be a hidden spy. "This is an emergency channel only!"

"Fuck your watches! .......need backup!"

Everything went silent. Whoever was out there must have turned off their radio; it was several minutes before I heard anything else. This time, the person hiding at the top of the hill made a violent sound that was probably a curse word I couldn't make out from so far away. Quite a bit of rustling and scrambling followed, and then the noises faded, and once again the world was silent.

## LESSON LEARNED

*Silence isn't always golden.*

# Interlude
## *How It Happens*

I keep repeating my name to myself, as if that will do some good. *You're Luke. Luke. Luke.*

It doesn't help.

I can feel the infection moving through my arm. I've felt it since the very beginning, really...starting in what was left of my fingers and spreading through me like a parasite. It's as if something is clamping down on my veins, one by one.

They didn't blindfold me when they were leading me to the school, so even if I don't turn, I know I won't survive this.

I wish I'd said more to Charlie, but at the same time I know she doesn't need me like I need her. It's scary, loving someone more than they can ever understand. Not that she doesn't love me - she does, I know that - but it's not what it should be. It's passion fueled by the adrenaline caused by the constant dangers we've faced.

I want to be okay with her not loving me the way I love her. It's better for everyone, really, because even before I understood that Jia never planned on letting me rejoin my group, I knew that I was living on borrowed time.

I'm hot, and it's not just the muggy weather. A fever is feasting on my body, and soon even the bandages that wrap halfway up my arm won't hide the fact that my blood is turning black.

That I'm becoming a zed, and there's no way to stop it.

At least I know more than Jia thinks I do. I know that she and Monika love each other. I know that Monika is a far kinder person than Jia. *But is she kind enough?*

When Monika told me that I was the one they'd be taking, she'd patted me down to make sure I wasn't carrying any weapons. I had this notebook and a pen on me, and I begged her to let me keep them. She was more worried about the pen, but I told her that I loved these people – *my* people. That I wanted to protect them and wouldn't do anything to jeopardize that. That if working with Jia and her group was what we needed to do to survive, I understood.

I meant all of that. I don't just love Charlie, I love all of them.

I know that she did it out of pity, but she let me keep these two small things, and I'm grateful. I will record what I can. I want people to know what it feels like to become a zed.

*******

This isn't quite what I was expecting. I'm locked in the nurse's office, of all places. They wanted her to look at my arm. I suppose I should be happy that she hasn't returned yet. I don't know how long I've been here, but it was getting close to sunset when we arrived and since then everything has gone dark.

At least there's a moon. I figure I've got several more nights of decent light because of that. Problem is, it's also bright enough to see that the infection has already moved too far up my arm for my bandages to cover it. My mind is fighting to stay awake, but my body is telling me to give in and go to sleep. I'm not sure how much longer I can fight it.

*******

I fell asleep, and now it's morning. I don't think I've been disturbed. My entire arm has gone numb, but I still feel the dull pain of the spreading poison as it moves down my chest and up into my neck. I thought I would have longer.

*******

The nurse finally showed up. Monika was with her, but Mrs. Downing told her to leave as soon as she saw my...condition. Ha, that's some positive thinking. 'Condition.'

I don't know what Monika saw before she left, or what she'll say to anyone else. I don't think she's a bad kid, and Mrs. Downing isn't so bad either.

She asked me if I'd known what would happen when they took me. I told her the truth. I mentioned that she'd met Charlie and Daniel, and her face softened. I think she's a good woman who's been put in a bad spot. We talked for a while, and I helped her work out the few kinks in what was, to be honest, a pretty good plan already. If some of my people get here within the proper time frame, there's a damn good chance everything will work out for the best. You know, for everyone except me. Ha. Ha. Ha.

Jesus, thank God I'm right handed. This pain is...well. It's bad, and I can handle pain. Or at least I thought I could. If someone finds this notebook, please understand that no matter how fast we turn, no matter what awful things we do after that...getting there was horrible, too.

*******

I met Dominic. The nurse wasn't here at the time, but I think they did that on purpose. He told me that she knew what was happening to me. He told me that they were 'prepared'. I guess I'm not thinking straight, because I don't know what that meant. He still locked the door behind him when he left.

Mrs. Downing came back and gave me a turtleneck to wear. It's hot as hell and the shirt didn't smell good to begin with, but I have it on anyway. I want to hide this just as much as they do. She locked the door, too, but then, it's only the end of my first full day here, and I know now that we're all just biding our time.

*******

Jia visited me in the middle of the night, asking me about the zoo, about my people. I could barely concentrate and I think she assumed her people were starving me, because she called for food and water and told me to get my shit together for tomorrow.

I'm not hungry, and water does nothing to stop the burning feeling that has crept up my neck and down toward my heart. I can't even look at what's happening, so damn right I'm thankful for this miserable turtleneck.

Even if it feels like there's a hand wrapped around my throat, slowly squeezing the life out of me.

Mrs. Downing showed up again — Jia must have sent her. She was supposed to make sure I ate.

She asked me if I'd touched the food. I hadn't. "Good," she said, and I know that means they have other mouths to feed. Probably too many. She reminded me that I had to do my best to stay lucid, and then she was gone.

Why are they so concerned with me getting my shit together or being lucid when it's all these other people who should worry about staying in one piece? The whole damn time she was here, all I could do was concentrate on when she would leave again. She smelled more like food than the plate of baked beans and canned carrots Jia left for me.

I don't want to hurt Mrs. Downing, but I have to assume that I will. So yeah, Charlie, if you ever read this...I'm already rethinking the whole thing.

*******

A sort of paranoia that I've never known before has gripped me. I almost tore every page of this notebook into shreds a few minutes ago, because what if someone discovers it before I can even do the damage I'm supposed to do?

Instead I hid it for a while and focused on finding a way out of this room. Not that that mattered or changed anything - Dominic came back and told me that he'd be standing guard at my door this evening. Most of my second day here is gone, and I don't even know how it happened. All I know is that the kid kept his distance and a military regulation knife in his hand the whole time he talked to me.

I asked him how he knew it would happen that night. Apparently Jia came to visit and found me sleeping, so she stormed off to make the nurse come check on me. Dominic didn't have to explain that somehow, some way, Mrs. Downing had staved Jia off.

I'm more worried about the fact that I don't remember falling asleep. I don't remember waking up. All I know is this fire in my head, this feeling that my heart is shrinking in on itself.

And when I blink my eyes, sometimes I see nothing but shades of red and black.

But at least it's still just sometimes.

*******

Dominic has been outside the door for a while. He's left it open. I hope he's prepared, because I'm not. I've lost so much of myself, and I know there's no way to get any of it back. I'm going to die. I'm going to turn. Or maybe it happens at the same time, when you've been infected like this. I wonder if Mrs. Downing knows. I wonder if any good can come of this. I don't care about being a martyr or a sacrifice, I just want to know that my friends are safe. I couldn't keep Cheryl safe, couldn't keep Joey safe, couldn't even keep myself safe.

But Charlie can do anything. I both love and hate her for that. So if you find what I've written here, if you run into a woman named Charlie, make sure she knows how it happens. And know that if anyone can protect you, she can. Just don't assume that she'll agree to do so.

I won't be able to write again. The door is open. Night has fallen. It won't be long.

# Chapter 12
# Fight

*There could be more than one of them.*
*Bullshit. You only heard one radio.*

Holden had long since sat down, still on alert but no longer as interested in things beyond the gate as he was in me. I knew that I shouldn't abandon my post, tried to tell myself that maybe Lauren and Mike had witnessed something and that she would be back soon.

In the end, my impatience got the better of me. I waited as long as I could, waited until the sky went from gray to pale pink, and finally decided that enough was enough. I ran back to the office building, Holden easily keeping pace by my side. Virginia was guarding the door now, her expression changing from merely watchful to concerned as she saw me approach. She stood and walked toward me, holding out her arm until I was forced to a stop. "What happened?" Her voice was worried yet stern in a way that made me more angry than anything else.

"I don't know. I don't know. I think they must have only had one person watching the gate. Holden, he heard something, and then I did too – a radio, they were calling for help at the school. Whoever was there ran off. I waited but didn't see or hear anything else, and maybe I should have kept waiting until someone came to get me, but we need to get moving. Even if that call had nothing to do with Luke, there's *something* going on at the school. What matters is that we're not their first priority right now."

"What about Lauren and Mike?" she snapped.

"When did they leave?"

"Hours ago; it couldn't have been long after Richard came back. He had me take Daniel's place here so that Mabel wouldn't be alone."

I tried to do the math in my head. "If they were able to take an almost straight route to the school, it was a couple of miles at most. A little over an hour, less if they didn't have any problems." *More if they did.* I shook my head, refusing to waste time on bullshit worries like that right now.

"Then we have to hope that Lauren is on her way back. But I'll need to take Daniel with me. And Richard, which means you're left guarding Bobby."

"No. Richard needs to stay. I'll go. Ethan can watch the door. We'll have to hope no one shows up at the front gate."

*Or in the back pen.*

I kept that thought to myself, too.

"If you insist on going, then I think you and I can handle this ourselves," Virginia said pointedly.

"You know I respect you, but you and I can't do this on our own. We need a third person. We need more than that, really, but three will have to do."

"And Mike? Do you think he'll want to come back here and just leave us to it? Four's better than three, if you want to play it that way. Or he can be the third person."

"Much as I hate to do it, I'll give him the choice of joining us or coming back to the zoo. But we..." I paused and bit down hard on my lip. I couldn't bring myself to say it, couldn't bring myself to point out that we had no idea what had happened or that either Mike or Lauren were safe. I needed Daniel, which means I had to assume that Lauren was safe and on her way back to the zoo.

Otherwise I was a monster who was putting Mabel's only remaining parent in danger.

"I don't like this," Virginia grumbled.

"Neither do I," I admitted. *But I didn't like letting Luke go either, and that happened anyway.*

If anything this was a reminder of how soft Virginia, Ethan, and Richard were. Would she even be able to handle herself once she was outside the safety of the zoo?

Virginia's voice brought me back to the present. "Charlie? Charlie, I thought you said we needed to get moving."

"Yeah. Yes. We need weapons. Guns. Knives. My bat, if it's still tucked away somewhere."

"I'll get Ethan. You go take your minute with Bobby, and then it's on you to convince Daniel to come with us."

"He'll come. In the end this is all about protecting this place, protecting our people. And his daughter is one of our people." *Do you hear the words coming out of your mouth right now, Charlie? Jesus, you sound like Luke.* "But hey, thanks for the last-minute chance to talk to the kid."

"If you think I don't know sarcasm when I hear it, you're wrong. But I need to find Ethan, you need to warn Richard, and we need to find out if Bobby knows why their guards would be called back to the school."

"Fine." I opened the door, but before I could step inside Virginia cupped a hand over my shoulder.

"Charlie, don't undo what Richard and I have done."

"What's that supposed to mean?" I asked, wondering if I should be merely annoyed or outright angry.

"Be *nice*," she insisted.

"I'll try my best. Go find Ethan and gather up as many weapons as you can carry." I turned and let the door slam behind me before she could give me any more unsolicited advice.

I found Richard sitting in a chair in the room where he'd once held Luke captive, only now it was Bobby in the cage. "We're moving," I told him, barely glancing at Bobby.

"What do you mean?"

"I mean that I was at the gate and whoever was watching it got a call on their radio and ran off, so some of us are going to see what's happening at the school."

I heard Bobby scoff. "You have no idea what you're dealing with."

I stepped forward, practically pressing myself against the bars of his cage. "Oh, I think Jia is the one who has no idea what she's dealing with. Luke – the man she took? He was bitten quite a while ago. We tried to fix it, but we couldn't. And yeah, she left someone guarding our gate, but he's gone – got an emergency call on his radio and ran back to headquarters. My guess is that anyone else watching this place got the same call...and yet...you're still here. Why do you think that is?"

He tried to shrug me off. "Doesn't matter. Jia wouldn't have left me here if she thought I wasn't safe. You want to make the first move? Hurt me, and she'll do ten times worse to you."

"I can handle Jia." I forced a laugh. "But can she handle a zed in her wannabe safe zone? After all, what else could cause her to recall her guards?"

"Charlie." Richard's tone was one of warning, but I refused to heed it. Instead, I crouched down in front of the cage and stared at Bobby.

"Your friends who were watching this zoo are gone. Jia took the wrong person captive. Luke was infected, and now your people are suffering. Even if Jia herself survives this, we know that we have sympathizers in your ranks. You *had* more people – but you don't anymore." I was mostly playing a guessing game now, and the worried look that crossed Bobby's face probably made me feel better than it should have. "Richard, can you go talk to Virginia? We're going to need you to...play a different role, for a little while. Hopefully not too long."

He hesitated, but I stared him down, hoping that he could see how important this was, that I wasn't just trying to trick him into leaving the room – although of course part of my goal was ending up alone with Bobby. "I won't be far behind you," I finally promised, and with a frustrated grunt he stood and left us.

"What, he's gone so now you're going to torture me for information?" Bobby's expression was once again vacant, as if he wasn't at all concerned about his fate.

I laughed. "Why would I need to torture you? We've already gained the upper hand, kid. No, I've come here to tell you that we'll be bringing you back to the school. That way you can see firsthand what happened to your fellow child soldiers."

"Child soldiers?" he repeated, his eyes glinting. "Fuck off. You know nothing about us."

"Oh, I don't know much, you're right about that. But I know enough. And I know you're coming with us."

The truth was, it wasn't safe, leaving him here. Unless by some slim chance Lauren returned before Virginia, Daniel, and I left, Richard would need to watch Mabel, which meant leaving Bobby alone. I wasn't ready to do that, and even if I was, I knew that this kid needed to witness Jia's downfall – that if he didn't see it firsthand, he probably wouldn't believe that it had happened.

And I didn't want Bobby to still be here at the zoo if for some reason I didn't return. That was always a possibility – my not returning – and it was one that I accepted wholeheartedly. My people had been very clear that they didn't expect me to protect them; I still felt like I *should* do so, but I had to imagine that Luke was gone, had to remind myself that if I came back to this place it wouldn't be a permanent thing. *Not anymore.*

Maybe I'd been lying to myself from the start, believing that we could stay anywhere for more than a brief period of time.

It was probably a good thing that Virginia came in to fetch me just then. "Let's wrap this up and be on our way," she said. "He can be left alone for a little while."

Now came the hard part. I turned my back on Bobby and followed Virginia back to the office, where everyone – even Mabel – was gathered. They were already separating what weapons we would carry with us, but when I cleared my throat they all turned to look at me expectantly.

"We're bringing the kid with us. We don't have enough people staying back here to watch him, at least not until Lauren returns, and that could be minutes...or hours. And he should witness this, anyway. Otherwise he might never believe that Jia could fail."

I was surprised when both Richard and Virginia nodded their assent. Daniel looked half-panicked by the idea, but the two people who had spent the most time with our "hostage" knew why it needed to be this way. *Maybe they were even about to suggest it themselves.*

"My bat?" I finally asked. Ethan handed it to me, and as he did so he looked me in the eye and wished me good luck. "Thanks," I said, smiling despite myself, smiling because I could see that he believed in me – in *us*. "While I'm gone, keep Holden close, okay? Take care of him for me." Ethan nodded; it was hard to resist the urge to reach out and take his hand; instead I smiled again before bending to tuck knives into each of my boots. I then grabbed the first gun belt I could find – it was one of my father's that we'd brought from the farm, all soft, tooled leather that was meant more for show than anything. I had to poke around for another knife, the smallest one we had left, and punch a hole through the belt strap several inches from where the last one had been. "*Shit*," I mumbled when I tried to put it on. It took two more tries to get it perfect, at which point I added a gun to each hip. A pistol on the left and a revolver on the right. Nothing special, but it was what I could carry if I wanted to move fast.

Daniel chose a shotgun and added a couple of sheathed knives to the belt that was already barely holding up his pants, then picked up a golf club we'd snagged from a sporting goods store when we were still at the farm. Virginia had her rifle and a belt with a pistol and a knife, as well as one of the zoo's original homemade maces. While I forced myself to zip myself up into a leather jacket, Daniel insisted that he would be fine in jeans and a t-shirt. Virginia was somewhere between us, wearing horribly dirty khaki pants and a long-sleeved running shirt with a high collar. They knew that I wasn't happy, that I would prefer us to suffer a bit on the trip to the school if it meant staving off zed teeth and nails along the way – *and once we're there* – but there wasn't really any time to argue, especially considering how much it bothered me that I couldn't remember how much Jia and her people had taken from us, couldn't remember how much we were leaving behind. *Not enough*, I mused, and it took everything in my power to tear my eyes away from Mabel.

Lauren would be back, I *had* to believe that, and she had weapons, too.

We were lucky that the zoo had had security guards. There was a pair of handcuffs, old but never used, for Bobby, and I cut a strip off one of our thick blankets so that I could blind him. Wide enough to cover his ears, as well, and hopefully muffle out whatever sounds the rest of us could hear.

"He knows where he's going," Daniel reminded me. It was obvious that he was forcing himself to say as much.

"I want him seeing and hearing as little as possible until we get there. I want to remove this blindfold and show him the fall of *his* sanctuary, because I know he imagined the fall of ours."

"It's already fallen," Daniel replied sadly.

All I could say was, "I know."

I watched him kiss Mabel goodbye, watched him hug her tight in a way that I couldn't remember my father ever hugging me. And then we left her with Richard and Ethan and went to gather Bobby. He didn't even bother trying to fight us, and I wasn't sure if the smirk on his face was forced or if he really believed we couldn't beat his people, couldn't conquer the school, couldn't oust Jia. It didn't really matter. Even if he was right – somehow, some way – we needed this last stand. We couldn't survive in this zoo if we were forced to give and give and give while we received little or nothing in return.

Bobby was handcuffed before we even led him outside, and blindfolded as soon as Ethan locked the zoo's gate behind us. Virginia clutched her son's hands through the bars; not a word passed between them, but I knew it was their goodbye. *Is it just in case, or does she know she won't come back?* And then we led our captive away from the zoo, my knuckles white as they gripped the thick rope we'd wrapped around his waist. He had to be my responsibility.

We stalked through the woods, the sun already pouring through the canopy, dappling the path in front of us as we moved around the zoo, cut through the back end of the park, and made our way up the river toward downtown. We veered to the west not long before we reached that more popular area, though strangely enough, we didn't encounter any zeds. Not long after we left the zoo I could hear distant popping sounds; not constant, but enough that when Daniel, Virginia, and I shared a glance, it was obvious that we all knew what they were.

It seemed like hours had passed before we finally hit a point where the woods ended and we were forced to make our way through a block of what were once high-end apartments. A large portion of one of the buildings was nothing more than a burnt husk, and I couldn't help but eye the windows of the other buildings as we half-walked, half-jogged through the back end of the complex's parking lot. Hands cuffed behind his back and eyes covered with a blindfold, Bobby had trouble keeping up with us even with me dragging him along, but I barely slowed down as I kept an eye on our surroundings. Most of the lower apartment windows were shattered, and there was no movement to be seen.

Finally we were back in a stand of trees, struggling up a hill through the underbrush before bursting out into the parking lot of a former café. We snuck between it and its old brick building of a neighbor, following the road another quarter of a mile north.

All the while we heard the telltale sounds of a battle going on somewhere nearby, which was probably the only reason that the few zeds I caught sight of were far away and not paying us any mind. We took another left through the parking lot of a much taller apartment building, shards of glass crunching under our feet. I motioned for the others to slow, pointed to my eyes, then at the building. If there were any guards outside the school's fences, this would be a perfect place...*assuming that Jia took it over.*

Even knowing so little about her, I had to assume that she'd done so.

Despite taking our time to curve around the apparently deserted building, we soon reached the edge of its property. I crouched down in the brush that separated it from the school fence by a couple dozen yards, dragging Bobby to his knees with me. Virginia and Daniel followed my lead; this brush was the only shelter we had as we gazed down a small hill at Jia's once seemingly impregnable fences.

Only now, chaos rained.

I nodded to Virginia, who removed Bobby's blindfold just in time for him to see a large group of zeds flatten a section of the school's barriers, pouring over it and each other as random gunshots split the air.

But the kid only laughed at us. "You think we haven't had them inside our walls before? In the beginning – "

This time I was the one who laughed. "This isn't the beginning anymore," I said, nodding toward the zeds that were rushing the school, many of them moving faster than some people could. "And I told you about Luke. I wonder how many of the people inside are dead now too, thanks to him?"

When Bobby turned and spat in my face, I merely stared at him as I dug a scrap of cloth out of my pocket and wiped my cheek clean. "Not very good aim," I sneered.

"*Charlie*," Virginia warned.

I barely stopped myself from rolling my eyes. "Two of us need to stay here with him, the other needs to do a perimeter check and hopefully find Mike before we make our move."

"You should go. You're fastest." I knew that Virginia was right, but I shook my head.

"No. Daniel, you up for it? You've been here before too, and Mike will know more about Lauren." There was always the chance she hadn't made it here, that any news like that would render Daniel useless, but I knew that Mike wouldn't lie to him.

And I knew that I would.

He gave a quick nod. "The zeds seem to be wandering in from the north; I'll move around to the south first. Hopefully by the time I circle back around most of them will be on school grounds."

"Thank you," I told him, reaching out and gripping his hand. "Be fast. Be careful. Be safe."

He gave me that lopsided grin of his that reminded me of country upbringings. "I'll do my best," he drawled, squeezing my hand hard before letting it go and turning south, jogging along the curb until he reached the far end of the lot and disappeared through a row of trees.

Virginia glared at me; of course she'd wanted me to go. Because of Luke. Because of Mike. But mostly because of Bobby. But I moved around to stand in front of the kid as I tucked his blindfold between his lips and tied it around the back of his neck. "Can't have you making any noise." He stared up at me, his gaze disdainful. I turned my back on him, still holding the rope, its knot tight around the front of his waist where he had no chance of reaching it. When Virginia glanced at me again, I cocked my head and ran my fingers across my lips, zipping them shut, so to speak.

"How long?" Virginia asked, after we'd waited maybe a quarter of an hour.

"Not much, depending on if he finds Mike." I stayed focused on the zeds; a small horde had approached from the north, but most of them were inside the fences now, leaving only a few very slow ones trickling in. We were close enough that I could see a difference; some of them were newly changed, moving awkwardly, looking like they were following some sort of beacon and couldn't quite keep up. But many weren't new zeds – they had the determination to reach the place they were drawn to, but they were half-dragging themselves there. "They're rotting away," I observed. "Virginia, look at them. The slow ones. Some of them are...fresh. But..."

"By God," she breathed. "You're right. You haven't seen this before?"

"If I did, it was so rare that I didn't really put two and two together. But now...so many of them...the ones we call 'super zeds'...must already be inside. But these older ones...I think I've just never seen so many all at once."

"I imagine they're easier to take down."

"Like slicing through months-old road kill," I agreed.

Virginia grimaced. "Something like that."

Still we waited. Another ten minutes passed before anything happened; then suddenly there was a disgusting *smack* to my right, and I turned to see Daniel and Mike sprinting towards us. My stomach flipped, but they were bulldozing through the stragglers as they made their way through the trickle of zeds that was still heading for the school. A few of those stragglers turned their attention our way, but I knew that we could take care of them; as soon as our friends reached us, I relinquished Bobby's rope to Daniel and Virginia and I rushed forward to cut the zeds down. When it was done, when we were certain we were safe – at least for the moment – I bent down to inspect one of them. I'd bashed its head in with my bat, and I'd swung much harder than I needed to. What was left was a mass of blood and pulp and bruised, rotting flesh. The zed was missing half an arm, too, and it hadn't been torn off – I knew enough to understand that it had simply fallen away.

I heard Virginia gagging and turned to lead her back to our group, immediately taking the rope away from Daniel and then turning to Mike. "Lauren?" I asked.

"She headed back to the zoo hours ago. Daniel told me you left there not long after dawn, but with all the noise from inside the school, we had a hard time staying in one place. I can't imagine she had an easy trip back; we'd settled in just northwest of here. The zeds, Charlie...there were so many of them."

"He saw me and came down from a tree," Daniel explained. "There's no way Lauren would have gotten back before we left, and they came a different way, so we wouldn't have seen her." But even as he spoke these words, his expression was one of forced relief. He didn't really believe that his wife was safe...and I didn't have the time to reassure him.

"There are good people in that school. Let's hope some of them survived." I nudged Bobby to his feet and handed Mike one of my guns. Daniel had already supplied him with the axe he'd carried all the way from the zoo, and after making sure we were all properly armed, I wrapped the rope around my fist and yanked my prisoner toward the broken fence. "Be careful with the downed ones – they can still bite," I reminded my friends.

We rushed down the hill and headed straight for the break in the fence, me leading with Bobby in tow and the rest of my warriors – *because that is what they are* – trailing close behind. We stumbled over the pile of zeds that had been caught up at – and in – the fence, me slamming the head of my bat into some, hearing knives sink into the skulls of many more. Every one of us had boots, and pants tucked into those boots, but when I heard someone curse behind me I knew that we had a problem.

It was Virginia, and her shoe was caught in a pile of several zeds. I knew that if she of all people was cursing, it was a real problem...and in that moment, I had to make a choice: let go of Bobby and help her, or simply hope that she could help herself.

"*Fuck,*" I swore. Mike was the closest, so I tossed the rope in his direction. "Don't let him get away!" I shouted as I turned back to grab Virginia. I stomped down on the closest head; it smashed under my foot like a soft peach. Disgusted, I reached for the older woman; as soon as we'd grasped each other's arms I pulled her toward me. Her boot slipped off, but we stumbled free of the zeds with everything else intact.

"Good thing I'm wearing socks," she joked, yanking off her second boot.

Just then Daniel cried out, and when I spun around it was like everything was in slow motion. I saw Daniel pointing, saw that Bobby was bent over Mike, and it was like something exploded inside of me. I rushed forward, tackling Bobby to the ground. Mike was gasping for breath – Bobby had been trying to choke him with his knees – but when I finally dragged our hostage to his feet, I understood that his decision to attack Mike was likely because he really didn't have anything left to lose, that he must have stumbled into a zed at some point; there was a chunk of flesh missing from his left arm.

"Do whatever you want to me now," he laughed maniacally. "It doesn't really matter, because we're all screwed."

I saw where he was looking and realized that he was right.

Dozens of the zeds that had been focused on the noise inside the school were now focused on *us*.

"What do we do?" Mike asked as he scrambled to his feet, his voice hoarse from Bobby's attempt to kill him.

"What we always do," I growled, dropping Bobby's rope and bending to pull a knife from my right boot. "Leave the weak behind, and finish our job."

I heard Daniel moan, heard Bobby laugh again, and then a roaring filled my ears. I couldn't look at my friends, couldn't be bothered with Bobby. He was already doomed and basically a stranger, anyway – and not a nice one. As so many of the zeds stumbled toward us, far too many of them the fast ones who had evolved but not yet started to rot away, I had to focus on my own survival.

Only then would I be able to save anyone else. *If I even have the chance to do so. If they use their guns...*

But no, my people were smarter than that. Even Virginia, who'd been holed up in that zoo from the very beginning, went after the zeds with a knife in one hand and her makeshift mace in the other. I glanced over my shoulder to see Bobby running off to the right, his gait awkward. "Follow him!" I shouted as I swung at a zed with my bat, barely connecting with its shoulder as I spun and followed the kid. I heard footsteps pounding behind me and could only hope, as I whipped my knife up to stab a zed under its chin, that those footsteps belonged to my friends.

And then we got lucky. A flurry of gunshots sounded from inside the school, causing most of the undead to turn away from us. A few stragglers were still stumbling across my path, but after taking a moment to shove my knife back in my boot I charged forward with my bat in both hands, bashing them out of the way without any thought of actually finishing them, my only goal being to catch up with Bobby. *How did you let him get a head start?*

Suddenly Mike and Daniel were by my side, but I knew it had to be me who reached the kid first. I tackled him to the ground, dropping my bat as I once again pulled out my knife and stabbed it into Bobby's thigh. I would have stabbed again and again and again, but the sounds of my friends staving off more zeds behind me brought me back to my senses.

Even with the bite on his arm and the stab wound in his leg, Bobby was petulant when I dragged him to his feet. "Show us where you were going, or I'll tie you up and let them have you," I hissed. "It won't take more than a minute."

"You're a *cunt*," he growled. I smirked at him.

"You're not the first person who's called me that, and I'm sure you won't be the last. Thankfully, it's just a word, no matter what it means. Now show me where you were going, or you die. Maybe in a few minutes, maybe in a few hours...just know that it will be painful."

"I don't give a shit about pain, but if you want inside so bad, fine. We still have more people than you."

I looked toward the school, where the mob of zeds was already pressing against not just the walls but the doors and windows as well. The glass was thick, but not thick enough; I imagined that it was probably already cracking. "Not for long."

Still, he shook his head, his jaw clenched. It was Virginia who changed the tide. "You're a little shit, kid," she mused, wiping the blade of her knife on her loose khaki pants, staining them with the black ooze of zed blood. "You may be done for, but there have to be some people in there who we could save. What'll it be?"

Bobby looked at me, then at Virginia, then at me again. "I'll show you the way in," he finally said. "But you'll still lose."

"Sure we will," I replied, rolling my eyes, doing everything in my power to keep him from seeing how concerned I actually was. "I guess I'll have to console myself with the fact that you're a goner no matter what happens."

"That's *enough*, Charlie," Virginia insisted. She reached out and took hold of the rope that was still bound around Bobby's waist. "He's mine now. We lead the way."

"Dissension in the ranks!" Bobby cackled.

He was right, but I couldn't let him know that. "More like you're close to being expendable and I need my hands free to make sure Virginia doesn't get hurt."

Just then Daniel and Mike surrounded us. "We have to *move*," Daniel ordered. "We lost most of them, but..."

I nodded. "We're moving. Bobby is going to show us the way in." I dogged the kid's heels as he led us around a corner of the school building and past a blocky addition that had been attached partway down its north-facing side, turning toward the wall where a large, dark, solid door was located.

"If things are really bad, it'll be unlocked. If they've got everything contained, though...good luck opening it." He shrugged.

I tested the door, pressing down on the heavy button at the top of the handle and pulling.

Nothing happened.

"Guess they're doing better than you thought."

"Does everyone know about this door?" Mike suddenly asked.

"Of course not. Just the people who work guard shifts. In fact, we've only had to unlock it once before, and we survived that. Just like we'll survive this."

"Just the people who work as guards, hmm?" I tapped my chin theatrically. "I think Daniel and I met a couple of them. They didn't seem too fond of Jia. Or of the people close to her."

Daniel groaned. "Now is *not* the time, Charlie. If we have to shoot that door open – "

I held up my hand. "We don't. It's just a big, heavy, metal door that hasn't been opened in a while. Daniel, Virginia, you're on the kid. Mike, let's try the door again. Together."

"I hope you're right about this," Mike mumbled as we grasped the handle. I gave him a reassuring smile and pressed my thumbs down on the button.

"Pull," I said. Our arms brushed against each other, and I could feel the strain of his muscles under his skin. I dug my feet into the ground, anchoring myself with my right heel so that I wouldn't fly backward if the door swung open. It gave a rusty creak and I felt it grinding against its frame. "It's giving!" Not knowing what was waiting for us on the other side, I gestured for Mike to move off to the right. He remained close, weapons at the ready, as I braced myself for one more hard pull.

Even though it was no longer stuck, the door was still heavy, and the hinges cried out as I dragged it open.

Nothing greeted us except for blackness and the distant sounds of zeds and fighting. "We stay together. Get inside. I'll shut the door. We'll leave it unlocked. Then we move. Mike, bring us to the nurse's office. We can lock Bobby up in there. Maybe he'll live and someone will be able to do something for him...though losing an arm nowadays is far worse than it would have been before."

"It's just an arm," Bobby said, and even though this time I didn't think his words matched his tone, I decided not to bother with a response.

"Let's move."

I let Mike lead the way, positioning Bobby between myself and Virginia, Daniel following behind. "We'll take the long way around," Mike whispered over his shoulder as he shuffled down the dark hallway to our right. "It sounds like that may keep us away from most of...whatever's happening."

"Just until we get rid of our little friend here," I responded insistently. *We have to find Luke.*

*Or what's left of him.*

I pushed the thought from my mind as best I could and tried to focus on our surroundings. It wasn't as dark as I'd first thought; there were classroom doors with narrow glass windows not far from where we'd entered, and light filtered through them, patches of it making the long, stark hallway more dim than dark.

"Never thought I'd see the inside of a high school again," I mused. Virginia snorted, but if anyone else heard me, they didn't acknowledge my awful attempt at a joke.

Eventually we took a left, and while the gunshots had stopped, I hoped that this was only because the people with the guns were down for the count. Even if they'd merely realized how much attention they were drawing from outside, that still gave us the upper hand.

*Hopefully we're the enemy they* don't *know about.*

"Here we are," Mike said, turning and stopping in front of a door on the left.

"It's gonna be locked," Bobby practically promised us.

"You wanna do the honors?" I asked Mike. He nodded and reached forward to twist the handle, which moved easily and allowed him to push the door in.

"Told you, kid. Not everyone wants Jia to win. There's probably shit going on that we don't even know about, and as you've seen by now, we knew enough."

"You've just gotten lucky so far," Bobby said as we shoved him into the office. The windows here were larger, looking out into the school's inner courtyard. "Mike,

Daniel, grab some meds and supplies, whatever you can find that isn't locked up. If any of it is. But be quick about it. Virginia, stay on Bobby. I'm going to look for a way to shut him up in here. We've got a minute, maybe two. Make it count."

I watched Bobby out of the corner of my eye as I roved the office looking for something to keep the door shut. I peered at some of the knickknacks on the desk and then made my way around it, searching every drawer, knowing that unless we had a way to melt the lock – and we didn't – then we would need the spare keys. I wasn't sure how many there were to this room, but maybe, if Mrs. Downing had truly left that door unlocked on purpose...

*Ha!* And there it was, a single key, worn with use, scuffed from the effort it must have taken to remove it from its keychain...hiding under a stack of post-its in the smallest desk drawer. I pocketed it and moved to help Virginia tie Bobby to a metal chair; as soon as we were done I called out to Mike and Daniel. They returned to my side, both zipping up bags that now looked quite a bit more full than they had before.

"A few things were locked up, but we got plenty of bandages, gauze, tape, sanitary wipes, even some OTC stuff," Daniel told me.

"Perfect. But now we need to go. Virginia, Daniel, you first." They left the room, and I took Mike's hand, both of us backing out the door slowly, our eyes on Bobby the entire time. I released Mike only when we were through the door and I had swung it shut, locking it as swiftly as possible.

I turned to my friends. "Now comes the hard part." I knew that I didn't have to tell them to avoid using guns unless it was completely necessary, and every other bit of advice just stuck in my throat. "We need to take care of Luke," I reminded them. "But *I'm* the one who will do it, understand? No matter where you are, no matter where I am, unless I'm completely incapacitated – " *or dead* – "leave him to me. All of you can whistle?" They nodded. "Good. Do that, loud as you can, if you see him first." I paused, staring each of them down in turn. "Promise me."

At first no one said anything, but finally Mike whispered, "Promise," and within moments the others followed suit.

"Mike, you and I will lead the way. Virginia, Daniel, keep an eye on our backs as we move." With that I gestured to Mike and turned to his left. We jogged this time, our feet seeming to slap the floor in an offbeat staccato that was far louder than I cared for, but the noise of what we were running toward soon drowned out any sound we made. The hall was slick with blood in places; I almost slipped once but Virginia grabbed hold of me and helped me regain my balance. I could see a turn up ahead, light flowing around the corner and highlighting our first true obstacle.

Bodies. Nearly a dozen, from what I could see. Mike skidded to a halt, and when I looked at him, his jaw was trembling. I laid a hand on his arm.

"Make sure any zeds are totally dead. If any of them are still alive – *actually* alive – find out if they've been bitten. If they have, take care of them. No matter who they are." *No one deserves to turn into one of them,* I told myself, but another part of me whispered, *Not even Bobby? Not even Jia?*

It was Virginia who moved first, Daniel on her heels. I followed, pulling Mike with me. "You don't have to do it if you don't want to," I told him. "Just help me figure out what's what, okay?" He nodded stiffly; knives in hand, we each headed toward a body. I was disgusted with myself when I felt relieved that mine was a zed, and already gone, at that. Mike's must have been as well, because he didn't say a word or do anything before moving on to the next one. Virginia and Daniel were ahead of us, and I heard the sickening sound of one of their knives taking care of someone. *Or something,* I reminded myself.

The next body I found was a young kid, younger even than Mike, I guessed. He was already gone, but I forced my knife through the base of his skull anyway.

I had to make sure that he didn't come back.

I heard a groan. By now Virginia and Daniel were beyond the bodies, poised for movement but waiting for Mike and I. It was Mike who'd groaned, Mike who was bent over a body but not moving.

Zed or human, it was someone he knew. I stood, wiping my own knife on my pants before kneeling next to Mike. "I've got it," I told him.

It was a teenager, a boy shorter and stouter than Mike, with a shaved head where Mike had kept a short crop of curls the entire time I'd known him. But they looked about the same age. "Your class?" I asked.

"A friend," he admitted.

I reached under the boy's head. He was unconscious, breathing shallowly, but he'd been mauled. There was no life after what he'd been through – *no* alive *life, anyway.* I was about to push my knife through the base of his skull when Mike stopped me.

"Please," he murmured. I let him push my hand aside. I saw his knife. I knew what he meant to do. I rested my hands on my legs, keeping my own knife at the ready – but I didn't need to. Mike took care of his friend, stood, wiped off his own blade, and moved forward without me. It took me a moment to follow, but finally I forced myself to my feet, dodged the rest of the bodies, and just barely caught up with my friends, who were pressed against the corner of a sharp turn in the hallway.

*What just happened...it's nothing compared to what lies ahead.*

## LESSON LEARNED

*At some point, there's no turning back.*

* * * * * * *

I turned the corner and the first thing I noticed was that the front entrance to the school was clearly the biggest problem. The ceiling was high, the wall all glass doors and windows, and the sun was reflecting off the hundreds – possibly *thousands* – of glass shards that littered the floor, almost making the mob of people and zeds fighting each other glitter as they moved.

And then I realized that many of them were coated in tiny bits of glass and wet with sweat and blood.

Everything in the grisly scene before us *shone*.

All of us had stopped again, staring at the dozens of bodies on the floor and the fighting happening no more than a hundred yards away. "Jesus," Mike hissed.

"Capture them if you can. Kill them if you have to," I ordered.

I rushed forward into the fray.

Zeds were still pouring in from outside, and I had to fight my way through the mob to reach the small group of people who stood in a circle with their backs to each other. I came face-to-face with the mousy girl who'd remained at the zoo's gate with Virginia mere days ago. I couldn't recall her name, but I knew her allegiance – I rushed at her, knife in hand, but she was shoved out of the way just in time. I spun to my right, weapon at the ready, but this time it was Dominic who I faced. We both stopped just short of attacking, and there was a moment when time stood still. Finally I inclined my chin just slightly, and we turned away from each other. I never knew what he did next, but I myself was faced with a group of zeds, a mix of new and old that moved so sporadically I couldn't even keep count as I slashed with my knife and swung my bat one-handed, merely hoping that it would do the damage I needed it to.

I saw Virginia fall, scramble, get back up. She was bleeding from her side, so heavily that the zeds were already turning towards her. "*Run,*" I mouthed, but she shook her head and plowed forward. I had to turn away when I heard a loud whistle. It was Daniel, beckoning me toward the far corner of the entrance hall – and Mrs. Downing was by his side. I ran, then, shaking off everyone – *everything* – that touched me.

"He's tied up, shut up in a room with Monika guarding him," the nurse hissed at me as Daniel and I pretended to hold her down. "'Round the corner, two doors down on the left. Jia took some people outside to try to thin out the pack, but she could come back any moment."

I nodded my thanks and followed her without a thought for my friends. They could handle themselves...but *I* needed to take care of Luke. Daniel had turned away, turned back toward the handful of fighters and zeds left behind us. *He and Virginia and Mike will have each others' backs.*

I ran then, dodging kids and zeds, sparing the time to take two of the latter down as I went. Mrs. Downing could barely keep up with me even then, and so I rounded the corner alone, swinging preemptively with my bat, which thankfully met with nothing but air. The noise and mayhem in the front entrance was obviously keeping the zeds from roaming the school, but even here there were bodies on the ground and blood – both human and zed – coating the floor and speckling the walls. I slowed to check the first body I saw, but Mrs. Downing grabbed my left wrist and pulled me toward the door she'd mentioned. "We took care of these," she hissed. "Now get in here, quickly. There will be noise, and it will draw more soon enough."

She cracked open the door and dragged me through it behind her; I didn't even have time to steel myself against what I would see. The classroom had larger windows than the nurse's office, windows that looked out into a small courtyard. All of the shades were wide open and for a moment the light from them blinded me; I saw only a tall person standing with their back to me. "Luke?" I said softly, hopefully.

But then the person turned, and my eyes adjusted to the light behind her. Monika. "He's in the teacher's closet," she said, her chin trembling, her gaze mistrustful, angry. "What have you *done* to us?"

"What we had to," I snapped, making for the closet at the back left corner of the room. I could hear the noises now, and my stomach turned. I jiggled the handle, but it was locked from the outside. I turned back to the two women, young and old. "Give me the fucking keys," I ordered.

Mrs. Downing looked up at Monika. "Give her the keys, dear."

"Don't call me *dear*. Who left that door open for him? You think we don't know how you and some of the others feel?"

In one swift movement I dropped my bat and pulled my gun, pointing it at Mrs. Downing's head. "Give me the keys, or I kill your nurse."

Monika stared me down. "She betrayed us. What do I care if she dies?"

"She betrayed *Jia*," I insisted. "And maybe some of the other assholes who follow her around either because they're shitty people too, or they have some awful form of Stockholm Syndrome. You know what that is?"

She nodded, but still didn't look at Mrs. Downing. "Say what you want, but Jia keeps people alive."

I laughed. "But she's no nurse. Who's going to take care of the people who actually survive this if I kill Mrs. Downing, here?"

That gave Monika pause. She finally looked over at the nurse, who spread her hands out in an apologetic gesture. "If I die, I die knowing that I tried to save you kids from Jia. She's not right, Monika. You of all people – "

"*Don't* talk to me about Jia," the girl hissed. She turned away, stalking back and forth, but after watching her for a few moments I knew I couldn't let her think this through any longer. *My people are out there, in danger. Other good people are, too. Kids, and not all of them like Bobby.*

I clicked off the safety. "You have to decide, Monika. Save this woman, or don't, but know that if you let me kill her, it's likely that far more of your people will die than if you choose to let her live."

The girl took a deep breath and faced me. "You're the one who chooses if she lives or dies," she said, but then she reached into her pocket and took out a small key ring with a single key on it and tossed it into the air. It hit the floor and skidded to a stop just a few inches from my foot.

Still, I didn't put away my gun. I bent to pick it up, my eyes on them the whole time, then stood slowly. "Thank you. Mrs. Downing, keep a hold on her, please."

"But – "

"*Do it!* Do you think I was kidding about killing you?" I wasn't even sure if I was lying anymore. For a moment there I'd really thought that I would need to pull that trigger. "Do it for yourself, if not for anything else. I could still kill both of you."

Neither of them seemed to be thinking about the fact that if I shot my gun, especially more than once, it was likely to draw attention. Or maybe one or both of them did understand that and simply didn't care. What *I* knew was that they were both afraid of me. *I think I probably would be, too.*

I fumbled to unlock the door, my neck craned over my shoulder so that I could watch them. Mrs. Downing had taken hold of Monika's hands behind her back, but I knew that the girl could probably wrest herself out of the nurse's grip quite easily. Finally I felt the handle move smoothly under my hand and tore the key from it, shoving it into my pocket and only turning away from the others to pull the knife from my right boot.

"Either of you come near me, and I'll let him loose," I said over my shoulder as I opened the door, holding my gun awkwardly in my left hand. I fumbled again, trying to turn the knob with a knife in my hand, but the only noises I heard were from Luke struggling on the other side of the door. For those few moments, I had to believe that Monika was not Jia and that Mrs. Downing was more trustworthy than I ever could have expected.

As it turned out, they weren't what I really had to worry about, because when I finally saw what was in that closet, it wasn't Luke.

Not anymore.

The thing that stumbled towards me was a zed. It still looked like Luke, for the most part; other than some new scratches on his face and neck he appeared to be whole. His arm was even still mostly bandaged, but his veins were almost black, stark against his now-dull skin, and though he was too newly turned to move very fast, his mouth was opening and closing as he tried to approach me, his teeth clacking together in an odd beat, an airy growl sounding from his throat.

*No. **Its** arm. **Its** veins. **Its** mouth. **Its** teeth. **Its** throat.*

I stepped back out of the closet, shoving my gun into its holster and scooping my bat up off the floor. "If either of you move, I *will* kill you," I promised Mrs. Downing and Monika. They merely stared at me with wide eyes. I spun back around to face Luke and shoved the narrow end of the bat between his teeth – *the zed's teeth* – as it opened its mouth again. I pressed it toward the back of the closet, feeling its hands grab at me, catching on the seams of my leather jacket. It couldn't scratch me, and it lacked the dexterity to take hold. It still took all of my strength to keep the bat between its teeth as I pressed myself against it – *against him*, some part of me screamed – and maneuvered the tip of my knife around to the base of its neck. "I'm sorry," I whispered, hating the tears that streamed down my cheeks. "I loved you, in my own way."

I braced myself and shoved the knife up through Luke's neck, deep into the base of his skull. There were a few seconds of struggle, and then he went limp in my arms.

It took everything I had to not start sobbing. Instead I released the body and let it fall to the floor, knowing there was a chance that I'd never see it again. When I turned to face the nurse and the girl, they were still standing in the same spot, watching me fearfully.

"Do either of you have any weapons?" Both of them immediately nodded. "Hand them over." This time they hesitated, but when I moved forward, zed-blood-coated knife in hand, they moved fast, each of them setting several knives on the closest desk. I picked up the knives one by one, shoving them into my boots and belt – wherever they would fit. "Stay where you are, and don't hurt each other," I told them, heading back toward the classroom door. I knew what Monika had given me – the master key. No wonder Jia had everyone under her control; with this, she could go wherever she wanted, lock or unlock any room. So I shut the door and locked it behind me. I knew there was a chance that Monika would go after Mrs. Downing, or vice versa, but I had to continue hoping that neither of them was that stupid – *or that horrible. Not everyone can be as cold as I am. As cold as Jia is.*

Most of the fighting was still contained to the entrance hall, but a few zeds must have heard some of the noise we'd made. They'd rounded the corner and were making their way toward me, but there was nothing of *me* left anymore, really. I took hold of my bat with both hands, my knife pressed against it, a useless close-range weapon in circumstances like these. The first few zeds were fast; I spun and swung and spun again, sending them to the ground but not truly *killing* them. It didn't matter – there wasn't enough time. I took out two more of them, slower ones, before rounding the corner, where a large semicircle of people was fighting off the zeds that continued to stumble through the broken doors and windows. The ones still left were a mix of newer and much older zeds, slower ones that had been at the back of the horde, and this group of people working together took them down almost *easily*. I saw Daniel and Mike and Virginia still fighting, and for a moment I felt almost elated.

And then Jia appeared, leaping into the fray, tumbling expertly across the floor and then springing to her feet in a perfect gymnast move. Several of her people were right behind her, and though they were still working to take down zeds, I knew that this sort of peace wouldn't last.

I raced forward, dodging between two kids I'd never seen before, cracking my bat against a zed's chest hard enough to send it reeling backwards into someone. It was the mousy girl again – *Allie*, I suddenly remembered, *her name is Allie* – and I made the split-second decision to let the zed go as I sprinted toward Jia, Allie's screams echoing behind me.

Jia saw me coming and spun away, out of the range of my bat, ducking under a zed so that it tripped over her and went sprawling to the floor. When she stood, everything seemed to move in slow motion. Her teeth were bared in a feral grin as she pulled a gun and tried to aim it at me. But I was fast, too; I dove to the ground, my hip slamming into the blood-slicked tile flooring. I slid several feet, pulled out my knife as I rolled over, and stabbed upwards almost blindly. Jia dodged me again, but not quickly enough – my knife sliced along the back of her left knee and she fell hard, the gun flying out of her hand. Still, she somehow had a knife in the other one before I could do any more damage, and even though those tendons in her left leg were ruined, she performed an awkward backwards flip to escape me...

And ran right into a zed.

At first I thought that Jia even had this under control; she recovered herself quickly, rising to her knees, her hand whipping up to stab the zed in the face – but then I heard something whizz by my head and Jia jerked forward, her arm automatically falling to her side.

There was a knife implanted in the middle of her back. I spared one look over my shoulder and saw Daniel lowering his arm, staggering backward as a zed threw itself at him.

And then there were screams, male and female both. I almost turned back to make sure that it was Jia screaming and not some other girl, but something pulled me toward Daniel instead. I knew he was being mauled, and I was angrier about that than I was about Jia.

*Apparently there's still some human left in me, after all.*

Saving Daniel – truly saving him – was out of the question; I knew that before I jumped to my feet and ran towards him, throwing myself on top of the zed and slamming my knife into the soft spot just below its right temple. It still took all of my strength to finally hit some part of the brain that would actually render the damn thing inert, but finally it went limp beneath me. I rolled away, pulling the body off Daniel as I went, and then scrambled over it to be back by his side.

"Ch-Charlie," he choked out. The zed had been shorter than Daniel, short enough that it had very likely been a recently turned school kid – there was a shallow bite, probably the first one, taken out of his bicep. But when he'd fallen, the zed had latched on to his neck. There was blood everywhere – I was drenched in it up past my wrists as I tried to hold my hands over his wound.

"I'm sorry," I said, and I meant it.

"Just...end..." He choked again, leaving things unsaid...but I knew what he wanted.

Everything around me was red. I couldn't hear anything but Daniel's labored breathing and his words – "Just end" – echoing in my head.

I wiped my blade on my pants, cleaning it as much as possible, and then leaned down, placing the point of my knife at the back of his neck. "Lauren and Mabel will be cared for," I promised him, trying to force back the tears that were pricking at the corners of my eyes. "You are one of the best men I've ever met. Goodbye, friend."

Still pressing on his wound with my left hand, I leaned into my right and drove my knife through the base of his skull. I felt sick, being thankful that there were no horrible death throes – that I'd done it right, that I'd ended his suffering as quickly as I could.

And of course there was no time for mourning. There never is, in the zombie apocalypse. As soon as I was certain that he was gone, I was on my feet, pivoting around to face the front entrance, planting myself in a fighting stance with my knife at the ready. But by now the flow of zeds had slowed to nothing more than a trickle, and I could see Virginia and Mike fighting with Dominic and several other kids from the school to take the last of them down. Not that it mattered – the school was breached, and unless they had some way to board up the broken glass and fix what were likely several downed sections of fence within the next day or two, it would be a while before anyone could live here and feel safe doing so.

*Find Jia*, I reminded myself, scanning the bodies littering the ground. Suddenly I saw something moving off to my right, and sure enough, there she was, somehow still alive. The blade of the knife still glinted where it was stuck in the muscle just to the left of her spine, and she was pulling herself along the floor, covered in both human and zed blood. I knew she must have been bitten, but I couldn't risk her doing any more damage than she already had. *For Daniel,* I thought as I rushed toward her, though I knew that deep down this was really mostly for me. When I reached her side I planted my boot on her back to stop her, then reached down and pulled her blade out of her hand. When I lifted my leg and nudged her onto her side, I wondered how she'd even still had hold of the knife at all — half of her right cheek was missing and she was coughing up even more blood, her breathing shallow and wet.

"I'm sorry it had to come to this," I said.

She spat at me, but there was no strength behind the gesture, and most of the red-tinged saliva just dribbled down her chin. "You're a monster," she replied, glaring up at me with red-rimmed eyes. *Maybe she has some human still left in her, too.*

"I do what I have to, to take care of those I love." I bent down, clenching both of her slim wrists in my left hand as I showed her the knife in my right. "You can't survive that bite. Do you want — "

"Just fucking do it. Even if I didn't want you to, *you* want to."

I sighed, knowing that in a way she was right — but also knowing that if she didn't tell me to do it, I wouldn't be able to whether I wanted it or not. "Monika is safe, or at least she was when I last saw her. She's in a locked room, and I have the master key."

Jia's eyes softened, then, and I knew that I'd been right all along — that Monika was her weakness. "I don't want her to see me like this. Just make it quick." I nodded and released her hands, knowing that my jacket was protection enough now that she was disarmed. Still, I kept my exposed neck and head as far away from her as possible as I reached around the back of her head, taking care of this teenaged girl who had caused us so much trouble in so little time in the very same way I'd just ended any sort of life – or afterlife – for my friend Daniel just moments before.

"That was a bad idea," a familiar voice called out.

*What the fuck?*

I didn't bother trying to pull my blade from the back of Jia's neck – I left it where it was and in one fluid motion I stood, drawing another knife from my belt, moving faster than I thought was possible as my heart slammed an erratic beat in my chest. I stumbled a bit as I backed away from Jia's corpse, my eyes finding Bobby. His left arm was pinning Virginia close, his right hand – handcuffs still dangling from that wrist – pressing a knife against her throat.

His left hand was missing.

Even from a dozen feet away, I could see that he was weak, barely even able to hold himself up...but at the same time, it doesn't take much strength to slit someone's throat. And no one had been watching for him, no one had been thinking to keep an eye on a hallway we'd already cleared. I wasn't sure I even wanted to know how he'd found a way to cut off his own hand, but then, what did it matter? I'd killed his friend, and at the moment he had control over *my* friend's survival.

"She'd been bitten," I stated. "And you were too, remember? It's over, Bobby." *There's no reason to keep fighting. Let Virginia go.*

He only laughed. "It's not really over, though, is it? There's life beyond this. For me, anyway. Maybe for this old lady. But not for Jia. You took that away from her."

It took me a moment to understand that he was talking about turning into a zed, and when I realized this, for a moment I didn't know what to say. *He can't be serious!*

But looking at his face, I knew that he was. He was desperate, and angry, and now more than ever I wondered if he'd ever been truly sane. "Jia didn't want to be one of them," I finally replied. "She didn't want...people...to see her like that."

"Bullshit," Bobby spat. "She didn't want *Monika* to see her like that, because Monika is weak. But she also didn't want to *die*."

"She was already mostly there," I said gently, my hands held out in supplication, pointing my weapon at the floor as I moved to take a step toward him.

"Stop!" he ordered, pressing the knife against Virginia's throat. She was staring at me, but she wasn't scared. I think I knew what she meant to do before it happened, but still I hesitated.

For a moment, I willed this to not be real.

And then Virginia stomped on Bobby's foot and quickly pivoted around to her right, releasing herself from his grip as he sliced her throat open with his blade.

He wasn't fast enough, though. She'd already been half-turned toward him, and in that moment before she lost control of her body, she jerked her right hand up and Bobby slumped inward as her knife found his lower abdomen. They fell together, and I wasn't the only one who ran to their aid – out of the corner of my eye I saw Mike diving toward Virginia, while a couple of the kids from the school split off from a larger group that was huddled against the wall behind Bobby. I dropped my knife and pulled out the pistol that hung at my right hip, pointing it at them as I dropped to my knees beside Virginia and Bobby.

"Back. The fuck. Off."

"I'd do what she says," Mike warned them, and after looking from me, to him, and back again, they slunk back to their group, though they didn't take their eyes off us. I jerked my chin at him, and somehow he knew what I meant. He reached for his own gun and trained it on the group of kids; I kept mine in hand as I pushed Virginia off of Bobby. I was too busy pinning the kid's arms under my knees to keep an eye on anyone else.

Suddenly, Virginia reached out and grabbed my wrist. "Bring me...zoo...don't..." She was choking on her own blood, now; there was nothing I could do.

"I will. You won't come back."

"Ethan..." she gasped. "Make sure...knows..."

"That you fought? " I asked, hoping that was what she meant. She was fading too fast to tell me anything else.

Her chin jerked down to her chest, and I slid my wrist from her grasp to take her hand in mine.

"You are a warrior, Virginia. You are a friend."

But in the end, as much as I would like to believe she heard those words, I'll never really know.

Bobby was still there, breathing shallowly, not even bothering to struggle against me pinning him to the ground. I still had the gun, but I knew that using it was a bad idea. The noise would only draw whatever zeds were around back to the school, and I had to get Mike out of there, and maybe others as well – at least the people who had helped us.

Mike seemed to have read my mind. "I've got it, Charlie," he promised, and I looked up to see that he still had his gun trained on the questionable group of kids.

I tucked my gun back into its holster and reached for my last knife, the one tucked into my right boot. Bobby wanted to turn, but I couldn't let that happen – or at least that's what I told myself, the reason I repeated over and over again in my head as I took my third life that day. And yet it wasn't the intimate thing that I'd had with my friend or that previous enemy. I felt cold, I didn't care. I was removing a monster from this world, and all the while I was wondering if I should be removing myself from it, as well. Suddenly I just felt so damn *exhausted*. It took far too much strength and energy to remove my blade from the base of Bobby's skull, but in the past few minutes I'd tossed away every other knife I'd been carrying, and I knew better than to leave this place with nothing more than my guns to protect myself. Still, I couldn't use this same knife to take care of Virginia; after wiping it off on Bobby's shirt, I tucked it away and searched the floor around me for another one. It didn't seem to have been used recently, but I wiped it down gently, anyway, with what seemed to be the last clean bit of my shirt.

And for the second time in just a few minutes, I made sure that someone I cared about wouldn't turn into a zed. When it was done, I caressed Virginia's cheek. "Thank you," I whispered.

*Treat your fallen heroes with care.*

# Chapter 13
# The Last Lesson

I clambered to my feet and called for Dominic.

"Here," he replied from behind me. I glanced over my shoulder at him.

"I need a shovel and the largest cart you have. Something from the A/V department, maybe? Just be careful – of zeds, and anyone else you might come across." He nodded and rushed off to do my bidding, while I moved to Mike's side and then turned in a slow circle, addressing the handful of people who were still in the entrance hall. "All of you, stand over against that wall." I gestured toward the group of kids that Mike was still holding at gunpoint. "We *will* use our guns if we have to, but trust me, you don't want that any more than we do."

I watched them carefully, taking note of the ones who obeyed immediately and who also moved as far away from their fellow school residents as possible. I'd have to talk to Dominic and Mrs. Downing, but it seemed there were more than a few kids still standing who likely hadn't cared much for Jia or for the people who clearly wanted to protect her and her friends.

After that, everything was a blur for a while. I gave Mike the master key and told him where to find Mrs. Downing and Monika; he hesitated at first, but I insisted. "We need to wrap this up. Fast." He finally agreed, albeit reluctantly, and by the time he returned, following the nurse and the young girl, who both had their hands up in the air like actual prisoners, Dominic had already showed up with a decrepit shovel and a large flat-bottomed cart.

"All right. I have to trust you guys more than I'd like to just now. Monika, get over there with everyone else. Mike,

Dominic, Mrs. Downing, keep an eye on them. This is going to take a while."

"Where are you going?" Mike asked suspiciously.

I sighed, hating everything about what I needed to do just now. "I'm going to bury Luke here. It's going to be hard enough to take Virginia and Daniel back...and besides, without Luke, we wouldn't have been able to rid ourselves of Jia, of the threat she and this place posed. He *should* be laid to rest here." *Like the martyr he had to be.*

Mike obviously didn't agree with me, but I couldn't see another way out of this, and Ethan and Lauren deserved to see their loved ones again, to say whatever goodbyes they could.

To bury them near Joey in what would now be the zoo's own little graveyard.

I took the shovel and made my way through the broken front doors of the school. There were landscaped areas on either side of the wide walkway; I turned to look back at the entrance and chose the area on the right, quickly scraping away a wide swath of the loose mulch and then digging into the soft, giving soil underneath.

It was late afternoon when I started; by the time I'd dug a grave that was just barely deep enough, night had fallen and I knew we were stuck at the school until dawn. The zeds were simply too active at night. I made my way back inside, so sweaty that my skin was streaked not only with dirt, but also with blood that had never really dried. The survivors were still standing in their little groups by the wall with Mike, Dominic, and Mrs. Downing watching them. One of them had found a chair and I assumed they were taking turns sitting down, though I had a feeling it was probably just Dominic and the nurse who were doing so – Mike looked completely exhausted.

"We're stuck here for the night," I murmured. He grimaced and nodded. "Let's move Virginia and Daniel into the room where..." I trailed off, rubbed my temples, and had to take a deep breath before continuing. "Where Luke is. We'll lock ourselves in there. But first we have to take care of the rest of these kids." I turned to the nurse. "Are there enough classrooms that I can lock up if we split them into groups of two to three? You and Dominic will stay with us, though. We need to talk."

Mrs. Downing nodded warily. "To be honest, they should stay together," she whispered, jerking her head toward one cluster of teenagers, the ones who had taken the most offense to me killing Bobby. "If we do that, and if you trust me to split the others up, there are enough rooms. But if I were you, I'd keep Monika close."

I glanced at the tall girl, who was sitting with her back to the wall, staring at Jia's dead body in the middle of the floor. Her eyes were red-rimmed, and she didn't even glance at us as we made our plans. I nodded. "Mike, Dominic, use that cart to get Virginia and Daniel to the room, and then board yourselves in there. Unfortunately, I'll need the master key for a bit longer, but don't worry, we're going to make sure no one else has anything dangerous to use against us." With that, I beckoned to Mrs. Downing, and the two of us made fast work of taking away the others' weapons. I passed some of them off to Mike and Dominic before they wheeled the cart away, doing my best to not look at the pile of limp bodies that was made up of my two dead friends. I handed the rest of the weapons and the master key off to Mrs. Downing, who scurried off to dump them in the room where we'd be spending the night. When she returned we herded up the group of kids and moved them in the opposite direction of Mike and Dominic.

We passed by several rooms and had almost reached the end of the corridor when Mrs. Downing finally unlocked a door and pointed at the handful of teenagers who she'd said needed to stay together. I didn't care for the arrangement, but I had to trust her, had to assume that she was doing this so that they couldn't try to harm anyone who might be on our side – *or who at least hadn't been on Jia's side.* We then continued around the school and locked the rest of them up in pairs and trios until we'd secured up five classrooms' worth of people, with only Monika left to us. I was bone-tired, and I knew I would need at least a few hours of sleep, but as usual our work wasn't done. Thankfully when we reached 'our' room and knocked, we heard the scrapes of furniture being moved away from the door almost immediately, and within moments Dominic had cracked it open enough for us to squeeze through one by one. Mrs. Downing went first, then Monika, and finally me. I shut and locked the door behind us – *thank God for double-sided locks* – and turned to see the rest of them standing in an awkward circle, eying each other uncertainly in the dim light of the camping lamp Mike had brought with him and set on the desk.

"Mike, get some sleep. Or at least try to," I corrected myself when he gave me a worried look. "Please. I'll need you to keep watch in a few hours so that I can rest, too." This would be a lot of responsibility on his shoulders, but after everything that had happened, I knew he could handle it. *Even now – or maybe* especially *now*. He moved to the back of the room and sat on the floor, propping his backpack in a corner and leaning against it. For the moment he was awake, but he had to be as exhausted as I was, and I hoped he would be able to sleep for at least a little while. "All right. The rest of you, take a seat." I waited until they'd dragged some of the awful little school desks into a semicircle, then pulled a desk toward myself as well, never taking my eyes off of them, glancing from Dominic to the nurse to Monika and back as I finally sat down. "Mrs. Downing, Dominic, will you want to remain here at the school?"

"Hell no," Dominic swore. The nurse glared at him, but he ignored her. "This place was a shithole before, and it's even less safe now."

I looked at Mrs. Downing. She sighed and shrugged. "Dominic, you should watch your language," she told him. "But you're right." She looked at me. "He's right. We can't stay here. Problem is, we weren't trusted to be out and about, so we have no idea where to go."

"Are there others like you? People who fought against Jia before, or at least...today, yesterday, whatever." I had no idea what time it was; I'd hated watches before the zombie apocalypse and since it had begun I'd continued to wear one as little as possible.

"Yes, to both parts. Some of them I'm not completely sure about, mostly because it was only when the tide turned that I noticed they were following mine or Dominic's lead rather than that of Jia's people. I'd say they're just kids, but that's not really it. They've always just...been trying to survive."

*I know that all too well.* "After I've gotten some sleep and buried Luke, I'll need you to take me to them." She nodded her agreement, and I finally turned to Monika.

"You were Jia's girlfriend," I stated. She just stared at me defiantly, and finally I shook my head in frustration. "I know you talked to Luke at the zoo. Can you look me in the eye and tell me that you agreed with what Jia was doing here?"

The girl's chin trembled. She looked at Mrs. Downing, then down at the floor. "Jia wasn't a bad person."

"That's not what I asked."

"Fine!" Monika hissed. "Fine. No, I didn't agree with what she's been doing lately. But it wasn't like this at first. We had a lot of infighting early on, after we'd let some outsiders in, and Jia did what she had to do, then. She just..."

"Continued to act like some combination of dictator and fucking prison warden after?" Dominic interrupted.

I could see that Mrs. Downing was about to chastise him again, and I shook my head at her. "Let Monika tell us her story, Dominic. Trust me, I believe that Jia was horrible, and I need to know why Monika remained by her side."

"I knew what she was, but I loved her. That's it. Do what you want with me, but I'm not going to lie and say that I didn't care about her."

Truth be told, that was probably the best answer I could have asked for...but it also made things that much more difficult. "We're going back to the zoo in the morning. Mrs. Downing, Dominic, you are welcome to join us. We'll see about the others who seemed to be against Jia first thing in the morning. Monika...well. It's up to you. You can stay here, but we will leave you with minimal weapons in a place that is no longer protected...and I'll be taking the master key with me, of course. Or you can come with us, but if you do, it will be as our prisoner, at least until we can determine whether or not it's safe to let you truly join us. Your choice, but you only have until sunrise to make it."

"I'll go with you," she said. "I know who you're probably leaving behind. I'd rather not take my chances with them."

"If she joins us, you have to promise not to harm her," Mrs. Downing announced. I sighed.

"That's our policy. Unless she gives us cause to take her out – trying to run away, hurting one of my people – she'll be under our protection. But we come first, understood? Not just before her, but before any of you who come back to the zoo with us. And Monika here probably won't be the only one who comes back with us as a prisoner. You have to trust me that they'll be taken care of to the best of our ability, and I have to trust you to be honest about who can come back with us as friends."

The nurse leaned forward, an earnest look on her face. "You believed that we would be on your side, and we were

– but still, you didn't have to help us. You could have killed us, or locked us up with the others, but you didn't. We won't forget that, especially if you can bring us somewhere safe."

"Nowhere is really safe," I pointed out. "And we'll need as many of your supplies as we can carry…and even that may not be enough to keep everyone fed. We'll need to continue to work together."

"Sounds a hell of a lot better than what we had here," Dominic piped in.

"Yeah, well, we'll see about that, I guess. You guys should try to rest up, too. We have a long walk ahead of us tomorrow, and it won't be an easy one."

Despite the fact that all three of them found a place to lay down, only Mrs. Downing and Dominic eventually fell asleep. I stayed where I was, all of my attention on Monika, who was stretched out on her back not ten feet from where I sat. Her eyes never closed, but just as mine started to – against my will, of course – she spoke.

"Did she say anything when she died?"

"You really want to know?"

"Yes." There was a finality to her tone that I couldn't ignore.

"She'd been bitten, badly, but she was still trying to fight. I was the one who took care of that – of her. She was relieved to hear that you were safe. She didn't want you to see her injured, and I believe she also didn't want you to see her as a zed. She asked me to make it quick, and I did."

Silence. The minutes crawled by, and although I couldn't hear anything other than the deep breathing of those who were sleeping, I somehow knew that Monika was crying.

"Thank you," she finally said, her voice quavering.

"For which part?"

"I don't know," she admitted. "Maybe all of it." And then she rolled over onto her left side, facing the wall, and that was that.

When I knew I couldn't stay awake any longer, I gently shook Mike awake. He still jerked away from me, his hand automatically moving toward the knife that he'd set on the floor next to him, but once he'd blinked the sleep from his eyes and realized that it was just me, he settled down. "Can you keep an eye on things for a while, and get me up before sunrise?" I asked.

He cleared his throat and blinked hard, looking around the room. "Yeah," he finally said. "Yeah, of course."

"Thanks." I flashed him what I hoped at least looked like a genuine smile, and within minutes of settling down into the corner he'd occupied, I was asleep. Unfortunately, it seemed like only a few more minutes had passed when I heard his voice again.

"Charlie. Charlie, it's almost sunrise. Please wake up."

"Hmm?" I mumbled, reaching up to rub my eyes. "Almost sunrise?"

"I've been trying to wake you up for a few minutes. I was afraid to startle you..."

"S'fine," I assured him sleepily before craning my head to locate the others. They were already up, Mrs. Downing and Dominic standing together while Monika perched on the edge of the desk, wringing her hands nervously. I dragged myself to my feet. "Mike, Mrs. Downing, Monika, you stay here. Dominic, I need your help with Luke."

The kid looked a bit sick at the thought, but I couldn't bring myself to leave him and the nurse and the girl alone together. He approached me hesitantly while I unlocked the closet door. The stench overwhelmed us at first, but when I held my breath and stepped inside, Dominic followed my lead. Together we dragged Luke's body – *no, the* zed's *body* – out into the classroom. "We'll have to carry him outside. You up for it?"

Dominic grimaced, but nodded all the same.

"Charlie, wait!" Mike said, rushing to my side. "Please...I just...let me say goodbye."

I reached out and took hold of his hand. "Of course." Mike fell to his knees and grasped the zed's shoulder. I couldn't hear what he said; I doubted that I wanted to, anyway. Soon he stood and backed away, his hand shaking.

"I'll be back soon," I promised. Dominic and I dragged the body out through the door, which I then locked behind us. I wrapped my arms around the zed's chest, Dominic took its feet, and together we staggered to the entrance hall.

A few zeds had stumbled in during the night, but it was the work of a moment to set down our burden and take care of them. I grabbed the shovel that I'd left leaning against the wall and laid it on top of the body before we picked it back up and brought it to the grave. "Right here," I said, lowering Luke's shoulders to the ground. Dominic followed suit, gentle as could be, and I nodded my thanks. "Keep watch for me. Please."

I took my time going through Luke's – *no, the zed's* – pockets, but in the end I only found a small notebook. I shoved it into the back of my jeans and then, before I could waste any more time, I rolled the body into the grave. With one quick glance to make sure that Dominic was still keeping an eye on things, I took up the shovel and filled in the hole, using the flat of it to pack down the earth when I was done. Then I snapped the head off the damn thing and shoved it into the ground at the top of the grave. The handle I now wielded like a spear, only planning on passing it off if I found my bat before we left.

The sun had broken over the horizon, though it was still early enough to hide behind the rolling hills and the copses of trees that dotted them. "We need to get going."

Dominic followed me obediently, and once we were back with the others I gave my orders. "Mike, bind Monika. You and Dominic will take her, Virginia, and

Daniel to the front entrance. Keep an eye on her, but try to collect as many weapons as you can. Mrs. Downing, you come with me. We'll gather up who we can and use them to carry supplies. Everyone carries something, got it? Even the ones we don't quite trust. We need to bring everything we possibly can back to the zoo."

It took about an hour, but finally we were all gathered in the entryway. Even the handful of kids whose hands were tied behind their backs were carrying packs of supplies, but there was so much we had to leave behind...and I knew it would be a long time before anyone would be willing to return to the school. What was worse, we had to secure Virginia and Daniel to the cart, knowing that eventually the thing would have to be carried at certain points. It would hinder us, but I couldn't just leave them behind.

No matter what I told myself, leaving Luke here was bad enough.

We made one hell of a parade, with Mike leading the way, a few kids behind him, followed by Mrs. Downing and several more people. Dominic had the third group, while I brought up the rear with Monika and a couple of students that Mrs. Downing had sworn were trustworthy. The rest of them were in the middle of the line with the cart that carried Daniel and Virginia, but I was on edge, and for good reason – I knew that we were making too much noise, and I still couldn't bring myself to trust anyone from the school completely.

Not even Mrs. Downing or Dominic.

But in the end, we encountered next to no trouble. We ran into a couple small groups of zeds and lost a few kids along the way – two of the ones we'd tied up, and one of the boys Mrs. Downing had vouched for – so of course I was relieved when we finally reached the road that led to the zoo's gate.

Until I realized that Lauren was the one guarding it. I rushed to the front of the group and with one look from me, everyone stopped. I walked up to the bars and before Lauren could say anything, I said, "Please let us in."

"Charlie...where's Daniel?"

"Lauren, please. Open the gate."

Her mouth fell open and she began to cry. "No...no..."

"I need you to open the gate. I brought his body back, but you need to let us inside."

She finally nodded, fumbling with the key ring but eventually getting the padlock open and yanking the chain away. I slowly pushed the gate inwards, gathering the key ring from Lauren as I did so, leaving just a few feet for everyone to filter through. Once they were all inside, I made quick work of shutting, chaining, and locking the gate behind me, trying to ignore Lauren's outcry and subsequent sobs as she found the cart and bent over Daniel's body.

I stepped forward and laid a hand on her shoulder. "I need to get these people to headquarters and lock some of them up. Can you stay here with Daniel and Virginia? Once I take care of all this bullshit, I'll tell you everything."

Lauren stared up at me, her expression blank even though tears continued to run down her cheeks. Once again she nodded, and I took that to mean that she would be okay here for at least a few minutes. Together Mike and I herded the rest of the people from the school back into the zoo – to our headquarters, our little sanctuary.

Ethan was guarding the door with Holden by his side. "Where's my mom?" he asked immediately.

"She didn't make it," I admitted, somehow knowing that it was better to be straight with him from the start.

"Who are they?"

"Some of them are...captives. Some are friends. Is Richard inside?"

"Yes, in his office, with Mabel."

Mike stepped forward. "I'll come back and take over here in a few minutes, and you can go see your mom."

Ethan nodded. "Okay."

Mike went in first, and Holden watched me as I ushered the kids in. "Stay here, boy," I said. He let loose with a pathetic whine, but remained at Ethan's side all the same.

"Take what these ones are carrying, get them into the cell, and keep an eye on them. I'll take the rest to Richard," I told Mike.

What followed was nothing short of a mess. Mrs. Downing, Dominic, and the handful of kids they'd vouched for cringed in the corner of Richard's office as he freaked out about how many people I'd brought back. Meanwhile Mabel huddled in the corner and watched everything with wide, fearful eyes. I hated what we were doing to her, but it was obvious that sometimes Richard's wrath knew no bounds – and this was one of them.

"We can't take care of these people!"

"I brought back supplies!"

"And I can tell you that it won't be enough. What were you thinking?"

"Oh, I don't know, that some people deserve a chance to *live*?"

"Like Luke did? Or Daniel? *Virginia?* Jesus, Charlie."

"Listen. Once we've buried Daniel and Virginia, I'll go out and look for supplies, okay? I have half a tank of gas in my car. I can cover a lot of distance."

"I'll go with you."

I turned around; Mike was in the doorway, and I had no idea how much he'd heard. "No, you won't. You'll be needed here."

"Screw that. You decided to trust some of these people, and anyway, Richard and Ethan and Lauren can take care of themselves. We can go back to the school, go wherever, but I'm coming with you no matter what."

"We'll talk about that later. You need to relieve Ethan so that he can come with Lauren and I to bury Virginia and Daniel. Richard, can you lock up this room?"

He rolled his eyes and nodded.

"Good. The people from the school will stay here. We'll take Mabel with us; I'm sure her mother wants her to be there. Everyone okay with that?"

It didn't seem like many of them were, especially when Richard and I moved through the group and took all of their weapons. But they didn't have any choice, and we didn't either. We locked them in the office, grabbed a couple of shovels from the storage closet, and by the time we made it back outside, Mike was at the door and Ethan had disappeared. Holden was still there, and I bent to scratch him on the head. "Stay with Mike. I'll be back soon, boy, and I won't leave you again," I promised.

We made our way back to the gate, Richard carrying Mabel while I remained vigilant, wielding a shovel in each hand. When we arrived, Lauren was still kneeling by the cart, clinging to Daniel's limp hand, while Ethan stood off to the side, an impassive look on his face as he gazed at Virginia. "Lauren, you need to take Mabel. Richard and I will get the cart and the shovels to the graveyard."

"Graveyard," she repeated softly, her eyes not even focusing on us.

"Lauren. *Your daughter*," I insisted. She finally looked at me, then at Richard, and struggled to her feet. She reached for Mabel, who practically leapt into her arms, and the five of us made our way up the left-hand path toward Joey's gravesite.

Richard, Ethan, and Lauren took turns digging while I kept an eye on Mabel. I held her for a while, but she squirmed so much that I had to put her down, and the rest of my time was spent trying to stop her from wandering off. The sun was setting by the time they'd rolled the bodies into their graves and covered them up, at which point I insisted on putting Mabel in Lauren's arms again. We stood silently, looking down at the fresh mounds of dirt.

"Long story short," I finally said. "Daniel sacrificed himself to take out Jia. Virginia sacrificed herself to take out Bobby. They didn't have to do these things, but they did, because they were brave, and selfless, and they wanted to keep us safe. Just like Joey. And now they all rest together, hopefully knowing that we are still here, and still safe, because of them."

I didn't really believe the bit about them resting together and knowing we were safe, but what mattered was that Lauren and Ethan believed it...and, I supposed, Richard as well.

We stood in silence for some time, until finally I knew I couldn't wait any longer. "I'm leaving the zoo."

Lauren choked back a sob, but didn't look at me. Ethan remained impassive. I saw Richard's jaw working, and just as I was about to walk away he spoke. "We need you here. We don't know these new people. There's too many of them, not enough of...of *us*."

"But you need food, and to be honest, I can't stay here. Not permanently. Don't allow them any weapons, keep everything hidden and locked up, and these people will be little to no threat – Ethan, you know what to do."

"Yup."

"When I come back, it will be with supplies. I'll take my car, I'll bring Holden so that no one has to watch him. I'm sure I won't be gone long."

I knew that I was lying, knew that if I returned to the zoo it would be to drop some things off in front of the gate and then be on my way again. I couldn't stay here – I didn't *belong* here.

*Truthfully, I don't belong anywhere.*

Again, silence. This time I waited a little longer before finally saying, "I won't be gone long. Goodbye."

There was no point in saying anything else; I could only hope that they focused on me saying I wouldn't be gone long, rather than on the finality of the word 'goodbye'. I turned and headed down the left-hand path, listening for footsteps behind me...footsteps that never came.

I'd hidden some of my own supply caches throughout the zoo, one of which held my car keys, so all I had to do was collect Holden and be on my way. Mike was dozing in the chair by the door to the office building, but jerked awake at my approach.

"Hey." I forced a smile. "I'm going to take Holden and keep an eye on the gate for a while. Richard, Lauren, and Mabel are still by the graves. Why don't you let Mrs. Downing or Dominic keep watch so that you can get some real sleep? Just don't give them any weapons. I don't think Richard would like that."

Mike cracked his neck and stretched. "Don't you need to sleep, too?"

"No rest for the weary, kid. I doubt I could sleep, anyway."

"Okay." He gave Holden a scratch behind his ears and then went inside. I knew it wouldn't be long before someone returned, so I called Holden to me and headed back toward the front of the zoo, collecting my hidden supplies along the way. Every time I rounded a bend in the path, I expected to see Ethan or Richard or Lauren and Mabel – or all four of them. But I made it to my car without running into anyone else, and it was the work of a few minutes to store everything inside and get Holden into the backseat. The only thing left was to unlock the gate, let myself out, and then lock it again and toss the key inside. It was the worst part of my plan, but it was all I had.

As I was pulling the chain away from the gate, I heard a shout. *Fuck.* I could have handled Richard or Lauren – but it was Mike who was running toward me, calling my name. I heard Holden go nuts in the car, whining and clawing at the inside of the door as he tried to get to our friend, but still I refused to turn around and face the kid. I gathered the chain up in my arms and carried it around to the driver's side of my car, but by the time I'd climbed in and arranged the damn thing in my lap, Mike had reached me.

"What are you *doing*?!"

I was certain I'd never seen him quite this angry, and there was no point in lying. "I'm leaving. I'm going to find supplies, but I'll only be back to drop them off. I'm done with this place."

"If you're done with it, then I am too," he announced, running around to the passenger door. Thankfully it was already locked.

"Charlie," he pleaded, yanking on the handle. "Charlie, let me in. Please. I've been with you since the beginning – you can't just leave me here!"

"Yes, I can. You're safer here than you'll ever be with me, and Richard needs all the help he can get."

He stomped around to the driver's side and wrapped his hand around the corner of my doorframe. "This is fucking *selfish*," he said. "Leaving us here to deal with all of these people..."

"I told you, I'll bring back supplies."

"By yourself? No way."

More than anything I wanted to slam my door shut and drive away, but Holden was whining, trying to jump into the front seat, and with the damn chain in my lap it was all I could do to keep him from escaping the car and running to Mike.

"Mike, please, just let me go. I've already told Richard and Lauren. The people from the school, they won't have any weapons and you guys can easily keep them locked up. But all of you need food, and there's not enough of it here."

"If you go, you're not going to come back."

I squeezed my eyes shut and sighed, knowing that there was no point in lying to him. *So just keep it simple.* "I will. I'll be bringing back food and supplies."

"And after that?"

I shrugged. "Like I said, I'm done with this place."

"And like I said, if you're done with it, than I am too. C'mon, Charlie. It's been you and me since the beginning. I don't want to stay here alone."

"You're safe here." Mike raised his eyebrows. "Well, safe enough. Safer than you'd be out there. C'mon yourself, Mike. Don't do this to me."

"Too late. Also, you dropped this. It's why I came after you."

He reached into his pocket and pulled out the small notebook that I'd found on Luke. *Luke's body.*

"Just give it to me, Mike. Please."

"No way. You can have it if you let me come with you."

"What's going on here?"

"*Shit*," I mumbled, glancing over my right shoulder at Richard and Lauren. The vet was practically running toward us, and instead of angry, he looked *worried*. "Don't worry, Richard, I'm just letting myself out!" I called, reaching to pull the car door closed.

But Mike held it in place. I could have forced it shut, but there was no such thing as a quick getaway, now.

I sighed and gave in.

"I'm going with her," Mike told Richard.

"That's what it looked like. Mike, we need you here. All these people..."

"It will be worse if you don't have any way to feed them. What if Charlie gets out there and gets hurt, or killed? Then there's no one to bring back whatever she might find. She'll be safer if someone else is with her, anyway."

Richard must have caught the look on my face, because suddenly his own expression went blank. *He knows.*

"Yes, you're right. I think you should go, Mike," he said.

"But what about the new people? You need more of us here to keep an eye on them."

"I think Mike is right – someone needs to keep an eye on *you*. Now give me that lock and chain and the key, and let Mike into the car. I'll close up behind you."

I knew there was no point in arguing. I unlocked my car doors and Mike rushed to get in. The moment he was seated, Holden popped up between us and started licking the kid's face. "See, Holden didn't want you to leave without me, either," Mike grumbled. I didn't bother responding, just put my car in gear and rolled through the gate, stopping to make sure Richard was able to secure it. I watched in the review mirror as I drove away; he, Lauren, and Mabel didn't move, but then I turned a corner and that was that.

Neither Mike nor I spoke until I reached the park's exit, a place I hadn't seen since we'd ended up at the zoo. I stopped and put the car in park. "Last chance to change your mind, kid."

He looked at me, his eyes sad. "No way. I'm with you, Charlie. Beginning to end."

"Okay, kid. Okay," I finally agreed, tears burning in the corners of my eyes as I shifted back into first gear, taking a right onto the main road and leaving everything – and everyone else – behind.

## LESSON LEARNED

*In the end, there really are no rules.*

# Epilogue

I was changed before I left the zoo, that much is obvious...but it was only later, when I finally read Luke's last words, that I fell off the edge.

I don't know what I would have done, had Mike not been with me. Certainly not gone back to the zoo. In fact, all I wanted now was to return to my family's farm. Even if it meant the end of me, I had a one-track mind. *Get back to the place where you found Luke.*

But Mike *was* there, and he was the one who directed me to local stores and gas stations and even, once, back to the school. Most places had been thoroughly ransacked, but we found random useful items here and there – mostly in houses and cars, although once in a while we fought our way through small groups of zeds trapped in stores and were able to gather everything from junk food to the occasional half-assed weapon, like a tire iron...or six.

I won't get into what we went through to get those.

Or what it feels like to siphon gasoline.

At one point we even made it back to my old condo, something I'd wanted to do since leaving the farm in the first place. If the zeds who'd been trapped in their own homes were still there, they weren't up to making noise anymore, and I wasn't about to check on them. I merely gathered up a few personal and clothing items I'd been missing and then we were on our way again.

We did go back to the zoo, eventually. We separated out most of what we'd found to leave there, and we also brought information – mainly that many of the zeds were slowing down again; some of them were almost entirely immobile. Mike and I were gone for several weeks, and during that time we saw far fewer of what we'd once called 'super zeds', and even less of the newly-turned ones. Instead we came across rotting bodies, many of which were almost entirely immobile. Even if they were still standing, it was often just barely, and we rarely had to truly exert ourselves to take them out.

It was early evening on a late-spring day (and hotter than it had any right to be) when we finally returned to the zoo. I was hoping, probably stupidly, that the gate wouldn't be guarded...but no, Ethan was there, with Monika – of all people – by his side.

Mike gave me a wary look; we'd already had our discussion and he knew that I wanted to go back to the farm. I'd tried to convince him to stay at the zoo, but he remained adamant about remaining by my side.

I hated that and wanted it at the same time.

I left Holden in the car as we unloaded everything we'd collected for the zoo. "You came back," Ethan said as we carried our first load of food up to the gate. I set down my burden and turned back to gather the rest of what we'd gathered. "But you're not staying."

Mike and I both remained silent, but when I brought the second armful of supplies back to the gate, I admitted, "No. We're not."

"Is everything okay here?" Mike asked, looking from Monika to Ethan and back again.

"Yes," Ethan stated.

Monika gave him a soft smile. "We're low on food, but everyone is helping. We even fixed the breach in that back pen. Had to let El loose to forage, though. Sometimes she comes back to the gate and we let her in for a while."

The fact that the elephant was still a thing was most telling of all. These people were fine; probably, as I'd always believed, better off without me.

I turned to Mike. "You sure you don't want to stay?" He rolled his eyes, and this time my reluctance to give in was completely fake.

"Keep an eye on Lauren and Mabel for us," I told Ethan.

At first he just nodded, but when Mike and I turned to walk away, he called out, "Thanks, Charlie!"

I turned around and smiled. "You're welcome. Take good care of yourselves, okay? Make sure everyone knows that the zeds seem to be...shutting down, for lack of a better term. You still need to be careful, I'm not sure how permanent this is, but it's not like it used to be."

Monika looked so hopeful that I had to turn away. I wasn't sure how solid her position was at the zoo, but clearly they trusted her. *At least somewhat.*

Nothing more was said. Mike and I returned to my car, and this time I didn't bother looking in the rearview mirror as we drove away. Even Holden remained silent and still, stretched out in the backseat as if nothing had happened.

"You okay?" Mike eventually asked.

"Just fine."

"So...the farm, then?"

"Yeah," I said, flashing him a quick smile. "The farm, then."

# ACKNOWLEDGEMENTS

It's pretty much impossible to publish a book without a lot of help, and while I certainly learned that when I wrote and published my first novel, this one was quite a bit more difficult to complete (for a lot of reasons).

To everyone who read one of my many drafts of *How to Start Living (in the Zombie Apocalypse)*, I cannot thank you enough...but special thanks have to go out to my friend Tykina for being both beta reader and editor and giving me such great feedback.

I also received an outpouring of support in other ways from two very important people – first, my mother, who is my rock, one of the strongest people I know, and who forced me to face hard truths...ones that led to my completing this book a lot faster than I would have otherwise. Second, to Brian, who upended his life for me and in doing so gave me time to focus on not just this story but on so many other things that I love to do.

Finally, while the characters in *How to Start Living* are of my own creation, one who wouldn't exist without a lot of real-life inspiration is Charlie's dog Holden. He is an amalgamation of my two amazing dogs, Wendy and Rigby, who more than anyone or anything else have kept me kind of sane and fairly grounded throughout the past few years. The "Who rescued who?" question associated with rescue pups applies to these two babies more than they could ever possibly know.

T. L. Walker has a B.A. in history and a long-established passion for writing. In addition to being an author, they are an event planner, fandom and geek culture expert, and public speaker. They founded Ice & Fire Con, the first ever *Song of Ice and Fire/Game of Thrones* convention in the U.S., as well as the genre lit webcast/podcast Sagas & Sass.

T.L. has written for the internationally recognized pop culture news site TheGeekiary.com, as well as co-hosting their webcasts "Feelings…With The Geekiary" and "The Bitching Dead".

They have spoken about geek culture at San Diego Comic-Con, C2E2, MegaCon, Dragon Con, Ohio State University, TedX Sarasota, and more. You can find some of their most recent panels on the A Geek Saga webcast and podcast.

A New Englander born and raised, they currently hail from South Carolina, where they live with a plethora of rescue pets and work in Continuing Medical Education while continuing to webcast/podcast, organize events, and of course write in their free time.

Find them across the web: @ageeksaga

Made in the USA
Columbia, SC
15 February 2022